Brothers Black 7
Johnathan The Fixer

Blue Saffire

Perceptive Illusions Publishing, Inc.
Bay Shore, New York

Blue Saffire/Perceptive Illusions Publishing, Inc.
P.O. Box 5253
Bayshore, NY 11706
www.BlueSaffire.com

Publisher's Note: This is a work of fiction. Names, characters, places, and incidents are a product of the author's imagination. Locales and public names are sometimes used for atmospheric purposes. Any resemblance to actual people, living or dead, or to businesses, companies, events, institutions, or locales is completely coincidental.

Ordering Information:
Quantity sales. Special discounts are available on quantity purchases by corporations, associations, and others. For details, contact the "Special Sales Department" at the address above.

Brothers Black 7: Johnathan the Fixer/ Blue Saffire. -- 1st ed.
ISBN 978-1-941924-03-7

I don't have to see you every day to feel you. While I miss your face, these last five years have been driven by your guidance. There will never be another mother like you, and I'm so happy you were mine. In God I trust, he knew exactly how to create me and who to place around me to get the right results.

–Blue Saffire

Good Morning

Roni

I can't breathe, but that's the intention. His tight grip on my throat has cut off my air supply. My body coils tightly as it's sent somewhere between heaven and the unknown.

He's done exactly what he set out to do. Clear my thoughts of anything other than him. I wrap my hands around the harness suspending me in the air as John rocks into me.

"Stop fighting it. Come," he commands in my ear.

His warm breath tickles my skin, causing me to shiver. When he moves to look into my eyes, his are dark with lust. Their golden color has rescinded to the very edges.

I'm not alone. Not that I could possibly ever think I am. His thick dick by itself ensures that's not the case. To think there was a time I thought I'd never stretch enough to take him whole.

Now the pleasure and pain just intensify the sensations running through my body. I want to close my eyes as I soar toward the ultimate release, but I know if I do, he'll snatch it from me.

John bites my chin in warning before kissing the sting away. If nothing else, he has just set flames to the fire already consuming me. How can a man wield sex like a weapon?

He slaps my ass, pulling the last of the defiance from me. I give up the fight and come all over him. It's so intense, I sag against his body as much as the harness will allow, placing my head on his shoulder.

"That's my baby," John croons and kisses the top of my head. "Now you can stop stressing. The baby is reacting to it."

I sigh. I know she is. She's been crying constantly. Dry diaper, she's fed, and still, she hollers unless John holds her.

If only he knew. Great sex isn't going to fix this one. Although, I know some punishment sex is on its way. When he finds out the entirety of what's been going on behind his back, he's going to kill me and Torque.

What he knows now is nothing. Torque has been taking the brunt of his ire. I feel so guilty. I'm testing John's patience on a new level.

He's been patient but of all the trouble I've gotten into, it's never been anything like this. I could kill Torque. If it weren't for his age and understanding his motives, I might have.

John and I have a baby to think about now. Torque should have thought about—

"Do I have to fuck you again?" John cuts into my thoughts with his words, running his fingertips down the center of my spine to the crack of my ass.

He slides a single digit between my cheeks and brushes it against my puckered hole. My body quakes, the harness sways with the motion. I lift my head and look at him.

"She'll be up soon for her next feeding," I say.

"My cock is already hard. I'll be quick about it."

As if on cue, he pulses inside of me. I'll never be able to understand how he does that. I felt his hot seed erupt with my climax, and he's still rock hard already.

"John," I groan.

He rolls his eyes and pulls out of my body. Like a pro, he cradles me to his chest as he releases me from the harness. When my arms are free, I wrap them around his neck.

"Let's get you taken care of and I'll go get her before she wakes."

I only murmur my consent. I'm so exhausted from the baby, stress, and getting back into the swing of things with work. When John dragged me in here to the playroom, I thought I'd pass out before he could get me wherever he wanted me.

I think he picked the harness with that in mind. Not that I'm complaining. It's been a while since we've been able to start full play again. I know this morning is only a taste.

This morning. Ugh. We'll have to start our day in a few hours. I wonder what's in store for us. I have to make a decision before John finds out what Torque has done.

"Why don't you just talk to me?"

I focus on John from my perch on the en suite bathroom countertop. He placed me here before starting the water in the tub. He rests his palms flat on either side of me and locks me in his gaze.

I reach out to touch his face. God, this man is so beautiful. It's a family trait, being so gorgeous. All of the Blacks and their cousins are handsome, but John takes it to new heights. He's stunning if you can say so about a man.

"I will. When I'm ready."

Reaching for my thighs, he pulls them apart and stands between them. His eyes are searching. Looking for my secrets the way he always does. It's hard to hide from him when he's like this.

Luckily, his phone begins to ring in the next room. He narrows his eyes at me but turns to go answer the call. I release a breath of relief, hopping off the counter to stop the running water.

I decide to climb in. Time is always of the essence around here. Either work or the baby can change everything in the blink of an eye, although John has continued to try to limit my work schedule.

"No, it's fine. I'll call mom to babysit. We can take her there and head in," John says, a hint of frustration in his voice.

I lift a brow at him. He never gives in so easily on my working. Must be something important.

He hangs up the call. "We're needed for a five-man op. It's a recovery mission. In and out."

"So, one of ours?"

"Yeah, Dad's handing it off. I'll call Mom to see if she'll look after the baby."

"That's not going to work. Your mother has a girls' day thing with Jennifer and Hope. I'll give Kaye a call. I think she has plans with her mother at the church or something, but maybe she can keep her for us," I say.

John works his jaw a bit before he nods his consent. So much for a long soak. I climb from the tub and step into the towel he holds up for me. He kisses my forehead and that sense of guilt rises again.

"We're going to have a talk when we return. I want to know what's going on with you," he says.

I sigh and nod. It's better to get this over with. So much for the peace we've had around here.

I Need Help

John

"I thought this was Torque and Torque alone. You were involved and didn't tell me?" I seethe as I barely contain my anger enough to fly this helicopter. "Do you understand who we're dealing with here?"

"Stop talking to me like I'm your child, John. I'm not in the mood for it."

"Not in the mood? Not in the mood? Roni, I swear to God…" I clamp my mouth shut because my temper is through the roof.

I lied to myself a few months ago back in Italy. When I said I didn't know how we got here, that's bullshit.

This has been who we were from the beginning. We were both in denial from the start, but Roni has always been the world to me, that's how I'm still wrapped around her finger and distracted anytime she comes in harm's way.

"I told you I had no idea what Torque was up to until it was too late. He was supposed to stand down."

"Fuck that. You should have come to me when Misha first called you. I should have known what was going on. Since when do *we* hold shit like this from each other?"

"Since you became a father who has a little girl to worry about. I'm not sending the father of my child out there to fight my battles. Especially when I don't know what they are or how dangerous," she snaps back.

"What the hell does that mean, Roni?"

I clench my jaw. She's stubborn to a fault. She's yet to understand I'm always here for her. She doesn't have to carry everything on her own.

This thing with our daughter needing me more than her, I don't get it. She's willing to stick her neck out as long as I'm there for our girl. I'm still trying to make this one make sense.

Insanity.

"What don't you understand? In order to keep our family safe, I need to know everything. Secrets expose us, they leave us vulnerable. I can't protect you or anyone else if I don't know what the fuck is going on."

I take a glance over at her when I get no reply. Her dark eyes are fixed on me as she glares. Her full lips are pinched, those long lashes lowered as she narrows her eyes.

"What?" I bark.

She points a finger at me. "Johnathan Dillion Black, don't make me choke your ass. Who the hell are you talking to?"

"You'll be begging me to choke and spank you after this." I snort.

"What's that supposed to mean?"

"The only time you hand over your trust and obedience is when I'm fucking you. Wait, that's a lie. You even find a way to defy me then."

"Maybe because I'm not a dog or better yet, I'm a grown ass woman."

"A grown ass woman who has one of the most dangerous men in the world pissed the fuck off and demanding you come see him," I bellow, losing my shit all over again.

I've been pissed since I got the text from LaSalle asking what the fuck has Roni gotten herself into. Her and Torque are going to send me to an early grave. Fucking hardheaded and stubborn as fuck.

"Misha?" I growl. "You get mixed up with Misha of all people, behind my back," I say incredulously.

"For the record, I wasn't trying to get involved with him. He reached out to me and Torque has gotten it in his head that he should be protecting me," she huffs and rubs her forehead.

She continues more to herself. "He's in over his head. He's barely twenty, I shouldn't have let him get involved in all of this."

I blow out a breath. "No, that's me. I shouldn't have let either of you be dragged into this. I should've found another way."

This time she snorts. "As if you had a choice. You were never the one calling the shots on all of this. You looked out for us, but this has never been your show to run."

"You underestimate me. I could have and should have found another way."

"John."

I turn to glance at her again. Her eyes soften and I can see how tired she looks. She's a mother now. Everything has changed. Exactly why shit like this shouldn't be happening.

"I'll fix it. Whatever it is, I'll fix it. I always do," I promise before she can say another word.

"You don't have to always rescue me."

"It's what I do. I come to the rescue, but it would make my life a whole lot easier to know when things are going on, for me to rescue you from them before they get this out of hand."

I see her shrug out the corner of my eye. She turns away to look out of the window. The weight of the morning's mission and that text press down on both of us.

"I don't remember a lot, but I remember the distance between me and my father. I… I don't think he protected me. Not like you do, not like I see you do for our daughter.

"We made promises to each other in that place. Natasha and Torque, we became family. I understand why he won't give up on her and why he's the way he is with me. He's not right in how he's going about it, but I understand," she says.

"I get it, baby. I do. But what I'm asking from you both is for you to let me fix this. It's what I do. The secrets and the bullshit have to stop. I would have been able to handle things better from the beginning.

"Let that guard down. You and Torque have to give me the trust you say you have in me. Then I can help. I'll find her."

"John, I already have a—"

Her words are cut off as Felix's voice fills our headphones. My blood runs cold as his words sink in. I'm turning the chopper around before he can finish.

"I'm headed your way," I say.

"Good. Noah, Brax, and Toby have been hit. We're down a few hands."

"I'm calling in my crew," I reply and nod to Roni to make the call.

She's on it. I push as fast as I can go to get there. However, my panic rises as the next voice comes through the headset.

"I need some help up here. Carmen's hanging off the side of the building and I'm holding on for dear life. Wyatt, can you get here, bro?"

"My hands are a bit full down here. I'm trying."

"Fuck," Ryan bellows.

I find my voice to let my little brother know I'm on my way to him. "Ry, this is John. Roni and I are in the bird. We're headed your way. You hold on. We're coming."

"Shit, if you can speed the fuck up that would be great."

"We're coming."

I work my jaw as I focus on getting there as well as a plan to get Carmen off the side of the building. Shit. This can't be happening. This is like the day from hell.

I still can't believe I almost got my head blown off. I have to focus this time. Carmen means too much to Ryan for me to fuck this up.

"We're going to have to work together on this," I say to Roni.

"Already ahead of you," she says as she unfastens her seatbelt. "I'll get in the harness. You just get me close to the building. I got her."

I nod as the hospital comes into view. We are so close but so far. My heart is pounding.

"Baby, relax. Be still for me," Ryan's voice comes through the headset.

He didn't close the connection. The emotions in his voice cause my throat to tighten with my own. Carmen's sob nearly guts me.

"Ryan, I don't want to die."

"Who's dying? How many times do I have to tell you I've got you?" Just like my little brother. He'll keep a cool head for Carmen, although I know him well enough to know he's freaking the hell out.

Always the joker. I don't know how Carmen deals with his ass, but I get why he has resorted to jokes. The fear in Carmen's voice is vibrating through the connection.

Ryan calls me out of my thoughts as I try to tone his crazy out. "John?"

"Almost there," I reply.

I can see their figures over the side of the building. Fuck, I need to move faster. I don't know how much longer he'll be able to hold her at that angle.

Clenching my jaw, I listen to Carmen's pleas and screams. It's as if everything has started to move in slow motion. We're getting closer. The sound of Roni opening the door causes my adrenaline to spike.

We draw nearer still and I hover over the hospital, not yet able to breathe. "Don't. Let. Go." Is the last thing I hear Ryan say before Roni jumps out of the helicopter and time seems to still.

Roni

Everything halts around me. The world seems to have taken a pause. My focus is on one thing.

Carmen is slipping. Ryan isn't going to be able to hold her at this rate. Wind blows in my face as I leap down to wrap my body around hers, to press her to the building long enough to latch onto her and secure her to my rig.

I'm a breath away from her when I see it happening. Carmen slips right from Ryan's hand. She starts to drop.

"You're not dying on my watch," I mutter to myself as I thrust my body forward and wrap around her, flattening us both to the building with a thud.

Jesus, I've got her. Thank God, I've got her. I haven't failed my friend.

"I've got you," I say as I secure her. "I've got her, John. Pull us up, I'll get her on her feet, and we can go in to help."

"Copy."

It's a single word, but I can hear the relief in his voice. Carmen is trembling against me. If I'm not mistaking, she's murmuring praises.

I don't get us on solid ground before Ryan wraps around us both. I do my best to unhook Carmen so they can have their moment. I've just gotten out of my harness after I release her when I give John the thumbs up to land.

That's when the door to the rooftop bursts open. Instinct tells me to pull my Glocks and cover Ryan and Carmen with my body. However, instinct nor my training could prepare me for what comes through the door.

My past. The one that's been so fuzzy, strolls right through. It's like a bolt of lightning hits. Everything floods back to me in this very moment.

Then the sound of a gun firing rips through the air. Everything slows down. My breathing, this moment, my thoughts. In the wind, along with the whistle of the bullet, are the last words I remember from the past who's looking at me.

CHAPTER TWO

 Toxic

Roni

I walk into the house feeling amused and sort of excited. I've been shopping all morning, trying to find the perfect lingerie. I want to lose my virginity.

"Tonight's the night," I whisper to myself as I cross the threshold of my boyfriend's house—if I can call him that.

I moved in a month ago on my father's suggestion. Yes, totally not normal. It should have been my boyfriend's request, but my life works different.

For starters, I'm in a relationship I'm completely conflicted about. My father has controlled every detail of my life since he came to get me after my mother died. Lately, I've been feeling like I have no power over my own life.

My need to please my father has suffocated the woman inside. I feel like a child. Yet, I rarely speak up, if ever. At least not out loud.

"You marry Darius then." That's one I've said in my mind a lot lately.

I'm defiant in my head. Will tell my father and Darius off in a heartbeat. Not so much to their faces.

I snort as I take off my sunglasses, slowly folding them to place them into my bag. I look around the house. Everyone's moving around to help with plans for some dinner party Darius is having tomorrow.

"Not going to be here for that one," I mutter under my breath.

"What was that, Ms. Pérez?" Darius's butler says.

"Oh, running through my to-do list," I reply with a forced smile.

There I go again. Funny thing, I wasn't always this way. A people pleaser.

"Your mouth hangs on the hinges of hell," my mother used to tell me as she'd glare at me.

I was always on punishment for something I said. Life was different then. I had nothing to lose.

And there lies the problem. I have become so complacent, who I am is a blur. All so I don't lose my father again.

Which is why I plan to give away the one thing my father has always been insistent I hold onto. It's that or I walk away from it all. I haven't gained that level of strength yet. I'm still waiting for the day he tells me why he left in the first place.

I guess that's why in the past I'd been trying so hard to please my dad. Hoping he doesn't push me all the way away. Twenty-two and still seeking my father's approval.

Daddy issues much?

"One day needing daddy's attention is going to bite you in the ass," I mumble to myself.

"Miss?"

I turn my attention to Norwood, the Butler. "Nothing. Is Darius here?"

"Yes, in the study. I'll get these bags to your room."

With a nod, I flip my freshly silk-pressed hair over my shoulder and turn for the study. My heels click against the floor as I make my way down the hall. Raised voices cause me to slow down and silence my steps as I go.

"You're catching feelings for her," Richie, Darius's younger brother bellows. His Dominican accent thick. "I warned you about that shit."

"Give me a break."

"No, you give me a break. If you fuck this up, you'll get us both killed."

Darius scoffs. "I doubt that. I think you are forgetting who we are. They came to us."

"You are going to fuck this up."

"What is there to fuck up? We want her to fall for me, don't we? Isn't that what everyone wants? I don't see the problem," Darius says as if he's bored.

"I know you, that's the problem. You're getting attached. Soon you will start to change things. Everything is set up to go as planned. You need to do your part."

"I've been doing my part for over a year. Have I not? Her father has given me the green light to propose and I will. *Carajo*, give it a rest."

Richie snorts. "I should have been the one to do this."

Darius laughs. "Ah, sí, we are getting to the problem here. I see now."

"No, you don't. I wouldn't become attached. You and I are very different."

"Yes, we are. I will get this done because I have to. My feelings will not play a part. I haven't worked this hard for it to all fall apart."

"As if this all has been such a hardship on you."

"You think it hasn't? Her father has watched our every move since *you* almost fucked this up. Oh, and the icing on the cake little brother, he threatened me to leave her a virgin until we marry.

"Come on. Have you seen her? She walks around in those heels and she's always showing off her tight body, I've wanted to fuck her from the beginning," Darius says like an angry child.

I stumble back. At this moment, I'm grateful to my father for ensuring I remained a virgin until married. I have no idea what's going on, but I don't like the sound of it in the least.

Both brothers are handsome with their dark hair and hazel eyes against tanned brown skin. Darius being the taller of the two has a nice build and keeps himself well dressed. It's why losing my virginity to him wasn't the most revolting idea.

With Darius, it's always been his attitude holding me at arm's length. He can be a lot like my father at times, other times he's overly attentive. Something that has always raised the hairs on the back of my neck.

I don't think I was ever able to place it before now. It's an arrogance, a smugness that has always kept me at bay. I can be distant, but I'm also observant. Pieces begin to fit together, and those red flags start to fly high.

"Like you're not getting your dick wet plenty—"

I can't. I can't hear another word. I may not be in love with Darius, but I've been committed to him. I've given him a chance as my father demanded. When my father suggested I move in with Darius, I did it because Papi thought it was a good idea.

"You will do this. It's for the future. You understand," my father had said.

"Yes, I do."

Now, I question myself and my father. I've had this feeling in the last few weeks. Before I thought it was all my lack of control. Instantly I know it was my bullshit meter going off.

I'm so pissed, I don't bother to go get my things. Fuck it. Darius paid for them. It's not my loss. I can go shopping again with my own money. I'd prefer it that way.

My phone rings as I step out of the house. I lift a hand to signal for my car as I pull the device from my bag. I don't know the number and nearly ignore it, but nagging in the pit of my stomach causes me to answer.

"Hello."

"Hello, is this Cherone Pérez?" the person on the other end says.

"This is she."

"Ma'am. You were listed as the next of kin for Eliam Pérez."

"Okay... that's my father."

"I'm sorry to have to inform you he has passed. Would you be able to come and identify the body?"

My father may be a cold man, but he's my father. I love him despite his inability to show me love. My grandmother once told me I would become like him if I wasn't careful. Cold and guarded.

I wish I could be cold at this moment. As the woman on the phone's words sinks in, I start to feel alone in this world. My grandmother passed last year. It has only been my father and me. I have an aunt, but she doesn't come to visit much. I've never really gotten to know her.

I have no one. The reality of my loss, and now, my loneliness chills my bones as the woman's words replay in my ear. He's gone. This can't be real.

The weight of the truth presses down on me. A breeze passes by and something about her words ring with a hollow truth. I faint.

John

"I think we should talk," Missy says.

I stand staring out the window of Missy's apartment, my mind telling me to slow down and evaluate some things around me. This arrangement I'm in being one of them. Between work and family shit, I haven't given much thought to it.

Well, not until recently. Something has changed. I'm questioning everything about my life.

This shit ever get old to you?

Wyatt's words have been ringing in my head for days now. Yeah, this is getting old. Not just old but draining and disheartening.

I've avoided looking at the real reasons for the way I am. There are two factors that I've allowed myself to consider over the last few days. One of which most people wouldn't expect. Honestly, I'd never say it out loud.

My mind takes me back to my teenage years. The first time I craved control and dominance. That can happen when you feel used.

"Have you seen John today?" I overheard Lauren the eleventh grader I was dating say from around the corner of her house.

"God, he's so gorgeous," one of her friends gushed.

I couldn't help but smile. It was no secret that girls found me and my brothers attractive. I reached for the handle of the gate to enter the backyard and let myself be known. However, I froze with the words of another of her friends.

"I still can't believe you're dating a ninth grader."

"Come on, like you don't know I'm dating him to make Billy jealous." Lauren laughed.

"I still think it's mean," a third friend said, it had to be Allison from the sound of the voice.

"How? He gets to tell all his friends that he's getting into an eleventh grader's pants, he gets regular blow jobs, I get amazing sex, and Billy has been losing his shit. It's a win for everyone if you ask me."

"John's sweet. You're using him like some toy because he's pretty and Billy's afraid of Wyatt and Noah," Allision retorted in disgust. "It's a shitty thing to do."

"Shitty because you had a crush on him or shitty because you plan to go after my sloppy seconds?"

"It's just plain shitty. Sure, I think he's supermodel gorgeous and totally had planned to corrupt his life, but you're wrong," Allison replied.

"Fine, I'll break it off, but not until after the dance. He looks way better in a suit than Billy. We're going to be the best looking couple there."

I backed away from Lauren's house and went home. The next day at school I dumped her in front of everyone and became a legend. What no one ever knew was how that made me feel, how out of control I felt.

"Are you listening to me, John?" I turn from the window and look at her.

Missy and I aren't compatible. She's not who she sold me on in the beginning. She put on a good show at first, but she's vanilla as a pint of Häagen-Dazs.

I stare at her and again something that's been nagging at me comes to mind. I've never been in love. Not with any of the girls I've been in arrangements with. I was always intrigued by the life, but that shit with Lauren pushed me fully into it.

I tilt my head at Missy and squint my eyes. She isn't the one, but I have this feeling like I'm missing the one that is. I know I don't know her, haven't met her, but she's out there.

The one that will enjoy my lifestyle and all that comes with me. When it comes to Missy, I've known for a while that she's not into all of it. That's why I think it's about time I end this arrangement.

"John," she barks out my name.

And still, I can't see her. I can only see the mounting reasons for moving on. She puts on airs to please me. That's not the type of Sub I want. I want someone that enjoys every aspect of our relationship as much as I do.

Suddenly, we're in her apartment, but the atmosphere is much different. Yeah, I'd been planning to break things off, but for this one night, I wanted to chill. Blow off some steam. After all, that's what our relationship is for. It was what we agreed to.

"John, I said we need to talk," she says from her couch.

My nonchalant mood from when I arrived goes up in smoke and I home in on the minor details. I begin to calculate the facts I'm taking in. Her hair is a little messy and she looks nervous. How did I not notice she's not ready for our date? Something is off.

Can she sense that this is going to be our last date?

God, don't let her ask me to extend our arrangement. I'm over this. Ready to move on and find someone that takes me there. Someone that can handle all of me.

Shit.

She's going to make this more difficult than I planned. In an instant, I decided that maybe this should be the end. I can go to dinner alone.

A year is a year. That's all we consented to. Knowing what I know now, I have no plans on extending things. They shouldn't have lasted as long as they did.

"Yeah, I was thinking the same thing," I reply with my decision made.

"Let me go first."

I assess her a little more closely. The long sleeve shirt she has on is pulled down over her hands. She starts to fidget and stands to hold one hand out. Covered by her sleeve is some type of plastic stick.

Now, don't get me wrong. I'm not slow or anything, it's quite the opposite. However, it takes my ass a few beats to connect with what's in her hand.

I lift my gaze to hers. "What the hell is that?"

"You know I'm on birth control, but… I don't know what happened. I'm pregnant."

I look at Missy like she has two heads. Pushing a hand through my hair, I damn near growl. In my going on twenty-eight years of life, I've been with multiple women.

I can't count how many dungeons I've been in. How many sex parties I've hosted and been a guest at. I've slayed more pussy than Buffy did vampires.

Never, ever, have I—

"Fuck," I bellow.

I close my eyes and I want to stab myself with hot pokers. My father has warned me repeatedly about my lifestyle. Hell, my mother hasn't bitten her tongue either.

"It's going to bite you in the ass one of those days, John. Have fun, but don't lose yourself in it. Mistakes happen, mistakes you can't take back," my father warned.

I groan remembering that talk. I'm sure Mom coaxed him into giving it. She may not say it out loud, but Mom fears that my brothers and I will never settle down and start families.

This has to be my punishment for all the shit I've done. My father was right, this shit is biting me in the ass. I pay for Missy's doctor appointments and the birth control she's on.

It was a part of the agreement. This has never happened before. Why the hell is this happening now?

"I'm just as shocked as you, John, but you're—," Missy starts.

I pin her with a glare. I bite back my temper because, at this point, I want to lose it. It's not fair to her. Missy has always been honest with me in the past—yet.

Don't be a dick, John.

I shake my head clear, not letting the doubts that rise take root. I've never had a reason before not to trust her. This is just my frustration trying to cloud my head.

This type of relationship requires trust. I want to believe she didn't break that, so I hold back the questions that rush my head, pushing at the surface.

"This is… wow, fuck."

"I know, but is it such a bad thing? I've always wanted a family and you're always so supportive of your family. We could make this work," she says, her voice sounding like white noise to me.

If only she knew, I'd come here to end this relationship, our arrangement is almost up. I had wanted to end it early actually, not change its terms and get in deeper. What a fucking mess.

"I need to think," I say as I start for the door.

"You don't want to stay and talk?"

"No."

With that, I'm out the door. I pass by her disheveled roommate as I leave. She looks a lot like Missy did when I observed her.

I push that thought aside and focus on my own issues. Something doesn't feel right about this to me. I'm not trying to be a dick, but it doesn't sit well with me at all.

Of all the women I've been with, Missy is the last one I would want to start a family with. I've stayed friends with a lot of my old Subs, and I'd marry one of them before I'd even think about such a thing with Missy. The main reason this was over for me weeks ago. Hell, this is the first time I've seen her in almost three weeks.

"Aw, fuck."

CHAPTER THREE

 Goodbye

Roni

I look up at the sky wondering if my father is looking down on me. Does he know about all of the unanswered questions I have? There are so many that I'll never have the answer to.

He's gone.

Tears spill as I take in a breath and start for the waiting limo. My heels sink into the soil beneath me, causing me to walk awkwardly. I grind my teeth when someone wraps their hand under my arm to steady me.

I don't have to look to see that it's Darius. I haven't forgotten what I overheard, and he still doesn't know that I heard it. He's been trying to console me and cozy up.

However, now I can see right through the act. I've been allowing him to think it's my grief causing my need for distance.

29

It's more a matter of me wanting to know what he and his brother have planned.

"We should go back to my place. I can draw you a bath and we can have a talk about what you want to do next," he says with that smile that used to be charming.

I fight not to roll my eyes. Stopping once we arrive at the car, I tug my arm from his hold and take a step away from him. He creases his brows as he searches my face, my sunglasses blocking his view of my eyes.

"I'm going home. As a matter of fact, I think this should be the last time we see each other," I reply.

"What?" He almost growls but catches himself and closes the distance between us. "You are upset about your father. That is understandable. Don't do this. We can talk."

"Talk about what?"

"Cherone," he says in warning.

"Yeah, about that. I hate it when you call me that. My name is Roni."

"I will call you anything you like. Just stop this. Come home with me. We can work out whatever is going on here."

"I doubt that."

I push past him to round the car door as it's opened for me. Darius grabs my arm, stopping me. I turn slowly, looking down at his hand on me.

Clearly, he has no idea where I'm from. The woman he knows is the one that was raised with my father. The girl that was raised with my mother is still very much alive and coming back to life slowly as if my father's death has been that Roni's resurrection.

"Get your hand off me. I've said all I have to say. Now leave and stop making a scene at my father's funeral before you get yourself hurt," I hiss with a healthy dose of warning in my voice.

He narrows his eyes at me. "Is that a threat?"

I pointedly look around at the men watching us. My father's men as well as his closest friends. The few that my father exposed me to and that know who I am are paying very close attention.

"Why would I need to threaten you? You're putting your own life in danger."

He releases me and takes a step back, buttoning his suit jacket and smoothing his hands down the front. "Exactly," I say.

As the word leaves my mouth Richie walks over with disdain on his face. "We should leave," he says next to Darius's ear.

"Yes, you should."

When he turns his attention to me it's the nail in the coffin. "You're an entitled brat. *Perra sucia.*"

"I've got your dirty bitch," I snarl, balling my fists.

"Richie," Darius snaps at his brother as he glares at him.

My driver has placed a hand on my arm to hold me back. I remember where we are and calm down. Years of charm school have gone out the window.

"This isn't over. We will talk," Darius warns.

I snort. "Yeah, don't hold your breath, *Joder, muchacho.*"

His eyes grow hard. "Not this time," he says tightly before clamping his lips shut.

His hazel eyes hold a ton of things he wants to say, but I don't stay to hear any of it. I get into the car and settle in for the ride back to my father's house. This day has a weight of its own.

It's once we are out of the cemetery gates that I allow myself to breakdown. I know this is only the beginning. Of what? I have no idea. Although I get the heavy sense my father left me to handle something way bigger than me.

"How could you leave me again? No one ever stays."

CHAPTER FOUR

Devastation

Roni

I sit staring at my motorcycle helmet sitting on the edge of the desk. I'm tempted to pick it up and take off for a ride. My father would chide me about being ladylike.

It's my one guilty pleasure he has never been able to chastise me out of. As I think of it now, it's my escape. A way to be free. What I would give to have my father boss me around at this moment.

I jump out of my thoughts as the sound of clinging pulls my attention. "Thank you," I say to my father's assistant, Taine as she sets a cup of tea in front of me.

"Do you need anything else before I go?" she asks.

It's her last day. I'm grateful to her for staying on for this long. It's been three months since my father had a heart attack and died.

I'm still in shock. My father was so healthy. Or at least I thought he was.

He was always telling his guys they needed to eat healthier. It's been so hard to wrap my head around all of this. It feels like I'm numb.

"Why on earth did he leave all this to me?" I mutter more to myself.

I look around at all of the papers on the desk in front of me. So, this is what drowning feels like. Half of this shit doesn't make sense to me.

"He always said that you were good with numbers. Given his system, I think that's why," Taine replies.

I groan and place my head on the desk. I'm not a quitter. I'll figure this out, but damn. What the hell was he thinking? No warning, no training, no map to help me out.

All of this was meant to confuse anyone that might stumble across it or worse case scenario if it ever fell into the hands of his enemies or the authorities. My father kept me out of his business. Which is why I can't for the life of me figure out why he left it all to me.

I sigh, lifting my head so I can dismiss her. "No, I don't nee—"

My phone rings cutting me off. When I look at the screen, I groan. It's Darius again. He's been blowing my phone up every day, all day since the funeral when I told him I was through.

He has come to the house, but I gave orders for neither him nor his brother to be allowed on the property after we had that heated exchange at the funeral.

Richie has tried to reach out to me since. I don't know what for. Hell, before standing outside that door and overhearing them, I knew he had a problem with me for one reason or another. The feeling was and still is mutual.

His words at the cemetery sealed my dislike for him. I'm no one's dirty bitch. I don't take being called one lightly. He's lucky Darius reeled his ass in before I popped him in his mouth.

I reach to ignore the call and turn back to Taine. "No, you can leave if you like. I'll figure this mess out tomorrow or the next day."

That's what I tell myself every day. Although I know the end isn't in sight with any of this. People that did business with my father want answers.

People that I'm finding have no problem showing that they can be dangerous and intimidating. I've held my own so far, remembering the things my father used to tell me. *Never let them see you sweat. You're a Pérez, things will always come naturally to you.*

Oh, and my favorite. *I've made you a hard woman to handle hard situations. Know when to be a princess and when to be a savage. It will save your life.*

So, I've been walking into these meetings as a savage. What these men don't know is that I grew up having to fight. Before my father came to get me when I was ten, I was raised by my mother.

We didn't have my father's kind of money and connections. Charm school wasn't on the agenda in the hood. I was bullied, tormented, and neglected at times.

My mother was always chasing the next Eliam Pérez. When she died, I thought I was going to live a better life with my father. Unfortunately, my father coming for me only created a different kind of savage. And still, I don't think I belong here in the middle of all of this.

"Keep your head up," Taine pulls me from my thoughts as she wraps her arms around me. "Your dad loved you a ton. I know he had a weird way of showing it, but he did."

"Thanks. I needed to hear that."

She releases me and straightens. "Call me anytime. I'm here to help. If you decide you need me, I'm here."

"Thank you."

Taine isn't much older than me. Goes to show my father loved having pretty faces around him. Although he did make sure they were pretty faces with brains.

Hell, I'm only twenty-two and I'm already working on my Master's. My father was big on education. Yet I don't know what I'm doing with any of this.

The truth is, I'm letting Taine go for her own safety. If things go south, then she won't find herself in the crosshairs.

I have to learn to do what my father grew up doing and there are a lot of eyes and ears open, waiting to see if I can pull it off. The problem is, many of those people didn't know I even existed. My appearance has ruffled some feathers.

"Oh, by the way, don't forget the two associates from New York that want to come in to meet with you," Taine says as she heads for the door.

I sigh. "When was that again?"

"You'll have to give them a call to set it up. I left the information in the notes."

"Right," I say and nod, reaching for the notebook she made for me. Nothing more than a few contacts and numbers. All made to look like either exotic car clients or parties interested in throwing events at one of our clubs. "What were their names again?"

Yet another reveal to the world. Some don't seem too happy to find out about me. I get the feeling they thought that they would be able to move in on my father's business after his death.

"La—"

My phone rings again, halting my thoughts and Taine's words. I purse my lips and wave for her to leave. I'll get that information on my own. I get ready to hit ignore on the call until the number catches my attention. Relief washes through me.

It's my father's sister. I've been trying to get in touch with her for months. From the way my grandmother told it, my aunt and father spent a lot of time around the business when my grandfather ran things.

Hopefully, she can help.

With a sigh, I answer. "Hello."

"Cherone, what has happened?" she says in Spanish.

My anxiety shoots through the roof. My Spanish is terrible. Okay, wait. My father and aunt are Dominican. So, the Spanish I speak is totally foreign to her.

I hate going to DR. My dialogue is one of the first things that's pointed out. So much so that I don't speak to anyone while there.

They have come to think I'm rude and think I'm better than everyone, but it's been my way to not feel completely embarrassed in front of everyone and my father.

"Roni, Aunt Grissel, you can call me Roni."

"Ay, tell me what's happened. Is it true? Your father is gone? What has happened to my brother?"

I swallow past the lump in my throat. For only a single moment, I've forgotten my loss and the pain. It's like having alcohol tossed into an open wound as she brings up the stark reminder.

"He's gone," I murmur.

"Gone, what do you mean gone?" she asks before going into full Spanish as she freaks out. "How? Why?"

Tears slide down my cheeks. I don't know how to say the words out loud. I still don't believe them. Every time I have to say them, I swear I've stabbed myself with a sword—or at least it feels that way.

For my aunt, I fall on that sword once more. "He had a heart attack."

"What? No, you can't be serious. I was away. I've been traveling. I had no idea.

"Dios mío, Roni. You must be devastated. *Cariño*... I... I don't know what to say. Eliam has always been so healthy. *Mi hermano*." Our sobs mix as I release the pain, I've been feeling.

Three months and it's still so fresh. "I don't know what I'm doing. I don't know what to do. His business... what do I do with it?"

"Oh, *cariño*. This must be so overwhelming. Why don't you come to Dominica? Come see your *tía*. We can figure this out together. I... can't believe he's gone. I missed telling my brother goodbye," she says in broken English.

The idea isn't so bad. I could use the chance to clear my head and find my footing. Maybe a short trip, miles away will help me sort all of this shit out.

"I think I would like that, *tía.*"

"Good. We are family. We need to stick together. You come to see me, and we will make everything right as a family. I should have come to visit more. I'm so sorry."

My father has told me before that Aunt Grissel travels the world all the time. She has no husband or children I know of, and my father wasn't the type of brother you dropped in to see all the time. My aunt spends most of her time in Europe. I wasn't surprised that I wasn't able to reach her right away.

"It's fine. My father was a hard man. He didn't make it easy for you to get close to him. I understand the distance," I reply.

"My brother and I were once very close. So many things changed."

There's something about the tone of her voice that alerts me. I'm not sure what it is. Once she begins to rattle off plans for my visit, I push it to the back of my mind. I haven't been around her enough to know her moods or tones, I could be reading too much into all of it.

At least now I have someone to go through this with. Most of all, I can put some distance between myself and Darius. I want to be ghost before the calls turn into more visits. Something I know is coming soon, now that I'm ignoring him.

John

I sit with my arms spread against the back of the couch, stewing in my own anger. The scene before me doesn't register as my thoughts play last night over and over.

What the fuck did we even argue about?

One minute I was trying my best to spend time with Missy, still trying to get to know her on a new level. The next thing, she started a fight that I still don't understand for the life of me. One thing led to another and I was gone.

"Want to talk about it?" Remi asks.

I turn to him and frown. Do I want to talk about it? No, I don't. I want to forget the last few months ever happened, but I sigh and start talking before it all chokes me.

"Missy called me this morning. She said she lost the baby," I say tightly, guilt clawing at me.

I should have kept my cool. She was probably going through some hormonal shit last night—not actually being a complete psycho. I could have been more patient. I should have been more patient.

Remi gives me a nod. He and Ramses are the only ones I've told about Missy and the baby. I couldn't bring myself to tell my brothers.

I don't want Wyatt and Noah to be disappointed in me and I couldn't stand for my younger brothers to know that I was irresponsible. They look up to me.

"I thought I'd be relieved or something, but all I feel is guilt. I wasn't there for her and the baby is gone. The last three months have been nothing but stress, but I still should have at least been there," I say.

"I think you're being too hard on yourself. You have been doing your best."

"Have I? It's no secret that I didn't want to enter a relationship with her. I've been acting as her boyfriend for the last three months and I've been miserable."

Miserable because nothing has changed. Everything I've come to understand about Missy has only been magnified. We're not compatible at all. I question what she was doing at that party we met at in the first place.

Then there's that feeling still tugging at my soul. That knowing that someone is out there that is a match for all my desires and needs. It's starting to feel like I'm drowning, waiting to find her.

"Maybe things can go back to normal now," he says.

I pull a face, twist my lips to the side. "That's the thing. Will it go back to normal?

"She's been calling all day. I stopped in to check on her. It felt like the right thing to do, but when I got there it... something was off and I was uncomfortable... I don't know. I left to clear my head," I grumble.

I feel like a pussy. I should be facing this head on. Missy needs someone now that she's dealing with this loss. I know she doesn't have any family. She was so excited about the baby.

As if speaking to my thoughts, Remi says. "And here you sit."

I look at the scene before me. The gorgeous redhead would have turned me on any other night as she gives herself over to Ramses. They make for a captivating scene. My head just isn't here.

"Honestly, I don't know what brought me here."

"This is where you think, where you thrive. I'm not surprised that you've come here."

I grunt and reach for my scotch. The smooth burn reminds me of simpler times. Times when I came and went as I pleased.

"Do you know I've never been in love?" I blurt out.

I turn to see the expression on Remi's face. His amber eyes are focused on me. His face is unreadable.

"You want to know something I've learned about love?"

"What's that?" I say.

"It can be cruel. We think we want it... that it's necessary to our happiness. Yet when we find it, it takes our souls and sucks away our happiness with it. Love, my friend, is overrated."

"That, *my friend*, sounds like there's a story behind it." I give a chuckle and take another sip.

He shrugs. "We all have our stories. I think you should take this as a sign from Allah. Take this time to reset.

"Follow what your instincts tell you. You have a way of always getting things to work out the way you want. I don't think this will be any different."

I snort but say nothing more. I try to train my focus back on the scene before me. I'm almost lost in the moment until my phone buzzes.

Fucking great, she's not going to give me time to process this. Again, it comes to me that something isn't adding up, but I don't know if she's in the right state of mind for me to ask questions. Maybe I should ask anyway.

Don't be a dick, John.

How is this my life?

CHAPTER FIVE

Not Happening

Roni

It's burning hot as I sit in the back of the car on my way to my aunt's home. It's been a while since I've been to DR. I wish I could say that being here has eased my mind.

That's yet to be the case. Since I stepped off the plane, I've had this funny feeling in the pit of my stomach. I haven't been able to shake it.

"Is this the right way? These roads don't look familiar," I say in Spanish.

My chest tightens as I speak the words. I suck my bottom lip into my mouth and start to chew on it. These roads definitely look off.

When the driver doesn't answer me, my pulse starts to race. It occurs to me that I shouldn't have ignored Anthony's suggestion that I have someone come with me. The head of my father's security was not a fan of my decision to come spend time with my aunt alone.

I had texted Aunt Grissel once I was in the car to let her know I had landed. As we continue on a road that becomes increasingly unfamiliar, I pull out my phone and send her another text while my panic surges. Something is off.

When I don't get a reply, I start to sweat. My upper lip is damp, and my palms are wet. I look around for anything that might look familiar and give me a sense of calm.

"Are we going the right way?" I ask again.

My Spanish may be slow, but I'm sure he can understand me. Which means he's ignoring me. I wish I had one of those guns I found in my father's office.

It doesn't take long before we turn into a set of gates and stop in front of a beautiful home. However, it's not my aunt's home. It's been a while, but not long enough for me to forget the house she lives in.

I know she hasn't moved. She told me so in one of our conversations as I prepared to come here for this visit. I gave the driver the exact address she gave me.

"You get out here," he finally speaks.

"This isn't the address I gave you," I say firmly.

He looks in the rearview mirror at me. "You get out here," he repeats.

"Take me to the address I gave you. I'm not getting out of this car until you do."

The door to my right opens before he can reply or I can make any further demands. I'm grabbed by my hair and dragged from the car faster than I can blink.

Pain sears through my scalp as I'm jerked from the vehicle. My vision blurs with tears as I fight to get free. The person holding me only tightens their grip.

I reach behind me to try to scratch their eyes out. I connect with soft flesh and start to claw. The guy howls in pain.

"Enough," someone bellows with a familiar sounding voice.

I freeze and turn my head as best I can toward the house. Stepping out of the entrance is a tall dark-haired man I know I've seen before. I try hard to place him through my burning eyes. He scowls as he gets closer.

"This is not how we were supposed to meet," he says as his eyes roll over me. "I should have done things myself. You're like a wild cat. I would have enjoyed putting out that fire."

My stomach turns in disgust. He reeks of slime ball. Although he might be handsome to some, I find the smug grin on his face revolting.

"What the hell is going on? Get this guy off of me," I snap.

He laughs. "Feisty, I like it. This really is a pity. You have two options, Roni. That's what you like to be called?"

"Fuck you."

He looks me over from head to toe. "Unfortunately for me, that isn't one of the options." He shrugs and licks his lips. "Marry my friend Darius. Allow him to take over your father's business. You can live your life spending as much money as you like and I will make all of your problems go away," he says with an underlying tone as if my problems are greater than the situation I'm currently in.

"You and Darius can go to hell," I seethe.

"Wrong answer. Option two is a bit nasty."

He closes the distance between us and lifts a hand to touch me. I slap his hand away, causing the guy with the tight grip on my hair to grab my arms and restrain them behind my back. I struggle but it's useless.

"One thing that can't be denied, you do have a nice body," he says as he releases a laugh.

He reaches out again, this time running his finger from my chin down my throat, between my breasts, stopping right at the waistband of my pencil skirt. He tilts his head to the side and licks his lips. My stomach rolls again at the sight of lust filling his gaze.

"Is it true?" he asks with a gleam in his eyes.

"Is what true?"

"Daddy's little girl is a virgin? Eliam kept a great secret from the world. At least he thought he did. My employer had thought that Roni was a Ronaldo for years. Did you know that?"

"Do I give a shit?"

He makes a face and nods his head. "Fair enough. I still want to know if it's true. If you ask me, I think the García brothers were lured in with your beauty and the promise of your tight pussy. Too bad your father never saw them coming."

I tighten my jaw and lift my head in defiance. This causes him to roar with laughter. He palms my waist and looks over me hungrily.

"I should keep you for myself, but if this is true, I'll get more for you."

"What?"

"Choose, Roni. I get what I want either way. It's up to you whether that's the easy or hard way."

"Go to hell. Let me go, you animal. I will never marry that asshole. You can't get away with this."

"Ah, that is the wrong answer," he purrs in Spanish, despite having some other accent. He removes his hand from my waist to squeeze one of my breasts. "What a shame. I think Darius actually liked you."

I spit in his face. "Fuck you. Keep your filthy hands off me." My hatred for this man soars to new levels with each second. "This is not going to end the way you think. I can promise you that."

He glares at me, grasps my face and squeezes hard. "It will end the way I want it to end, Cherone."

Before I can reply, he backhands me, sending pain through the side of my face. Something pricks me in the neck and my vision fades. Next, I'm hit in the head, for good measure I guess, or because I spit on him.

Whatever the reason, I don't get to analyze it because I completely blackout.

***

I wake with a pounding headache. My left eye is throbbing. My entire body feels so heavy.

When I try to open my eyes, my left one won't open. The vision I do have from the right is blurry at best. The cold of the floor beneath me seeps through my skin.

That's when I realize I'm naked and on a cold concrete floor. I search my brain for any indication of how I've gotten here. Nothing is clicking into place.

Disoriented, I test my tongue in my mouth. It's a little swollen as if I've bitten it. Slowly, I lift and turn to sit.

"Easy," comes the sound of a soft voice.

I blink my good eye and a young girl comes into view. At least she looks to be young. The throbbing in my head causes me to close my eye.

"Where…" I cut off as my dry mouth feels like I have sandpaper inside of it.

"I'm Natasha," she whispers. "You've been taken like the rest of us. What's your name?"

My name?

I wrack my brain to answer the question. It doesn't come to me as fast as it feels like it should. My name. What is my name?

"Roni," I test it on my lips.

It feels right but doesn't at the same time. I wince as my brain fights against me. A chill runs through me and I tentatively lift my arms to cover myself.

"It's nice to meet you, Roni," she says softly. "They don't like us to talk to each other. If they catch us, they'll drug us. So, we have to be quiet."

I tighten my hold around my knees that I manage to draw into my chest. Gently, I nod my understanding as the slightest movement feels like I'm rattling my entire brain. I swallow thickly.

"Where are we?"

"I don't know. The men here all speak Russian, but I don't know if they've taken us that far," she replies.

"Russia?" I frown.

"Yes, I was traveling in North Korea with my family when I was taken. They ambushed my family one night. Where did they take you from?"

I go to answer but realize that I have no clue what the answer is. I don't know. I try to think, but everything is a fog. I can't link anything together.

What the fuck? I start to hyperventilate. My body shivers.

"Hey, I'm sorry. I asked too many questions. You should rest. The drugs are in your system, they've been drugging you all this time. Try to get some rest. I'll keep watch," she says.

All this time. How long have I been here? How long have these people had me?

I fix my gaze on her hazel eyes. They look innocent, but upon looking deeper there's a wisdom you wouldn't expect to find in such a young girl. Her brown skin is smooth, and her cheeks are slightly chubby, showing the youthfulness of her heart-shaped face.

Her dark hair is braided, reaching her shoulders. If it weren't for the eyes, I'd think I was looking at an illusion of my younger self. I nod as my lid grows heavy.

I don't have a choice in the matter. I still don't remember much as I try to push through the fog. I lie down and close my eye, hoping that when I wake again this nightmare is over.

John

I open the door to my apartment and look at Missy on the other side. She looks at me with the saddest puppy eyes, and still, I feel like it's all an act.

It's been two weeks since the miscarriage. I've gone by her place to check on her a few times, but she's been so hot and cold. Even her roommate has been acting funny.

"I have work to do. Can we do this some other time?" I say as I hold onto the door, not opening it further to welcome her in.

"I was hoping for only a few minutes of your time. I promise I won't be long," she replies.

I want to tell her, no, but I'm trying not to be a dick. There used to be times when I didn't find her presence to be so annoying. With a sigh, I step back and allow her in.

"Can I get you anything?"

"Water please."

I nod and head for the kitchen to pour her a glass. She wanders about my living room, looking at all of the photos. I get distracted as I watch her.

Trying my hardest to place what's off to me, I narrow my eyes and home in. Missy is still attractive. None of that has changed.

She's wearing her hair in long highlighted blonde locks this week. It's not strange for her to go back and forth between brown and blonde.

Despite being around four months when she lost the baby, she's still tight and fit. Long legs, toned arms…

Four months. Wait a minute, when was the last time we slept together? I start to do the math in my head.

"Are we still going to join your family for dinner next week?" she asks, pulling me out of my calculations.

"What?"

"The dinner with your family. I mean, you invited me before… I assumed we'd still be going."

"Uh, yeah. I don't know about that. I had planned to introduce you under different circumstances. Things have changed," I reply as I walk over and hand her the glass of water.

"Oh." She takes a sip of the water and sits. "I know my emotions have been all over the place. You know, with losing the baby and all, but I was sort of looking forward to meeting your family."

The last thing I want is to get into another argument with her. I've been feeling completely drained dealing with all that is Missy. The little things that caused me to want to call it off before the pregnancy have only amplified.

She's gritting on every nerve I have with the mood swings and signs of some real narcissism. For crying out loud, I showed up at her place in the middle of the night after she sent me a text that she was depressed and wished she had ice cream to drown her sorrows in.

When I arrived, she accused me of trying to check out her roommate who was sitting in the living room. At one point, I thought I had by the way she spun the shit. I almost felt guilty until I sleepily thought about it.

Needless to say, I turned right back around and left. I'm getting tired of the whiplash. None of this seems normal.

I want to ask Mom if I'm being insensitive, but if I open that box, Cassidy Black is going to want details, or she'll beat them out of me. What do I know? Maybe Missy isn't psycho. Maybe she needs a bit of time to deal with all of this before she can move on.

I sigh at my thoughts. "We have time. Nothing needs to be decided today."

"So that's it? Are you breaking up with me?"

I bite back my quick response. Lately, it's felt like I'm channeling my inner Ryan and Brax. I grimace as I hear the reply I want to give in my head.

We'd have to be together to break up.

I've wanted off this ride for a long time now. I don't intend to drag things out. That is until she hits me in my weak spot.

"John, this hasn't been easy for me, you know. I've lost so much already. If I lose you… I don't know if I can go on living."

Fuck.

Something else to know about Lauren from high school. Since I never told my mother why I dumped Lauren in front of everyone, she reamed my ass good. I've never been able to make a girl cry without cringing since. It's my weakness because I saw how hurt and disappointed Mom was even though I had a reason.

I reach to wrap an arm around Missy's shoulders, and I do what I always do. I fix shit. I make it so that others hear what they need to be whole. What they need to hear so I get my way and they remain happy.

Tonight, I want to get back to work as much as I want to keep her from harming herself. Which is why I kiss the top of her head and rub her arm soothingly. Then I reassure her.

"It's going to be fine. I'm here. It will all be all right."

CHAPTER SIX

Bonds

Roni

I really don't know how much time has passed since I was taken. However, I have been counting the days since I've woken. Two months, that's how much time has gone by give or take.

I've learned a lot since then, although I still can't remember much about before I arrived. I've tried. I've tried very hard.

"They are coming to take more girls away today," Natasha says in Spanish as she walks by my cot.

I nod my head slightly. I've watched plenty of girls come and go. Among a few of the other girls, Natasha and I have remained for a few different reasons.

"What did she say?"

Raven, the girl on the cot next to me asks. She's new. She's only been here for a few days or so.

I take in the dark circles under her worried eyes. Her right eye is black, marring her gorgeous brown skin. She looks like she could be Gabrielle Union's little sister.

That's one of the first things I've learned. If you are defiant, they won't hesitate to put you in your place. Those who are rebellious also seem to have it rougher and remain longer. It's as if they want to break us before taking us wherever the others go.

"They will be moving more girls soon," I murmur low.

Her eyes grow panicked. She draws her legs into her chest and starts to rock. I know that look. I've seen it so many times before.

I lean in and catch her eyes. I give a slow shake of my head to warn her not to freak out. They hate that and the beatings are more severe for it.

"You're safe for now. You're in this room which means you're valuable to them," I whisper.

I've also realized there's a difference between the holding cells. Thin walls separate us into small groups. They don't like us to talk to each other, but I've figured out that the cells hold different individuals for different reasons.

I've watched through the glass panel of our room as they've ushered the young boys to and from the room next door. Natasha has told me about the others. Apparently, we are broken down by race, sex, age, and virginity.

I look around at all the brown faces in this room. Anger is the only emotion I can find as the thought of our future makes me sick. We mean nothing to these people.

"Each of us has a price," I say to Raven.

"I've seen the girls in the other rooms," she whispers. "I don't want to be like them. Those men stand in line—"

Her last words are choked off by her emotions. I've only been out of this room a few times. They made me shower and dress up before they forced me to take pictures, some of them were nude.

"I don't think your fate will be anything like theirs."

It won't be. The girls in this room are different. I believe I understand why I'm here, although I seem older than most of the girls they bring here. Something about knowing I'm a virgin feels right. Not that I remember much.

I think the drugs they pump in us have kept me from remembering. The dried blood on my head when I finally was able to sit up and stay awake was also an indication.

That seems like forever ago. The one thing I know for sure is they're saving me for something. Although not everyone stays, Natasha and a couple of other girls have been here for as long as I have.

I don't know why or what they are waiting for, but I know it's something big. Yes, a few of us are defiant. We fight back when they come to take check-in, and they want to get rough.

However, I know it's not our fight that makes us special. It's something different with us. From what Natasha has overheard, we believe there is a buyer that has reserved us or an auction that we are being held specifically for.

I can't help but hope that Raven has made that list and they won't take her out sooner. I have to believe she's like Natasha and myself. She'll be around long enough for us to find a way to escape. I don't know what it is about her, but she has grown on me in the short time she's been here. Sort of like Natasha has.

"How do you know so much? I've never heard them speak English, not much anyway," Raven asks, breaking into my thoughts.

I chew on my lip, what seems like old instincts kick in. Never show your hand to everyone. I don't want Natasha to be placed in danger by the jealousy or desperation of any of the others.

Of all the girls here, Natasha is the most unique and valuable to the guys that are keeping us. From what she has told me, they aren't sure whether she should be auctioned off. Which I can totally understand.

Natasha and I stick together. We share our stale food, especially when they want to punish one of us to go without. She watches my back and tells me what the guards are plotting.

"I speak many languages," Natasha answers for me. "I can understand everything they say."

"Like them," Raven nods toward the girls in the back of the room.

They are the Black Russian girls. A few are ARMY brats, others from villages throughout the country. They tend to stay away from me and Natasha.

I think they believe they're better than us. As if the fact that they're Russian will get them out of this somehow.

Natasha gives a slight shake of her head. "No, they're all native Russians. A few speak English as well since their parents are US military."

"Oh."

"They use me to translate sometimes, Spanish, Portuguese, and Mandarin. I've been thinking, I believe that's why they took me. My family used mostly Mandarin while on our vacation. I'm thinking they scout their targets."

"Oh," Raven says and nods. "That's why they brought you in when we first arrived, and the Chinese girl was freaking out." Natasha nods and takes a seat on my cot. We all look around out of habit to see if we're being watched. I pick up the brush from the little makeshift table they provided and hand it to Natasha.

"This is the one thing they allow us. If we need to talk, we have to be careful. I brush her hair, but we hide the fact that we're talking."

"Okay," Raven whispers.

She picks up the brush from her table and comes to sit behind Natasha to join us. While Natasha releases my two braids to brush my hair, Raven nervously does the same to Natasha's.

"How did they get you?" Natasha whispers.

I know she's talking to Raven because we both know I can't remember a thing. Raven is so silent; I don't think she's going to answer at first. However, she begins so quietly, I have to strain to hear her.

"I was on vacation with my family. Our room at the resort got messed up or something. A man offered us his villa that he and his wife would no longer be using.

"My father agreed since we had no place else to stay. It was in the middle of the night on the second night. Men came in and snatched me from my sleep." Raven starts to sniffle.

"The next thing I knew, I was here. I haven't seen my family since. I don't know if they're okay or..." She trails off. I know how that ends.

At least she knows she could have a family out there looking for her. I get the feeling I may not. That fact keeps me up at night. It's up to me to figure out a way out of here. No one's coming to my rescue.

The door to our room opens and we all stiffen. Four of the men come in. Immediately, I know something has changed. They head straight for one of the new girls and two from the group that came in before Raven and the other new girls.

"Oh, no," Raven breathes when the last of the guards looks around and his gaze falls on her.

I don't know why, but I jump to my feet and stand between the two. He narrows his cold eyes on me and storms in our direction. My heart is pounding, but I'm not letting him take one of these girls.

"No," I yell when he goes to shove me out of the way.

I stand my ground despite him being bigger than me. He growls at me, but he's not quick to hit me like I've seen him do with the other girls. Taking note of this, I quickly take advantage and back up to cover Raven.

"Move, little girl. This is none of your business."

"Yes, it is. You're not taking her."

"Don't make problem you don't want," he says with ice in his voice, his English broken.

"Leave her. She's not ready to go." I don't know what else to say. All I know is I have to protect these two. They are just girls. I may not remember my age, but I know I'm older than them both.

"Take me," I blurt the words out before I can think.

He rolls his eyes over me. I straighten my shoulders and lift my chin. Do I want to be sold or in one of those rooms with the crying girls and lines of men? No, but I can feel it in my bones that I can't allow them to take these two.

He snorts, reaching out to touch my loose hair. He goes from caressing it to grabbing a handful and tugging my head to the side. Leaning down, we come face to face as he seethes.

"I would love to take you, but we are not allowed to touch you. Don't make problem for me. I can't sell you, but I can make life miserable."

With that, he tosses me to the bed. He glares at Raven, looking her over. When his gaze lands on her eye, he frowns.

Waving a hand, he turns his back. "She is damaged now. Keep her this time."

I breathe a deep sigh of relief at his words. Raven and Natasha both throw themselves around me. However, the victory is short-lived.

When the asshole says something in Russian, Natasha stiffens. The word *no* whimpers from her mouth. My stomach sinks as one of the other men tosses the girl in his hold to the guy that was coming for Raven.

He's bigger, much bigger than me. When he reaches us, he grabs me and tosses me over his shoulder. I try to kick and scream but it's futile.

The one I assume is the leader snarls at me in his broken English. "There are ways to break you without touching you, da. Let me prove."

John

I've put this off for a little more than two months. Hoping that Missy would pull it together in that time and we'd have the talk. That hasn't happened and then, the guilt starts in.

"That was so nice," Missy chirps from the passenger seat.

I tighten my hands on the steering wheel. I'm conflicted. I feel like I've spent the evening lying to my family. They saw right through me.

I'm surprised my mother didn't call me on my shit. I noticed the look she gave me. I think I held my breath the entire night waiting for her to lay into my ass.

Still, this is the happiest I've seen Missy since she lost the baby. She has a sparkle in her eyes, and she looks better. She looks more like the fresh-faced girl I met that first night.

"Nothing out of the norm," I reply.

It wasn't. Despite getting looks from everyone for bringing Missy home and introducing her as my girlfriend it was the Blacks as usual—boy, did I get looks. Everyone and I do mean everyone in my family knows about my lifestyle.

My mother gives me shit about it all the time. Not in front of everyone, but when she gets me alone, she definitely ribs me about it. I'm her *kinky little fucker*, her words not mine.

For the life of me, I can't see why Missy thought my family was so great. They practically went on like she wasn't there. My family wasn't going to change because of her presence, but it wasn't like they rolled out the welcome wagon either.

"I wish I had a big family like yours. Sisters or brothers. It must have been so neat growing up with all of them," she gushes.

Not in the fucking least. I love my brothers, would kill for them and die for them, but there was nothing neat about growing up with six brothers. Half the time I wanted to kill one of them.

As the third oldest, I was sort of the mediator between the older brothers and the younger. While Wyatt has the whole, *do it because I'm the oldest and I said so*, I was the one that tried to hear them out and get the other side to listen. Shit drove my crazy.

However, I don't tell Missy all of that. It's not something I've ever shared with anyone. Truth is, that's the second reason why I think I am the way I am. My need for control comes from my role as the third son.

I'm not quite the middle child, but I have my own issues. I've never lacked love or attention from my parents, but I have always had a sense of responsibility and I take my responsibilities seriously. Always have, always will.

I grunt to myself. And that's why I'm here in this situation. I can't walk away without making sure Missy is okay. It's starting to feel like a character flaw on my behalf.

"Want to head to your place?" Missy pulls me from my musing, reaching to run a hand through my hair.

I nearly cringe. Reaching for her hand, I place it on my thigh to keep her from doing it again. The last thing I want is for her to have roaming hands.

Although, when she locks her fingers through mine, I see the mistake I've made. I glance at her and she's smiling more than she has all night. I'm not trying to deepen this connection she thinks we have.

My goal was to get her back to a healthy place and gently break things off with her the way I'd planned before finding out about the pregnancy. Too bad goals aren't always met. "I have a bounty I need to head out on. Dad handed it over before we left," I answer her question.

It's the truth. I do have a guy to track down. Some shit show with parents that cut him off and now he's on the run, skipping bail.

"Oh."

I sigh, hating the disappointment that starts to roll off of her. She was just on such a high. The last thing I want is for her to digress.

"Maybe next time."

The words are out before I think better of them. It wouldn't be my first mistake tonight. Mistake number one was calling her my girlfriend in front of her.

"Maybe I can come along to Sunday breakfast. Now that your family has met me, it would be good for them to get to know me more," she says, the excitement returning to her voice.

This is my point. I couldn't *not* call her my girlfriend. If I would have brought Missy home as a friend, there was no way I was making it through the night without an interrogation. I don't bring "friends" or Subs home to meet my family.

I totally took a chance with the girlfriend title. It was my hope that they would think she meant enough to spare an ounce of her feelings—this time. And here, she wants to go back.

"I don't know about that. I'll be busy for the rest of the week. I don't know if I'll be going. If I do, I'll be popping in real fast and heading back out, so Mom doesn't kick my ass."

I'm going to kick Brax's ass for mentioning Sunday breakfast in front of her.

"Oh," she says, the chipperness in her voice dies down.

I'm grateful when the exit for her place comes up. I turn off and we make the rest of the ride in silence. When I release her hand, she crosses her arms over her chest.

Pulling up in front of her place, I turn the car off. She turns to me and stares for a beat. Why do I feel like I should get out of the car and let her have it?

"Are you going to come in?"

"No, I told you, I have to work tonight."

"Right, fine."

With that, she jumps from the car and slams the door hard enough to rattle the glass. I throw my head back. I have to figure out a way to cut ties.

The problem is, I know I can be a dick. How do I break up with someone that was pregnant with my baby without coming off like a complete douchebag? I groan and want to kick my own ass for the millionth fucking time.

This is some John shit for sure. Fuck!

CHAPTER SEVEN

Craziness

John

Mom pushes her hand through my hair as she sits a plate of muffins in front of me. I lift my head and look her in the eyes as I sit in her kitchen at the island. I can't count how many times she's done that exact gesture throughout my life.

"Ye look exhausted," she says. "Talk to me. What's on ye mind?"

"Nothing I want to talk about," I mutter.

"But enough to keep you awake at night. Ye have circles under the eyes. What's going on? Is it that lass ye brought here? Something's off about her."

"Don't make me have to drag her ass up and down this street. She has crazy eyes, but I'll show her what crazy really is, I will."

I chuckle. "Relax, Mom. I don't need you kicking anyone's ass... again."

She sniffs. "I'd do it again. No mother is going to accuse me boys of something they didn't do. Ye and Wyatt were right under me nose all day."

I release a deep laugh as the memories surface. One of the moms on the block tried to blame me and Wyatt for beating up her son. We'd both had some stomach bug or some shit and hadn't been out all day. Mom was fine until Mrs. Delaney threatened to call the cops.

Mom whipped her ass back to her house. "Now if one of me boys had touched yers that's what it would have looked like," she snarled once she beat her to her front door. "Now ye have a reason to call the cops."

"I think that's when everyone on the block figured out our entire family is crazy." I laugh and wipe at the tears. "Dad stood on the porch and watched until Mr. Delaney stepped out like he was going to help his wife. I've never seen Dad move faster in my life."

"You damn right. Joe has never failed me," she says with a smile.

I return the smile. "Yeah, you and Dad have always had each other's back."

"We had to work for it."

I've always admired that about my parents. Family is important to them, but their relationship has always been something to marvel. My parents can finish each other's thoughts.

I remember when I was little and I'd get in trouble, they would mirror each other's expressions. Even when they don't agree on something, they show a united front. Yet as I got older,

I watched my parents closer and I could see the submissive side of my mother.

I also recognized a lot of myself in my father. Not that I want to think about my parents in the bedroom, but I've observed Dad enough to know he has explored his dominant side and my mother is no stranger to submission.

Well, that and I may or may not have learned about the life from getting into Dad's things. If only my brothers knew where those videos used to come from. I've been holding that one in for years.

Still, I envy dad. I can't knock my parents for any of it. Maybe that's what's kept them going strong for so long. The balance the life brings.

That's what I want.

"Ye want to know what makes it work?" Mom says, bringing me back to the room.

I look into her hazel eyes. They have softened. Instantly, I know she has seen right through me.

She cups my face and continues. "Your father and I bumped heads like bulls in the beginning. We had to work our way to balance, but the one thing we did know... we were made for each other."

"Did you know that from the beginning?"

"Aye, we did. I gave him shit, I did, but I knew from the time I looked into his eyes, I was his. I'm pretty sure it was the same for him. It's the same as the way you know that lass isn't yours," she says with a knowing look.

I blow out a breath. She's right. I've never felt anything real for Missy. Not anything that would make me want to change the nature of our relationship.

"Everything has gotten complicated between us. It's not the clear, clean-cut relationship I normally have. Usually, I set the rules and that's what we play by. Not this time," I admit.

"Well, I'll tell ye the first problem. Yer playing. What's the meaning of the word? Go on look it up."

I pull my phone out and pull up the definition to read aloud. "To engage in activity for enjoyment and recreation rather than a serious or practical purpose."

"Aye, let that sink in. Anything you play at you are not serious about. Yer twenty-eight, John. It's time to start thinking about where ye want to be in a year or two. Will playing be enough for ye?" she asks and tilts her head to the side.

"I don't know," I murmur.

I've often thought about my lifestyle. Do I want to keep bouncing from Sub to Sub? I've had a few that I wouldn't have mind seeing if I could enter longer arrangements with, but I still can't say I've been in love with any of them.

Mom covers my hand with hers. I look into her eyes as she gives me a warm smile. It hits me hard that someday I want what my father has. Someone to bear my children and help me to raise them with love.

"When you find the right one, she will understand you enough to allow you to be the kinky little fucker you are and be everything else that you need. Until then, kick that Maisha to the side." She frowns at the end of her statement.

I laugh. "It's Missy."

"Do I look like I give even the wee bit of a fuck?"

I bark out more laughter. "No, Mom you don't."

"Now eat ye muffins before Braxton shows up and eats them all. He's a human garbage disposal."

I snort and shake my head. I love my mother. I don't know what we'd do without her.

Roni

"Hey, you okay in there?"

I suck my busted bottom lip into my mouth. I don't know how many days have gone by since I've been down here. I haven't eaten in however many days that might be.

I try to stifle my cries. I think I'm losing my mind. I still can't remember anything and the anxiety of not knowing what happened to Raven and Natasha is weighing on me along with the anticipation of what they plan for me next.

"Hey, you okay?" The voice comes again. It's male, but young, not quite a child, but not a man either.

It's also not the voice I've been hearing, the voice I believe belongs to my father. I've been hearing that voice a lot and having dreams and visions of him and me as a young girl. I get the feeling that he wasn't such a loving man. Which leads me to believe even more that he's not coming for me and probably isn't worried that I'm gone.

"No... no," I choke out.

"You have to stay strong. We're going to get out of here. I'm Torque."

I furrow my brows. He sounds like he's barely entered puberty, but here he is trying to give me reassurance. My heart aches as I think of all the people here that have had their lives snatched away. Young girls and boys. This isn't right.

"I'm Roni," I say as I shove down a sob.

"Have... did... are you hurt?" he says in a softer tone. "Not the beatings. Did they touch you?"

My heart burns. From the sound of his voice, I don't even want to think of his reply. These sick bastards need to pay for what they've done to everyone. I ball my fists as I pull my knees into my chest.

The cold floor beneath me chills my body, but my blood boils with my anger. I haven't been raped, which had been my biggest fear when they first brought me down here. However, they have jerked off in front of me while making me watch, beaten me, splashed me with ice water repeatedly, and starved me.

"No," I say barely above a whisper, but I know he's heard me when he releases a relieved breath.

"Can I ask you something?"

"Yeah."

"There's a girl that they use to help to talk to the others. She's... um, Black, I think and pretty. Really pretty. She can understand and speak to almost everyone," he says cautiously.

I bite my inner cheek. He's talking about Natasha. I take pause and try to decide if I should say anything. This could be a trap for all I know. I won't put her in danger.

"Please. I need to know if she's okay. She saved my life. Have you seen her?"

"Yeah, you're talking about Natasha."

"Natasha," he says as if testing the name on his lips.

"Yeah, she was safe the last time I saw her."

There's a long pause before he replies in a low voice. "Thank you."

"You're welcome," I breathe before I close my eyes.

No telling when they'll return to torture me more. The restlessness is a part of their plan to break me, they never stay away for too long. If I can rest for a little while, maybe I can sleep the hunger and pain away.

Don't break, Roni. You're going to make it through this.

CHAPTER EIGHT

Misery

John

Pushing a hand through my hair, I head out of the bar. It's time for me to call it a night. It's been a long day.

First, there was that call from Nellie's ex. She's only been home for four months, but it's like old times. I remember the cute little kid that would run around with Bean, I was protective of her back then too.

That call had me boiling mad. "Piece of shit," I mutter to myself as I think about it.

I make my way to my car thinking of all the ways I want to torture that asshole apart. I'm at the driver's side door when my phone rings. I pull it from my pocket and growl.

The second reason it's been the day from hell. Missy won't stop calling. She knows she has me by the balls. I'm going to answer. Why?

Well, that's the next thing that has me wondering how the hell I got myself into all of this. Last week she called me sobbing. I was in the middle of a case and I couldn't take the time to find out what the hell was going on.

The next time my phone rang it was her new roommate freaking out as she screamed that she didn't know what to do. Missy had swallowed a bottle of pills. Yup, she tried to kill herself.

"Hello," I answer the phone, trying my best not to allow my annoyance to show through.

I still can't believe she tried to kill herself. I'd told her to give me an hour and I'd call her once I was done with work. It hadn't been fifteen minutes before that next call came in.

I know she's been unstable, but I never thought she would take it that far. Now I'm walking on eggshells to keep her from harming herself again and I'm miserable. It's starting to feel like I can't breathe.

"Hey," Missy replies. "Are you still out with your brothers?"

I roll my eyes at the bitter way she says that. When she'd asked to come along, I'd danced right out of that. Nellie had been all of our priority.

Missy would have made the night about her. It's something I've learned about her that I hate. We could be in a conversation about cats and somehow the cats would remind her of something she wants or needs.

Not a greater need or want than the topic in discussion. It comes off odd and egotistically at times. Most times to be honest.

"Actually, I'm heading home. I'm exhausted," I reply. "How are you feeling?"

"Lonely, I was hoping you could come over and hold me again. You know like the night you brought me home," she says hopefully.

I'm enabling this behavior. I know I am, but the guilt I feel won't allow me not to do anything I can to make sure she's safe, mentally and physically. As I climb into my car and start it, I prepare myself for an even longer night.

"Yeah, I'll be there," I murmur.

Once I end the call with Missy, I stare straight ahead, unseeing. I'm like a bottle ready to explode. The lid is ready to pop right off.

My thoughts race. I'm seriously trying not to be a dick, but something about her suicide attempt was off as well. God, I hate feeling like I'm making all this up because I don't want to be with her.

"This has to end soon," I mumble to myself.

Roni

"You know who I am?" the tall man says.

He's handsome. Lighter than me and my mommy, with pretty light brown eyes. His nose looks like mine.

I squeeze the teddy bear he gave me to my chest before answering the question. Looking up into his eyes, I nod. He squats in front of me, coming down to eye level.

"You're my father," I say softly.

"Good, she told you about me," he says.

Cupping my face, he searches my eyes. My lips tremble. This is the first time that I can remember that I'm seeing this man in person.

I don't know if I can give him a hug. I want to. I'm scared and my mommy is gone. They said she's not coming back this time.

"Our plane is waiting." He nods and stands to turn. "We leave. It's time to go home." He starts walking without another word.

I gasp and jump out of my sleep as ice water hits my body. They're back. My teeth chatter as I tremble.

Yet I try to hold onto the dream I've been awakened from. It feels important to me. A much needed memory.

"Please."

The chilling cry causes me to snap my head up. It's then that I realize they have my cell door wide open and Natasha is now standing outside in the hold of one of the guards.

She's been beaten. I stifle the sob that bubbles up. She's naked, revealing the bruises all up and down her torso. They limit the damage they do to our faces, but our bodies are free reign.

"I want you to see friend. You two bane of my existence. It's time you learn place."

"Let her go," I say with as much force as my tired body will allow.

He snarls at me and tightens his grip. "I can't wait to be rid of you both. You cause me trouble and make others think they should too. Enough," Iosif, the one that ordered I be placed down here says.

He turns to leave, dragging Natasha with him. Someone slams the door shut before I can see where they are taking her. I immediately rush to the door and try to see underneath, through the crack between the floor and the door.

I can't see much, but I hear when a door is slammed shut. I wait for the sound of their footsteps to disappear. Weakly pressing my hands to the door, I close my eyes as Natasha's sobs grow louder.

"Natasha," I call out.

"Roni," she sobs and sniffles. "Oh my god, you're so skinny. They're starving you."

"Don't worry about me. Why are you here? What happened?"

"They came for Raven again. I overheard what they wanted to do with her, so I fought them," she says.

I close my eyes and try not to fall apart. At this moment, I vow that one day I'll get out of here and kill them all with my bare hands. For Raven, for Natasha, and for all the others. I'm going find out who I am and I'm going to make everyone pay.

That dream comes back to me. My father, he was a wealthy man. That much starts to tickle my brain. How did I get here? Were we on vacation? Why do I feel like he's not looking for me?

He was cold.

Is that it? Is my father too callous to care that I'm missing? So many thoughts are sparked.

"I'm going to kill them."

Torque. I almost forgot about him. His voice pulls me from my thoughts. The rage that comes from him almost matches my own.

"First, we have to survive, but yeah, one day…" I trail off on that promise.

Nothing more needs to be said. They will all die. I feel that in my bones.

CHAPTER NINE

Tortured

Roni

"Wake up." The words are snarled as warm liquid is tossed on me.

Right away I know it's not water. The stench turns my stomach, causing me to back away from the pool it's making around me. I tremble with anger. I've held my shit for this long, but this... this is about to be my breaking point and these two clowns are laughing before me.

"We thought you could use shower," one says.

I snap. As weak as I am, I get to my feet and charge them. I start to claw at the eyes of the one closest to me. That's when the other one hits me in my side so hard, I know the moment my ribs break. I gasp and fall back, dropping to the piss covered floor.

I barely have time to curl into a ball and cover my side before they start to stomp on me. I'm silent as I take the attack. I won't give them the satisfaction of my whimpers and tears.

I'm not sure how much time passes as they kick and punch at me. My mind begins to travel off away from here. It's as if I float out of my body, away from the pain and the torture. A distant memory is triggered.

"This world will never love you back, Roni," my mother said as she sat in the window.

The scent of lemon pine and honey filled the room. She had her hair wrapped up. It was a Saturday, her day to clean. No doubt one of her friends would be coming to visit.

"Your father took what he wanted and left me as if he never had any love for me. I thought he'd come back for you." She snorted. "Not even you could make him come back. Nope, this world will never show you love. It only knows how to take."

"Daddy sends me things," I said. "Maybe one day he will come back. He's just busy."

"Girl, you better get over that dream. He will leave you for dead like he did me."

"He'll be back."

She turned from the window and glared at me with her dark eyes. I stood twisting my fingers in my T-shirt. I hated when she got like this.

"The world revolves around money. You don't have it; it has no use for you. You keep waiting on your father. He will disappoint you every time. Money is the only thing that man is capable of loving. We are just pawns on the chessboard, pieces he can toss away," she said coldly.

"But—"

"There are no buts, little girl," she started to cough. That had started to happen a lot. "I'm trying to prepare you. We will never know your father's world. He keeps us here, hidden, with the bare minimum. I deserve better.

"Remember this. You have to fight with everything you have to get what you want. If you show weakness, they'll try to take everything, but there are times you will allow them to think you're weak so you can live another day to fight and win.

"Don't be like me. Don't love them more than you love yourself. You'll forget what you wanted in the first place."

I didn't believe her words. My daddy never met me. If he did, he would know I'm a good girl and I'm smart. Then he would want to take me away from here. If she wasn't so angry all the time, maybe he would come back and stay.

She jumped up and slammed her hand down on the kitchen table. "You listen to me, Roni. I'm teaching you how to survive. He'll never come to rescue you. You'll have to rescue yourself. Always rely on yourself. Trust no one."

"Roni, Roni," Torque's voice pulls me back to the present.

I look at the ceiling, but I can't focus. There's too much pain. I roll my eyes and try to breathe. It's not easy. My breaths are coming shallow.

"Roni," this time it's Natasha. "Can you hear us?"

I nod as if they can see me. My mouth is so dry when I try to make a sound. Rolling to my side, I whimper.

"I heard something," Torque exclaims. "Roni, you okay?"

I manage a groan. There's the taste of copper in my mouth as I roll my tongue around. So much pain radiates through my body.

"I hear her now. Maybe we should leave her to rest," Natasha says nervously.

"I'm here, Roni," Torque says softly. "I'm here. Don't let them break you. We're going to get out."

I close my eyes. Has my life always been shitty? The memories all have me so confused. Like puzzle pieces that refuse to fit together.

"Trust me, Roni. I'm here." Torque's murmurs are the last thing I hear as I pass out.

CHAPTER TEN

Enough of This

John

"I want to leave," Missy mutters.

"Okay, see you later," I say and go to walk back into my parents' house.

"Really, John," she shrieks at my back.

I whip around. "Really."

My body is tight with anger. I've had to step out of myself to evaluate this bullshit. I'm being manipulated.

My anger has burned away the guilt. Now that I'm looking with fresh eyes, I'm seeing things for what they are. Bullshit. This has been going on for months.

I've started to question everything and follow my gut. The PI in me promises that something is off with all of this shit. The only reason she's even here this morning is because she showed up on her own.

"Why are you being like this? Did you poison your mom against me? Why does she hate me?"

I narrow my eyes. "Missy, I don't have to poison anyone against you. You're doing a wonderful job of that yourself."

"What?"

"Look, I'm sick of this. Yesterday was the final straw. You asked me to come spend time with you. I've been with you since Friday night.

"Yet you accused me of seeing someone else and all that other bullshit. This is not what I signed up for. I told you in the beginning that I don't do drama and that was the reason for the arrangement." I pause and lower my voice.

"I can't keep doing this with you," I say in a hushed, but firm tone. "We had a baby between us. I'm sorry that you lost it, but *this,* all this other shit. I'm over it."

"John, wait. I'm sorry. My emotions have been so unbalanced since losing our baby. I know I haven't been myself in a long time. I'm so sorry. Please. I need you to get through this."

"You need to talk to a professional."

She whips her head back. My words aren't said harshly, but they are honest. She needs to talk to someone; this shit isn't healthy.

She looks down as if she's searching. I sigh. I know that look. She's probing for something in her feelings.

"Miss, I'm not trying to hurt you. It's just the opposite. I want you to get better. I want you to find some balance and peace with everything that's happened," I say.

"Which is why I need you. You're so great at making me feel better. I promise I'll go to see someone. Don't leave me, I don't think I could handle that too after losing our baby," she pleads.

I close my eyes and groan. The hook that keeps reeling me in. *Our baby.* I'm responsible for this.

"Listen, why don't you head home. I want to spend more time with my family. I'll come by later and we'll talk," I say more gently.

She searches my face with sad eyes, lips trembling. I reach out and tug her into a hug. Maybe I've been a little harsh.

Sometimes we manipulate people when we're most vulnerable. I could be misreading things. The least I can do is make sure she gets the help she needs and then I can start to create distance between us.

"John, I need ye to come help me in the kitchen." I turn to find my mother peeking out of the front door, with her lips pursed and a hand on her hip. "Ye be getting on, Missy. You don't want to get caught in that traffic during rush hour."

I bite my lip to keep from laughing. When I turn back to look at Missy, I almost lose the battle. The confusion on her face is priceless.

"But I don't live that far, Cassidy."

"Mrs. Black to ye. And it's the hour ye need to rush out of me house. Goodbye, lass. Don't worry about coming back too soon. John."

"I'll be right there, Ma."

"Humph." Mom glares at me before she turns back into the house.

"Why does she hate me? She told Nellie she could call her Cassidy."

"Nellie has been a friend of the family for years." I shrug.

"So why am I just meeting her?"

"Missy," I say in warning.

"Well?"

I grind my teeth and call on my patience. "Because she moved back home four months ago. She's been living in Seattle—" I cut off and work my jaw. "Why am I explaining myself?"

I grab her by the elbow and start off the porch toward her car. I've had enough for one day. It's time for her to go.

"What are you doing?" Missy whines.

Fuck, I've never noticed how much she does that shit. It's like nails on a chalkboard. Damn, the more time that passes and the more she forces herself on me, the more I'm finding things that drive me crazy about her—not in a good way.

I guess that's because we were never supposed to be more. Our relationship has been Dom and Sub. I've never mixed family and pleasure. Things have crossed the line on so many levels.

When you try to fit a square peg in a round hole it never fits. Missy has been trying to fit her way into my life and it's not working, no matter how she tries. It's only showing me how right I was to want to end our contract early.

"Listen, I'll see you later. Get home safely."

"John, wait—"

"Later, Missy. I'll be over and we can talk then."

"John, get ye ass in here to help me like I asked ye," my mother calls.

"Fine." Missy pouts and climbs into her car.

Thank God.

I need some room to breathe. I narrow my eyes as I watch her drive away. That feeling that I need to dig deeper pulls at me.

You're projecting, John. You don't want to be with her, so you're making up this feeling. Get her help.

One way or another I'm going to have to make it clear that things are going to end, but first I will get her help. She needs help.

CHAPTER ELEVEN

On A Mission

John

Four months later...

"Passport, keys, vest," I mutter to myself and twist my lips as I look around my bedroom.

Wyatt will be here to pick me up in about an hour. We leave tonight for this mission that has had us all on edge.

I already have so much going on in my head. The fact that Missy has been calling me all day hasn't helped. I clench my jaw at the thought of her.

As if I conjured her up, my phone rings and sure enough, it's Missy. I get ready to chuck the phone across the room. I don't get what she doesn't understand about me having to get my head straight to go out on a dangerous mission.

"Hello," I answer.

"Why do you sound so annoyed?"

"I don't know, maybe because I told you the last twenty times you called that I was getting ready to leave for work and had to get my head straight," I snap.

"I'm sorry. I was checking-in. I'm going to miss you. This is hard for me."

"Missy, you've been seeing that therapist for three months now. He has told you that it's a great idea for you to find things to occupy your time so that I'm not a crutch. This is a prime example of why that's so important.

"I need to focus on work. I'm going to be gone and I won't be able to contact anyone for two weeks. I need to know you're not going to do anything..."

I trail off. It took a month to get her to see someone after I first suggested it. The only reason she has been seeing a therapist is because she tried to kill herself again a few weeks after.

At least, I got the call from her roommate that she'd found her passed out with a bottle of pills. Once again, while I was away on another assignment. The main reason I had been sending her calls to voicemail all day.

"I'm going to stay with some friends up the coast until you return. I understand you need to focus on work. I only wanted to hear your voice once more," she says.

"Are you forgetting the talk we had?"

There is a long pause on the other end. At first, I question whether or not she's still on the line. Before I can speak up to check, she replies.

"I remember," she mutters.

I sigh. "It's for the best, Missy. It's time that you do this for you. Trying to start a relationship with me on top of everything else is unhealthy. I want to see you healthy and happy."

"You say that like we're not already in a relationship. We're not starting anything. We've been together for more than a year and a half."

"No, we had an arrangement for almost a year. We were adjusting to the fact that we were going to be in each other's lives a whole lot more, but we haven't been in a relationship. That's where you have things all f—," I cut off before I say too much.

"I don't understand. Where is this coming from?"

"I don't have time for this right now, Missy. I need to get ready to leave."

"No, answer me. You told your family that I was your girlfriend. We were becoming more."

"Missy, we talked about this. Dr. Farner agreed this is the right thing for you, for everyone."

"You know what, go on your trip. Don't let me weigh you down. If I hurt myself or not it's not on you at all," she replies and hangs up.

I throw my head back and push a hand into my hair. "Fuck."

Great, just what I need right before walking into a mission. My grip on the phone in my hand is so tight my knuckles turn white. The temptation to hurl it across the room is even greater this time. I swear I don't need this shit.

The guilt starts to rise, and I question whether I should call back. One thing I know for a fact is that I'll be in my head about this shit for the next two weeks. If something happens to her while I'm gone that will be on my head.

But you can't keep enabling this. Something more is wrong here. You know it is.

I turn and punch the wall, needing to get my frustration out. My chest heaves as I look at the hole I've created. I'll have to patch that up when I get back. A glance at my knuckles pulls a curse from my lips.

I start for my bathroom to clean my hand up, but the doorbell rings. Muttering to myself, I start for the door instead. When I open it, Noah stands before me.

"What happened to your hand?"

"Nothing," I mumble.

"Sure doesn't look like nothing," he says, reaching for my right hand and lifting it to inspect. "Where's your first aid kit? I can get this cleaned up before Wyatt gets here. You can talk while I patch."

"I'm fine," I say, snatching my hand back.

He pushes into my house heading for the kitchen. "I said get the kit."

I glare at his back. Wyatt and Noah have always bossed me around. Today's one of these days I'm considering kicking his ass over it.

"I can hear you thinking. Get put on your back if you want. I'll carry your ass to the car after I fix you up and put you onto the plane if I have to," he calls over his shoulder.

"What are you doing here anyway? And why didn't you use your key."

"Felt like spending some time with my little brother before this mission. I think it's time we all start ringing doorbells. Last thing I want is to see your pale ass in the air."

"Whatever." I snort.

"Let's get your head clear."

I groan. That's code for he thinks I need to talk it out. I'm not ready to talk. Talking is only going to piss me off more.

I make my way to my bedroom bathroom and collect the first aid kit. When I saunter into the kitchen with it, Noah has a sandwich made and is already scarfing it down. When he sees me coming, he brushes his hands off and waves me over to the nook area of my kitchen where he's sitting.

"Don't you have food at home?"

"Sure do, but I figured I'd help you out. This stuff will spoil while you're away."

"That's why I planned to eat it before Wyatt gets here."

"Oops. Shit was good though." He shrugs his shoulders. "Besides, there's plenty left."

I chuckle because he's right. There was too much for me to polish off on my own. I had planned to make sandwiches for the flight.

"Dick," I mutter.

He grunts. "You can have it back if you like. It'll even be nice and piping hot."

I give him the finger with my good hand. He takes the busted one and slaps a bag of ice that he had at his side on it. Grabbing the kit that I placed on the table, Noah opens it up and starts to pull out supplies.

He removes the ice, looks my hand over, and frowns. "You better be able to shoot when we need you," he says.

"I'll be fine. It's not that bad."

He grunts again and mumbles something to himself. "You want to talk?"

"No."

"Figured you'd say that."

"You want to talk about what's going on with Bean?"

He lifts his gaze to mine. I lift a brow, causing him to roll his eyes. Yet he nods his head and drops the suggestion.

"Keep the ice on it. It's swelling but the cuts aren't deep at all. Plaster?" He nods to the dust on my wrist.

"Yeah, will fix it when I get back."

"I hate when you bottle things up, but I'll give you your space. Just know I'm here. And the only reason I don't want to talk about Rebecca is because I'm not going to be able to resolve that shit until we get back and I'm already anxious about it," he says.

"Fair enough and thanks. This is something I'll resolve then too. For now, I want to focus on what we're walking into."

"Have you thought about this? What we're getting ready to do?"

"Yeah, I have."

"I don't know how it all sits with me. I get what Sam and Bobby are trying to do, but it feels like we might be trading prisons if you ask me," he says.

"Yeah, I know what you mean. I've thought the same thing, but if we leave them where they are, there's no telling what will happen to them. I think the options they have planned for them will be a hell of a lot better than where they are now."

"This is true. Nate did say he has an alternate plan for those that don't want to follow through with the program."

"It will work out," I say. "I trust Nate and Sam. Bobby has done his research inside and out. If he feels this is the right thing to do. I'm going to put my hat on it."

Noah nods. "You're right. We need to make this as clean as possible. Leave zero chance of this coming back on our doorsteps."

"I'm with you there."

His phone buzzes and he pulls it out. "Head in the game. Wyatt's out front. Let's do this."

Whether Noah knows it or not, he has helped me get out of my head a little. I push all of it aside and go to grab my shit. We have a job to do.

Roni

I awaken startled. When I open my eyes, I'm staring right into Natasha's. She lifts a finger to her lips and looks around the room.

I nod and she releases my mouth. I sit up on my cot and glance around at the other sleeping girls. I never thought I'd be so happy to see this place, but after spending all that time in isolation with only Torque and Natasha to keep me sane, I appreciate this holding cell more.

"We have to come up with a plan and fast. Earlier, they were talking about the buyer that's been holding up our sale. He's coming to collect. We have two weeks tops to figure out a way out of here," she whispers frantically.

"We have to get word to Torque. I'm not leaving him here."

"I got a peek at the list on the desk. He's going to be sold to the same guy."

"That might be a good thing. Maybe we'll be placed closer to Torque or something. We need to get more information. Maybe we can get out during the exchange or something. There has to be a way."

"That asshole that had us tortured said we all have to go. We're being sold the same time as the auction for the others. They are cleaning the place out. A truck will take the others to auction and we're going to the exclusive buyer or something like that," Natasha informs me.

"Okay, let me think."

We weren't drugged up while down in the bowels of this place. So, when they released us to return up here, I was able to observe some things. There's the underground where they kept us while trying to torture us out of our minds.

Then there's this level. It seems we're in some type of huge factory. The rooms they separate us in are on this floor.

This is the level where all the real security is. There are a lot of guys around, but they tend to focus more on the sex rooms. Those of us back here are so high, we don't pose a real threat or at least they feel we don't.

I noticed a back door, but I don't know what it leads to. We need to know what's beyond that door. Maybe we can escape through it.

I don't like that plan. Too dangerous.

"Maybe our best chances are to go with the buyer, and he might not have as many guards. Maybe we can get away in transport," I muse aloud.

Natasha shakes her head before I can finish my thought. "If the buyer flakes, he's going to auction us off with the others. He's scared or something. It seems like they move people in and out a lot faster and we're becoming a liability," she replies.

I tug at my hair. I don't know what to do. However, I know I have to get us out of here. A beam of light heads our way.

"Get back to your bed. We'll figure it out. I promise. I'm going to get us out of here," I whisper.

Natasha nods and gets low as she crawls her way back to her bed. I say a silent prayer. Two weeks. I have two weeks to figure out how to get these kids out of here.

I bite back a sob. That's going to be much harder than I let on to Natasha. Neither of us knows what Torque looks like. We know his voice, and he knows what Natasha looks like.

Hell, he could have been one of them for all I know, but something in my gut tells me that he's one of us and I'm not leaving one of us behind. We built a bond down there. These two are my responsibility.

I lost a piece of me down in that basement. However, they couldn't take away my determination. I'm absolutely determined to get the three of us out of here alive.

I roll onto my side and let the tears hit the pillow beneath my head. I flinch as my still healing ribs scream at me. "Please, God. Please get us out of here."

CHAPTER TWELVE

Hero or No

Roni

"I did it. I got the message to Torque. He's going to meet us," Natasha whispers excitedly.

"Good, are you sure he understands the plan? Do you think he'll get away?"

"He says he can. Besides, we're out of time. They're coming to transport us. This is it."

I can't believe she pulled it off. Luck is on our side. They've been needing Natasha in the boys holding cell to help translate for the last few days. She's been hoping for the opportunity to find Torque and get him the plan.

He revealed himself to her the first day she was in there, although they weren't able to talk. Thank God he knows what she looks like. Everything is falling into place.

"Okay." I nod. "Where's the milk?" Natasha winces and pulls a disgusted face. "I'm the one drinking it. Now hurry."

"Yuck," she mumbles and rushes to get the curded milk she's been hiding away for me.

She rushes back. "I think I hear them."

I grab the carton and say a prayer before I take a gulp. I almost upchuck it immediately, but I fight through and take a second gulp, holding some of it in my mouth. Natasha takes the carton and hides it.

"Are you okay?" I nod and try not to make a face.

"Everyone, let's go," the asshole they call Kodiak yells as he bursts into the room.

Nervous cries and whimpers ring out as the girls start to stand and file toward the door. I nod at Natasha and she falls in line. I go to stand behind her, but Kodiak walks up and places a hand on Natasha's shoulder.

"You to front. Now," he barks.

Natasha looks over her shoulder at me. I say with my eyes what I can't say out loud. We stick to the plan, nothing changes.

She licks her lips and gives a slight nod before turning to move to the front. I feel sick to my stomach and it's more than the curded milk, but this isn't the time for me to lose it.

We are all led out into the hallway. The first thing I notice as we walk the hall is that the other rooms have been emptied. All the doors sit open and the rooms are vacant.

My heartbeat races. I don't know where everyone has gone, but I don't think it's anywhere good. However, I'm not going to worry about that. I need to get Natasha and Torque out of here.

"Stop walking slow," Kodiak says in my ear before shoving me.

It's that one shove that screws up our plan. We're nowhere near the exit we wanted to be near when I start to lurch, but I can't keep from doubling over and letting it all go.

"Disgusting," Kodiak growls. *"Vstan', prodolzhay. Teper' vstavay."*

"I can help. She doesn't understand you," Natasha says.

"You, back in line," he barks. He then grabs my arm. "You come with me."

I don't budge. I continue to heave even though I have nothing left. Peeking up, I give Natasha a look of warning as I see Kodiak reach for his gun.

"I said let's go," he says holding the gun to my head.

"Please. She doesn't understand. I can help," Natasha tries again.

I still haven't moved. Wrong idea. Kodiak backhands me so hard I see stars.

My head explodes with pain. I swipe a hand under my nose, and it comes away with blood. This time when he tugs me forward, I go because my head is buzzing too much to fight back. My vision blurs, but I keep moving.

"Otvedi ikh v komnatu. Now," Kodiak barks.

"What room?" Natasha asks nervously.

"Shut up. You come with us," he snarls, yanking me forward.

I do my best to steady myself before we get too far away from the exit Natasha and I need. This will only get harder if we get out of range of the exit we planned to take. I suck in a breath before I throw my elbow into Kodiak's balls and take off running.

"Let's go, move, move, move," I say to Natasha.

I push forward as fast as I can. Doubling back toward the room they'd kept us in. We turn the first corner but don't get much further before he grabs Natasha by her hair and shoves his gun into the side of her head.

He turns the gun on me. "I kill you where you stand," he seethes, cocking the gun back.

"No," I shout.

I rush forward and block Natasha with my body. He points the gun into my face as I shield Natasha.

Misha

You want war, you build army. I respect what LaSalle aims to do. This is why I help.

"Would you like another drink, my friend?"

I look around this office in disgust. He sits comfortably in his leather chair, offering me a drink. His desk is handcrafted, I can tell, I've had one made by same artist.

Smug son of a bitch. I know what lies beyond these walls. The balls to bring me here tells me this piece of shit knows not to fear me. Lesson he will learn hard way.

I don't like business my father and his sisters are in. It is not the way to do things. I don't sell little girls and boys for profit.

I want to blow this vile place up and be done with it. However, I need to help LaSalle get those people out of here first. I'm not quite devil they make me. Tonight, I prove.

"*Da*, more vodka," I say to bastard sitting across from me.

Dead men don't need names. I have forgotten his because it's not necessary. I don't like him. He thinks I'm stupid.

"I'm so glad you could come, Misha. I think we can build lucrative business together," he says.

"But this is gun and ammo business, da. These rumors about selling babies, it's lie?"

"*Da, da.* I am not in the business of selling people. You shouldn't believe everything you hear."

I nod, but I know lie when I hear. It's written all over his face. He sells women, girls, and boys.

Nate and his team have been watching this place for two weeks. Tonight, they plan to take truck load of women and boys to auction. Too bad that truck will never make it.

"Do you mean to insult me?" I say and lift a brow.

"*Net*, I mean you no insult, my friend."

I glare at him. He has no idea that Bobby is private buyer that has been purchasing from him for almost year now. It was one of the things LaSalle asked me to set up for his brother to nail this prick.

"*Da*, I think you mean to insult me," I say.

"*Net*, my friend. Not at all. In fact, I have gift for you." He looks over my shoulder. "Iosif, bring gift."

The asshole that must be Iosif goes to rush from the room. When he pulls the door open, the sight before me nearly makes my head explode. I raise to my feet so fast, the chair I'd been sitting in falls to the ground.

"What is this?" My voice thunders through the room.

Bastard whips his head toward door. I'm seething as I watch girl guard another with her body. There is fucker holding a gun to her head. He grasps her arm and pulls her toward his chest. She's not the younger of the two, and young like some girls I've seen in surveillance pictures.

"Kodiak, take your friends home. You and all friends leave, now," this bastard behind me spats.

For a split second, confusion crosses Kodiak's face. Catching on to his boss, he begins to tug the girl away, nodding for other to follow. She tugs free and rushes toward me.

"Wait," she calls.

"I said shut your mouth," Kodiak growls, grabbing her by the arm to pull her out of my sight.

I turn to this lying sack of shit, then back to the open doorway. "Bring them here. I want to ask questions," I demand.

It is clear they are both unhealthy as their bones jut out in their faces. Although there are signs that curves once were there in the old girl, her body is well on the way to rail thin. Her clothes hang loosely from her.

Then there are her eyes. Her eyes are haunted and sunken. She seems to protect right side with one arm even as she tries to protect friend.

"They are nothing. Don't worry."

"I said bring them here."

"You are worried about nothing. They are nothing. Let Kodiak handle his personal life. Those two fight like this all the time. He has temper. She and little sister will be fine."

"In that case, Kodiak. You bring me gun. Now," I say firmly, daring him to defy me.

He looks between Iosif and his boss. Iosif gives him a nod that I narrow my eyes at. I go to reach for my knives, but Kodiak hands gun to Iosif who hands gun to me.

Before I can say another word, Iosif rushes out and slams the door shut behind him. I turn to this fucker as I place gun down and lean onto his desk. I will not be ignored.

"Please, Misha, don't overreact. This is nothing, my friend. Let's have drink."

I stand up straight and fold my arms over my chest. "Show me your operation. I want to see guns and factory. Show me top to bottom. Thirty million is on the line, da. Show me where my money goes."

He turns white as a sheet. Wheels turn as he tries to give me answer. Answer that he does not have. To show me factory is to reveal lies.

His face cannot mask his anger. Reaching for the walkie talkie on his desk he walks toward window away from where I am, out of range to hear. Murmuring orders into device, he keeps his back to me.

"My second in command will walk you through. I have business to tend to. I will meet up with you," he says when he turns back to me.

I go to protest, but phone in pocket buzzes. I retrieve from jacket. It is signal; they are loading truck. Truck that we've come for.

I clench my teeth. If they are loading up, what have they done with girls I just saw. I want to make sure they're on truck.

"Why not tell Kodiak and friends to join me?"

"I'm sure they are gone. Come, you want a tour. We will get you tour."

Roni

I can't believe how close I came to my own death. And still, I've failed. I failed to get us all out of here. Panic raises as Iosif grabs me. He snarls in my face, looking as if he's about to strike me too.

"I'll take her. Get that one and others to cars for transport."

"We are waiting for last of them to get to room," Kodiak replies.

"No time, any that have not gotten to room go to truck. If they don't make truck, they die."

I gasp. Immediately, I think of Torque. If he doesn't get away, if they catch him, they will kill him.

Kodiak looks pissed as he slides his gaze to me, but he nods, grabs Natasha, and turns away from us. Iosif starts in the opposite direction of Natasha and Kodiak.

"No," I cry out.

Iosif tightens his grip. "Don't test me," he seethes while listening to someone speaking low over his walkie talkie. Once again, we're going away from the escape exit.

"Where are you taking me?" I demand.

"Shut your mouth. You have cost us ten million dollars. If you have cost boss deal in there, I will kill you myself," he replies.

"What?"

"You go to auction now. You caused Kodiak to damage your face and now we can't chance taking you to holding room for virgins and exotics. They need to leave." He glares at me and licks his lips. "Maybe I break you in. No need not to touch anymore, deal is over."

That Kodiak guy already threatened to put a bullet in my head. I don't think he had plans to take me to that holding room once I ran from him. I'm not ready to give up.

I ball my fist, ready to swing. It's an instinct. Something in me comes to life and I'm ready to defend myself. I get this feeling that I'm more than capable of holding my own.

"We have to go back," I demand.

"Only place you go is truck. Boss needs you to disappear before you are seen again."

I open my mouth to scream, but he covers it. Pulling me against his chest, he leans into my ear. "You scream, I kill you now," he hisses. "Understand?"

I nod. Tears well as the truck backed up to a door comes into view. I need to go back for Natasha and Torque. This is not the plan.

Those thoughts are halted as we make a sharp turn and I'm shoved into a corridor. A few more steps and we enter a room. It's like we've taken a back route to the holding cells, it's exactly like the one we've been sleeping in. Cots lining the space.

It only takes a second for it to register what he plans to do. Before I can fight back, he hits me in my side. My ribs go from the dull flame that I've been surviving through to a roaring fire. I can't breathe.

He tears the front of my shirt open. "Not as nice as when arrived, but good enough. Tight pussy will be worth it," he says with a grin.

I blackout. Panic takes over. After all this time, the torture, the crumbling of my soul—piece by fucking piece—he's going to rape me now. I've lost everything in this place, my mind, my hope. Being tortured stripped me of my humanity.

Now, this. No.

He shoves his filthy hand into my too big pants. I kick out and plant my knee right in his balls. He folds and I bolt. Tearing the door open, I take off for the direction Natasha is in.

"Bitch." The word is snarled before a handful of my hair is grabbed and I'm dragged backward.

He covers my mouth as I start to kick and scream. However, he doesn't drag me back into that room. I cover my breasts as the night air hits me.

Suddenly, I'm airborne. I yelp as my body sails through the air. When I land, I gasp breathlessly. My entire body feels as if I'm being boiled from the inside out.

"Get away from her. No one touch her," the asshole that tosses me in here orders.

I ball into myself. There's so much pain, I might die before we get to wherever they plan to take us. They bark orders around me and there's a bunch of activity before the door to the back of the truck slams down shut.

I think it's then I lose the last of my sanity. The darkness, the pain, the loss of the only friends I know I have, knowing I failed them—it's all too much. My mind starts to shatter.

As it splits, the sight of cold blue eyes appears in my vision. I can't help but wonder if he was there to buy us. Is he the one that will take Torque and Natasha to some unknown place?

I shudder.

I wonder if he knows he sent me to my death?

CHAPTER THIRTEEN

Freedom

John

"Everyone, look alive, the target is in sight," Nathan Briggs says.

The command comes through my ear com, causing me to settle in behind the tree I'm using for cover. I focus on the scope that brings the truck into view.

"Toby, Wyatt, we move on your signal," Nate says.

"Got it," Wyatt replies. We're all in our positions ready to go. "Let's get this over with and get back home. Bro, we go on three," he says, talking to Toby. "One, two, three."

In sync, they take out the tires of the truck with the cargo we've come for. The vehicle comes to a stop, looking as if it might turn over at first. From there, I move in fast.

The back door to the truck opens and two guys jump out. I take out the first, then the second without a single thought. Screams come from inside as I run up to the opening.

"Clear," I call out as I secure the back of the truck and climb in.

The first thing to grab my attention is a body curled up on the floor. I quickly scan the young faces around me. Anger ignites in my blood, not for the first time in the last two weeks—or since we agreed to take this on if I'm honest.

They are all huddled together except for a boy that's frozen a few paces from the others. I lock eyes with him, if he's sixteen I'd be surprised. I think of my little brothers and what I'd do if anyone ever tried to harm them.

He breaks eye contact to look down toward the floor at the body I noticed when I first stepped in. Following his gaze, I find that the fragile looking figure is a girl. Her clothes are too big and she's too still.

My heart aches as I come to the biting realization that we might have been too late for one of them. I glance around at all the terrified faces; they're all looking down at her too.

"We're here to help," I say.

"Help her, they wouldn't let us go near her. They tossed her in here like garbage. Please, help her," the young boy says.

"Torque?" It's a whisper, but I vaguely hear the girl on the floor murmur the word. Her voice has a rasp to it that sends a chill down my spine.

I frown and ignore it. Moving closer, I squat beside her as Noah and Nate climb into the cargo hold of the vehicle. Reaching out to check her pulse, I scan her figure quickly.

That is my first mistake. She starts to scream and flail about. She's clearly hysterical. She catches me in my side, but I'm hardly fazed.

I'm not too worried about her attack. However, I am concerned about her hurting herself. It's clear how weak she is and that she's favoring her right side a bit.

Although, it's her ripped shirt and exposed breasts that cause something possessive in me to rise. All my tactical training and everything I've learned as a Dom mix together and kicks in.

"Easy," Noah says.

She continues to pound at my chest. I hold my hand up to warn Noah off and give him my rifle. Once he takes it, I grasp her by the face and restrain her hands behind her back. In one swift motion, I bring her chest to mine to shield her. We're face to face now, her eyes locked on mine.

I breathe her in as she freezes, breathing heavily. I note her wince of pain and loosen my hold. She bares her teeth at me. As tough as she's pretending to be, I can see the fear deep in her eyes.

"Get the others out of here," I say to Nate and Noah.

We're on limited time. They begin to usher the others out and into the transportation, we brought with us. The sound of Wyatt's voice reaches me, but I stay focused on the scared brown eyes in front of me. "I'm not here to hurt you."

"Then get off me," she growls.

I nod. "Are you going to stop swinging?"

She nods and I slowly let go. As soon as I do, she swings at my head and grabs for my balls. I block her hand quickly and restrain her again.

Noah's ass chuckles somewhere nearby. I want to kick out and put him on his back, but I keep my eyes on the woman before me. Woman, she's not a girl.

Up close I can see she's not as young as many of the others. She looks like she could be in her very early twenties, but she's not a girl like a lot of the others. She also looks like she's on the verge of starving, but she's still beautiful.

There's something about her eyes. Though sunken, something about them calls to me. I get pissed at myself. This is why I'm in the situation I'm in back home. I always need to fix shit.

At the moment, I want to fix what placed that look in her eyes. I want to erase the haunted glare that's staring back at me.

She starts to scream, and I move to cover her mouth with my hand. Her eyes harden, almost causing me to smirk. She's tough. That means she'll make it through this.

"Listen to me. You're safe. I would never hurt you." I pause to let my words sink in. She searches my eyes for a moment, and I can feel her relax when she finds whatever she's looking for.

"We don't have much time before they come looking for all of you. We have to get you out of this truck and to safety. Do you understand?"

She nods and this time I do give her a small smile. I note that she's trembling. I loosen my hold again.

When her eyes lose some of the fear, I continue. "I'm going to release you and this time you're not going to swing on me or try to grab my shit. I'm going to take off my shirt and give it to you to cover up. I'll turn my back to give you some privacy."

She gives me another nod.

"Guys, we need to move," Nate warns.

"We're coming," I grunt and turn to shield her with my back as I get my things off to give her my shirt.

Making quick work of taking off my hustler, I hand it over to Noah. I take off my vest and place it between my legs. Next, I peel my black thermal off and hold it over my shoulder.

"Thank you," she murmurs.

"You're welcome."

I start to tug the vest on over my tank shirt. When I go to reach for my hustler from Noah, I feel more than see her reach for my blade in my leg hustler. Damn, she's not going to give it a rest.

I spin out and grab her hand with the knife, placing it behind her back. With my free hand, I grab the back of her neck and lean down until we're face to face. She bares her teeth again.

"Let me get you out of here and I'll let you kick my ass all you want, but we don't have time for this now."

"I'm not leaving without her," she says in a sob.

"Leaving without who?" I ask and wrinkle my brows.

She lifts her chin. A snot bubble forms at her nose. She's trying to hold it together. That's clear, but it's also clear that she's holding on by a thread.

"I have to go back."

"Sweetheart, the only thing left back there is death. If whoever you're looking for is still there, our other team will find her."

"I'm not your sweetheart. I can't leave her. I can't leave them. I have to find them." She tries to pull away and a yelp tears from her lips. They begin to tremble; more tears flow down her cheeks.

I draw my brows in deeper. My hold isn't that tight. Releasing the back of her neck, I gently place my hand to her side.

She collapses into me. Any fight she has left goes up in smoke as she passes out. I catch her and hold her close. Looking down, I lift her shirt enough to expose her middle section.

Her torso is bruised. I'll give my life savings she has broken or bruised ribs. The adrenaline has probably started to wean.

I scoop her fragile body into my arms and start off the truck. Noah reaches for her, but I don't want to release her to anyone. I look at the jump down and grind my teeth. To jump it would be to jar her.

Instead, I hand her to my brother long enough for me to get out of the truck and on solid ground. As soon as I'm out, I take her back and carry her to the waiting bus. Climbing in with the crowd we rescued, I settle in.

"We're riding in the SUV," Wyatt says as he comes from the back of the bus, probably ensuring everyone is secure.

"Yeah, I'm not anymore. I'm fine here."

He looks like he's going to protest but thinks better of it. He steps off the bus, tapping the side of the doors to signal the driver to close them and take off. I train my eyes on the face of the woman in my arms. Guilt twists in my stomach. I want to protect her more than I do the woman that was pregnant with my child.

What does that say about me?

As the smell of urine hits my nose, I'm not sure. Yeah, I noticed before I got her out of that truck that she peed herself. And still, I'm not letting her go until I know she's completely safe.

Roni

We haven't stopped yet and I haven't opened my eyes. I'm in pain, but the real reason I won't open them is because I know I'm in his arms. I don't think I can handle looking into those golden eyes again.

Especially knowing that I've probably soaked his lap with pee. I should be embarrassed, but all I feel is... numb. Something about being in his embrace has calmed the storm inside my head.

I should freak out from not knowing where he and his people are taking me, but I don't feel that sense of danger. Sort of like when I looked into his eyes.

I do my best to remain stock still. He moves with me in his hold. His warmth surrounds me as he leans into my ear.

"You don't have to pretend to sleep. I know you're awake." His breath fans my temple and raises goosebumps.

It's a strange feeling I can't say I've ever had before. Kind of like the comfort. It's foreign to me, but I want more.

"I'm here. I'll be with you until you're safe. We're going to get someone to look at those ribs," he whispers again when I make no move to open my eyes. "I'm John. No matter what happens, remember my name. You call it, I'll come."

The promise in his voice causes the tiny spark of hope I have left to flicker. It's his words that wrap me like a blanket and allow me to go to sleep.

CHAPTER FOURTEEN

Aftershock

Roni

I wince as I make my way to breakfast. These halls are so long, it takes forever to get anywhere. It's like being at an academy or something. I've been calling it the assassin's academy in my head. I might change that to toy cop academy after sitting in on a few sessions.

Every morning for the last week, I've walked these halls from my room, hoping I'll get a glimpse of *him*. I refuse to ask anyone for him. He lied.

He said he'd be with me until I was safe. I'm not safe. I might not be in the hands of sex traffickers, but these people sure as shit ain't normal.

I walk into the cafeteria and go to get my tray. Since the first day, I've kept my head down and stayed to myself. I'm not able to join the physical training yet, but I go to the classes on my schedule.

I like the mathematical stuff. I seem to be pretty good at it. Then there are the computers. I've tried to see if I could remember anything about myself to search for answers, but not much comes to mind. Although I get the feeling I was really good at school.

"Hey."

I turn to see a fresh-faced kid on my right. He's cute. The longish blonde hair suits his pretty face. There's an innocence about him, causing the two dimples in his cheeks to make him adorable as he gives me a nervous smile.

His eyes aren't quite green, but not quite blue either. He's on the lanky side. A bit taller than me despite not looking more than sixteen or seventeen years old. He's a handsome kid. His cheeks turn red as I stare at him.

"Roni, right?" he says when I don't speak. "It's me, Torque."

I drop the tray in my hand on the counter and wrap my left arm around him. I have three healing ribs, so I don't squeeze him as hard as I want to.

When I release him, he's blushing twice as hard. This is not what I was expecting to find when I found him. No wonder they were trying to sell him. He's pretty in an almost feminine way, but still masculine enough.

John's face pops into my head. He was a pretty man too. Definitely masculine. The way his back flexed when he took his shirt off to give me made my mouth water.

His broad back had muscles that melted into muscles. He had to be over six feet, making it all fit together like a well-made puzzle that snapped in place effortlessly. However, his face, I'll never forget his face.

"How are you feeling?"

I chew on my cheek as I focus back on Torque. I've been trying to tell myself to stop obsessing over the liar that left me here. He doesn't deserve my thoughts.

"I'm fine, I guess. Given the circumstances."

He shrugs. "It's not so bad," his voice breaks, causing him to blush again. "They're pretty cool. Besides, I have nowhere else to go. So, this place is great."

My heart breaks for him. "Does that mean…"

"They were killed," he says, looking down at his feet. "Nate said they were found with their throats slit. The authorities kept it quiet on the island because there was a rise in kidnappings and murders, but they didn't want to ruin the tourism."

Right, God forbid that happen. Such bullshit.

"I'm so sorry."

"I'll be okay, I guess. I mean, come on. They offered to teach us how to be badass private security guards in return for living here. This place is like the X-men academy or something."

I chuckle and turn to grab my tray as a line starts to head our way. I grab a muffin and grapefruit. Torque starts to load his with bacon, eggs, toast, a muffin, cereal, grapes, and apple juice. I snicker.

"Hungry?"

He turns to me with these adorable dimples and that blush. "We work up an appetite in the morning training," he says.

"How old are you?" I can't keep the words from slipping out.

"Fifteen, I'll be turning sixteen soon."

Wow. That rage that's always right below the surface rises. He's a baby.

"You don't have family that would take you in? Did they even offer you that option?"

"These guys are the real deal. They knew everything about my family by the time we arrived here. I have a grandmother, but she's in a home. She couldn't take me in. She can't even wipe her own ass," he says.

I give him a stern look and the blush comes back. "Sorry," he murmurs.

We make our way to the table I've claimed every day since we've been here. I've made sure to give off the vibes that I don't want to be bothered. For the most part, people have stayed clear.

"Shouldn't you have gotten more food than that?" Torque says cautiously.

"Not in the mood to eat much."

"You'll need to build your strength for when you can start training. How much longer will it take for you to heal?"

I tilt my head at him and stare. Like I said, I don't talk to anyone. I find it interesting that he knows so much about me.

He shrugs his shoulders. "You and Natasha are my family now. I asked about you."

I nod. I don't want to ask, but I have to. I need to know.

"Is she here?" I say and look around. "Have you seen her?"

"No," he says as his lips tremble. "They got away with a few of the girls that were being sold outside the main auction."

I wrinkle my brows. "I heard your voice. When they came for us in the truck. Why were you in the truck and not with Natasha? She said you were being sold with us."

He frowns. "Something was changed at the last minute. When I went to break free, I lost my chance at the last second. I was placed on the truck not long before…" He trails off.

Not long before I was tossed inside, I assume. He must have been in transport at the same time as me. I pick at my muffin as I think about what this means.

Natasha never made it out. That John guy told more than one lie. Anger consumes me and I ball my fists on top of the table.

"Hey, she would want us to make the best of this," Torque says, hurt and anger in his voice. "We have to make the best of this for her."

I look across the table to see the blaze in his eyes. A look no fifteen-year-old should have. I want nothing more than to protect him. From the past, from these people, and from his own anger and bitterness.

He should not have this rage on his head. Something occurs to me as I look him over. It's something I've pushed to the back of my mind for a long time.

"Torque?"

"Yeah."

"If you don't want to answer you don't have to. But… did something happen to you there? Did… they…"

He drops his eyes to the table. If my rage could filet the skin off my body, I'd be nothing but flames. My head starts to hurt from the fury coursing through me.

"Never mind. You don't have to answer."

"We'll find her, right?" he murmurs, lifting his gaze to mine once again.

I sit and stare at the look in his eyes. In this moment, he looks all of fifteen if not younger. I don't want to lie to him, but I don't think we will ever see her again.

"We don't even know where to start," I reply.

"They're training us to secure, track, and hunt down people. We can use that to find her and we can make them pay for everything they did to us," Torque says.

"We're learning to be security."

"Badass security. We can use it."

His words sink in and take root. Something inside of me sparks, I don't think I've ever been a quitter. He's right, we could take what we learn and track Natasha down.

"How long would that take? She could be in danger now." I think aloud.

"I don't know, but I know that I'd want out no matter what or when. If I were still there, I'd be praying every day that someone would find me and get me out of there," he says softly, a haunted look in his eyes.

I swallow hard as if his words are a pill. I know he's right. When they were torturing me—even with Natasha and Torque in the cells beside me—I felt like I was crumbling from the inside out. I prayed every day that someone would end it all or come and get me out of there. I start to look at all of this differently.

I look at Torque, eyes filled with a new resolve, and give him a nod. We'll do this, we just have to be smart. We'll find her.

"All right. I'm in. We need to figure out where to start."

"Cool. For now, we train and learn. Something we learn is bound to help us, right?"

"That's what we have to hope for."

He lifts the plate of bacon from his tray and pushes it toward me. "That means you need to get better. Eat up. You'll need your strength. They kick our asses in those sessions," he says with a smile.

"Okay, kid. Okay."

John

I woke up with a gasp. It's been the same every night for the last week. The same brown eyes and raspy voice.

Each time she's reaching out for me to help, but I'm too far away. Right out of reach. I've tried hard to get her out of my head.

The dreams show her with all the details I remember and more. The bruises on her torso, her torn shirt, and the haunted look in her eyes. She wasn't the only one that looked as if they'd been abused, but she's the one I can't get off my mind.

"Fuck," I huff and push a hand through my sweaty hair.

I think to call Wyatt, but I'm sure he's either sleeping or wrapped up in Nellie. Besides, they're in Seattle. Noah is next to come to mind.

Same with him, he has Bean now. He's probably asleep or has his mouth full. That leaves one other option.

It's the middle of the night, but I know nine times out of ten Dad is up. He's thinking about a case or lifting weights in the garage, thinking up ways to cover the schedule. Dad breathes Black and Lock.

I pick up my phone and shoot him a text. It only takes a second for my phone to ring. I smile.

"Hey, Dad."

"Aye, my lad. What can I do for ye?"

Hearing his accent, I know he was asleep. I curse and chide myself for texting. "Shit, you were sleeping."

"No. Dozing, not sleeping."

"It can wait. I'll call you in the morning."

He sighs. "John, don't you hang up this phone. You never bother me unless you need something. I'm your father. I'll welcome you to my grave to talk to me as long as you like. Come, tell the old man what you need."

I chuckle. "You're not old."

"Bullshit and you're stalling."

I blow out a breath and sit up in the bed to draw my knees into my chest. I have so much going on in my head. Funny, but Missy isn't at the forefront the way she was before I left. Not that she hasn't been calling and texting since I got back.

"I've been wondering about the ones that chose to work for Nate. You know, how they're adjusting."

"Ah, the lass with the busted ribs."

"How did you know?"

"Wyatt and Nate debriefed me on everything. She's healing you know. They were broken and already healing when you found her."

"Yeah, I heard as much. Dad, I've never seen anything so fucked up in my life and I've seen some shit. She was so shattered, but she had so much fight left in her. They were all broken.

"There was this one boy, he seemed to watch her. Almost like he was ready to protect her from us if he had too. He was a kid, but I could see the fear and protectiveness in his eyes," I say as I relive that night in my head.

"Nate has said that we're welcome to drop in to see how things are going. I think he was encouraging it."

"You don't think I'll be a disruption to the process?"

Dad chuckles. "You mean, do I think the girl will be distracted by your presence? No, I think you may be a familiar face she trusts and needs to see. She's not training with the others yet and that has to be a little difficult for her."

I sit, silently thinking it over. I could pop in and see how the program is going. Maybe I can help with the training too.

"I might go out."

He laughs tiredly. "Do what your heart leads you to do. I'll cover for you here."

"Thanks, Dad. Nothing's written in stone. I'll think about it."

"Aye, I know ye will. Goodnight, John."

"Goodnight, Dad."

CHAPTER FIFTEEN

New York Bound

John

I end my shower feeling like this morning has been a waste. Usually, I can get in a workout and clear my head. Not today, the dream from last night has lingered in my mind and I can't focus on anything else. A trip to New York doesn't sound so bad.

I can pop in and pop back out once I put my mind at ease. I'm sure I'll be able to forget about those eyes and the woman they belong to after I reassure myself that she's fine. My phone rings as I war with the decision.

"Hello," I answer the phone without looking at it, tucking it between my head and shoulder as I wrap a towel around my waist and head into my bedroom from the bathroom.

I regret it instantly. "I feel like you're avoiding me," Missy says.

"How can I be avoiding you when we've talked almost every day since I've returned?"

"But you won't come by and you keep telling me you're too busy for me to come to your place."

I pinch the bridge of my nose. "Missy, taking a break for you to get yourself together and for us both to process and grieve doesn't work like this," I say slowly, hoping for once she gets what both I and her therapist have been trying to tell her.

"So, we can't even be friends?"

"You're seriously trying to sell me that you only want to be friends?"

Every time she's around me, she tries to cling to me. That's not the nature of our relationship, but she insists on trying to push it there. I'm not having it; she knows this and yet it never fails.

"I'm not trying to sell you anything. It's the truth."

"It's unhealthy. Neither of us are getting to work through this properly. Give it some time, Missy. Allow us both time to figure out how we feel," I say with as much patience as I have left.

"Okay, I won't call as much, but how about we go for coffee? We can catch up later today?" she says happily as if nothing I've said has gotten through to her.

I bite my fist. This has gotten way out of hand. I need to clear my head because I'm at my breaking point.

"I won't be in town later today. I'm actually getting ready to fly out." As I say the words, I walk into my closet and retrieve my travel bag.

I need to get away. I'm going to take Dad's advice and head to New York. I need a break from everything here in California. I can still work from there. All of my cases involve me and my laptop for now.

"You're leaving again? Will you not be able to contact anyone again?"

I think to tell her a lie, but why should I? I honestly don't have to tell her anything and damn sure don't have to lie. I'm over it.

"I'll have my phone, but I'd prefer if you didn't call. I'll check in with you in a few days or something."

There's silence on the other end. I wait for her to flip out, but instead, she hangs up. I blow out a breath and shake my head.

Without thinking about it, I plan a trip to New York and get ready to head out.

***

When I walk into the state-of-the-art facility that the Briggs train in, I look around at all the new recruits. Some look focused, others are smiling. It seems they are adjusting fine to this new change.

A group of young girls and boys are on some mats, listening intently to Kelly Briggs. God, they're so young, ranging from six to twelve. Most people would wonder why we didn't just take them home to their families.

It's because these are all the kids that were sold into trafficking by their families. If we took them back, they'd only be sold again.

It's a shit life, but Nate did his research and that's the stories he found. They'll have a much better life here. In time, they will be given the option to go out in the world or stay and do what they're being trained to do.

"Good to see you, John," Bobby says as he walks over to me. I reach out for his hand and he pulls me into a one-armed hug.

"Good to see you too."

"I wanted to thank you guys for helping with all of this. We were able to help a lot of people and put a few behind bars," he says.

"Yeah, but they got away with a few. You didn't get Sidorov?"

"Oh, we got him. However, his right hand did get away with a few girls." Bobby frowns.

"Tough shit to swallow," I mutter.

"Yes, it is."

"Those are babies. How could their own families sell them to those monsters?"

"You'd be surprised. Some do it to eat the next day, some because they have too many mouths to feed or…" He pauses and shakes his head. "So many reasons. Not the world you and I know."

That's when she appears out of nowhere. The glare in her eyes says a million words. I look down at her, she looks better. She could still stand to gain more weight, but she looks healthier.

I have to keep from reaching out to tug her toward me for a hug. I don't know where the urge comes from. I'm glad to see she's up and moving, but it's more than that. It's more of a pull I feel in the pit of my stomach that makes me want to shield her in my arms.

It's the same pull from that night. I wanted to hold her near and ensure she was okay then. It's twice as strong now.

"Where'd you come from?" she asks in an accusatory tone.

"Home," I say with a grin.

She frowns back. "I thought this was your home. Why would you talk me into coming here, doing this, and you're never around? The one person I thought I could tr—"

She cuts off and waves a hand at me before turning to walk away. This time I don't hesitate to reach out and halt her. I regret it the moment I see her wince.

Releasing her arm quickly, I close the gap between us. "I never said I lived here. I don't live in New York."

She tilts her head back to look up into my eyes. My cock twitches in my jeans. Shit, that look is perfect. It's exactly how I'd want her to look up at me in my playroom, bound, gagged, and soaking wet.

I take a small step back and shake my head clear. I don't know where that thought came from. After all she's been through, the last thing she needs is to have me perving out over her.

Get your shit together, John.

"Where do you live?"

"Cali," I answer the question before I can think better of it.

The crestfallen look on her face has me closing the space between us again. Those eyes. They say so much. I lean into her and dip my head.

"Are you okay? How are you adjusting? You're ribs... are they healing well?"

She inhales sharply and takes a step back, looking away from me. I go to ask more questions, but I remember that Bobby's watching us. I turn to find his sharp gray gaze locked in.

"So what? You're here now to make sure I'm being their good little slave."

Her words pull me back to her. She's staring at me with blaring determination. I part my lips as the word slave vibrates in my head.

I wonder if she knows that she oozes submission even in her defiance. That defiance would be such a turn on to cut through. Her full lips thin into a line, but it does nothing to remove those sexy lip lines of hers. It's not the first time that feature has stuck out to me.

I love a woman with a sexy mouth. Those lip lines make her mouth even sexier. I know, I'm an odd man. It's the smallest things that turn me on—long lashes, full lips and lip lines, Cupid's bows—fuck if she doesn't have a perfect bow.

Come on, John. A sex slave? That's what you saved her from. She's not yours and never will be.

"They don't want to make you a slave. The people here are family. They treat everyone that works for them like family. They protect their own," I say.

"I'm not their own. I have n—" she stops short, her nostrils flaring.

I narrow my eyes, looking for the end of her words. That's when Bobby clears his throat. I turn to him again.

"I'm going to head out. Good to see you, John. Roni, so you know. Once you stepped through those doors, you were family whether you wanted to be or not," he says and nods, turning to leave.

Roni, cute name.

I turn back to a glaring her. A mix of spite and hurt cover her face. There is also… lost, confusion.

What is it about her?

Roni

I feel like I can't breathe and it's more than my healing busted ribs. It's looking at him. He's so gorgeous. Handsome would be the wrong word. He's more stunning than I remember and for the love of God, he smells so damn good.

When he stepped into my space and I inhaled, I thought my knees would go weak. How did I not pick up on that before? His scent is lick worthy. I drag my tongue across my lips slowly. He allows those golden eyes to drop down to my mouth to watch the action. Frustrated with my reaction to him, I roll my shoulders back.

"What were you going to say?"

"Nothing," I murmur.

He narrows his eyes at me more. With a shake of his head, he closes the gap between us. I tilt my head once again to look up at him.

I'm five seven, he has to be six one or six two. The fact that I have to look up at him makes my belly flip. Goosebumps rise across my skin.

"I know that's a lie. I don't do lies. Since you and I are going to be friends, I think we should establish that upfront."

"Who says we're going to be friends?"

"You have no one," he finishes my earlier words. "Or so you think. Now you have me."

"You don't even live around here, how are we going to be friends?"

He places a hand on my shoulder gently and I swear my belly drops. With a small squeeze, he locks those eyes on me. Again, like that first night, I see something I feel like I can trust.

Trust.

I haven't felt like… I can't remember the last time I trusted someone. I try to recall a time when I was able to hold onto that feeling. To trust someone, to have someone in my corner. The recollection doesn't come, but I know this is that feeling.

"I don't have to be here all the time for us to be friends. Besides, I'm here now and that's what matters. You seem like you could use a friend and I'm here. Question is, do you want me?"

I part my lips to say yes, but not in answer to his real question. I don't know where the thought comes from. I've never been so drawn to a man in my whole life.

I pause as I have that thought. It seems right. I don't remember much, but that thought feels accurate.

"Don't you have to get back home?"

He shakes that pretty head. His hair spilling onto his forehead. I want to reach up and push it back into the neat waves he had it combed into.

A look crosses his eyes for a moment. Then he does something that steals all the breath I have left. He smiles, showing a pair of white teeth. Perfection.

Damn.

"I'll go back when I have to. For now, I'm in town to hang with some friends. Problem with that?"

I roll my eyes. "Have fun with your friends. I don't trust you," I lie and storm off.

CHAPTER SIXTEEN

A Friend

John

It wasn't my plan to be here more than a few days at first, but I haven't been able to force myself to leave. I'm finally breaking through to Roni. The tension between us has started to die down. Well, not the sexual tension. That's only growing by the minute.

With each day that passes she's taking on more weight and her face is becoming fuller. God, she's gorgeous. That heart-shaped face has starred in my dreams on many nights. Even now, as I walk into the gym her face is the first thing I'm looking for.

A slow smile comes to my lips when I find her. She's jumping rope as sweat drips all over her skin. Skin I've wanted to touch on more occasions than one.

Her sports bra shows off those nice plump tits that are glistening with her perspiration. What I'd give to lick every single bead that's dripping between her breasts. Roni falls between a redbone and bronzed brown God crafted just for me. A color I wouldn't mind seeing across my sheets as her silky skin calls to me.

"Hey, John," someone calls out, but I don't stop long enough to see who.

I wave and allow my feet to carry me to the corner of the gym where my new friend is focused on her task. She looks great. Her ribs have healed and she received the all clear a few days ago.

I was glad and a bit disappointed, to be honest. For two weeks I've had her to myself during training sessions. Now, I have to share her with everyone.

Sort of.

"Good morning," I say as I stop in front of her.

"If you're here to chastise me, you can leave. I said what I said."

I shrug my shoulders. "Not my business," I reply.

She stops jumping and turns her pretty eyes on me. I'd sell my right arm for the chance to pull her in for one kiss. It would be a long and deep one.

I'd only let her up for air after I had my fill, but something tells me I'd never have enough of Roni. Which is why I beat back the urge to grab her and pull her into my chest. She's one drug I'm wary to sample.

"Bull crap and you know it. They sent you to talk to me. I thought we weren't going to lie to each other, *friend*."

"You're assuming things, *friend*."

She folds her arms over her chest, causing me to drop my eyes to her full mounds. Fuck, she's put on weight in all the right places. I look lower to her curvy hips. Those thighs are thick enough to cradle me for the long hours I'd spend putting in enough work to get a paycheck.

"You didn't come to breakfast?" she says, changing the subject.

She's good at that. Nate did inform me that she's been difficult today. She was pretty aggressive in her physical combat training. Although she's been cleared, Nate's worried about her injuries.

"I had to get some work done to send back home."

She chews on her cheek for a few seconds. "Are they asking you to come back?"

"No, not yet."

"Oh."

"You want to talk about what's going on? You seem... high strung. You should be pacing yourself."

"I thought you weren't here to talk about that," she says with a pointed look.

I hold my hands up. "I'm not. I actually wanted to see if you want to get out of here. You, me, and a bar. What do you say?"

She looks up at me cautiously. I smile and tilt my head to the side. I know she's been wanting to get outside these walls. I figured it would be good for her and admittedly, I thought I'd find out what's going on in her head.

"You buying?"

I broaden my smile. "Always. It's not in me not to treat."

"Fine, but I need something to wear. I'm not going out in one of those Men in Black suits."

I reach into my back pocket and toss her the other reason I'm here. I watch her face as she drops the rope and catches the item. It's adorable how confusion turns into realization, back to confusion.

"A wallet?" she says as she turns the blue custom-made leather gift over in her hands.

I shrug. "There's some money and a few cards in there. You'll have to hand the cards back over after, but you're welcome to use them to get whatever you want while you're out."

She wrinkles her brows. "They give you this?"

"Does it matter?"

She slants her pretty eyes at me. I hold her gaze as I grin. No, the money, cards, and wallet didn't come from Nate and his team. The ID did, but the rest are on me—and man, did I have to go to bat so she could have them.

I needed her to have this. No, I couldn't tell anyone why because I've been avoiding that answer myself. Along with the answers to why I'm still here, why I want to spend more time with her away from here, and why I can't wait to see her in something other than workout clothes or the suits everyone here wears.

"Yeah, it does." She pauses and licks her lips. "It does, John. I don't know why, but it does."

And we add another to my millions of questions. Nate has nothing on Roni or where she's from. She hasn't told him a thing to help with the background check.

It's like she never existed before she was taken. No facial recognition has come up, her prints didn't get a hit. She's a mystery. Yet, the way her words come out tells me something deeper is at the root of everything about her.

"The ID is from Nate. I asked him to get it for you."

She pulls the ID from the wallet and frowns as she reads it. "Roni Black?" she says, looking up at me. "That's some racist bullshit."

I laugh and shake my head at her. "Black is my last name. I've had brothers all my life. Now I can say I have a little sister."

Her face crumbles and I'm not too sure what to think of it. "Little sister?"

I open my mouth to reply when Torque walks over. He's the only other person Roni talks to. The kid seems to cling to her.

"Hey," he says as a blush takes over his cheeks.

"What's up? Listen, I need to make a few calls and get some more work done. Paige, Bobby's wife will take you out shopping. Be nice."

"Yeah, whatever," Roni murmurs.

I stand watching her for a moment before I smile and nod. One way or another, I plan to get answers about the anomaly before me. Roni has history and I plan to pull it out.

Roni

I look in the mirror, fidgeting with my T-shirt. Biting my lip, I wonder if I'm reading too much into this. If I am, this off the shoulder black Tee might not be appropriate.

For that matter, the skintight light blue jeans and patent leather crisscross heels probably make me look ridiculous. I shake my head at the reflection in the mirror.

With a sigh, I think of how much more I look like I did when I first reached that place they kept us in. My cheeks are fuller, my eyes aren't sunken in. My hips are even almost back to normal.

Damn girl, those jeans are tight.

"But this feels right," I mutter and push the silver bracelets up my arm.

It does. John aside, when Paige took me shopping, I knew what I wanted in each store. It would seem I have expensive taste. Although Paige made sure to take me to high-end shops.

"Oh, girl please, I was told to make sure you get whatever you want. Sky's the limit. If I were you, I'd relax and enjoy it," she'd said while I looked nervously around the pricey shop.

"I don't know if I should. I don't feel comfortable."

"Listen, honey. The men around here are protective and providers. I may not know John as well as some of the others, but I haven't met a man connected to my husband that hasn't spoiled his woman," she replied.

I gasped. "Oh, no. You have this all wrong. That's not my man. I'm not his anything. Which is why this is ridiculous."

"Okay, you keep telling yourself that, Ms. Black. I'm going over here to look at these shoes. By the way, there's a twenty-thousand-dollar credit limit on each card from what I'm to understand," she said with a secret grin and walked off.

I stood in silence, glued to spot she left me in. The words retail therapy whispered in my ear, but it wasn't my money to spend. All I wanted was something to wear to the bar.

I wouldn't need twenty grand for that. Besides, John had that wallet ready for me before I said I wanted to go shopping. Yeah, we had talked about me going out before, but the wallet, the money, and the last name. What the heck does all that mean?

He trusts you.

Running my hands down my thighs, I let that thought take root. John trusts me. He has to. I could have taken the money and cards he gave me and ran off.

Not that it hadn't crossed my mind. Drain the cards of the cash advance and go as far from here as I can. Then I thought about Torque and Natasha.

Torque looks happy here. He's thriving. We have a mission to complete before I can decide where I'll go from here.

A knock comes to my bedroom door. "Roni?"

I nearly jump when John's smooth voice carries through the solid wood door. Frowning at myself, I start to mumble. I have no idea why I'm reacting to him like this. We're friends.

"Coming," I call out and rush to get my purse and jacket.

One more glance over my shoulder, and I poke my lip out. I should have done something with my hair. The long coils are hanging free. Not much life or style to them. I push a hand into the front and flip a mass of it over to the right side.

It will do. Turning to leave, I move forward with a stomach full of nerves. I stop at the door and take a deep breath before opening it. It's time I remind myself of the things I know.

Trust no one.

Always be on guard.

Never show emotions.

I stop as that last one springs up. The dreams I've been having of the man I assume to be my father come to mind. The handsome yet stern man that always seems so detached in my dreams.

"Roni, you all right in there? You need more time?" John calls, disrupting the train of thought I get ready to sprawl through.

I toss my jacket over my arm and tug the door open. "Yeah, I'm ready."

Wow, I pause as he comes into view. John always looks great, but he's putting a hurting on the black jeans with the tears in the knee and thigh and that tight black T-shirt that stretches across his chest beneath his black leather jacket. I suck my lip into my mouth as I allow my gaze to roll over him.

Damn it, Roni. Cut it out.

I know I'm caught when I bring my gaze to his. He has a grin on his lips as he stares back at me with those eyes. I go to step out of the room. However, he doesn't move.

I wait for him to back up, but he remains in place as he returns the favor of taking me in from head to toe. I lift my head despite feeling a little self-conscious. That is until he takes a second pass and his gaze lands on my hips. A groan comes from his mouth.

"I think you were safer in your uniform," he murmurs.

"What?"

He shakes his head. "Nothing. Come on."

He takes a step back, allowing me to step out. Taking a peek up at him, we lock eyes. I search his, wondering what he's thinking.

Already, I'm forgetting my list. He is a means to an end. As long as I'm here, I need someone to… what do I need John for?

Comfort.

I clench my teeth. Comfort is for people that don't have to watch their back. I may not remember where I'm from or who I am, but I've had this feeling for the longest that I need to watch my back.

Nope, comfort is not for me. You slip up when you're comfortable. I have nothing to be comfortable about.

"Roni."

"Yes?"

"If it's not with my brothers or my parents, I hardly ever let my guard down."

With that, he turns and starts down the hall. I stare at his back as he goes. Slowly a smile comes to my face.

Twin flames.

I gasp as the memory hits me hard. I sat in a kitchen with a plate sitting on the table before me. The cinnamon-colored face across from me wore a smile.

"One day you will find the mirror to your soul, Roni. You will know it from the spark that carries between you. Almost like a light goes off. When you find that flame, hold on. Don't be afraid of it. See where it will take you."

"Yes, Abuelita," I said and smile.

I hold onto that memory as I move to catch up with John. I don't want to dig too deeply into what it all means. For tonight, I'm getting out of here.

CHAPTER SEVENTEEN

Temptation

John

"You sure you don't want to move to a table?" I ask as I stare at the profile of Roni's face.

I thought she was beautiful before, but tonight those jeans and that top give away her personality. The more I look at her, the more I want to know about her. This side of Roni is sassy and sexy.

I sit back on the barstool beside hers with my gaze still glued on her. She's been nursing her third beer for the last hour. I get the feeling she's holding back to keep from loosening her tongue.

"I'm fine here," she replies, not looking at me, which I'm starting to think is on purpose.

She has her back to the bar, tapping her foot to the pulsing beat of the music. This place is pretty laid back, but it's not some dive either. There's a mix of college students, the after-work crowd, and a few couples.

"Tell me something about you," I say, drawing her attention from people watching.

She turns to me. "What?"

"Tell me something about you."

"Nothing to tell," she says and turns back to look over the small crowd.

I grin. "Okay, how about this? I'll tell you something about me," I say. I've caught her attention with that. She holds my gaze.

Not waiting for a reply, I continue. "I have six brothers. I'm the third oldest. My mother is Irish, and my father is a Scot. My family is huge outside of my immediate family as well."

"Okay."

I snort. "Okay, now it's your turn."

She tips her head to the side as she looks at me. "I thought they told you everything about me. I guess I was wrong."

"I was told you haven't given over anything that will help with the search for your past life. You do know they're trying to help. If you talk, they can see if you have a safe life to return to. You are not obligated to stay here if you have a family to return to."

She searches my face, her eyes growing sad as her thoughts race across her features. I lean into her, feeling protective. I can see something is off.

"It's not that I don't want to tell you about me. There's nothing to tell because…" She pauses and licks her lips. "I can't remember."

"As in you have amnesia?" She nods. I crease my brows. "Nothing?"

She looks down at the floor and shrugs. There's a long pause. At first, I think she's shutting down on me already.

"I can't remember anything before waking with those people. I've been having these dreams. I think they're memories, but I'm much younger. A girl. Nothing that will help me figure anything out. I figured my family may have been killed like some of the others," she says.

I clench my hand holding my beer. I have to tell myself to reel in my anger. There's nothing I can do about all of that at the moment anyway.

"Wait, your memory was gone when you woke?"

"Yeah, I had a head injury and they were drugging me. Sometimes I get these flashes of things, but never enough to pull real pieces together," she says.

"Okay, so it seems there's a chance to regain your memory. I mean, I'm no doctor or anything, but the flashes and the dreams are a good sign."

"Maybe I'm not meant to remember that past. The one I do remember is painful enough," she says and turns away from me again.

I can see the tight set of her lips even in profile. Seeing the tension in her body, I want to kick myself. I should have known this wasn't the right conversation to have.

We've been having fun for the most part. As much as I want to know and understand this woman. I still wanted her to chill tonight.

The song changes to "In Those Jeans" by Ginuwine and I grin. Placing my beer down, I stand and hold a hand out. Our eyes lock and it's like I'm sucker-punched in the gut.

Something in her eyes calls to me as it always does, but at this moment it's more intense. It's like I can see her thoughts and for the first time in my life, I want to allow someone to see mine.

"Come on." She lifts a brow at me. "Come on. Dance with me."

She turns to look down at my hand. A second longer and she submits, placing her small palm in mine. When she lifts to her feet, I guide her out to the little dance floor.

She stands awkwardly, looking up at me. I give her a full smile and draw her body close to mine. I know I'm playing with fire the moment I do.

She feels too right in my arms. Her breasts against my chest cause all my thoughts to go to my playroom. I still haven't broken it in since I purchased my house.

I dance my eyes over her dark hair and imagine it spilled across the pillow. Her thick lush locks are begging to be wrapped around my fist. I inhale sharply and shove away the feeling.

Without warning, I start to guide her hips to a slow rock with mine. Her lips part and her eyes widen. I can't help the wolfish grin that comes to my face.

I wink. "Stick with me and I'll show you things," I say.

She slides her arms around my neck and relaxes into my hold. I tighten my arms around her and slide my leg between her thighs. That tension that has been building between us takes over the entire place.

I've been ignoring it as much as I can, but with her in my arms, I can't deny that it's there. As if holding her isn't enough, she decides to turn, placing her back to my front. Her plush ass fits into me, causing my jeans to tighten as I grow hard.

I believe she's intent on teasing me as she looks up and over her bare shoulder and locks gazes with me. I splay a hand against her belly as I keep our heated two-step sway in play. Again, she reaches up to place her arms around my neck.

My lips turn up in the corner as I read her gaze. "Trust me, you don't want that."

"Want what?"

"Me to fuck you."

"Why not?" she says, that rasp to her voice feels like a caress.

I growl and cup her throat. I want to close the distance between her lips and mine. Instead, I kiss her forehead and move to whisper in her ear.

"I'm bad for you, Roni."

With that, I squeeze once before letting go. The flicker in her eyes almost sucks me right in. Her brown orbs spark as if the gesture turns her on as much as it does me.

I lick my lips as I drop my eyes to her lush mouth. Lifting my gaze, I remind myself of everything she's been through. That's enough to make me back off.

Keeping eye contact, I reluctantly take a step away. This might not have been a good idea. One dance and I'm ready to strip her down and feast on her gorgeous brown skin.

"We should head back," I say huskily.

"Yeah, okay."

Roni

John hasn't said much since we left the bar. I've been as much in my head as he seems to be in his. His words are on repeat in my head.

Me to fuck you. My heart raced as he said these words, but it was the ones after that confused me. *I'm bad for you, Roni.*

John has been a nice guy from day one. I don't know how he could be bad for me. All I know is that I want to know what that means. Being in his arms made me feel safe and the way my body felt... still feels.

"I'll see you in the morning," he says as we stop in front of my room.

"Will you tell me what you meant?" I blurt out before I can stop myself.

He searches my face before replying. Reaching up, he brushes his thumb across my lips. I'm surprised by the whimper that tries to leave them.

"Go to bed."

I frown. "What if I don't want to?"

He crowds my space until my back hits the door. Leaning down, he stops when we are nose to nose. His cologne surrounds me, causing me to close my eyes to take him in.

"Never pour gasoline on a fire you're trying to squelch. We're going to let this go for a number of reasons. Goodnight, Roni."

"Because you think those savages ran through me?" I say bitterly, opening my eyes.

His eyes soften. He cups my face and for a moment I think he's going to kiss me. I hold my breath, but the kiss doesn't come.

"If I could kill them all, I would. The thought of anyone touching you against your will... anyone touching you period makes me see red, but I would never blame or shame you for something out of your control," he says.

"They never touched me. I was one of the virgins. They weren't allowed to touch us, not like that," I say before I can trap the words inside.

He narrows his eyes for the briefest second before pushing off the door behind me and stepping back. I feel his loss in my belly as if someone stole from my womb. I want to reach out and pull him back to me.

"You just proved me right. I'm not for you, baby. Not at all," he says, kissing my forehead and turning to walk down the hall.

I stand staring after him, fighting back the urge to release angry tears. The sting of rejection brings me back to reality. I don't need John in my bed. I need to focus on learning how to find Natasha.

Don't ever forget that again.

I turn and head into my room. Flipping on the light, I find Torque sitting on my bed. He has a laptop in his lap as he looks at me with his big pretty eyes.

"What are you doing in here?"

"I wanted to show you what I learned today. I think I found a way to start searching for Natasha," he replies.

I sigh. Exactly, this is what I should be focused on. Unfastening and kicking my shoes off, I stroll to the bed and sit beside him.

Maybe this is what I need tonight. A distraction from that sexy ass dance and the man that accompanied it. I take a pause.

The man that was able to read my thoughts as if he's known me for years. Now that I think about it, I know this is for the best. I can't afford to get attached to anyone here and a man that can read me like a book is way more than an attachment.

CHAPTER EIGHTEEN

John

"John, I understand that you want to help her acclimate, but the money... we don't know anything about her. Handing her money and credit cards is a risk to everyone," Nate says as he sits behind his desk in his office. "She's already undermining my staff."

"I'll talk to her about that. I think she's been rebellious based on the circumstances she's come out of. Come on, Nate. She's still a human. I only wanted to make sure she felt that way. I made sure she returned the cards."

"By giving her almost a hundred grand in finances. I never would have approved that. That's not what we agreed to. I can't believe Paige didn't come to me first," he grumbles.

"I went to her husband. I told Bobby how much I wanted her to have. He approved it," I reply.

"Yeah, I'll be having a talk with him," he mutters. "Do you understand the kinds of things we've been teaching her? She could track you right to your front door once you leave here."

I shrug. "If she needs to, so be it."

He narrows his eyes at me. I lift my hand up when he goes to retort. I already have a feeling I know what he's going to say.

"Listen, I'm a big boy. I can handle her if she shows up on my doorstep. I'm more concerned with her having the need to. Maybe this isn't for her and I shouldn't have talked her into it. I had no idea she had no memory. We don't know who she is. I don't like it."

He glares at me for a moment. "That's a concern of mine as well. Hell, the last thing I want to do is send her on a mission and she runs into her past," he says and frowns.

"Exactly."

"Still, that has nothing to do with what you've done. I don't like the idea of you giving her so much free reign. Fact is, we don't know who she is and that's dangerous for a lot of reasons."

"Any solutions?"

"Yes, I'm placing her into mandatary therapy sessions, for starters. I want to see if anything comes up. By the way, thanks for finding all this out. We thought she was guarded because she didn't trust us yet. This is a new ball game."

"No problem. I'll do anything I can to help. I'm not trying to make this harder on you guys. If you like, I'll take sole responsibility for her."

He sits back in his chair. "I can't ask you to do that. We've taken this all on. We'll handle it."

"You're not asking. I'm offering."

"Why?"

This time I narrow my eyes at him. The fact of the matter is, I don't want to admit to him or myself why. Last night I almost said fuck it and entered that room with her. However, when she told me she was a virgin, I knew I needed to walk away.

I'm not for her. My tastes, my lifestyle—I wouldn't corrupt her innocence with it after what she's gone through. Then there's the fact that I've never been in love and I wouldn't want to drag her into my failure to connect with women in that way.

But you've already connected with her.

"I want to help her. Did you see how badly she was beaten or how they starved her? Now on top of that to know she doesn't remember her life before all of that. I want to help, simple as that," I reply.

He tilts his head as he examines me more closely. "But you only found out about her memory last night. You gave her the money and accounts before that."

"When I see something that needs fixing, I fix it."

He narrows his eyes. "Friend to friend, Black. I'm going to warn you to be careful with Roni. This could blow up in your face. Are you sure you want to take this on?"

"I'll take full responsibility for her. If she doesn't take to the program, I'll be the one to figure out something else for her."

He releases a whistle before sighing. My phone interrupts whatever he's about to say next. When I pull it from my pocket, I see it's my dad.

"Hey, Dad, what's up?" I answer.

"Wyatt needs you in Seattle."

I sit up straighter. "What's going on?"

"It's Nora. She's not doing well. Wyatt doesn't think she has much time left. He wants to marry Nellie before… he's been planning the wedding for a week or so. I wanted to wait until he had things locked down before I bothered you. It's time, he's asking us to be there for him."

"Say no more. Does he need anything? What else can I do?"

"I think he needs his family more than anything. This isn't going to be easy for either of them. Your brother loves that lass with everything he is. Her hurt is his hurt and she's going to be devastated. I talked to Steve before calling you.

"Nellie had no idea the cancer returned. This was all a shock to her when she and Wyatt arrived. She's had, what? Three weeks to digest that she's losing her mother," Dad chokes out.

"Damn," I say, and hang my head.

Mrs. Nora had always been so nice to us when we were younger. I was happy to see her and Steve marry. I almost missed the wedding because of school, but I remember that day like it was yesterday. I'd never seen Steve look so happy in my life.

"I'll see ye soon, aye," my father says, pulling me from my racing thoughts.

"Yeah, I'm on my way."

"I love ye, John," he says the words with such emotion, his accent so thick, I know this is tearing him to pieces.

"I love you too, Dad."

"Everything okay?" Nate asks as I hang up.

"I need to head out to Seattle. My brother is getting married."

"That's a happy occasion, no?" Confusion fills his eyes.

"I don't know for how long. It seems I'm heading to a wedding and a funeral. His girl's mom is dying from cancer."

Nate jerks as if I've punched him in the chest. He swallows hard and nods a few times. His eyes grow distant for a moment.

"Go handle your business. Your brother will need you."

Roni

To say I'm annoyed is an understatement. I've been waiting for John to show up all day. I've thought of him as many things, but never a coward.

If last night wasn't something he wanted, fine, but for him to avoid me after is pure bullshit. I guess I can't trust him. I feel stupid for thinking that I could.

"Hey, Roni."

I stop jumping rope to turn and find Torque's wide eyes on me. His cheeks are flaming red. I smirk and laugh to myself. He's a teenager. It's not the first time I've caught him staring.

"What's up?" I say, choosing not to embarrass him any further.

"You weren't in the cafeteria. I came to check on you."

I shrug. "Not hungry."

"Is it because he's gone?" he says in a whisper.

"Who's gone?"

"That guy. John."

"Gone?"

"Yeah, I saw him heading out during my groups' morning run. He had his bags when he got into the car. He looked like he was in a hurry," he says.

Anger rushes through me. It's as if my head is going to explode. He couldn't be man enough to say goodbye.

"Whatever," I mutter.

"Do you think he'll be back soon? I thought you could trust him. Maybe he can help us?"

"I don't know if he's coming back. I'm sorry, kid." Feeling completely disappointed in myself, I shut down.

I drop the rope I'd been jumping with and kick it aside. Torque calls after me, but I hold my hand up to warn him off. I need some time to myself to think.

Heading straight for my room, I mumble to myself. Natasha needs me and I've been thinking only of myself. Starting tomorrow, Torque and I will use what he showed me last night to figure things out on our own.

"Roni," my name is barked from behind.

I spin to find the one they call Thomas. From the whispers I've overheard, he's related to Nate. Some say his dad. I can totally see that. They may be worlds apart in complexions, but they have the same face.

I fold my arms over my chest as he closes the distance between us. He's a tall man. I have to crane my neck back as he gains on me. That seems to happen a lot around here.

"I have a letter for you. Sorry I'm just getting around to finding you. My son asked me to hand it off before he had to head out this morning," he says, holding out the letter.

"Your son?" Hope blooms maybe they were wrong, and this guy is John's dad.

"Nate. Rita and Nate are my two," he says with a smile.

"Oh, okay," I reply in disappointment, reaching for the letter.

"Let me know if you need anything. I'll be here for this week's shift. My door is always open."

"Thanks," I murmur and turn to head toward my room.

Nate is probably fed up with me and now that John is gone, he's going to put my ass out. I have the money. I can use it to get out of here and start over.

First, I'll need to get away from here and get a place. Then, I'll work on how to make my own money. Torque will need to go to school. I'll have to figure out how to make that happen. I'm not leaving him behind.

Closing the bedroom door behind me, I go to sit on the floor on the side of my bed. I'm still sweaty from my workout. I don't want to sit on the bed before I shower, but I want to know what this letter says.

Roni,

I'm sorry I had to rush off without a word. My brother needs me in Seattle. I've placed my number at the bottom of this letter and a new phone will be delivered to you in a day or two. Behave. You can trust them.

John

I grind my teeth. He could have told me in person if he had time to write this stupid letter. I know it's total bullshit.

I swipe at the tear that falls. So much for my *friend*. I get up and head into the shower to wash this day away so I can get some sleep. Hopefully, the dreams will give me peace for at least this one night.

***

"Sit up," my father says as he sits at the head of the table. His eyes and demeanor are cold. "You will always sit straight. When people see you slouch, they think you're weak. You are a Pérez. We have no weakness."

I sit up quickly, not wanting to disappoint him. I want him to like me. He has to like me, or I can't stay. I want to stay with him. I have no one else.

"How was school? Are you learning anything there?"

"Yes, sir. I'm learning."

He drops his fork and knife. His expression seems hurt for a second. He goes to say something, but his hand is covered, drawing my attention to the older woman sitting across from me.

"Give her time, Eliam. She will come around," she says gently. Abuela, she's always gentle with me.

I wrinkle my brows in confusion, knowing I've done something wrong, but not knowing what. My stomach tightens. I'm so nervous, but I won't show it. I'll be just like him. I won't show emotions. That will make him like me.

"I have work to do," my father says and stands.

He pauses beside me for a long moment. I sit nervously, thinking I'm in trouble for something. However, he pats the top of the chair I'm sitting in and walks away.

"Roni," my grandmother calls.

"Yes?"

"How about you start to call your father, Papi or daddy? Do you think you can do that?"

My heart swells at the thought of being able to do so. I've been so nervous; not knowing how he will react. It's only been a month since I've been here.

"Yes. I can do that."

"Sí, ustedes dos estarán bien."

I wake with a gasp. Running a hand through my hair, I try to hold onto the dream. Were her words true? Were me and my father ever fine?

It bothers me so much that I can't remember. All I have are these pieces I get in my dreams. It's not enough to tell me much, they only give me more questions.

"*Coger.*"

CHAPTER NINETEEN

Breaking Rules

Roni

"I don't know about this. They watch our every move. You're not going to get out of here without them catching you," Torque says nervously.

I mess his hair and kiss the top of his head as he sits at the desk in my room. "You watch and see. I can be determined when I want to be," the words float out without me thinking, but I know them to be true by instinct.

He turns his head up to look at me and that adorable blush is on his face. "What do you plan to do when we get there?"

"Who said anything about *we*?" I frown at him.

"You might need me."

"Need you to stay right here and continue learning. I'm not leaving for good. Not yet."

"I don't like it," he says and pouts.

I tap his nose. "You don't have to. You're staying here. My plan only works if you're here covering my ass."

"Why do you have to go?"

I freeze. I've given John enough time to contact me. Okay, it's been a day. The phone came this morning. I haven't called him because if he sent the phone, he has to have the number. He should be the one to reach out, not me.

However, I want to know the truth. Is his brother really in some type of trouble or did he leave because of what happened between us—or should I say what didn't happen between us. Whatever the case may be, I want to hear it from his mouth face to face.

Which is why I had Torque track him down and I'll be purchasing a plane ticket to Seattle. That much he told the truth about. Torque was able to trace his credit card there. He's staying at some swanky hotel.

Curiosity is killing me. Why a hotel? What's going on with his brother? Why leave and not say something?

I trusted him and he left. I don't like the way that feels. So, I'm going to get answers.

"You have training in the morning. You should head to bed. You're doing so good. Thanks for the help," I say.

He stands and tugs me into a hug. I force myself to relax and hug him back. I think this kid has grown since we've been here. I'm sure he's about an inch or two taller now.

"Be safe. I... I don't want to lose you too."

I cup his cheek. "Hey, I'm going to be fine. I'll be back before you know it."

"What if they don't let you come back? What if I can't get to you if they find out and tighten security around here?"

Moving my hand to his chest, I smile up at him. I don't miss the fact that his heart is pounding. Giving a reassuring pat, I lock eyes with him.

"You worry too much. Nothing can keep me away from you. I'll be back for you or I'll die trying. And we didn't lose Natasha. I have to believe we'll find her," I say.

"Is that why you're going to Seattle?"

I open my mouth to say no, but I lie instead. "Yeah. If I can make this happen, I have hope we'll find her sooner than later."

Well, it's not a complete lie. I do plan to find out if John's full of shit or if he'll be willing to help us. If he's not, I'm absolutely ready to take this all on by myself.

Torque pulls me into another tight hug. "Be safe. If you need me, log into that app I downloaded to your phone. I'll be watching."

"I'll be fine. Get to bed."

I watch him drag his way out of my room. Releasing a long breath, I get ready to put my plan in motion. I grab my small knapsack and slip out of the room. The halls are quiet. Everyone's fast asleep for the night.

Great, that's exactly what I need. I'll slip out the back and head right through the brush. Looking down at my phone, I see my ride will arrive in ten minutes. That should be enough time to get into place.

I pause as I hear heavy footfalls ahead. Clinging to the wall, I don't take a breath. As the tall guy walks past, I can hear the music coming from his headphones.

I relax and slip through the shadows, avoiding making a sound or getting caught. I jog silently down the stairs and dart to the back door. The alarm system blanks, informing that it's engaged.

"Thanks, kid," I mutter to myself as I use my phone to disarm the thing.

Torque really is learning fast. He's been so eager to learn more. I know it's because he thinks we can use it to find Natasha.

I'm hoping he's right. It's come in handy so far. If only I knew where to start, I'd find her and kill the rest of those bastards in the process.

I grind my teeth as my thoughts go back to the shit we had to go through. I can only hope that Natasha is hanging in there while I figure things out. Once through the bushes, I find new hope. I made it out.

"I might be able to pull this off." I grin as I jump into my ride. Once in the back seat, I pull up the website to purchase my plane ticket. My smile grows as I enter the numbers from one of the cards John gave me by memory. Apparently, I have a thing for numbers. "John Black, here I come."

John

"What's up, Nate?" I breathe as I answer my phone, tossing my arm over my face.

"I think you have a visitor heading your way," he replies. "Told you the money was a bad idea."

I sigh and sit up. "How do you know she's heading to me?"

It's a dumb question. I know Nate's team is one of the best. If I didn't have my brothers to have my back, I'd want to have Nate's crew.

"Watched her walk right off the property. Had one of my guys follow her to JFK. She boarded a flight to Seattle about five hours ago," he says.

"Roni," I groan.

"Told you, you were taking on more than you bargained for," he says.

"Yeah, I know. Listen, the wedding is in a few hours, but I'll handle this. I'll get her back to you."

He snorts. "Good luck." With that, he hangs up.

I get up and swing my feet over the edge of the bed. If Roni boarded her flight five hours ago, I have about an hour before she lands. That gives me time to shower and check-in with Wyatt before she'll be able to receive calls.

I dial Wyatt first. I want to see if he needs anything before I get my day started. We've all been moving around to get last minute things done for him and Nellie. I haven't had time to sit down with my brother or his bride to be.

"Hey, John, what's up?"

"Checking in. You ready for this?"

"Yes and no."

"Want to talk about it?"

He sighs. "I feel like Nora is holding on for today. I wish there was a way to drag it out and keep her here longer for Nellie. Man, I've never felt so powerless in my life," he says, pain clear in his voice.

"Bro, this has to be hard. I'm here when you need. Whatever you need," I say. "Maybe you and Nellie should take a vacation when things settle. It's on me. My gift to you guys."

"You don't have to do that."

"I want to. Let me do this for you. Wherever you guys want to go."

"Thanks, man. I'll let you know. First, I need to get Nellie through today. I want this to be perfect for her. It has to be her dream wedding."

"Are you kidding? Do you see the way she looks at you?" I chuckle. "This wedding could be in a cave with no light and not a crumb of food and she'll still be happy as long as she's married to you."

"Yo, that reminds me. What happened to Missy? I would think she would have loved to come to something like this. She seems to like having her ass at family functions."

I groan. "This is your wedding day, so I'm not going to answer that."

"We're going to talk about it sooner or later. I've had questions since you first brought her around."

"Not today. Listen, I'm heading into the shower. I have some shit I need to handle before I head over to the house. See you soon. Love you, man."

"Love you too."

I toss the phone on the bed and head into the bathroom for a shower. My mind chucks question after question at me the entire time, almost causing me to lose track of time. The biggest question on my mind—what the hell does Roni plan to do when she gets here and how did she plan to find me when she took off?

Could Nate and I be assuming things? Maybe this is home for her. It's possible that my mention of Seattle in the letter I left sparked a memory.

And you know that's bullshit.

Do I ever. Which leads back to my other questions. What does she plan to do when she arrives?

I walk out of the bathroom, wrapping a towel around my waist. As I look at the clock, it's clear that I totally lost all sense of time. I grab my phone from the bed and scroll to the number I saved for the phone I sent to Roni.

As I'm dialing, a notification comes up for one of the credit cards I gave her. I furrow my brows. She returned all the cards after her shopping trip. I move to my wallet to count and make sure I have them all.

Sure enough, I have the card she used. I open the notification up to see what the charge is for. A little digging and I find all I need to know. She has purchased a plane ticket and rented a motorcycle.

Only a few seconds and I'm able to get the plates and VIN number for the bike. Deciding not to call in a favor, unsure of sending a stranger to intercept her, I log into the GPS I had placed on the phone I sent her.

I'm glad I don't need Felix or Wyatt for this. I shake my head as I see she's indeed heading for me. However, I won't be here when she arrives.

I contemplate sending her a message, but she's on a bike. Her safety is more important to me. I don't want her distracted.

A plan forms and I head over to the hotel phone to call the front desk. The perks of being in a suite will work out for me today. I grin as I think of Roni's face when she finds out I'm two steps ahead of her.

"Good morning, Mr. Black. How can I help you?"

"I have a guest arriving this morning, but unfortunately I won't be here when she arrives. Her name is Roni Black. I'll provide you with a picture for reference."

"Yes, sir. We will be on the lookout for her," the concierge says. "Will there be anything else?"

"Actually, I want her to join me at my brother's wedding. She'll need a dress and heels. Please see to it that she's provided with both and a car. I'll drop the address at the desk when I depart along with that image. Place all charges on my account."

"I'll be happy to assist," he says.

"Thank you."

I hang up and realize I'm smiling much more than I should be. I should be totally pissed at Roni for this little stunt, but the truth of the matter is that I'll be happy to see her. I miss our talks about nothing.

She may be guarded, but she's funny and a quick thinker. One of the things I like most about her is that she doesn't mince words and she lets you know how she feels. It's refreshing.

"But why are you here, Roni?" I shake my head at that question. I'll find out soon enough.

CHAPTER TWENTY

No Place for Me

Roni

I stand in this fancy hotel room and stare at the dress the smiling woman is holding up for me. What the hell am I doing here? This is not what I came for.

"Mr. Black requested I find something in yellow. Now that I see you, I understand why. This will look gorgeous against your skin," Julia, the woman who introduced herself as my personal shopper upon my arrival says.

I was more than surprised to be intercepted by the concierge and handed a note from John. Him and his fucking notes. Along with the smiling concierge was this one, with her too-white smile. I'm sorry, not sorry, but I can't trust anyone that doesn't have a single stitch out of place.

This chick is like an iBot, but that's not the weirdest thing going on at the moment. John knew I was coming, and he wants me to join him at his brother's wedding. The butterflies I had after I first read the note have disappeared as reality sets in.

"I don't think I'll be needing that dress," I say.

Her smile falls. "Oh, I was hoping to get to see you in it. I know Mr. Black would have approved."

She moves to place the dress and the bag she's been holding on one of the accent chairs in the living area of the suite. This room is huge and not what I was expecting. None of this is what I expected.

"Weddings aren't my thing." I shrug.

Actually, I don't know if they are or not. What I do know is that I'm not going to that wedding to be judged by John's family. Some black chick that can't remember a thing about herself.

There's no telling how they will treat me. Nope. I'm not doing it and fuck John for being an ass. He probably knew I wouldn't want to go in the first place.

"Shall I cancel the car then?"

This gets my attention. "Do you have the address the car was supposed to take me to?"

"I believe all of that information has been given to the driver."

"Thanks. I'll go down and let him know I won't be needing him myself," I say and grab the keys for the bike I rented.

Looks like I have a wedding to crash.

John

I look at my phone for the millionth time. Roni should've been here by now. Finding her a dress shouldn't have taken that long. I wish I knew her size. I would've given it at the desk along with my request for the color.

The more I thought about seeing her, the more I envisioned her in something sexy and yellow. A dress I could spend the day imagining peeling off. I may have no plans of touching Roni, but I can sure think about it.

"What's up with you?"

I look up to find Ryan with his eyes narrowed on me. Oh great, of all my brothers to home their focus in on me it had to be Ryan. This kid doesn't miss a thing. I think it's because he's the baby in the family. He's beyond observative, even for a PI.

"Nothing," I grumble.

"You've been watching your phone since before the wedding started. Something's up."

"It's nothing. Isn't there someone else here you can harass?"

"Nope," he says, popping the p. "You're distracted. Where you been lately? Dad hasn't been too forthcoming with details about your schedule. That's a little odd."

"I've been minding my own fucking business. Something your ass needs to learn to do."

He draws his brows and immediately, I feel like an asshole. I'm frustrated. The GPS on Roni's phone has her pegged as a few miles from here. She was on the move toward me and then she just stopped.

At first, I thought she was in traffic, but that thought went out the window two hours ago. I haven't had a real moment to call her. I already know when we talk it's not going to be a quick conversation, so I've chosen not to start it until we are face to face.

Honestly, I'm starting to wonder if something has happened, but I've pushed that thought down to keep from losing my shit. She's stubborn. She's doing this to be stubborn, I know it in my gut.

"I'm only concerned about you. This isn't like you, but I'll mind my damn business," Ryan says.

"Ry, I'm sorry."

"Eat my ass." He goes to turn away from me, but I grab him by the arm and tug him into me. Damn, this kid has outgrown us all. He's at least five inches taller than me, but he still melts in my arms like the big baby he is. He wouldn't let on to anyone, but I know I've hurt his feelings. "I love you, Ry. I'm annoyed with some shit. It's not you."

He pulls away and looks me in my eyes. "Damn, we're going to have another wedding," he says.

"What?"

"Whoever she is, she's different. You think she can handle all your kinky shit? Wait, that's the problem, you like this one, but she doesn't know."

I roll my eyes. "Goodbye, Ryan."

"Hold on, what the fuck is going on with Missy then? She's been blowing me up. You said you told her about this, and she didn't want to come. I call bullshit."

I clench my jaw. First, I don't know how or why Missy has been calling and texting my brothers. Yes, I talked to her the other night when I arrived here in Seattle. I was exhausted and told her I was handling some personal shit with my family and I'd check on her in a few days.

I don't know why I lied to Ryan. I guess it was because I knew he would pry. My phone grabs my attention as it vibrates with a text. It's Roni.

I'm here.

"Hey, we'll talk later," I say to Ry and take off before he can grill me any further.

When I get out front, I'm expecting a town car. Instead, I find a motorcycle roaring its way up the street. When it stops Roni climbs off in a pair of tight-fitting jeans, a T-shirt, and boots. Parking the bike, she removes her helmet, gets off, and leans back against the motorcycle. She's not dressed for a wedding at all.

Moving down the driveway, I stop in front of her and shove my hands into my pockets to keep from touching her. Not only would that be inappropriate, but I've come to learn she's not fond of people in her space. I want to respect that as much as I can. Our dance the other night was definitely out of her comfort zone, which made me cherish it even more.

"You left. You left and didn't say a word," she says, her words coming off oddly detached.

"You followed," I say and grin.

She shrugs. "I wanted answers and I wanted them in person."

"What happened to your dress? I told them to get you a dress and heels," I say.

"I don't want to go to a wedding," she seethes. "I don't know them, and I apparently don't know you."

I close the gap between us. "Yet, here you are."

She pushes at my chest, causing me to take a step back. Not from the force of the shove, but because it's what she wants. She glares at me, her nostrils flaring.

"You could have told me to my face. I never thought of you as a coward," she spats.

"Wait, how am I a coward?" I say, wrinkling my brows.

She widens her eyes. Not for the first time in the last few minutes alone, I want to tug her in and kiss that sexy ass mouth. Even as she's pissed off, I note that she looks good, healthy.

I can't help thoughts of reaching for that single braid she has resting over one shoulder. I love that it's not perfect. It's fuzzy strands rebel against the weave she's forced them into. Her curls as defiant as she is.

"How are you not a coward? We had a thing. Then you run off. Why?"

"I told you in the letter, my brother needed me."

She looks past me to the house, drawing her brows together. When her confused gaze comes back to me, I think I understand where her thoughts are. I ball my fists in my pockets because right now, all I want is to reach for her.

"You didn't know he was getting married? You couldn't have told me sooner that you were leaving?"

That ache in her voice is my undoing. I take my hands from my pockets and place them on her waist, bringing her to me. Kissing her forehead, I keep my lips against her skin as I speak.

"It's a complicated situation. We all had to come in at the last minute. If you'd have worn the dress like I asked, you would've understood. I could have explained…" I trail off the moment I know I've lost her.

Her body stiffens and she pulls away slowly. I run through my words to find which ones were the trigger. Fuck, I have to learn to be more careful with my words when it comes to her.

Roni

"First, John, you didn't ask me shit. You left yet another note and some strangers to tell me that you wanted me to come to this wedding where I don't know anyone, and they don't know me. A bunch of white folks that would make me feel out of place," I snap.

He laughs. I mean, a deep belly laugh. I eye him in disgust. Okay fine, I'm not disgusted by anything I see. He is wearing the hell out of that tux. I want to grab the lapels and kiss those sexy lips of his.

I hate how he always makes me feel this way. Other people, I don't give a fuck about. I could go days without talking to anyone, but when it comes to John, he makes me crave something I don't think I've ever had.

It's more than a sexual attraction. It's his attention. I want his attention. It sounds so needy, but it's the only way I know how to describe how I feel about him.

Then he laughs and goes from gorgeous to breathtaking during said laugh, but he's laughing at *me*, nonetheless. Which only pisses me off more. *Jerk.*

"Come on, come inside with me. I want to show you something," he says through his laughter.

"No, I'm not dressed for a wedding."

He rolls his eyes over me and I swear he's seeing me naked. "It will be fine. No one will care."

"If no one cares why the dress and personal shopper?"

He frowns. "Are you forgetting that you took off from campus without a word to anyone or permission? You are the one that got on a plane and followed me here. You are the one that used a credit card no longer in your possession. You are the one that went to my hotel for... what? Why did you come here?

"You know what, don't answer that. I thought if you were going to be here for this, you could be my..."

He cuts off. I can see him trying to wrangle his temper. Note to self, that temper is hot. I might want to trigger it again sometime just to watch.

"Date?" I finish his words and narrow my eyes at him. "Yeah, that's a no. I'll be at the hotel when you're finished. I never should've come here."

"Roni, wait," he calls out as I throw my leg over my bike and reach for my helmet to tug on.

I don't stop to hear what he has to say as I turn the key and start the bike. For over an hour, I sat a few miles away pondering whether or not to come here. I was right the first time. This is no place for me.

"I'll get my answers later," I mutter to myself as I take off down the street.

CHAPTER TWENTY-ONE

Heat

Roni

I sit with my jeans unzipped, a hand over my full belly, and the remote in my other hand, while the plate that held my finished steak, seasoned green beans, and baked potato sits on the couch beside me. I'm stuffed and grumpy. I still can't believe I went to that wedding like a fool. Better yet, I don't get why I'm here.

"You're batting a thousand, Roni," I mumble.

I frown and flip through the channels. My phone buzzes with a notification. I look down to see its Torque and the app he placed on my phone. I smile.

The kid is really worried about me. He should be sleeping. I'll get to his message in a little while. My brain is currently occupied with a ton of shit.

The door to the suite opens and in saunters John. My lips part as my gaze roams over him. His hair is tousled, and his shirt is gaping open to his mid-chest with his tie loose around his collar. He tosses his tux jacket over his shoulder as he leans against the wall, watching me.

"I see you made yourself at home," he says.

He sounds tired and looks it too. I didn't realize how tired I am until now. I shrug through my own exhaustion.

"Nothing else to do."

"You could have danced the night away with me," he says and gives a crooked smile.

"John—"

He holds his hand up to halt my words. "I've been drinking, and I need a shower. I'll take the pullout. You can have the bed."

I chew on my lip. I didn't think about the sleeping arrangements. I've been waiting with all intentions of getting answers and getting on a plane to head back to New York.

He pushes off the wall and moves closer. Tossing his tux jacket onto the accent chair, he then starts to release his cufflinks. The man oozes sex. Even the way he stands commands attention. As if sensing my stare fixed on him, he lifts his head.

The way his gold eyes look through his long, thick lashes sends my pulse racing. Although John is pretty, there's something dangerous about him. A shiver rolls through me. He pulls his bottom lip between his teeth.

His eyes are distant for a moment as if he's not looking at me but through me. When he shakes his head and mutters a curse, I swallow hard and scoot to the edge of the couch. He follows the motion with his gaze.

I don't know where I'm going or what I plan to do. All I know is within seconds this room is charged with so much sexual tension, I can't breathe. He clears his throat and swallows.

"Where are your things?"

"Huh?"

"Your clothes… bags?"

I rub my palms on my jeans and point to my knapsack in the corner. "I didn't bring anything. I hadn't planned to stay long," I reply.

He nods. "I'll give you something of mine to sleep in. Do you want to shower first?"

Before he can fully get the words out, I'm picturing his big body pressed to mine. He has a hold of my throat like he did in that bar. Only this time he's squeezing tighter, longer.

Yup, I need to shower first. My panties are so wet, I think they may soak through to my jeans if I sit here any longer. I stand and almost tip over, but I play it off, wrapping my arms around my middle.

John closes the distance and cups my face, brushing a thumb across my lower lip. I lock eyes with him and hold my breath. He searches with that sharp gaze.

A smile comes to his lips, but this smile is different. It's almost sad or… pained. Suddenly, I wish I knew how to read minds. I crave to know what he's thinking.

"I've always wondered what you'd look like," he murmurs.

"What?"

"Nothing." He shakes his head, drops his hand, and takes a step back. "I'll get you something to wear."

He turns to walk away, but I reach for his arm and stop him. Turning his head, he looks over his shoulder. I part my lips, but I can't find the words that I need to say so I release him.

Wordlessly, he turns for the bedroom and I follow like a silly little puppy. I stop in the doorway and lean against it as he goes to the closet and pulls out a dress shirt. Walking back to me, he hands me the shirt before kissing my forehead and turning to leave the room.

Those forehead kisses are going to kill me.

"Take all the time you need. I'll wait," he says.

I stare after him for a moment, wondering if his words could mean more. Then I realize that he's the one that said this couldn't happen between us. I'm not the one pulling the breaks.

You should be.

John

I flop down on the couch and drop my head into my hands. My chest is tight. She's the one, the one I've been waiting for. How can this be happening and now?

When I walked into this suite to find her sitting on the couch waiting for me, I knew. All this time I've been wondering what she would look like, what her voice would sound like, and now... it's all right before me. It's her.

Yet this can't happen. Roni has too much shit on her plate and so do I. Hell, I don't even know how old she is. I'm assuming she's legal, but I could totally be wrong. Most of the girls we saved weren't over twenty.

"Fuck," I mumble as my phone buzzes in my pocket.

I know without looking its Missy. I'm tired and frustrated. Even if Roni and I didn't have a shit ton of cards stacked against us, I wouldn't go after her until I've cleaned up this shit with Missy. It's not my style.

Still, I can't stop thinking about Roni and that look in her eyes. You ever know something belongs to you, but you have to wait in line to get to it. That's how this feels.

With a sigh, I throw my head back against the couch and close my eyes. I get so lost in my thoughts I don't realize how much time passes. Not until the scent of my body wash hits me.

Only, it's altered by her natural chemistry. My nostrils flare and I open my eyes turning my head to her. I'm hard instantly and it's like someone turned up the heat.

She's in my white shirt and looks like an angel fallen from heaven. Her hair hangs damp and loose around her shoulders. Those lips. I clench my teeth and fist my hands.

"Roni," I say in warning as she looks back at me with the same lust I know I have in my eyes.

"I'm not ready to go to sleep. I thought I'd wait for you to be done in the shower. Give you privacy in the room."

I close my eyes and take a deep breath. Everything in me tells me she belongs to me, *take her*. Damn, the shit I'd do to her. Tie her up, fuck her hard, choke her until she comes so hard, she passes out.

Oh, I don't have to talk shit about my dick game. Older girls were always willing to teach me what they knew and then there was my father's stash of videos I found. That's where it all went left and I've never turned back.

I open my eyes as soft fingers touch my cheek. When I look into her eyes, I see her cautiousness, but there is also determination, desire, and… innocence. Tough Roni is gone and in her place is a vulnerability I've never seen.

"Tell me what you're thinking?" she says.

"You don't want to know that."

"Yes, I do. I wouldn't have asked if I didn't." She drops her gaze to my lips. "Talk to me. Why'd you run?"

"Run?" I snort. "I didn't run. My brother's mother-in-law is dying. He wanted to give his wife a wedding before she lost her mother.

"She's... she's not doing well so we had to act fast. Know this about me. When my family calls, I go running. It will always be that way."

She looks down. "Oh."

I place my hand beneath her chin and lift her head. "I don't run from shit, Roni. I told you the other night. I'm not good for you."

She lifts her head defiantly. "Why not?"

I grasp her throat and drag my tongue from her cheek up to her ear, nuzzling the soft skin behind it. Inhaling, I relish in her scent mixed with my body wash. I want nothing more than to leave my essence all over her body until she smells like nothing but me.

"I don't make love, baby. I fuck. I fuck hard and dirty. I take your pussy; you'll belong to me. You'll submit to me and when you defy me, you'll pay in ways that will bring us both pleasure.

"Oh, and I know you'll defy me. It's what draws me to you. I want to spank that fat ass now for coming here when you should be in New York. I'm not for you, sweetheart. Let it go," I breathe in her ear.

Even as I say the words, they burn in my mouth like acid. When I look into her eyes, they are wide and filled with so much lust, my cock twitches. Between her wearing my scent and shirt and the wide-eyed look she's giving me; I'm holding on by the thread.

"What if that's what I want?"

The sound of her voice is my undoing. So swiftly, she releases a small yelp, I grasp her wrists and pin her beneath me. Her thighs cradle me as I settle in. I groan as her heat burns through my tux pants.

I roll my hips into her before I can think better of it, bringing a whimper from her mouth. I hover over her sexy mouth, feeling her breath fan my lips. I've never wanted to kiss anyone more in my life.

"Careful what you ask for, baby," I say and drop a kiss against her neck. She whimpers my name. "Shit, you're going to drive me crazy. We can't do this."

"Why?"

"How old are you?"

I look into her eyes and she scrunches up her face at the question. Her gaze loses focus for a moment. I can see the wheels turning. I sigh and release her.

"You're proving my point. We can't do this. Not until you figure some things out and I get my shit together."

"How old are you?"

"I'm twenty-eight."

"I don't know the number, but I know I'm legal," she says.

"Not good enough for me."

She sits up and tucks her knees beneath her, wrapping her arms around her middle. "So, that's it. I don't remember my age so this can't happen?"

I run a hand through my hair. I'm silent for a long moment. There's so much I want to say, but I've had too much to drink. I shouldn't have let things get this far.

I stand and pinch her chin between my fingers. She parts those sexy lips, enticing me to take them and make them mine. Instead, I kiss her forehead, allowing my lips to linger.

"Let's talk about this in the morning. I have some things I need to handle on my end. After that, when you understand me, then you can decide if you want me. It will be your choice, always yours, but only when you understand what you're asking for."

She looks up at me with desire still overflowing in her eyes. I count my blessings that she didn't follow me back to Cali. If we were in my home with all my toys, I don't think I would be resisting her tonight. Fuck it all, I'd take her and make her mine.

"You have to stop looking at me like that, it's not going to help this shit," I say tightly.

"Like what?"

I shake my head. "Go to bed."

"Don't you want the room to shower?"

"Go to bed, Roni. Now."

CHAPTER TWENTY-TWO

Over It

Roni

I toss and turn for the millionth time. I should get up and get dressed. It's already after ten. John's loud snores have been ringing out through the suite since he passed out last night.

I haven't slept all night and it's not because of the chainsaw in the next room. My thoughts haven't shut the fuck up. I came to Seattle for answers, not dick.

However, it seems we've opened a door that I don't think is going to close so easily. I can't unfeel him on top of me or the bulge in his pants as he ground his hips into me. I can still smell the alcohol on his breath and feel the warmth from it against my face. Not to mention how much I crave his kiss.

I fuck hard and dirty. Did he really say that last night? What does that even mean? *Ugh.*

I flip onto my back and kick my feet. This is total bullshit. Sucking my lip into my mouth, I think about slipping my hand down between my legs to handle my current situation myself.

It's not like I've never done it before.

Oh, where'd that come from? I stare at the ceiling as memories of writhing in pleasure come forward. The shit that I can actually remember. I groan at myself as my pussy throbs and tightens with need.

"Fuck it," I mutter.

I peek at the doorway and note that he's still snoring out there. Quickly, I unbutton the rest of the buttons on the dress shirt he gave me. Running my hand down between my breasts, I close my eyes and sigh.

Goosebumps rise as I remember the feel of his weight over me. When my fingers meet my slit, they're greeted with my juices. I moan quietly.

I'm better at this than I thought. I bow off the bed as I push two fingers inside. Soon my juices are dripping between my cheeks as I pump in and out of my core.

A groan that's not mine fills the room and I snap my eyes open. John is standing in the doorway with his arms above his head, holding onto the top of the doorjamb. The way his legs are spread and planted makes me shiver. His shirt is gaping open and I can't miss the thick, fat, long, outline of his dick.

"Don't stop," he commands.

I go to defy him, but the stern look on his face warns me not to. I gush against the sheets as I continue to touch myself. Pinching my left nipple with my free hand, my eyes roll back.

A voice in the back of my head asks what the hell I'm doing, but I silence it as he saunters closer. I start to pant in anticipation. However, he doesn't climb onto the bed like I expect him to.

Instead, he folds his arms over his chest and watches my every move. The way his eyes lock onto me feels like a caress. I narrow my eyes at him.

What the heck is he waiting for?

"Make that pussy come for me," he says, his voice thick and husky with lust.

I bite my lip and work harder to get there. I want to please him. It's almost like it becomes my mission.

I start to moan loudly and that seems to pull a response from him. He shoves a hand through his hair. Lifting his eyes from my center to look me in mine is all I need. It's like he's pulled a trigger.

I cry out and soak my fingers and the sheets. His face twists with desire and he licks his lips. I lift and peel the shirt from my shoulders, but he shakes his head.

"I'm not going to touch, baby. I told you that last night."

I pause and glare at him. Did he really just watch me masturbate to tell me no? He gives me a cocky grin and I swear, I want to charge at him.

"You can't be serious."

"You want to shower first?" he says as he looks my body over.

I snort. "It's all yours," I say, jumping from the bed and snatching up the dress shirt to toss it back on.

He doesn't take his eyes off of me. I grab my phone and go to stomp out of the room, but he grabs my arm and halts me. I stare daggers down at his hand.

"Give me fifteen. I'll order us breakfast. Then we can talk."

"Whatever."

I yank my arm from him and storm out into the living area. I pace the floor mumbling to myself. This was all a bad idea.

I don't think straight around John. As I pace a memory flashes in my head. I pause and stare into space.

The memory is of my father. It's so clear I can smell his cologne. I can even feel the distance between us. It's not the physical space, it's more his demeanor.

The look on his face is so harsh. I don't fear him, but I do feel as if at that moment I've disappointed him. However, it's as if I too had been annoyed.

He's sitting at the head of the table as always. It's only the two of us. He placed his wine glass down and looked at me.

"One day you will learn you can't trust everyone," he said coldly. "Especially these little boys."

"But we were just friends—"

He holds up his hand. "Concentrate on the things that will get you ahead in life. Boys will come and go. If they think they can get to what's between your legs, they will sniff around longer, but never for long. Focus on your priorities. Be smart."

I blink the memory away and turn to stare at the bedroom. Of all the memories to come forward now. I should be looking for Natasha. That should be my priority. I harden my resolve to leave John alone. It's time I go.

I rush into the room and get dressed, keeping John's shirt. Yup, I'm the coward this time. Or maybe I'm just being smart.

Either way, I'm over it.

John

"Roni," I call out as I step out of the bathroom drying my hair with a towel. "How about after we eat, we go shopping since you need something to wear? We can—"

I stop short when I walk into an empty living area. The first thing I do is look for her little bag. Like her, it's gone.

I clench my jaw and turn back for the bathroom, where I left my phone. Sure enough, I pull up the GPS on her phone and find it moving toward the airport. The sane part of me says to let it go. Let her go.

Then there's the part of me that won't allow me to. We need to talk. She's not leaving without us having a sober talk.

Clearly, there is something between us and I don't think ignoring it is an option. Shit, I'm hard thinking about her beneath me last night. And this morning, watching her please herself in front of me with not a care in the world, ready to give herself to me.

"Argh." With a groan, I turn to head back into the bedroom to dress as I call her phone.

It goes right to voicemail. I fold my arms across my chest as I wait for the beep. I grin at her message.

"Hey, whatever." Her raspy voice slides over my skin.

Fuck this. I need to go after her. However, that doesn't stop me from leaving a message.

"Roni, when you get this message call me. Don't get on a plane, don't try to avoid me. We need to talk. Face to face. I'll meet you at the airport."

I'm in the middle leaving the message when my other line beeps in. I rush to check the call, hoping Roni has come to her senses, instead of running off like a brat. I sigh when I see it's Dad and not her. I switch over.

"Hey, Dad. What's up?"

I swear I feel his pain before he replies. "It's Nora, son. She's gone. Wyatt needs us. He has to go tell Nellie."

I'm already tossing on a pair of jeans and a T-shirt. "On my way."

"See you soon."

I hang up and spin in a circle, my thoughts are scattered. The need to go after Roni tugs at me, but my brother needs me. The bond I've had with my brothers since we were little tells me I'll have to let things with Roni go for now.

It's not like I can do anything about this thing between us. I have to settle things back home first. I huff and rush to put my shoes on as I make a plan in my head.

Once I'm moving out of the hotel, I bring up Nate's number on my phone. Braxton pulls up in the rental SUV we've been sharing. A hand lands on my shoulder and I turn to find Noah with a grim expression on his face.

"This is going to be hard as fuck," he grumbles.

"Yeah, I don't doubt that, but we're all here for them. We'll fix this."

He nods at me soberly. It's like the weight of the world sets in on my shoulders. Once in the car, I settle into the backseat. Instead of calling Nate, I shoot him a text to let him know Roni is headed back his way.

Then I pull up Roni's number. I stare at the phone, not knowing what to text. For the first time in my life, I don't have the answer to the problem before me. No quick band-aid, no long-term solution, nothing.

Me: Go back to NY. They'll take care of you. I'll see you soon.

Staring at the text with my thumb hovering over the send button, I think over the text and delete the last part. I don't want to make any promises I can't keep.

I throw my head back against the headrest. My head starts to ache. This is going to be a shit day.

"Fuck."

CHAPTER TWENTY-THREE

Shutdown

John

"Yo, John," Braxton calls through the office. "You have that file for me?"

"Yeah, I have it here."

He walks over to my desk and sits on the edge. I tap at the keys on my laptop to send him the footage that accompanies the file he's asking for. I'm glad to hand off the socialite. Of all the shit we do, I hate these types of cases.

Some people think money buys you truth, sometimes not knowing is better than knowing. This girl is in for a world of hurt when she gets the answers she's looking for. My thoughts turn to Roni.

I've been to New York a few times without making my presence known to her. It's probably best that way. She's taking to the program. Almost too well.

Nate has concerns about her. While she's one of his top trainees, she's still an X factor. We don't know where she's from or who she used to be. Her sessions with the psych team have revealed she has so much repressed anger, she's essentially a ticking time bomb.

"Hey, did you hear what I said?"

I draw my brows as I focus back in on Brax. He looks at me like I'm crazy. Releasing a sigh, I fall back in my seat.

"I missed that. What did you say?"

He narrows his eyes at me. "What's the deal with you? You've been spacing out a lot lately. Not to mention, I was just up front at Heather's desk. You're taking time off again. The schedule shows you out of the office for two weeks again. I didn't see any bounties attached to your load," he says, his words measured as if he's piecing together a puzzle as he talks.

Thank God this isn't Ryan. He'd be up my ass with the truth in a hot second. Although, if I don't create a distraction Brax will get there soon enough.

"Been talking to Dad about a side hustle. I need the time to research shit and make sure it's a move I want to make," I reply.

His expression almost looks hurt. "You're thinking about leaving?"

"No." I snort. "What the fuck would you assholes do without me? I'm exploring ways to challenge myself. That's all."

He's silent for a moment. It's not a lie. I've been thinking of starting something of my own. Not that Black and Lock doesn't pay well, and it keeps me busy enough, but I can't help wanting something to call my own. Something I might want to share with my sons like Dad has done with us.

When Brax looks like he's in his feelings, I try to find the words to explain. "Wyatt's married now. Hell, I think Noah will be next. There are seven of us. If we all have kids do you really see them all peeling into this place to work for dad?" I say.

"Well, yeah. Fuck yeah. Do you know how badass that would be to have our sons all work here? Little fuckers would run the world. Wyatt's kids are going to be geniuses between him and Nellie."

"We'd be buying a new office building, cause we'd need a hell of lot more space."

"I didn't even know you wanted kids."

I freeze. To be honest, I don't know when I started to think about my future and having a family of my own. I mean, it's been a fleeting thought for some time, but I've been planning in my head lately. Thinking about what I want for my future.

It's her. You know you've found her.

I shake the thought away and shrug. "We're all going to grow up someday, right? Mom and Dad are happy. They have a great life. We're a part of that."

"Someone order some fucking lunch. I'm starving," Ryan calls through the office, cutting off what Brax is about to say.

"Are your mouth and hands broken?" Heather snaps.

"No, but I've bought you ingrates lunch every day so far this week. My wallet is closed for the month," Ry grumbles.

I chuckle. "Order what you want. I'll pay," I say.

"In that case, I want two of everything you get, Ry," Braxton croons and jumps up from my desk to head over to Ryan's.

I shake my head and go to place my order but my phone rings, drawing my attention. When I see the New York area code I pick up quickly. Roni hasn't run off since Seattle, but you never know with her.

"Hello."

"Hey, John. This is Rita," a familiar voice comes through the line.

Rita Briggs is one of Roni's trainers. She's been one of the staff members that have been concerned with whether the program is right for Roni. From the sound of her voice, I'm sure this isn't a social call. This is about Roni.

"What's up, Rita? How's everything?"

She's silent for a moment. I sit up straighter, tuning out my brothers as they banter and laugh a few feet away. I'm already in the app to get our pilot ready to fly me out.

"I wish I could say great. It's Roni. Her aggression has gotten worse and now she has shut down on everyone. Including the therapists. She's not talking. She... she broke one of the other trainee's arms."

"Fuck, I'll be there tonight."

"Thanks, John. I think she needs a friendly face she trusts. Um... just a heads up. I think she knows you've been here without letting her know. Nate thinks that's one of her triggers."

I furrow my brows. "How does she know that?"

She releases a heavy breath. "The guy who's arm she broke. He's one of the Greek trainees from my uncle. He's an ass. He was taunting her in the ring. He mentioned you and she snapped."

I can't help the smile that comes to my lips. I shouldn't be smiling but the thought of Roni getting pissed and breaking someone's arm reminds me of the fire that draws me to her. Enough of this watching from the shadows, it's time I pay my girl a visit.

"I'll see you soon."

Roni

It's like a storm is building inside me and I don't know what to do with it. The dreams of my father are haunting me. The cold man and his distant demeanor are constant reminders that I don't have anyone that cares where I am.

I can't help wondering if he sold me like many of the others here whose parents traded them for a dollar. Yet my dreams reveal a man of means. I don't think my father hurts for a dime, so why? Why sell me?

"Because he didn't want you," I mutter breathlessly as I push my body to keep moving.

I bounce on my toes before spinning to kick the heavy bag. The force of the kick rings out like thunder in the empty gym. It's almost midnight. I'm the only one here.

I need to get my frustration out. Breaking that asshole's arm got me suspended from combat and weapons training. The only shit that keeps me sane and distracted from thinking about shit I need to forget, including John.

I'm so fucking pissed. He's been here and he hasn't come to see me or say anything to me. I know I was the one to run off, but I didn't think that meant he wouldn't at least remain the friend he promised to be.

I need someone to talk to. Someone to listen to the turmoil that I'm holding inside and no, I don't want to talk to their fucking shrinks. I feel like they tell the Briggs everything I say.

"Fuck them," I huff as I throw a punch combination.

"Lift your arms." I startle and spin defensive even as I know who the voice belongs to. If a glare could shoot fire, he'd be torched.

And still, he takes my breath away. He's more gorgeous than I remember. Right down to the way his dark hair is spilling into his face—longer and unkept—not what I'm used to. It looks like he's been running his hand through it or as if he has just woken from sleep or maybe a bit of both.

His long lashes somehow seem to be longer than usual as they fan out over his golden eyes. Eyes with a stare so intense, I believe he can see right through me. His nose is so perfect, well-proportioned to his full lips. Well, not overly full, but both his lower and upper are plush enough to make you want to stare and dream of them pressed against your own.

I stifle a groan as I lower my gaze down his body. The way he's standing with his arms across his broad chest and his legs parted wide makes my belly flip and drop low. His long body exudes power. The black dress shirt that's turned up over his elbows and black slacks that hug his thighs are like wrapping paper from an expensive high-end store. The perfect touch to perfection.

"You're looking great," he says, the sound of his voice rumbling through me.

I roll my eyes and turn back to the heavy bag. Yes, I know I was longing for him to be here only a moment ago, but now that he is, I can't help the anger I feel toward him. He tossed me aside as if I were nothing. That feeling has cut deeper than I want to admit and for reasons I'm still piecing together from dreams and faded memories.

Returning to my workout, I ignore him and my body's response to him. I wish I could forget that night and morning in his hotel room. I believe I've embarrassed myself in front of this man enough for a lifetime.

"I don't get a hello?"

I stiffen from his front pressed to my back. He wraps his arms around me, preventing me from swinging at the heavy bag. I hate that his arms bring me comfort. It's a battle not to sink back into him.

Once he places his chin on top of my head, I lose the battle. However, I don't show him that. I remain stiff as I absorb what I haven't realized I've been missing. Instead of letting him know how I feel, I lash out with my words.

"You've been here several times, and not once did you say hello. I'm returning the favor."

He releases a heavy sigh before moving to bury his face in my hair and inhaling. I grimace. I'm a sweaty mess. My hair has to stink of perspiration.

I wiggle a bit, but he only tightens his hold. "I didn't want to distract you. The first time I came I saw how focused you were. You didn't even notice me watching you."

"What happened to needing to talk?" I say bitterly.

I spun to face him. Bad move, my belly tightens as soon as I look into his eyes. Once he smiles, I completely lose my thought for a second.

"We did and still do. That never changed."

"Then what did?"

The words come out so harsh I have to take a step back from him to reel it in. He reaches for my taped hand. I should pull back, but my stupid brain won't listen, craving his comfort more than my sanity.

"My brother's mother-in-law passed away that morning you took off. I got the call as I was making plans to come after you," he says somberly.

"Oh," I reply, something about his brother's sudden loss triggers an ache within me.

It's almost like I know that feeling all too well. I knit brows. "I lost my mother at a young age. I think I went to live with my father after that."

The words fall out of my mouth without thought. I don't know why I share them with him, but it feels like I can. I look up into his eyes to find him watching me closely.

"Have you remembered where you're from?"

"New York," I blurt out and frown. "At least that's where I lived when I was with my mom. I don't know after that. I remember getting on a plane with... my dad? Yeah, the man in the dreams. He's my dad."

"That's good, angel," he says stroking my cheek.

I wrinkle my brows at the endearment, not really sure how I feel about it. "Did you handle whatever you needed to?"

He gives me a puzzled look at first, then realization lights his eyes. He rubs his forehead and shakes his head. "I've minimized the issue. It's more complicated than I care to explain at the moment. I'd rather you talk to me about you."

"What about me?"

"Whatever you want." He closes the space between us. "Tell me what's been on your mind. I miss talking to you. I've missed you."

I stare at him for what feels like hours. My mind arguing my needs over my wants and desires. In the end, I start to spill drop by drop.

"The dreams are more frequent. They mix in with the torture and beatings." As the words pass through my lips, the weight starts to rise a bit.

Well into the morning, I talk and he listens. Each word untwisting the feelings I have inside. It's not quite the peace I need, but it's a start.

CHAPTER TWENTY-FOUR

Be Honest

John

Without thinking, I cut off my car as I park in the garage of Black and Lock and dial the one person that can make me smile instantly after the crap day I've had. I rest my head back and close my eyes as the phone rings through the car.

"What do you want, John?" Roni sighs into the phone as she answers.

My lips turn up into the smile I was looking for. She's such a brat and that voice. It brings a smile all of its own.

"Stop trying to act like you don't want to hear my voice," I reply as I grin. It's clear in the sound of her words that she's not as put out by my call as she's trying to put on.

"I don't. You're only going to tell me to behave. Fuck that noise."

I bark out a laugh. In the last year, the one thing that I've learned and love about Roni is that she has an amazing sense of humor. "Are you behaving?"

"Am I a toddler?"

"You're a brat."

"Whatever. Don't you have some work to do? That's the reason you said you had to leave, right? But here you are always on my phone."

"Ouch, that hurts. I thought you'd be happy to hear from me. I know you miss me."

"I miss you breaking me out of here. That's about all."

"Jasper said some of the others go out to a local bar. Why don't you go with them?"

Silence greets me as I get out of the car and stroll across the parking lot to head upstairs. For a moment, I think I've lost her. Then I remember who I'm talking to. I chuckle.

"Okay, fine," I say.

The sound of her moving around on the other end of the call comes through before she speaks, reminding me of the time difference. "The days seem longer when you're not here," she says.

"Yeah, I know what you mean," I mutter.

It's been a long ass day for me. Starting with a call from Missy. She said she needed someone to talk to. Of course, me being me, I was there for her and listened for an hour.

It wasn't like my calls with Roni. I can't fall asleep at night without hearing her voice. We talk at all times of the night despite the time difference. If I don't call, she curses me out. We talk about nothing most of the time and that's fine with me. She could recite the alphabet and I'd be good to listen.

"Maybe I'll kick someone's ass to get you back here sooner," she teases.

"Roni," I groan, causing her to laugh.

It's beautiful. She doesn't do it often, but when she does it's amazing. My stomach coils and I swear my cock swells enough to rip through my pants.

"I'll behave."

"You better," I say with a smile.

I can almost hear her thinking on the other end as I stand outside the elevator. I know I'll lose the call once I get inside, but I'm not ready to let her go. I lean against the wall and stare at my boots as I get lost in thought.

"You'll be back soon though, right?" she says, pulling a grin from me. "I mean, I'm not rushing you. I... I want to ask you something when you come back."

From the sound of her voice, I furrow my brows and straighten. "Ask me now."

"No, I want to ask in person."

I'm quiet for a few beats. She's stubborn, if I push, she'll shut down on me. With a nod to myself, I start to rearrange my schedule to find a way to get back to New York sooner.

"Hello?"

"I'm here. Listen, I'll be there soon. I need to get upstairs and get some work done. I'll text later when I get home."

"John."

"Yeah?"

She sighs. "I'm not your responsibility. You don't have to check on me all the time. I like talking to you, but you have a life there, don't you? You don't—"

"I don't do anything I don't want to do. Later, Roni."

"Later, John."

I climb into the elevator with a smile on my lips. Not for the first time, I think about apartment shopping in New York. I've never considered moving away from my family permanently. However…

I'm snatched out of my thoughts by the sound of someone crying out in pleasure as I step off the elevator. I shake my head. That's Wyatt and Nellie for sure.

His office door sits open and I can see shadows moving inside. It's a strong reminder of how long it's been for me. There's only one person I want to be balls deep in and she's off-limits for the time being.

Somehow, Roni and I have fallen into a comfortable arrangement as we manage to ignore the flaming hot chemistry between us, but I swear to you, at this moment, I'd give my fucking kidney to have Roni screaming like that. I shake my head clear. It's been a while since I've had a chance like this to give my oldest brother shit.

With a grin, I sit on the edge of the reception desk and wait for my moment.

Wyatt

"Slow down, baby," I whisper in Nellie's ear as she cries out.

She releases a sigh and throws her head back. I nip at her cheek with my teeth before kissing the sting away, then move to her lips for a deep hot kiss. I have a tight grip on the back of her bra as she bounces on my cock in the reverse cowgirl position.

Everyone's out of the office, leaving us to steal this moment. A moment my wife needs. When she walked into my office to ask if I wanted to order something for dinner since we both planned to stick around and get some work done, I could see in her eyes that her thoughts were elsewhere.

It's that look she had for months before she came back to me when she was only a shell of herself. I've just gotten her back. I won't allow her to slip away from me again. The thought of her sinking back into that darkness has me thrusting up into her tight pussy harder.

"Oh my God, Wy," she cries.

"Fucking right. Call my name, baby. Arch your back for me."

She does so obediently, and my balls start to tighten. I drop my gaze to her ass spread in my lap, swallowing my cock with each rise and fall. Sucking my lip between my teeth, I groan. It's all I can do to keep from blowing on the spot.

However, what does take me over the edge is the way she starts to swivel and swirl her hips nice and slow as she squeezes her walls around me. I wrap my hand in her bra strap tight enough to pop the entire thing. Needing her close, I band my other arm around her exposed breasts and hold her to me.

Feeling her hard nipples against my arm, I wish she were facing me so I could pop one in my mouth. I didn't get enough when I first pulled the cups down to feast on her mounds.

"Wyatt," she screams as I pump into her hard and fast. It's all I need to release into her heat with enough force to leave my head spinning.

We're both panting as we come down from the heaven we always create together. From the first time she gave herself to me, I've known perfection and never want to know what life is without it. Inhaling deeply, I take in the heady scent of sex and us.

"I love you," I pant against the side of her face as sweat drops down mine.

"I love you too," she says breathily. With a small chuckle, she turns and pecks my lips. "Does this mean we're going home now?"

I kiss her forehead. "No, go clean up. I'll call for dinner."

"Make sure you order something for me too."

I look up to find my brother standing in the doorway with his back to us. His shoulders shaking with laughter. "John I'm going to fuck you up if you don't get your ass away from that door."

"You know I like to watch," he teases.

"Dude," I growl.

He throws his hands up. "Listen, I just got here." He chuckles and walks off.

I kiss Nellie's head as I lift and turn her so that I'm covering her body as I grab her dress off my desk. She begins to fix her bra while I turn her dress right side out. Lifting my gaze to look at my wife, I nearly burst into laughter.

Her wide-eyed expression is priceless. It's not the first time we've been caught fucking, but as always, her reaction is priceless. I hand her the dress before tugging her into my arms and kissing her lips.

"Relax, it was a joke. He didn't watch. That's not John. He's huge on consent and respecting boundaries."

"We have to stop having sex every and anywhere. This is getting out of hand," she scowls at me.

I snort. "You and I know that's a damn lie. Your pussy gets wet from the thought of getting caught. I know my baby's nasty," I tease.

She swats my chest. I laugh and kiss her neck. "Get dressed. I've been wanting to talk to this guy anyway," I say.

She nods as I release her to pull up my pants and fix myself up. I open the desk and pull out the wipes we keep in there for times like this. Like I said, we're not going to stop fucking in the office or any other random place for that matter.

Once I'm good to go, I walk out of my office into the main area, closing the door behind me. John is up front with a menu in his hands. I close the distance and slap him in the back of the head.

He turns to me with a smile in his eyes. "You do know I could have been dad?"

"And?"

He shrugs. "You guys looking to eat anything in particular? I'm starving."

"Not really. Nel didn't say what she wants, but we had pizza the other night."

"Thai fusion it is," he croons.

I stare at my brother as he places all but the Thai menu back into the desk. Something is up with him. I try to put my finger on it. I've picked up on it for a while now.

"Is Nellie right?"

He lifts his eyes to lock with mine. The storm that enters them so strong, he knows what I'm asking.

"Be honest with me. She says it's a girl. Some chick that was at my wedding. Why didn't you bring her inside to meet the family? From the way you've been acting lately, disappearing and shit. She has to mean something to you."

"You want to do this now?" he drools and lifts a brow.

"Answer me this? Is it the one from the rescue?"

He gives a small nod. I grimace and lean back against the desk behind me. Tossing the menu down, he leans to rest against the desk too, mirroring my stance.

"Roni," he says as if that's all the explanation needed.

"And Missy?"

He rolls his eyes, turning to glare off into space. "Complicated. Not my problem anymore if I can help it. If only I could get her to see that, my life would be golden," he mutters.

"What does that mean?"

He shrugs and turns to look me in the eyes. "Don't worry about it. I'll take care of it. How are you, how's Nellie holding up?"

I narrow my eyes. "John, one of these days you're going to learn to release shit before it builds and explodes."

"And one of these days you're going to learn that we all have to make our mistakes and do things our own way, not Wyatt's way," he returns.

"Fair enough, but I watch you fix everyone and everyone else's shit without thinking about yourself. I'm making sure you're not doing it again."

He releases a long breath and runs a hand through his hair, as he glances toward the office where Nellie is. When he locks eyes with me this time the storm is raging deeper and darker. It's as if he ages right before my eyes.

"If you knew Nellie couldn't remember anything before you and that she had no one to make sure she was safe in every sense of the word, could you stay away?"

I don't have to think twice. "No."

"Exactly. I don't know how to explain it. She needs me whether she'll admit it or not. Until she remembers something, or I figure it out, I'm going to guard her."

"Are you two a thing?"

"Wyatt," he warns.

Nellie comes out of the office and John shuts down, turning to grab the menu and focus on it. I straighten and take Nellie into my arms as soon as she reaches me. I kiss her forehead before looking at John again.

"If you need me you know I'm here," I say, pulling his attention.

"I know. You know the same, in this life and the one after."

I grin and nod. And the one after that. My family is my world. All I want is to see John happy. Right now, he's somewhere in between and I wish I could do more to help him get there.

"I'm fine, Wyatt," he says without looking up.

I pat him on back and nod. "I love you."

He turns his gaze on me. "I'm not taking that case. You and Noah were handpicked."

I roar with laughter. "Fuck you. This has nothing to do with that."

His pretty ass winks at me. "I know. I love you too, bro. Now you two let me know what you want before I starve."

CHAPTER TWENTY-FIVE

Forgive Me

Roni

I walk into the cafeteria beside Torque as he talks excitedly about his driving lessons. Looking up, I give him a smile. He's so tall now. Almost a year and a half can change a lot.

Each day I watch as the boyish look falls from his face and a young man appears in his place. He'll be seventeen this year. I can't help wondering if Natasha looks as healthy and well taken care of as Torque.

"We pair off in teams tomorrow. Someone said something about them mixing driving and target practice," Torque breaks into my thoughts with his deep voice.

I can't remember when that happened. It's like one day he started to speak and my eyes nearly popped out of my head from how deep his vibration registered. He's still a kid in so many ways, but he's not a baby anymore.

"That sounds cool. I'll be taking the chopper up again tomorrow," I say and give him a smug grin.

He frowns and his shoulders sag. "Man, you get to do all the cool shit."

I lift on my toes to pop him upside the head. "Aw, come on. You say tons of worse things."

"I'm also older than you."

"Sure, sorry," he mumbles. His frown deepens as he looks over my head.

I turn to see what has caught his eyes. When I find John with his arms crossed over his chest as he leans against one of the pillars in the cafeteria, my heart leaps. It takes everything in me not to show any of the emotions I feel.

I want to run to him and jump into his arms as I inhale his cologne, but I keep all that to my fantasies. Public affection seems so off putting to me. Or as if it's something to be rejected or shunned. Instead, I stroll over to him and look up into his handsome face.

"Look who flew in on a breeze. Thought you weren't coming around for a few weeks," I say as I stop in front of him.

"Go change. We're heading out." I knit my brows at his tone.

"What's going on?"

"I need to clear my head. You're coming with me."

I nod and turn to head back to my room. However, I bump into Torque's chest. He's scowling as he looks between me and John.

"Have you found anything that can help us? Are you even trying?"

I look over my shoulder to catch John shaking his head. "Not yet, Kid. I'm still working on it."

"I'm not a kid," Torque grumbles.

"Hey, I told you let me handle it," I say as I place a hand on Torque's arm. "I'll catch up with you later."

"Yeah, whatever. You're forgetting about her. We've done nothing in over a year, and he's been useless for a whole five months."

John's chest presses against my back as he closes the distance to get closer to Torque. "Kid, if this was easy, I would have found her by now. I'm doing everything I can. It would be a hell of a lot easier if I didn't have to cover your tracks, while you leave a messy ass trail."

Torque's cheeks turn red and his mouth pops open. "Yeah, that's what I thought. You have no idea who I am, *kid*. Don't test me, today is not the day."

"Fuck you," Torques snaps then storms off.

I spin around and glare at John. "He's just a kid. Did you have to talk to him like that?" I hiss.

He covers his face with both hands and exhales. Dragging them down and away, he grits his teeth and steps around me. I turn and grab his arm.

"Where are you going?"

"To talk to the kid. Go get ready."

I narrow my eyes at him, taking in the stress on his face. "Leave him. Give him some time to calm down. I'll meet you out front."

He searches my eyes for a moment before he nods. He reaches out as if he's going to lift his hand to touch my face, but he drops the hand as fast as he raises it. I watch as he turns and walks out, looking lost. Something I never thought I'd be able to say about John.

I knit my brows as I try to figure out what could have him so unhinged. John is always so unfazed. When I told him about how they tortured us, he listened without saying a word or showing a reaction, although I know he was boiling inside. The more I get to know him the more I learn to read him.

"Whose ass am I going to have to beat?" I say to myself as I narrow my gaze on his back.

John

"Fuck," I growl as I pace in front of the training dorms.

I was already pissed off when I arrived. Having that kid throw in my face that I haven't been able to deliver on the only thing Roni has ever asked me for gets so far under my skin, it feels like my flesh will burn off. Trying to find out what happened to her friend has proven to be like looking for a needle in a haystack. I never fail at a mission and yet, I can't find this girl, and if I'm honest it's because I've been so fucking distracted for the last five months.

"Hey, what's up?" Felix answers his phone.

He sounds exhausted. I know he has a huge workload and shit going on of his own. Which is why I haven't pulled him into this for help. That stops here though.

"I need a favor. I'm sending you a file. I need you to try to find this girl. I've hit wall after wall. Something isn't right about the entire thing," I say in frustration.

"Who is she?"

"She was a captive in that trafficking ring. Roni says she told them her name was Natasha."

"I'm assuming you found out that's not her name," he says.

"Not at all. I started with that name and the trip she told Roni she'd been on with her family, in North Korea. Never found a Natasha.

"But here's the thing… it's all fishy. The entire thing looks like one of your jobs. You know, if you were hiding someone or their trail," I bite out.

Felix releases a long whistle. "No moving forward or back," he says distractedly. I know he's looking through the file I sent him. "I'll get on it. See what I can dig up, but this girl looks like a ghost. Should I look into the assholes that got away?"

I tighten my jaw. "I did a little of that. As much as I can for now. The team that hit the warehouse found three guys with bullets in their heads and four of the girls the same way. None of the girls fit our girl's description. We're not supposed to bring that shit back on our heads, so we need to be careful."

"Yeah, I was thinking that."

"I feel like that whole mission was cursed. Like we're waiting for it to blow in our faces. It's only a matter of time."

"Yeah, Wyatt said the same thing. I wish I could have gone on that one to watch over you guys," he says.

I blow out a breath and turn to find Roni walking down the front steps. She's in jeans and a leather jacket that's cut to accentuate her hips. That's the distraction I truly need. Not the bullshit I have going on.

"Let me know what you find."

"Already on it. Call you soon."

"Thanks."

I hang up as Roni stops in front of me. I'm so tempted to kiss her. This is the strongest it's been in a long time. I thought I had this under control, but at the moment, I want her so much it hurts. She folds her arms over her chest.

"There's something I've never asked you," she says as she searches my eyes.

"Ask."

She purses her full lips for a second. "Do you have a girlfriend?"

I grin, unable to keep myself from reaching to cup her face. "I don't do girlfriends."

She frowns at me and knocks my hand away. "That's not an answer, dick. Yes or no?"

I snort. "Watch your mouth. No, I don't have a girlfriend."

"Okay." She nods, but there's a skeptical look in her pretty brown eyes.

"I was going to take you to that West Indian restaurant you like," I think aloud. "But maybe it's time you learn a little more about me."

"What?"

I wink. "You'll see."

And just like that, I make a decision that will ruin the comfortable existence we've created. I need to clear my head, so I'm going to combine the two things that help me do that. *God forgive me.*

CHAPTER TWENTY-SIX

John

I can't take my eyes off of her. Roni has been captivated by the scenes that have been playing out in front of her, one after another. I shouldn't have this much glee running through me from corrupting her.

I thought she would run after we finished dinner and I drew the viewing curtains back. I even went out of my way to bring her in without running into any of the open parties that would tip her off before we arrived at my room.

Yes, I keep a room at Club Desire. Brax loves his expensive cars. I hold expensive memberships to sex clubs. We all have our vices.

Roni scoots forward in her seat, her mouth open. "She's going to whip him?"

"Yes, Meana is one of the five Mistresses here. She prefers to be called Domina. Her skills with a whip are impeccable. She makes it look like an art," I reply, letting my gaze search her profile as she keeps her sights on the scene before us.

She turns to me and looks me in my eyes. "You would allow someone to do this to you?"

I tilt my head and study her with a smile on my lips. "I've never been topped. I prefer to watch this type of scene. Honestly, I've never thought about switching, but if it were something my sub needed, I'd allow it."

She sucks her button lip into her mouth and my cock twitches. I drop my eyes to her nipples straining against her tight T-shirt. I'm so tempted to pull her into my lap and help her release the tension I see in her body.

She tilts her head mirroring me. "Your ass is nasty as fuck."

Surprised by her words, I lift my eyes to hers. I expect to find disgust on her face, but I find interest and humor instead. She rolls her eyes over me.

"Damn, of all the things I thought you were into, this was not what I thought. Not at all," she says.

I release a roar of laughter. Reaching out, I do tug her into my arms as I shift to place my leg on the leather couch so that she can sit between my thighs with her back to my front. Burying my face into her neck, I nuzzle it.

"You have no idea," I whisper and lick her neck.

"This stuff turns you on?" she moans.

I release a groan. "Not half as much as you do, but yeah. It's more than that though. Most people think the life is all about the sex and kinks. It's…"

"About the release," she says when I don't finish.

I turn her face to look up at me, a puzzled expression on my own. "Yeah, how'd you know that was what I wanted to say?"

"You've been relaxed since we've been here. Whatever was going on when you arrived at campus, you've let it go." She pauses to bite her lip. "You haven't touched me, and you haven't touched yourself, so it's not about sex. It's mental."

I press my forehead to hers. "Does that freak you out? That I like... need this?"

She cups my face, breathing me in. "I believe the demons running around inside of me are darker than your secrets. You can see yours; I have no idea what mine are fully.

"I think I can handle this. If this is who you are, it's who you are. From my dreams, I don't think I know how to connect with people or show affection. If you can handle that, I can handle this."

In my head I want to call bullshit. I see how she is with Torque. She loves that kid as if he were her little brother.

However, I let the comment go. If I can teach her how to release and free herself, I can get her to see she's capable of more than she thinks. I go to take her lips, but it's at that exact moment that my phone rings. Closing my eyes, I tighten my jaw and ball my fists. It's probably for the best.

After all, my biggest distraction hasn't been handled. For the last six months, Missy has been clinging to the last thread of my patience and twisted guilt. Two suicide attempts and random threats to follow through have kept me from severing our connection completely.

"Are you going to answer that?" Roni asks as I stare down at my phone.

I heave a heavy breath before kissing her forehead and lifting to my feet. "Yeah."

Roni

My body is coiled with so much sexual tension, I think my head may explode. I was sure he was going to kiss me before his phone rang. I swear, I want to cut whoever that was. Not only did he look annoyed by the call, there was something else.

"You may not have a girlfriend, but there is a woman," I murmur to myself as I stare at the door he walked out of.

Anger starts to boil out all of the hormones raging through my body. Leaning forward, I rest my forearms on my thighs and stare at the dude's face as he's being whipped. He's so focused, so much intensity rests in his face.

I turn my attention to the woman whipping him. She's as focused as he is. Suddenly, she pauses, leaning in to whisper something in the guy's ear. He nods his head and that's when she looks out in my direction. I'm sure she can't see me.

From what John said, this room is one of many that can view the scenes below. Then there are the people that are on the main floor. However, it feels like she's looking me right in the eyes.

There's a fire and fierceness in her eyes. Strength that I recognize deep down in my soul. I'm thrown back in time.

"When will you understand the power, you have been born into?"

"Daddy, I—"

"Silence. You will do as I say, Roni. They treat you as princess, you let them. But what you let them see is the ruthless woman they will get if they cross you. You are a P—"

"Roni, Roni."

I shake my head as John calls me out of the memory. I focus and his golden eyes come into view. He looks pissed off.

"We're leaving."

"Why?" I say as I stand.

"I'm not in the mood to be here anymore. I should take you back."

I don't respond. Instead I watch him closely as he ushers me out. Something has changed and not from that call alone. The way he shields me protectively as we walk is more possessive than it had been before.

It's the first thing I pick up on as we walk out. If I didn't know better, looking from the outside in, I'd think I belonged to him.

Get a grip, Roni. You don't belong to no one. Listen to your father, you're a ruthless savage and that's how you'll survive.

It's the truth, my friend is still out there, and she needs me. I'm not giving up and I need to be ready when I find her. That's when I'll release the demons living inside me.

Let John and his problems have him. That's not for you.

CHAPTER TWENTY-SEVEN

All My Life

Cassy

"For fucks sake, Joe," I huff as I slap the bed with my palm. "I feel like we're failing our boys. Am I a bad, mum?"

My husband groans. Turning to look at him, he has his arms behind his head, his muscles bulging. His dark brown hair is a sleep mess atop his head, the natural golden highlights catching the light from the window. I ignore the looks of the fine lad I've come to love in ways I've never imagined possible.

If you would have told me that I would fall for a big hairy Scot when I was a girl, I would have tossed you the finger. I had a thing for green eyes and red hair before I locked eyes with Joe Black.

"I'm serious, Joe. I want to see them happy."

"Tell me something, love. When did they tell ye they weren't happy?"

I hear his tone. His accent slips a little. He's annoyed. "Joe."

"No, be truthful with yourself. Which one of them told you that they're not happy. They come to talk to you when they need to. So, which one?"

I glare at him. "They don't have to say it. Toby has been getting more irritable lately. For the life of me I can't put my finger on what's going on with him."

Joe grunts. I narrow my eyes. Does he know what's going on with that little shit? The look that crosses my husband's face happens so fast; I think I may have imagined it.

He reaches out and slips a hand under the covers to place on my thigh. His palm is heavy and warm to the touch. It's a distraction to me thoughts as he starts to caress my bare skin.

"Give him time to figure himself out," Joe murmurs, closing his eyes, his long lashes fanning his cheeks.

And this is why I worry about me boys. They're as gorgeous as their father. The world eats from their palms.

I refuse to raise a bunch of entitled little fucks, but the way the world yields to them makes my job that much harder. It's one of the reasons Ryan is a brat. I snort.

"What?" Joe sighs.

"Ryan walks around with his head in the clouds. He needs to grow up. He's twenty-three, the pain in the ass," I mutter and fold my arms over my chest.

My husband grunts again as he squeezes my thigh. I wiggle beneath the sheets a little, turning to glare at him. His face is expressionless as if he hasn't a clue how he's affecting me. I call bullshit, I tell ye. Bullshit it is.

"Ryan will become the man he needs to be when the time comes," he replies. "He hasn't met the right challenge yet. Ye remember how carefree I was when we met."

"Aye, I do. Don't know why I married ye," I tease.

He opens his eyes and pins me with those golden eyes I fell in love with at first sight. They're as intense now as they were back then. He quirks a brow.

"Shall I show ye?"

I grin. "Brax is going to get his heart broken, chasing after Heather. It will take a lion to tame her heart and all the other things going on with her," I say, ignoring his words.

He releases a deep breath and closes his eyes again. While keeping his fingers dancing against my skin, he nods. I don't think he's going to respond at first.

"I remember when Braxton was born. Head full of red hair. He came out hollering and kicking. If she needs a lion, she has one. I've watched the two together. Brax is not sniffing up a tree he can't climb, believe me."

"Aye, ye have an answer for everything this morning."

He peeks an eye open as he runs the back of a single finger up my inner thigh. "Aye, lass. I do. I'm just waiting for ye to get this all out yer system. Ye have yer own lion in yer bed ready to pounce."

I laugh and slap his broad shoulder. He flexes his muscles at me. Joe looks every bit of a man that works out nonstop. He's as fit as his sons. He'll still box one of them up if need be.

I bite my lip as I think of last night. I'm almost tempted to say let me boys figure their shit out on their own, but then I think of my oldest babe. He doesn't even know he's going to be a father.

"Wyatt will be fine. She's doing the right thing. He needs to focus on the mission he's on. If Nellie tells him about the baby, he'll be home before she can get the words out," he says, reading my thoughts as always.

"Ye think ye know me so well."

"Aye, I do." In one swift move, he plucks me up and brings me to settle over his waist. "You're worried Noah is going to break Bean's heart. The answer to that is never. He'd take his own life before allowing any harm to come to the lass. Felix will see his way through the challenges he's taken on."

With that, he rises and takes me lips in a searing kiss. My thoughts scatter as he pushes his fingers into my hair. Tugging my head back with a tight grip on my roots, he starts a trail of kisses down my neck.

A gasp leaves me lips. Joe has as much of an appetite for sex as he did when I first met him. I give all my boys shit, but I know where they get it from.

"Joe," I moan, when he drops one hand to my bum and drags my heat into his rock-hard erection.

I'm almost lost, but the bite of his fingers into my ass followed by a hard slap carries me thoughts to the one son he didn't reassure me would be fine. I cup my husband's face and look him in it. He groans and closes his eyes as he leans his forehead to my chin.

"That one I can't give you any guarantees on. The lass he's head over heels for can be as unpredictable as he can. But John is John. He will fix her and by proxy, himself. I think they are good for each other."

"Does she deserve me boy? He's a special one. That heart is softer than he lets on. I know that crazy one is still lurking in his life. I can just feel it."

"Aye, she's his perfect match. Fire and heart. The only difference is she doesn't show it like he does, but it's there." He nips my chin. "I keep an eye on all of our family, Cass. I take care of what's mine. Let me show you."

"Fine."

My worries are silenced as my husband captures my nipple in his mouth, sending me writhing in his lap. I lock my fingers into his dark locks and give myself over to it. If Joe says he has it, he has it.

Joe

All my life I wanted the love of a woman like Cass. I ache for this wee lass every day of my life. I've taught my sons to find a woman that leaves them breathless the way their mother has done me for the last thirty-two years. Cass was the worthy one.

My muscles shake as I thrust into her heat. Her small body shakes beneath me. All worries went out the window about an hour ago.

"I love you," I whisper in her ear as I take a tight hold of her red locks.

Rope after rope of my passion spills into her body as she arches off the bed. I don't see the woman lying beneath me, I see the soul that I live and breathe for. The mother of my sons, the protector of my sanity, the little warrior I fought to call mine for the rest of eternity.

"Joe," she breathes. The way it leaves her mouth, I know it's the equivalent of my words. It's a promise and a prayer.

I place my forehead to hers. "Woman, you're going to be the death of me some day."

"And a grand death it shall be."

I laugh and roll onto my back, tugging her into my arms. However, when I open my mouth to tease her back, an alert from my phone begins to blur through the room. I rush to grab the device from the nightstand. I'm on my feet before I can focus on what I'm seeing.

"What is it?"

"Nellie. It's Wyatt's."

"Go, Joe, go," my wife demands.

CHAPTER TWENTY-EIGHT

Red Alert

John

"Roni," I groan.

"What John?"

I lower my voice as I stand in line to pay for my things in the store. "You can't pistol whip a guy because he's staring at your ass," I growl at her.

"And why the hell not?"

I groan. "Because the Briggs train people for a living. Sometimes outsiders come in. Nate or Thomas would have talked to him if you would have said something."

In all reality. I wish I were there to pistol whip the asshole myself. However, I can't tell her that.

"Screw that. Are you still coming? I need to get out of here."

"I think they're all right. I spoil you so you think you can get away with this shit."

She scoffs. "You're not my daddy. As a matter of fact, the only reason I haven't left is because I'm waiting for you to help me with finding my friend. Otherwise, you all can kiss my ass."

"Be careful what you wish for."

"What?"

I grin. "I'll kiss your ass... after I spank the shit out of it."

The woman in line in front of me turns her green eyes on me and smiles as she ogles me. I lift a brow. A few years ago, I might have whispered in her ear and asked her if she wanted a try.

Today, I turn away and look out the window as I listen to the panting coming from the other end of the phone. I'm in San Francisco tying up a bounty. I plan to board the private jet from here to head out to New York.

"We're going to talk when I get there. Your temper has been one of the reasons you haven't been placed on a real assignment. You're the top of your class. There's no reason that you shouldn't be out in the field," I say in a hushed tone once again.

"Bullshit and you know it. Nate won't send me out because he has no clue who I am. You know what, John? You're getting on my nerves."

I laugh. "What's wrong, baby? I know it's been a while since you've seen me. I promise, I'll give you a big hug when I see you."

"Damn, she's lucky," the woman in front of me mutters as she fans herself.

"Fuck you," Roni hisses. "Get your ass on that plane so I can get out of here and have a beer or ten. I need a break."

I get serious. "I'm on my way. Stay out of trouble until I get there."

I hand my money over to the clerk that looks at me with big brown eyes. She's nothing more than a teenager. You would think she were staring at a movie star. The woman that had been ahead of me, looks over from the other register.

"Honey, I know. He's simply gorgeous," she says to my clerk.

"Um, that will be $10.27," the clerk says.

"Right... I gave you a twenty." I lift a brow.

"Oh," she says, looking down at the twenty in her hand as if she has no clue how it got there.

I shake my head and grin as I open the water I just paid for to take a sip. This is why I appreciate Roni so much. While I know she's attracted to me, I'm never left feeling like she's never heard a damn thing I've said.

Living in California it all gets really old, super-fast. In all honesty, I miss Roni and can't wait to get to New York.

"I'm going to my room. I have plans with that vibrator I ordered on your credit card."

I choke on the sip of water I just took. I know that she's memorized the card numbers from the first time I gave them to her. I don't mind that she uses them when she wants and I've never monitored her purchases, but there is something about knowing I've paid for a vibrator that will be between her legs.

"Roni," I say in warning. "Tell me you're joking."

She gives a small laugh. It makes my heart skip a beat. It's been a while since I've heard that laugh.

"Wouldn't you like to know."

"Angel, I promise you the real thing is better, but if you want to torture yourself—" Shit. My other line beeps. Probably for the best because I'm horny as fuck and now I have images of my face between her legs as I put that vibrator in her ass running through my head. "Fuck. That's not my other line. Roni, I have to go."

"What's wrong?"

"That's not a call. It's the alarm system at my brother's house is going off. I need to get there. I'll call you later."

With that, I turn to rush out to the car to head for Wyatt's. I don't have a good feeling about this. Fuck, I knew it's been too quiet.

Roni

I don't know what's going on with John, but I didn't like the sound of his voice when he hung up earlier. I already get the feeling he's not coming as planned. I stare down at my phone as I chew on my lip.

If his family needs him, I shouldn't be a pain. However, I can't stop the churning feeling in my stomach. I look up as I hear voices up the hall.

"Let's roll out," Earl Briggs barks. "Jas, you're with me."

"The Blacks stuck their necks out for us on this one. Do whatever you need to make sure everyone returns home safe," Nate says with heat in his voice.

I pick up the pace and rush down the stairs. I had been heading to the gym to blow some steam off, but now the only place I want to be is in one of the cars heading out. Hearing the name Black, I know something is wrong with John.

"I want to suit up. I want to go," I say as I come to a stop in front of a pissed off looking Nate, dressed in a tux.

That's right, there was a wedding today. He got married. I push that thought aside and straighten.

"Not this time."

"But it's John. Something happened at his brother's house, right? I want to help. Let me go."

"No," he barks and turns to leave.

"Hey, what the hell? Isn't this what you guys are training us for? Let me go. I can help."

Nate spins on his heels and moves to get into my face. "I'm telling you no because these assholes could be connected to the ones that we saved your ass from. You're a wild card, Roni. You listen to no one and your temper is all over the fucking place.

"John will be there, and his brothers' wives and their children need to be his focus. Not you. I can't guarantee that so, no. You can't go. Let the team do their job," he bellows.

I fight the tears that threaten to spill. I want to go even more now that I know those bastards could be there. I ball my fists and bite back my anger.

Nate sighs. "Listen, Roni. This is for the best."

"Yeah, whatever." I turn and walk away.

CHAPTER TWENTY-NINE

So Close

John

"John, what's your status?" my father's voice comes over the com.

"Keeping the southside clear. I'm the only one left standing. Do you need me to come to you?"

"No, I have the northside secure."

At that moment the doors to the warehouse burst open and two guys rush out. I don't even think twice before putting them both down. The feminine screams that come once both men hit the ground draw my attention.

I narrow my eyes on the entrance and find a brunette peeking her head out. My mind goes to Roni. These are the same guys that took her and her friends. It's a long shot. It's been over a year and a half, but maybe, just maybe her friend is here.

Rushing forward, I wave the girls to me. Three step out, all shaking like leaves. I scan the area to see if there are any more. My heart sinks in defeat when I find none. The pale faces of these three assure me that I've not found Roni's friend.

More shots ring out from inside, drawing my attention. "Let's move," I say to the girls. I need to get them to cover. "Dad, I have three girls here. They all seem to be in shock."

"Get them in a car and go. We have this. Get them to safety. I don't want any of these fuckers escaping and grabbing one of them like last time. Go."

I hesitate for only a moment. However, as the gun fire dies down, I know the team has this. I pull my earpiece from my ear as I usher the girls into one of the waiting SUVs. Noting that one girl is limping and has blood dripping down her leg, I pick up the pace.

I tear off my shirt to tie around the wound before I rush to the driver's seat and take off. With one last glance in the rearview as I drive off, I grind my teeth. My gut tells me there were answers back there.

However, my training tells me I need to get this girl some help and I follow my training. Pulling up the number I need, I arrange for a meet and stitch.

Natasha

"Dad, I'm sending a package your way," the tall guy with the golden eyes says as he moves toward me. I'm curled in a ball, not sure what's going on. One minute I was in the office with

Iosif shouting for me to get him something for his busted nose, the next he was dragging me out of the room by my hair.

I look to Iosif. The guy shot him. I'm so numb with shock, I don't think that fact has registered with my brain yet. I wish I were the one that pulled the trigger.

"Run for that door, honey. There's a man there that will get you to safety." I bring my gaze back to golden eyes.

I'm trembling as I stare up at him. This can't be real. I blink a few times. Golden eyes looks at me as if I've lost my mind before his face softens and he begins to talk to me in Russian repeating for me to run for the door and meet the man and safety on the other side.

I'm afraid to get my hopes up again. Then he says the words that I dare to latch onto. "You're safe now."

Without letting him know that I understood him fine when he spoke English, I nod and start to crawl toward the door. Once a few feet away, I scramble to my feet and race for the exit. I'm so close.

My chest tightens as I get a foot away, I can feel the cool air coming from under the door. And then, it's snatched away. Someone grabs my hair and pulls me back, I swing out, but I'm still dragged back.

"Where do you think you're going, pet?" Is snarled in my ear.

I hate the name the other girls call me because Iosif allows me privileges for my help. Privileges, I snort at the thought. They are jealous over nothing.

I'm spun around to find Nikita, one of Iosif's right hands, sitting on the concrete bleeding out from his side. He looks up at me with wild blue eyes. He swallows hard and waves his gun at me to come closer.

"They're waiting for me to come outside. If I don't go, they will come in," I rush out.

"You go," he says to Sarah.

I widen my eyes as I look at her and the smug grin, she gives me. "No," I cry out.

"You take good care of him, pet. Thanks."

With that, she turns and runs for the door. I go to chase after her, but Nikita grunts. "Don't." He inhales raggedly. "Come, help me. We leave."

CHAPTER THIRTY

Night Terrors

Roni

I look up from the magazine I'm flipping through as my father steps out on the back deck and takes a seat across from me at the patio table. Before I can return my attention to the magazine, he gives me a stern look that tells me he wants to talk. I place the magazine down.

It's not often that he gives me much of his attention. I was surprised when he invited me to make this trip with him to the Florida house. I mean, who wouldn't be up for a trip to Miami. Although I knew this wouldn't be some chance to bond or whatever.

"I have someone I want you to meet. I'd like you to become friends with him," he says.

My brows shot up into my hairline. My father doesn't involve me in his business and he hardly ever encourages relationships between me and the opposite sex. However, I don't point this out.

It's a chance for me to please him. Maybe dating this guy will get my father to open up to me. I look down at the magazine now resting on the table.

"Do I meet him when we return home?"

"No, he and I have business here. You will meet him tonight."

"What's his name?"

"Da—"

"No, no."

I jump out of my sleep as the masculine whimpers startle me. I'm confused and lost for a moment, until there's movement in the bed beside me. Shock, I slide back, ready to jump from the bed until I realize the thick blonde hair belongs to none other than Torque.

"Don't touch me," he cries out again.

Rage fills me. He's having a nightmare of his own. Scooting closer, I touch his arm gently and give a shake.

"Torque, Torque. It's me, Roni," I whisper. "Wake up. You're safe. Wake up."

He pops out of his sleep, looking around wildly. When his blue eyes settle on me, I give him an awkward smile. He flings himself at me and I stiffen at first, surprised and unsure of what to do.

The kid needs to feel safe, so I swallow and wrap my arms around him. The hug is as awkward as my smile. He rests his head on my shoulder.

"I've been having nightmares more often," he says. "I'm sorry. I didn't want to be alone and you went to bed early tonight."

"It's okay."

After Nate wouldn't allow me to go help, I came to my room and thought I'd take nap or something. Apparently, my nap turned into hours. I glance over at the clock and it flashes 4:45 a.m.

"I keep wondering if she's safe. Is she going through all that shit still? I hate not knowing. What if she's…"

"Hey, we don't know that. We have to stay positive. We'll keep looking and John is looking as well."

Torque pulls away and frowns. "You like that guy, don't you? Are you sure we can trust him?"

"I trust him."

He pouts. "You didn't answer the other part."

"Why are you asking the other part?"

His frown turns into a pout. "I may be the younger one, but you're still my sister. I have to look out for you."

I don't have the heart to tell the kid we're not really related. He says the words with such conviction. Instead, I run a hand through the front of his hair.

"I don't think I've ever had anyone care about me as much as you two. He's not out to hurt me. Our relationship is… it's complicated."

He nods as the wheels turn in his head. "Well, you should be careful. You know, you guys should use condoms and stuff like that."

I nearly choke as my eyes bulge. Slapping him in the shoulder, I laugh. "I'm not sleeping with him. Like I said, complicated."

"All right, but just in case. Remember what I said. We have to look out of each other."

"Lie down. You need more sleep," I tease.

He gives me that smile that will break a few hearts someday. If I can help it, this kid will have a normal healthy life. As a matter of fact, I need to start thinking more about that. He's happy here, but is this the place for him?

He turns onto his side with his back to me. Tossing an arm over him, I spoon his back. Torque snuggles into my embrace.

"Roni."

"Yeah," I murmur, sleepily.

"I love you. I never want to lose you."

My heart squeezes. Those words hit their mark and tears come to my eyes. I nod as I try to clear the lump in my throat.

"I love you too, kid."

"I'm not a kid."

I snort. "Yeah, sure. You'll be eighteen soon. I know just what we're going to get you."

He chuckles. "Sounds like a breakout situation. I'm game."

"Go to sleep before Nate bursts in and blames me for trying to break you out."

"He thinks I have potential. He says I need to stop rushing."

I sigh. "He's right. You need to think things through and slow down. Go to sleep, Torque. We can talk in the morning."

I don't know why, but I do something totally out of character. I lean forward and kiss the back of his head, tightening my hold on him. His body relaxes with the gesture and he reaches to lace his fingers with mine. Soon his soft snores fill the room.

You need to start making your own money, then you can get him out of here.

John

I'm exhausted. Nellie hasn't woken up, but she and the baby are stable. The family stuck around for Wyatt as long as we could. I plan to shower, pass out for a few hours and head back in to make sure he eats and has a change of clothes. I know he's not leaving his wife's side and I can't blame him.

I pull out my phone to see if I have any messages from Roni. It's so late, I'm not going to call her. Although I know she's probably pissed that I never caught my plane.

I'll explain in the morning. Sometimes I truly hate this distance and time difference. Hearing her voice would be perfect at the moment.

"Hey."

I look up in confusion. Missy is sitting on my front step. I turn to look behind me. I could have sworn I locked the gate since I was headed out of town.

"Um, hey," I reply, my brain too tired to catch up with what the hell is going on.

"So… um, I have a friend that was at the hospital tonight and saw you there. I was worried, so I came over."

I knit my brows. "Seriously? I mean, thanks, but you had to be here all night."

"I couldn't sleep until I knew you were okay," she says and bites her lip.

In the past, I thought that was sexy. It's this little thing she does that makes her mouth look hot. Tonight, even in my exhaustion it does nothing for me.

"Listen, it's been a long as fuck day. I'm so tired I can't see straight." On cue my stomach starts to growl.

"Sounds like you're hungry. How about I come in and make you something to eat while you shower? Kill two birds with one stone," she says.

Something rings off about the words despite her saying them sweetly. However, my head is starting to hurt, I'm starving, and I want to get in my bed as soon as possible. Instead of sending her on her way, I move around her and unlock the door.

Pushing inside, I turn on the lights and start for my bedroom. "I have some soup you can heat up. I'm in the mood for grilled cheese," I call over my shoulder.

It's a comfort food my mother used to make me when I wasn't feeling well or in a bad mood. I need some type of comfort tonight. My brothers almost lost the women and children they hold dear.

My mind goes back to Roni. If anything happened to her… I'm grateful to Nate for not placing her on assignment. I know she's been wanting to go out in the field, I can't say that I'm upset that she's not.

As I strip out of my clothes, I think about my own future. I have options. Dad has been talking me through the pros and cons.

The question is, am I ready and willing to cross that line. It's not an every now and then thing, it's not here and there. I'd be committing.

"All in," I grumble to myself.

Stepping under the spray of the shower, I clear my head and think of nothing. I channel the focus and control I have during a scene, allowing myself to just be. Placing my hands to the shower wall, I drop my head between my shoulders and let the water run down my back.

I release a heavy breath. Something has to give.

***

I wake with a hand caressing my back. Jumping up, I look down at Missy lying beside me. I squint at her as I try to recall last night.

Shit, I was so tired, I climbed out of the shower, wrapped a towel around my waist, and faceplanted on my bed. I never made it to the kitchen or to put anything on. Shifting my gaze down my body, I find my cock out and on display. Grabbing the edge of the bedspread, I yank it over my waist.

"What are you doing here?" I say tightly.

"I didn't want to wake you. So, I climbed in bed and waited for you to wake. You looked so peaceful."

"You should go. I need to get back to the hospital," I mutter.

She pushes up on her elbows, her blouse gapes open to expose her breasts. I look away and go to climb out of bed. Missy reaches for my arm, halting my exit.

"Wait, I can come with you. You know, for moral support. You didn't say what happened. Are your brothers okay?"

"I don't think that's going to be a good idea. This is a sensitive matter. I'll call you, but you should go."

With that, I head for the bathroom. Hoping for once, Missy will take a clue and leave when I ask her to the first time.

Yeah, today, I don't have it in me not to be a dick.

CHAPTER THIRTY-ONE

Not A Fit

Roni

"I don't think this is working out for me," I say as I look up at John.

He says he's here for a quick visit. I think Nate and Rita called him in. I've been mouthing back and not giving my all to training.

It's not like they plan to put me in the field. I'm no one, I have no past and that's dictating my future. I'm stuck in this void.

John sighs and pushes off the bookcase he was leaning on. We're in the library here at the Toy Cop Academy. It's the only place I could find to hide. Everyone knows I like to go to the gym when I want to avoid people and interaction.

Funny. If you know I don't want to be bothered why come find me. I needed a new hide out. So here I am. Don't ask how John found me.

"Then what do you want to do?"

I give him a side glance. "I won't be carted off to some third world country."

He laughs. "Where'd you get that from?"

"People talk," I mutter.

"First of all, the Briggs are half Greek. No one goes to a third world country. Some of the recruits that didn't work out went to work in Greece for a family company," John explains with humor in his tone.

"Yup." I let the "p" pop. "Ain't going to Greece either. Although I hear the men are good to their women."

I grin at the frown that comes to John's face. He comes to prop his butt on the edge of the table in front of me. I watch him as he stares at me.

"Come to L.A. It doesn't have to be permanent. If you like it, you come work for me," he says.

"Doing what?"

He shrugs. "Can't tell you that really. You'd still need the training here. You'd have to complete the program, but when you're done you would be with me."

I sit back in my chair and fold my arms across my chest. I suddenly feel so small in this huge library, as if this decision has taken on physical size. Lately I've been looking over the books for some projects Thomas put me on once he learned I'm good with numbers.

I get the feeling these guys do more than security. I narrow my eyes at John because I know he's talking about a job that's going to be more than investigations and bounties. The fields he claims to work in.

Not believing that bullshit.

"You don't have to be suspicious of everything. You know I wouldn't allow anything to happen to you," he says to my silent appraisal.

"So, I come with you to see if I like it and then I come back to this place."

He shrugs. "I'll talk to Nate. I don't think it will be a problem."

I narrow my eyes at him. He's leaving something out, but I don't push him. I'm curious.

"Okay. Let's go."

He laughs. "I have a few things to get in order. We'll leave tomorrow."

John

What is it about this girl? I can't seem to stay away. I should be back home helping out with everything that's going on. Instead, I jumped on a plane as soon as Nelly opened her eyes and I knew my niece would be okay.

Now here I am planning to take her home with me. Not that I haven't been thinking about it for a while. In theory, this will all work out.

"I've been waiting for you to come to me with this," Nate says, humor lacing his words.

"It's not like I haven't already taken responsibility for her."

"This is true. All right. If this is what you want. We'll train her when she returns, but I'm putting it out there now. That girl is a ticking time bomb."

I grunt. "I know. That's why I'm trying to diffuse the coming explosion," I reply.

"I hear you. I'm only telling you not to be the one laying on top of the bomb when it explodes."

"We all make our choices. Yeah?"

"Yeah." He shakes his head and chuckles.

CHAPTER THIRTY-TWO

Test Run

John

"I think I can get used to this," Roni says as we stroll out of the sushi bar, we just finished stuffing our face in. "Although this isn't better than that Jerk chicken place in New York, that's always going to be my favorite."

"Noted." I smile at her. "I wanted to ask, does anything about Cali feel familiar to you?"

Roni turns her face up to look at me. I can see the wheels turn. She has this distant look in her eyes for a few beats.

"Not really. Nothing that sparks a memory or anything." She shrugs.

"So, you're not from L.A." I nod.

"That's an assumption, but I think you can stick with it," she teases. "When do I get to work?"

I look down at her. I love that she's so eager to make her own way, but honestly, I don't have the type of assignment I plan for her to work with me on lined up. Not yet.

"Waiting for something to come down the pipeline. Are you getting tired of it here already?"

"No." She taps the back of her hand against my stomach a few times. "You promised me a job. I'm trying to see what all you're offering here Black."

I laugh. "Yeah, I hear you. For now, let's enjoy. How about that?"

"Yeah, yeah." She rolls her eyes.

I place a hand on her back to steer her out of the way of the drunken group heading toward us. It's a warm night. Perfect for an evening at the beach.

"Want to go for a surf?"

When I look down at her face, I have to hold back my laughter. If this moment were a meme, the caption would read, *if what the fuck was a person.* Her expression is priceless.

Luckily, I'm saved by her phone. It rings and a smile beams across her face. "Hey, it's Torque. I need to take this."

"No worries."

I watch her take a few steps away. I know this isn't going to become a permanent thing for her without Torque. I need to decide if I'm willing to take his mouthy ass on.

My phone rings and I pull it out. I groan when I see it's Missy. I shoot her a text instead of answering. I'm not in the mood.

She's one of the reasons that Roni and I are staying at a hotel. The other reason being my brothers. They will pop up unannounced whenever they feel the need.

I want to introduce Roni on my terms. Speak of the devils. My phone rings and it's my brothers Facetiming me.

"What's up?" I answer.

"Felix wants to barbeque and introduce us to the kid," Wyatt says.

"Dae-Dae, right?"

"Yeah," Felix replies proudly.

"Cool, I'm game."

I look toward Roni. This would probably be the right time to bring her into the fold. I'll invite her to come along.

"This weekend it is. I'm ready for some grub," Brax says.

"When are you not ready to eat?" Ry says.

Brax tosses him the finger. "Bite me."

"Hey, I'll catch up with you guys later."

They all say their partings and we end the call. I stand and watch Roni as she talks on the phone. Torque is one lucky kid. He pulls a smile no one else can get from Roni. She's gentle with him.

I think she'd make a great mom.

My mind goes immediately to her being swollen with my children. She would be gorgeous. *Damn, John, you're in trouble.*

Roni

"I'll be back soon." I laugh into the phone.

"It sucks here without you," Torque says.

"I know. I'm just trying to see if this is the right thing for us."

"He wants me too?"

My heart aches at the sound of his voice. It never crossed my mind that I would take a job with John and leave Torque behind.

The only reason I didn't push for Torque to be able to come on this trip was because I wanted to see if it's even something we should do. I didn't want to get his hopes up and find out I don't want to do this. I still don't know what this is.

"How is it?"

"It's cool. I haven't done much, but it's okay," I say.

"They're going to let me come with you, right? You're my sister. My family."

"I'll burn that motherfucker down if they try to stop us."

He laughs. "I can see that."

I turn and find John watching me. "Hey, I should go."

"Okay, I love you, sis. Be safe."

I'm silent for a moment. "Yeah, love you too, kid."

CHAPTER THIRTY-THREE

Try Outs

John

"We almost done here?" Roni murmurs.

I nod. I want out of this dank basement as much as she does. She's cagey and I can't blame her. This job was not what I had in mind for her first, but it's what came up.

"Good," she mumbles.

This entire try out hasn't worked out the way I intended. Everything that could go wrong seems to be happening. After the first week, Roni questioned our staying in a hotel instead of my home.

I could see on her face she didn't like my response. Shit, I didn't like it. How do you tell someone you have a psycho ex that pops up and gets on your damn nerves?

To top that off, I received a call from the ER about Missy. Apparently, she still has me listed as her emergency contact. Ever the nice guy, I went to see if she was at least okay.

However, by the time I got there she was discharged, and I couldn't get more information beyond that. Which was weird as I was her emergency contact to begin with. Thank God at the time Roni had decided to do some exploring on her own.

I've learned she likes being on her own. I tried to get her to come to Felix's barbeque and she totally blew me off. I'm not going to lie and say I wasn't disappointed. I felt Wyatt's eyes on me when he realized she wasn't going to show. I was sorry I even mentioned it.

However, I'm not going to lie and say it didn't feel good to find out that Felix already knows about Roni. It's actually a relief. She may not want to meet my brothers yet, but having Felix and Wyatt know about her feels right.

Now this.

I look to Ole, the asshole we were hired to recover. Actually, my cousins asked me to do this favor. I turn my gaze to Maximilian as he leans against the wall, watching his guys work over the dude we dragged back here with us. The triplets wanted to know who exactly targeted their business associate that we were hired to extract.

This poor fuck better cough up some answers while he still has a chance. They don't call the Triplets and their crew the Slaughter House for nothing.

"You should put some ice on that," Roni grumbles to Mil as he flexes his fists.

I can't help wondering where the busted knuckles came from. He hasn't hit the guy they're roughing up. He looked pretty pissed when we arrived, now that I think of it. However, I know better than to ask questions now.

"Thanks, love. I'll get it taken care of," Mil says to Roni.

"Not your love. And suit yourself," she replies.

Mil turns his eyes on her and glares a beat before he snorts to himself. He shoves his fists into his pockets and pushes off the wall to head over to his men and the ass whipping across the room. Again, I have questions. Maximilian is always decked out in a suit and converse. Usually, his appearance is impeccable—even after he kicks someone's ass.

Something is definitely up with him.

"I want to thank you for being so swift and discrete about this," Ole says, drawing my attention.

"Doing my job," I say curtly.

He lights a cigarette and squints his eyes at me, then turns his focus to Roni. He's been doing that a lot. I'm trying my best not to knock his teeth down his throat. That would be bad for business.

"You sure do have a pretty crew."

I turn to him fully and glare. Placing my arms across my chest, I look him over as if he smells like shit. "Sorry, I'm not into guys, but thanks for the compliment."

He chuckles. "While you are on the pretty side. I was talking about your little friend," he says, letting his eyes scan over Roni and licking his lips. "I guess that works. She sure did have that motherfucker distracted when you came for me," he says.

"I'll filet the skin off your fucking face," Roni hisses.

"Oh, yeah, I like you."

"Mil, you done with us," I bellow out to my cousin.

He turns to me and I can see all three of my cousins in one. He looks to Roni, grins, and gives me a nod. That's all I need. I turn to Roni.

"Let's go."

This all could have ended so simply. We get this guy from the very bad guys, we bring back someone from the very bad guys, we get our money, and we go home. Nope, I'm John. So, of course, this shit goes way the fuck left.

It's like it happens in slow motion. Ole reaches out for Roni and grabs her forearm. She spins and grabs him by the throat, lifts him in the air, and slams him on his back on the hard-concrete floor beneath us like it's nothing.

"Roni," I call.

It's like she's blacked out. She's beating the shit out of this guy. I have to grab her around the waist and tug her off of him.

"Don't you ever put your hands on me," she yells, her chest heaving. "You will swallow your *huevos* if you ever come near me again. You hear me?"

Mil pulls a gun and fires at the asshole on the ground. I look to him and knit my brows. Mil, puts his gun away and fixes his suit.

"Inevitable outcome." He shrugs. "You will still be paid. Nice to meet you, hell cat."

With that, he turns away from us and walks out of the room, leaving us all behind.

Roni

"Do you want to talk about it?" John asks as he sits across from me on the private jet.

I keep my gaze on my lap. "Did I lose the job?"

He scoffs. "That's what you're worried about?"

When I bring my head up to look at him, he's frowning back at me. I didn't mean to lose my shit. That guy was giving me weird vibes from the time we picked him up. Arrogant asshole.

"I blacked out. I don't know what happened. I cost that guy his life."

"You didn't cost him anything. Mil does everything with intent. That guy wasn't making it out of that place whether he touched you or not. I was on the verge of knocking his ass the fuck out. If you want the job it's yours," John says.

"Really?" I narrow my eyes.

"You have a bad temper. We'll deal with it. When you get back to the training center, I know all the things I want them to work on. That is if you still want this. It's not security and it sure as hell isn't safer than what Nate is offering. It's up to you."

"Torque and I are a package deal," I say quickly.

"I know. Trust me, I know."

"Good. Let's get me back to Toy Cop training then, shall we?"

He laughs and shakes his head. For the first time in weeks, I relax. I can do this. Training and then I go to work for John.

Yeah, that sounds right.

CHAPTER THIRTY-FOUR

Val

Two and a half months later...
I've been watching this chick and I see so much of myself in her.
She moves like a killer with a chip on her shoulder. We're the
most dangerous type.

She won't kill because she's told to, she'll do it because she
wants to, needs to. There's one problem. That anger is locked
inside, and she hasn't learned how to harness the rage within.

"What are you thinking?" Uri asks at my side.

I turn my gaze to him. Nate stands beside him with the same
curious look in his eyes. I tilt my head toward the *bella* that's
brooding in the ring.

"She's the best here. Why do you hold her back?" I say.

"Roni isn't one of mine. Not anymore. She's volatile. She also has no memory of who she was before she was taken. Too many unknowns with her," Nate replies. "She's better off in the situation she's going into. I hope."

He mutters that last part. I nod and turn back to watch her. "You do know you can't leave her like this?"

When nothing is said, I look to Nate. He stares at me in confusion. The man may be a trained killer, but there's a difference.

"Bloody hell," Uri murmurs and folds his arms over his chest.

I know my husband understands me. This girl is a mirror of me. She's been hurt. She needs to release the things clawing at her insides.

"Want to fill me in?" Nate says.

"You leave her this way, she'll explode. It's there, the signs. It's coming. Let me help her."

He narrows his eyes at me. I wait, holding my breath. I haven't been able to show the asset I can truly be here. This girl... I can show them the intensity their team lacks. The edge that makes me the hitter I am. What makes Uri who he is.

"Are you sure you want to take that on?"

I turn at the sound of the deep rumbling voice. A gorgeous face greets me. He's not as tall as Uri, but he's over six feet tall. Those eyes and lashes are amazing.

"John, this is Valentina Donati, Val this is Johnathan Black. You already know Uri," Nate says.

"Nice to meet you. You can call me John."

"Val."

He nods his head toward Roni. "She's stubborn. There's a lot going on in her head. Some of it she's still trying to sort out."

"Good. She can use it. I know I will."

With that, I saunter away toward the ring. It's time I free this phoenix before she burns up in her shell. This will be fun.

Roni

I feel the moment he enters the gym. I haven't seen John in over two months. I get it. His family has needed him, and I need to be here to train and get my temper under control.

That doesn't mean I haven't been angry and resentful. They treat me like a fragile doll here. I hate that John told them how I lost it on that mission.

I'm watched more closely and cautiously now. It's getting frustrating. Add the dreams, visions, and fragments of memories and I'm just pissed. Who cares about this training? I'm not going to be able to use it if I can't get my fucked up head right.

"Come on, Roni. Focus. You're better than this," Jasper coaches as we bounce around the ring.

I roll my eyes. Adjusting my stance, I barely raise my guard. I didn't want to be in this ring before John arrived, now that I've spotted him standing with Nate and that Uri guy, I could care less about being in here. It's a waste of my time.

"You fight like you're constipated."

I pause and drop my hands, looking to the side of the ring. This bitch. It's the Black chick with the blue eyes. I think she's the Uri guy's wife or something. Valentine or some shit like that.

"Get your ass in here. I'll beat the shit out of you," I say in annoyance.

"Shit, Roni, I don't think you want to do that," Jasper groans.

I frown and look her prissy ass over. I'll beat that weave right off her ass. She gives me a smug smile as she pulls her hair up into a bun before stepping into the ring.

Ignoring her, I look to John and Nate. They seem to be in a deep conservation. He hasn't been around in months and it's like I don't exist.

Why am I here? What am I training for? If he's not checking in on me, it's clear he's not interested in giving me the job anymore. I should leave and find Natasha on my own. I've learned enough now.

Fuck them. You don't have to work for any of them.

Pissed, I pull my gloves off. I'm done. I turn to walk out of the ring, moving toward the ropes. My back caves in and I stumble forward.

Reaching for my back, I turn to find this blue-eyed bitch grinning at me. "Never turn your back on me. I'm the last person you give your back to."

I grimace and look this crazy ass chick over. I toss the gloves in my hand down and step toward her. The gleam in her eyes tells me she's a damn nut for sure.

"Val," John bellows through the gym.

She ignores him. Calmly, as if she didn't just kick me, she looks at Jasper. "Clear the gym. Leave us."

"I'm done with this shit. Whatever you think you're about to do, you can save it. I'm leaving."

She laughs. I jerk my head back. When did I say something funny?

"You invite a snake into the ring and try to leave. I have much teach you, *bella*."

A quick glance around the gym and everyone's leaving. John, Nate, and Uri have moved to the side of the ring. Jasper has left with everyone else.

"Attention on me. Roni is it?"

"Fuck you. That's who I am."

She snorts. "You are pretty, but my husband suits me fine." She circles me, walking backwards. Her gaze taking me in from head to toe. She shoves me by my shoulder. "You are angry."

I ball my fists. I'm about to beat her ass. Let her touch me one more time.

"You're the best here," she says and taps my forehead with her fingers. I shove her arm away. "But you are locked in here. I can smell the vengeance on you. You want revenge, but you don't know how to get it."

"You know nothing about me."

She laughs again. "I am you," she says bitterly. "I've done what you want to. I've made them pay."

"Get out of my face." She's too close and I'm beyond pissed.

"Not until you fight me."

I grin and fold my arms over my chest. "Then we'll be here all day, bitch."

She smiles so wide her pretty teeth are on full display. "You want them to respect you, to set you free to be who you are? You fight me. Show you can gain control of that rage. Fight me." She pushes me.

I stumble back and ball my fists. Tears build as my anger simmers. I have nothing to prove to her or anyone else.

"If I want to leave, I'll leave. I don't need anyone's permission," I snarl.

"Yet you are still here. And you and I know that's not the freedom I'm talking about. I see you.

"You're haunted. You reek of it. It's in your eyes." She starts to circle me again as she continues, poking me in the chest with her words. "The freedom you need is in here. You want to go after the ones that hurt you, don't you? That means you need control of here."

She taps my temple again. I ball my fists tighter and narrow my eyes. My chest tightens. It's as if I'll choke on the rage that's clawing up.

There's a reason I'm here. I know in my heart that I'm not like the others. There's so much more to why I ended up in that sex trafficking operation, but I can't put the pieces together to figure it out. For the last few months that feeling has been getting stronger. She's speaking to the turmoil inside and I hate it.

"Fight me."

"No," I growl.

"Fight me," she hollers at the top of her lungs.

"No," I shout back.

She gets nose to nose with me. "You want revenge? Here is how you begin to get it. I will make you what they cannot. Your soul is already black. Accept it." She pushes me. "Fight me."

I don't move.

"*Argh*," she's screams in my face and backs me up. "*Argh*." She yells again, still backing me up, her neck straining. She's shorter than me, but she's a force, making me feel like she's bigger than I am. "*Argh*."

She shoves me and I snap. I'm back in that basement again, shivering from the cold water they threw on me. Being slapped around and punched. Having piss tossed on me.

Suddenly, my father's words fill my ears. It's so loud, it feels like he's right next to me. Not like the dreams or visions. This time the words vibrate in my skull.

"I've made you a hard woman to handle hard situations. Know when to be a princess and when to be a savage. It will save your life."

I'll never be that weak again.

I back hand the shit out of Val. Her head whips to the side and blood splatters to the mat.

"Val," her husband, bellows her name and starts for inside the ring, looking at me with a death glare. I glare back, my chest heaving.

Val holds her hand up, a huge smile on her face as she wipes the corner of her mouth. "There she is. Come on, baby. Fight me. I'm them. I'm who you want. Come get me."

A growl comes from deep down inside, rattling my chest. "Argh," I yell back.

Betrayal consumes me. I don't know who from, but I feel it. Loss swells inside. It too has a source I don't understand or remember. I black out.

Val

That's what I want. I know she no longer sees me, but her pain. Her eyes are distant and haunted.

She comes at me with so much force, I'm stunned at first. I block her first strike anyway. I'm ready for her when she spins and kicks out.

She's good. "Don't let the anger control you. You control it. Use it."

A grin comes to my lips as I watch her adjust. A gasp leaves my lips as she connects her feet with my midsection. Uri growls in the background, but I ignore him.

"That's it. Let it out. Come for me."

I see the moment it clicks, but I'm ready. Roni jumps in the air, intending a spinning kick. I jump and counter with the same kick in opposite rotation. We send each other spinning in the reverse directions, landing in crouching positions.

Her chest heaves as she looks at me. The tears spill over and she falls back onto her butt. She's done.

I crawl to her and sit behind her. My front to her back, wrapping her in my arms. Holding tight, I whisper in her ear.

"Let it out. That's it. You're safe now," I coo. "We'll get them. I promise."

She starts to scream as I hold her. The screams coming from deep within her soul. Uri and Nate turn their backs as if to give us privacy. However, John stares with a tightness to his jaw.

If I didn't know better, I'd think I were staring at an avenging angel. I nod at him, letting him know that I'm here to help. I'll get her ready for the day I know in my gut will come.

The day she settles the score with all her demons. She continues to scream out, just as I had done to get her to fight me. I tighten my hold as her body shakes.

I lock eyes with John as I whisper in Roni's ear. "This thing you want, what you want to do, it will not fix the darkness. That still lives inside, but it will free you." She nods at my words. "I will call you, *La rabbia della morte*. Death's Rage."

Time seems to pass slowly as she cries herself out. John enters the ring and stands over us for a brief moment before he squats down. He reaches to place his fingers beneath Roni's chin to angle her face toward him.

He kisses her forehead, causing me to pull back in shock. I look to Nate and Uri, and Nate shrugs his shoulders. "Angel, you want to get out of here?"

She nods and in the next breath, John has her in his arms as he stands to his full height. Nate and Uri hold the ropes open as John climbs from the ring with Roni held close to his chest.

It looks like he's whispering in her ear from where I sit. Uri walks over and hands me his handkerchief. I take it and wipe at my mouth.

"I get it, love. She's the reason you wanted to help."

I shrug. "Maybe." He nods and holds his hand out to help me up. "Are they a couple?" I ask Nate.

"They're something," he replies, shaking his head. "Now, *what* exactly? Well, your guess is as good as mine."

"Interesting."

CHAPTER THIRTY-FIVE

Bad for You

John

"This is your place?"

Turning from the freezer, I find Roni looking around. She seems... pensive. The wheels are turning and now I'm curious as to what she's thinking.

I can't help taking her in from head to toe. She has on a black short sleeve button up. It's tucked into a pair of tight light blue jeans. She kicked off her ankle boots by the door. Her bare feet give me a view of black painted toes.

I grin. Pink toes, not my Roni. Although from here I can tell they have a light sparkle to them. What I'd give to have those toes in my mouth while slamming into her tight pussy.

Damn, what did she ask me? Oh, my place. Right.

"Sort of. I've been playing with the idea of getting a place here. I'm renting to see how it feels. After six months, if I like it, I'll consider the purchase or extend the lease," I reply.

She moves to sit on the couch. I like how comfortable she looks in my space. I'm starting to like this apartment more with each passing second.

"The Toy Cop Academy not good enough for you?"

I grin at her nickname for the training facility. "It's fine enough, but I want a space of my own."

"How long is this training supposed to last? I thought I'd be coming to L.A. soon."

"You will, but I do business here. Having a place isn't such a bad idea."

"Mm." She nods. "How much does a place like this cost anyway?"

Closing the distance between us, I meet her in the living room and hand her a tumbler of whisky. She takes it and locks eyes with me. I lift my shoulder and pull a face. "A few grand a month."

"What's a few grand a month? Two, three?"

"Fifteen." I knock back the tumbler of amber liquid that reminds me of her eyes.

Eyes that fill with sadness as she drops her head, looking defeated. My curiosity heightens. Taking her tumbler from her hand, I place both on the coffee table.

She takes a seat, staring down into her lap. Taking the seat beside her, I cup her face and lift it until her brown eyes lock on mine. She covers my hands with hers and I search her gaze. "Talk to me."

"I can't afford something like this."

I furrow my brows. "What?"

"I have to find a place for me and Torque. Whether here or L.A. we need to find a place soon. This isn't for him. He's impulsive and he doesn't stop to think. He'll get himself killed out there. I want more for him."

I nod. Torque's birthday will be here soon. If he turns eighteen while here in New York with Nate, they're going to start handing him assignments. I've been thinking about that a lot.

She's right. I don't think he's ready. He's smart, he's decent at hand to hand and a damn good shot, but Torque rushes through things like a teenaged boy does. He hasn't gained the discipline needed for what's being asked of him.

I stroke her cheek. "You and Torque come to Cali whenever you say the word. I'll make it happen. Neither of you have to stay."

"I want to be able to make money and take care of us. If you decide…" she trails off and looks away.

"Is that what you think? You think I'll decide I don't want you guys? I won't help you?"

"I want to make my own money with my own skills. These are the skills I have now. This is what I know."

I bob my head. "And revenge, you know revenge."

She turns away, but I bring her face back to mine. "What do you want me to say? You do know when I find Natasha, I'm going after her. If those filthy animals still have her when that happens, I will kill every single one of them where they stand. If not, I will find them one by one and make them pay."

"And…" I say, narrowing my eyes.

"What makes you think there's an *and*?"

"There is. Val was onto something."

She turns away again.

Not wanting to push too hard too soon, I stand and go to fill our glasses again. My mind plays over her words and the incident in the ring. Val sees something in Roni. If I tell the truth, I've seen it as well.

When I go to return with our drinks and the bottle of Whiskey, I find her standing at the stereo. Music starts to float through the apartment, and I smile.

Placing the bottle on the coffee table, I make my way over to her. Once I hand her the glass, I reach into my pocket and pull out my phone to start one of my playlists.

I keep my gaze on her as she lifts her glass to her lips. It's written on her face that her thoughts have taken her somewhere.

"Come here," I say, reaching for her hand and taking her back over to the couch.

This time I sit across from her in the accent chair. Instead of sitting on the couch, she takes a perch on the edge of the coffee table. I give a little grin as she places one of her feet on the arm of my chair spreading her legs for me.

My grin grows as the song playing registers with me. "Bad" by Wale. It's perfect to explain why I don't need to do this with her.

"What are you smiling at?" she asks as she leans forward and rests an arm on her thigh.

I watch her closely as she knocks back another drink and places the glass on the table behind her. I sit up and lean into her, placing my hand on her thigh.

Giving a gentle squeeze, I appraise her eyes. She's in over her head with me and doesn't even know it. *Oh, Roni, the shit I'd do to you.* I forbid myself from saying the words out loud.

"You should pay attention to the lyrics. I'm bad for you, baby. I keep trying to tell you that."

She searches my face with those pretty eyes. It's clear she's tuned into the music. I bite my lip when her gaze notes she's caught my point.

"You've never made love? Is that what you're trying to tell me?"

"Now you're getting it. I've never been in love and I've never made love. Oh, trust and believe without a doubt, I can fuck. I'll fuck you senseless, but you deserve better."

She turns away and I sit back. It would be so easy to grab her by the waist and bring her into my lap, but I won't. Instead, I circle back to my earlier thoughts.

However, Roni has other plans. She stands and moves around the room, stopping to look out the window at the amazing view of Manhattan that sold me on this place. Not about to stay away from her, I put my tumbler down and go to stand beside her.

"Is Val right? Did you remember something?"

"No."

In one quick move, I spin her by one arm, grasp her throat, and back her into the window. She glares at me defiantly. Dipping my head, I rub my nose against hers.

"What did I tell you about lies?"

"We don't lie to each other," she breathes.

"Then let's try this again. Did you remember something?"

"No, let's try starting with the truth from you. It's been almost two years. If I was underage when you found me, I'm definitely legal by now." She reaches up to place her hands behind my head, pushing her fingers into my hair. "But we both know I've always been old enough."

With that, she closes the gap and presses her lips to mine. It takes me all of two seconds to take over. It's a starved and unrestrained kiss. It has none of the finesse I'm capable of.

This kiss is equivalent to an exploding volcano. It's been building all this time and now the flow won't stop. Her fingers tighten in my hair and I squeeze at her throat. The moan that comes from her lips turns me on so much I have to break the kiss to make sure she's real.

We're both breathing heavily. I'm so hard, I have to reach to adjust myself. Roni drops her gaze to the action and smiles. I go to say some slick shit, but my words are trapped in my mouth when she grabs the front of her shirt and tears it open.

Buttons fly everywhere, her smooth skin is exposed in a silky looking bra—skin I've wanted to devour for so long I don't want to count. I place a hand on the window to brace myself as I hover over her. Looking down at her, I call on my restraint.

Slowly I lower my gaze to her tits once more. With the back of my other hand, I run my fingers from the base of her neck down the center of her breasts. When she shivers, I abruptly raise my eyes to hers. There's so much desire in her eyes, it brings a smile to my face.

I drag my fingers over the bare skin of her right breast, causing goosebumps to bloom. Her breath hitches and her breasts rise. I can barely think straight.

"John," she whimpers.

"Shh, baby, let me take my time with you."

Gently, I slip my fingers into the bra cup and tug it down. Moving to the other side, I repeat the action. Cupping her full breasts in my hand, I massage them.

Not able to torture either of us any longer, I lean in and capture her nipple. She cries out and I suck harder. Watching

Val get Roni to release some of her demons caused me to want to free her of them all. I have the power to do that. I know I do.

I suck harder, while pinching and kneading the other mound. When I start to circle her dark nipple with my tongue, she laces her fingers into my hair. I take my time feasting on her smooth, full mounds.

"Please."

Rubbing my cheek against her nipple, I close my eyes and relish in the sound of her pleas. Dropping to my knees, I tug her waist forward as I begin to lap at her bellybutton. I groan from the silky touch of her skin. She smells like honey and something else sweet.

I suck her flesh into my mouth, leaving my mark. With a tight grasp on her ass, my fingers bite into her jean covered flesh.

Roni puts in extra hours in the gym to blow off steam. It shows in her tight stomach, but what I love about her body is that no matter how hard she works out, her ass and thighs remain juicy with a jiggle I'd love to see in a sundress. Yeah, my horny ass is special.

It doesn't take much to make me happy and this body sends me into a state of euphoria. Although as I kiss her stomach, the thought of ruining this tight belly with my seed drives me to the brink of sanity. I drag my tongue up the center of her body. She bends to bring her face to mine. Allowing me to drag my tongue over her chin to her lips.

"You're mine. Mine to ruin, mine to have whenever I want. We do this and you're mine, Roni. Do you understand that?"

"Yes." Her voice comes out husky. So sexy and needy.

I can't wait anymore. I need to taste her. First, I pop the button on her jeans and pull down the zipper. I spin her and go to pull her pants down from her waist, but freeze. Closing my eyes, I want to throw a full-blown fucking tantrum. I swear, I do.

Lifting to my feet, I straighten her and wrap my arms around her waist. Kissing the top of her head, I inhale. This is going to sting.

Leaning into her ear, I think of the best way to say this. "Baby, we can't tonight."

"What?"

"Come, you can shower in my bathroom. I have a pair of sweats you can put on. You've started your cycle. It's come through your jeans," I say gently.

She stiffens. I kiss the back of her head, then turn her to face me. I hate the embarrassment I see in her eyes. She never has to be embarrassed with me.

Lifting her into my arms, I carry her to the bedroom where the en suite is. She won't look at me. I don't force her to either. I give her time.

Once in the bathroom, I place her on her feet. "I've got it," she murmurs when I go to take her jeans down her hips.

"I'll make a run to the store. Tampon or pads?"

The bewildered expression on her face makes me close the space between us. I grab her face and kiss her deeply. When I pull away, I look her in the eyes.

"Mine. I take care of what's mine. Everything you need will be my mission to handle. Everything."

"Pads. The long, extra thin ones."

"You got it. The clothes will be on the bed. Take your time. I'll be right back."

Roni

With everything I am, I want to tell him to release me. I want to crawl into a hole and never return. Why is he so sweet and why does he want to spoon me, knowing I'm bleeding?

"If this makes you uncomfortable then I can go into the guestroom," he breathes against my neck.

"You don't have to go into another room. I'm… you can release me though."

He chuckles and rolls away, the bed dipping with his movement. I turn until I'm on my other side, facing him. He goes to reach for me again but stops himself.

"Sorry," I mutter.

"For what?"

"Everything. My stupid period coming early. Not wanting to be touched."

"First, you and Val were going at it pretty hard. You may have triggered your cycle during all of that. Second, if you're not comfortable at any time, tell me. That's most important in our relationship. I will always respect your boundaries."

My heart feels… it's a weird feeling. I ignore it, not wanting a name for any of the emotions swirling through me. Nervously, I reach for his hand and lace my fingers with his. It's the most I can give in this moment. He gives my fingers a gentle squeeze.

"Thanks."

"Get some sleep, baby. It's been a long day."

CHAPTER THIRTY-SIX

Tesoro

Uri

"Do you think they understand she'll never be like the others?" Val says as she pops another grape into her mouth while she sits naked in our bed with her back against the headboard.

I contemplate her words as I lie facing her from the foot of the bed. Reaching for her silky legs, I bring one to my thigh and begin to caress her skin. She has a bruise from the fight between her and that woman. I frown at it and purse my lips.

"What I want to understand is what you want with her. What happened to taking this job to right the bad you've done?" I reply, leaning to kiss the bruise.

When I lift my eyes to hers, Val's seem distant. I wait for her to come back to me. As her focus returns, she moves to crawl to me and straddles my lap.

"I'm still doing good," she quirks, then something in her eyes changes.

"Are you ready to get involved in all of this? It hasn't been a full two months since…" I allow my words to trail off, knowing she never wants to speak of murdering her stepmother again.

"This Alliance you want to keep me away from. It will need hitters. You will need hitters. Not just the soldiers Nate thinks he is building."

"His intentions have not been to build soldiers for the Alliance," I reply.

"*Marito*," she purrs. My cock twitches to hear her call me husband in Italian, my chest swells with pride, and then she pushes a pen in it. "You think so little of me and my resources. Nate may not know what he's building. Sure, he thinks he's preparing to take a step back. Sam has other plans. Plans that will not hold with the crew Nate is building."

I snort and give her a smile. And here I thought I was keeping things from her. I cup her face and flip her onto her back.

Placing a kiss to her nose, I breathe, "You are not to worry about the Alliance or what Nate is or isn't up to."

"Um-hm."

"Valentina," I say in warning.

"What? I heard you. I will not worry about Nate or the Alliance."

I groan. "Why do I have the feeling you will find a bloody loophole in that statement."

"You know I love it when your accent comes out. It's so sexy. I'm such a lucky girl. A British-Italian mash up, who could ask for more?"

"You're avoiding the topic. Listen to me. I saw your face when you were watching her. I don't need you trying to start some Bella Mafia. Get that thought out of your head now, love. I swear down, I mean it, Val," I growl.

"Ooohh! Bella Mafia. I like how that sounds. Ellen doesn't seem the type though," she says, tapping a finger to her chin. "I'll have to toughen her up."

"Ellen has no idea who her husband truly is. You will stop whatever you are thinking this instant, *capisci? Cosa mi sono preso?*"

"What do you mean, what have you gotten yourself into?" she says in Italian. "I've been behaving. Don't act like I haven't been on my best behavior. I haven't even cocked a gun in a week."

"Really, *Tesoro?*"

She nods with all seriousness.

I burst into laughter. I love my wife. However, my gut tells me it won't be long before she finds herself in some trouble. I question moving to New York and allowing her to take the training job with Briggs.

As I'm lost in thought, she sits up and leans into my ear. "Stop thinking of ways to tame me and fuck me before the baby wakes," she whispers.

Val

I stare at my sleeping husband as I hold our daughter in my arms. There isn't a word in the dictionary to express the love I have for him. Which is why I won't sit back and ignore my instincts.

Roni would make the perfect hitter. Not this security guard or whatever they are training her to be. *What is it John wants to do with her?* Humph, I will train her to her full potential.

"Vita, your papa has no idea the lengths I'll go to, to protect this family. You will never know the losses of my past. He wants to play Don. I will play *Donna Suprema*," I say and kiss my daughter's nose as she coos up at me. "*La rabbia della morte* is just the beginning. This will be our new way."

CHAPTER THIRTY-SEVEN

No PDA

John

I thought I knew Roni, but I'm learning so much more about her with each hour we spend together. Like now, we're walking through the streets of Manhattan and I have a smile on my face as she eyes my hot pretzel. Normally, I would hold it to her lips and let her bite it, but that's not a Roni thing.

"You have no problem with me putting my mouth all over your body, but you won't eat from me," I say, trying not to laugh.

She shrugs. "It's different."

"Why'd you say you didn't want one when clearly you do?"

"It didn't look good until you got one."

"Brat."

"Whatever."

I break a piece of the pretzel that I haven't bitten off of and hand it to her in a napkin. She takes it with a smile that lights up her entire face. A smile that I want to consume with my own lips.

I lean in to kiss her, but she ducks me. I wrinkle my brows and watch her closely. "What?"

She looks up through her lashes and bites down on her lip. I drop my eyes to her mouth, and she frowns, those lip lines becoming more pronounced. Licking my own lips, I meet her gaze again.

"I'm not into PDA."

My brain farts for a moment because she can't mean what I think she does. With the right person, I can be very affectionate. With her I crave it.

"What do you mean?"

"I don't do public displays of affection," she replies.

My expression turns to shock. "You're serious?"

I watch as she searches her feelings. She lifts her shoulders, a nervous look in her eyes. However, I don't press her. I'm willing to adjust.

"John, I'm trying, okay. This just isn't in my comfort zone. It feels like something that never has been for me."

Bumping her with my shoulder, I wink at her. "I'm not complaining. I can adapt. Maybe someday you'll be okay with me mauling you anywhere."

"You sure it's okay?"

"Once your little visitor is gone are you willing to let me cuff you to my bed and fuck you all night?"

"Dude, for real?" She barks out a laugh and tosses a napkin at me.

I laugh with her. "You're laughing, I'm serious as a heart attack."

"I know you are, with your nasty ass," she smirks at me. "I'm afraid to find out all the shit you're into."

Leaning into her ear, I whisper. "We. All the shit we're into. It's you and me now."

Roni

His words make butterflies take off in my belly. Again, I curse my period and it's shitty timing. Today, I'm more pissed off than embarrassed.

It's you and me now.

Why do those words make me feel so giddy inside? His eyes say so much as he looks down at me. I want to let my guard down and be cool with this, but there's a nagging voice in the back of my head telling me not to get too close.

I know it's crazy. This man went to get me pads, he washed my clothes and give me one of his shirts to wear today. Although he hasn't said the word boyfriend, I'm pretty sure that's who he's become.

"So, what else should I know, Angel?" he says breaking into my thoughts.

"What do you mean?"

It's like a lightbulb goes off and his eyes light up. "Tell me you will let me spoil you at least."

"Huh?"

"I want to take you somewhere. You can't tell me no once we're there. I can buy you whatever I want. You game?"

"Isn't there supposed to be a safe word between us?" He roars with laughter, causing people around us to turn and stare.

"We can discuss that later, but you should be thinking about it," he says through his laughter.

"Come on you," I say grabbing the front of his T-shirt to get away from all the stares.

We get a few paces up the block before I release the fabric. When I drop my hand to my side, John brushes the back of his against mine. I look up at him, and the smile on his face causes my cheeks to warm.

I nod to let him know the small gesture is okay. I can handle it. His smile broadens.

He gestures for me to follow him as he hails a cab. We jump inside the first one that stops for him. He pulls up an address on his phone and gives it to the driver.

I'm a little nervous and unsure about where he's taking me, but I trust John, so I sit and watch as the cars and buildings go by. When we pull up in front of a Ducati dealership, I turn to look at John with wide eyes. He can't be serious.

"You brought me here to do what?"

He reaches to stroke my hand. "I've been thinking. When Nate gave me your license, I was curious. He mentioned later that you took interest in the course.

"He took a guess that you knew how to ride and made sure to get your license with the motorcycle rating. When you came to Seattle, you went straight for a bike. You rode like it was second nature." He looks over my face. "You like motorcycles."

I never thought about it. When I needed a ride, I wanted something quick. I had gone for the bike without thinking. It was so second nature; I hadn't even thought about being licensed to ride or not. Honestly, I still wouldn't have given it a second thought if he didn't just bring it up.

I ride at the compound all the time. If I'm not in the gym, most times you can find me on the track. However, that doesn't mean I want him to buy me a freaking bike.

"John—"

He shakes his head. "Didn't I tell you once we were here, I'd buy you whatever I want?"

"You want to buy me a Ducati?"

"I'm going to buy you a Ducati. I want to see you smile and if I can't kiss you right now, then I'll spoil you instead. It will be as close as I can get to my own pleasure."

"Come on, man. Stop playing."

He laughs. "Get out of the car. I'm not playing."

I do as he says and an hour later, I have a custom bike being delivered at the end of the week.

CHAPTER THIRTY-EIGHT

Little Helper

John

Four and a half months later...

"Roni, I know you're upset. Baby, I'm sorry. I promise to make it up to you. Call me back. You can't ignore me forever." I sigh and end the message.

I get it. This is the fourth time I've had to cancel on her. I haven't been to New York in months. With all that's going on, Dad has needed me to pick up some of the slack. I've had three bounties today alone.

The first two were simple. This last one, I can feel it in my bones I'm going to have to get my hands dirty. This guy is a real shitbag.

And still, all that's on my mind is my girl. I miss her face. Seeing it through a computer or phone screen isn't enough.

Knowing that she sleeps in my bed every night and I'm not there drives me crazy. Once Torque turned eighteen, they moved into my apartment in New York. However, every time I try to head to New York something gets in the way.

Now, she's ignoring my calls and I'm ready to say fuck it all and go to New York to see what the hell is going on. I push out of my car grumbling to myself. This is some straight bullshit.

"You ready now?" Ryan asks as he leans against the roof of the car.

I nod. "Yeah, let's get this over with."

"All right, all right, all right, let's get us a scumbag today," Ryan chants.

"Your bitch ass better not make us chase you," I mutter to myself as we come up on the house we've found Baron Jones at.

Sure enough, we're on our way into position not even ten feet from the house when the door swings open. Baron comes out with a cigarette hanging out of his mouth as he laughs over his shoulder and calls something into the house. As soon as he turns and lands his gaze on me and then bounces to Ry, he lets the cigarette fall from his lips and takes off around the house.

I pull my taser gun and take chase, waving Ry to try to cut him off from the other side of the house. This dude isn't going to outrun us. He's about five packs a day out of shape.

I stop at the back of the house and flatten against the washed-out siding. The sound of grunting sends me into action. Apparently, Ryan moved faster than I expected.

When I peek around the corner with the taser aimed, the mix of emotions that runs through me almost makes my head explode.

"Roni, what the fuck?"

"Not now," she snaps back at me.

Roni takes this dude, twice her size, down so fast I think my head spins. She sends a hand into Baron's throat before she spins and kicks him in the gut. He stumbles back but shakes it off and tries to charge her.

Roni fucking runs up his chest, locks her legs around his neck and spins so they both rotate as she takes him to the ground. I don't get to blink as she pulls cuffs and slips them on his wrist. She then sits on his back, looking up at me expectantly.

"Really, Roni?"

"You know her?" Ryan says as he comes around the corner.

"Yeah."

Baron grunts. "Get this bitch off me."

Roni pops him upside his head. "Watch your mouth."

I pinch the bridge of my nose as she stands, moving out of the way for Ry to lift Baron to his feet as he eyes her suspiciously. Roni, on the other hand, completely ignores Ryan and the prick that's hurling curses at us all. Her attention is fixed on me.

"What are you doing here?"

"The kid has gotten good at tracking." She shrugs.

I throw my hands up. "That's not even what I meant. Wait, Torque tracked me?"

"Isn't that what I just said?"

I point a finger at her. "Don't even. Is he here with you?"

"No, he made this cool shit. It's like the ear comms from the Toy Cop academy, but better. I think he's found his calling—"

"*Roni*," I drag out.

She tilts her head to the side. "I thought you'd be happier to see me."

I close the gap between us. "You just show up on a dangerous bounty out of the blue. You cuff a guy twice your size. Hold on… where did you get the cuffs."

She pats my cheek. "Always be prepared." She winks at me.

I narrow my eyes at her. I don't know whether I want to kiss her or spank her. As my anger starts to wane, I'm leaning more toward kissing her senseless.

"By the way, I'd like my cuffs back, dude," she calls over her shoulder to Ry.

"Who are you?"

Roni turns to look Ry over before she turns back to me. She has a little pout on her lips as she looks up at me. I go to reach for her, but stop, remembering her PDA rule.

"What?" I say gently.

"He looks like you. Your brother, right?"

I nod. "Yeah, the youngest."

"And he doesn't know about me." She nods and moves to walk around me.

I reach to stop her, but Ry's words halt me. "Excuse me, but we're still on a job here. Thanks, by the way." He looks between the two of us and gives me a shit-eating grin.

"Yeah, whatever," Roni says as she keeps moving.

"Roni," I call after her.

"Handle your business. I know where you live."

I stare after shaking my head. What the hell just happened? Rubbing the back of my neck, I mutter to myself.

"Damn, she has some guns on her. Nice ass too," Ry quips.

I turn to him slowly and glare. Yeah, Roni has a tight chiseled body. Not overly done, but you can see her dedication to her training. Her arms are one of her assets that draw the eyes, and that ass and those thighs are another, but I can't help feeling possessive as Ryan's words ring through the air. He's my little brother, probably closer to Roni's age than I am.

He lifts a hand up in surrender. "You ready to get out of here before someone comes out of that house or something?" Ryan says.

"Shit, yeah. Let's go."

Roni

I have this feeling in my gut that tells me I never should have come here. Okay, maybe I shouldn't have popped up on John the way I did, but I'm tired of him canceling on me. I wanted to come in person to see if maybe things have changed.

"Did you break into my home? How did you disarm the alarm?"

I look up to find John leaning against the wall with an amused smile on his face. He looks sexy in the bulletproof vest and cargo pants. I tried to ignore that fact when I first saw him earlier.

I don't know. Something about his bounty badge, the cuffs, gun and other gear are a turn on. I bite my lip as I get lost in my fantasies.

He pushes off the wall and starts into the room. As if he's a magnet, I stand and move toward him. He cups my face and looks down at me.

"You didn't answer the questions, baby."

"Yes, I broke in. Torque handled the alarm."

He crushes his lips to mine almost as soon as the words are out of my mouth. I groan and lock my fingers into his hair. My period has come and gone this month.

There's nothing stopping us from doing this this time. Not unless he doesn't want me anymore. There is an ache in my chest as I think of how that could be a reality.

"God, I've missed you," he says against my lips and the tightening in my chest loosens.

"Then why didn't you bring me here yourself?" I say as I finger the stubble on his face.

His brows wrinkle. "I don't know why I didn't think of it."

"Could it be the same reason you didn't tell your family about me?"

He takes a step back and folds his arms over his chest. "Babe, I haven't seen you in months. We can fight or you can let me shower and feed you. Then we can make up for last time."

"I'm not trying to fight. I just find it weird that you've never once mentioned me to your family."

He reaches for the back of my neck and draws me into him. "I've talked to my dad about you. The rest of my family has had their own shit going on. Trust me, I think about you all the time."

He plants a soft but firm kiss on my lips. "I guess I never thought to fly you in before because, again, things have been crazy, and I know you don't like weddings." He grins down at me. "I'll be leaving for one in Ireland the day after tomorrow. My brother's throwing a huge engagement party tomorrow night. I'd love for you to be my date."

"Yeah, not going to happen." I snort.

"You see. I knew that would be your response. I knew you wouldn't want to get involved in any of the shit I have going on. That doesn't mean I haven't missed you like crazy."

I give a little smile. "You could do better at showing it."

His face gets serious. He bobs his head. "You're right. I'm sorry. Let me take a shower and I'll make up for my fuck up."

I roll my eyes. "Yeah, okay."

He kisses me once more before releasing me and starting to take off his vest. His black T-shirt clings to his chest and biceps. I try not to ogle him as he goes, but I can't help it.

"Baby, as I matter of fact, there are some menus in the drawers in the kitchen. The one next to the sink. Pick something and order. I'll eat whatever you get," he calls tiredly.

I chew on my lip feeling a little bad about dropping in without warning. I walk to the kitchen knowing that all the things I had planned to do and say aren't going to happen tonight. He's exhausted.

My thoughts turn to all the dirty talking he does over FaceTime and the phone. I'd planned to see if he would make good on it. A girl can take but so much talk.

"Ugh, fine," I mutter to myself.

I'm not going to pounce on him tonight. Although I make no promises for tomorrow. Those kisses were as heated as I remember.

Touching my lips, I smile. I shake off the silly feelings stirring inside and go to call for some pizza. I make the call quickly, ordering a few sides in case John is extra hungry.

Now that I'm more relaxed. I move around his place, taking it in. He has so many pictures. I noticed earlier that his brother looks so much like him. Looking at the pictures around his home, it's clear all of his brothers favor him. However, John is the pretty one of the bunch. Not that the others aren't gorgeous. John simply has a softer face.

Suddenly, an idea pops into my head. We have some time before the food arrives. I toe off my shoes and get ready to follow in the direction I saw him go.

The ringing of the doorbell stops me in my tracks. I wrinkle my brows. That's sort of fast to be our food.

I pad my way to the door. When I open it, there's a girl standing on the other side. Her eyes fix on me and her lips pinch.

"Who are you? Where's John?"

Folding my arms over my chest, I glare at her. "Who are you?"

"Missy, John's girlfriend."

I rock back on my heels. My father and my mother's voices play in my head. *Trust no one. Be smart.*

They may be from dreams and pieces of memories, but my parents were right. The bitter truth burns right through me. This is why he never offered for me to come to see him.

Acid rises from my stomach. I'm the world's biggest fool. Here I am chasing after some guy and he's been playing me all along.

"Baby, what did you order? I'm starving." John's voice booms through the house.

Quickly, I double back for my shoes, not bothering to slip them back onto my feet. Ignoring the blonde at the door, I storm out past her. She can have him.

John

I frown when Roni doesn't answer me. She should be able to hear me from here. Rubbing the towel through my hair, I head for the living room where I expect to find her.

Instead, I come to a halt as I find Missy sitting on the couch with a tear stained face. My mind is spinning as I turn in a circle to look for Roni. My heart sinks because I know she's gone.

"Fuck," I bellow.

"Who is she?"

"What did you say to her?"

Missy wraps her arms around her middle and looks at me like a kicked puppy. My head is ready to explode. I turn back for my bedroom to get dressed.

I have to stop Roni before she gets on a plane and leaves. With the trip to Ireland and Toby's wedding, there's no way I can go after her once she's gone.

"Who is she?" Missy screams.

I turn to her with my brows drawn. "You need to leave."

"I want to know who she is?"

"Why the hell are you here? Why would you come to my home this time of night?"

Her face turns red. "Are you sleeping with her?"

"Un-fucking-believable," I hiss. "Who I do or don't sleep with is none of your business. What the hell did you say to her?"

"I've been so patient. I've given you time and space. I thought that was what you needed so we could get back together."

I look at her like she's lost her mind. I don't have time for this. I turn back to get dressed. I'm losing time with each second I spend here arguing with this nut.

I toss on a pair of jeans and a T-shirt. Why can't anything ever be easy for me? While in the shower I had been thinking of how right it felt to have Roni here in LA with me.

She was right, I should have brought her out to spend time with me. I don't know, New York sort of became our place. I never allowed myself to think about bringing her here. Now, I feel so stupid and at the same time, I know the real reason why.

I rush from my bedroom with my phone in my hand. I'm about to call Felix to get him to help me out when something catches my eye on my kitchen floor. I stumble to a stop.

"Son of a bitch," I breathe.

"John," Missy calls out weakly from the pool of her own blood. She has slit her wrists with one of my kitchen knives.

I rush to call 911 instead. In the back of my mind, I know I'm not going to get to stop Roni from leaving. I have this sinking feeling in the pit of my stomach.

Fuck me.

CHAPTER THIRTY-NINE

Distance

John

"I just want to know how she is," I say into the phone as I pace the edge of the wedding tent.

It's been five days since Roni disappeared from my place and Missy tried to kill herself in my kitchen. Five days that I've had to put on a smile that I don't feel.

Roni won't answer my calls or text. Between the engagement party, flying to Ireland, the two days we've spent with family leading to the wedding and the wedding, I've felt like I'm spinning in a tornado. I know the shit that's being torn up outside of all of this, but I'm helpless to do anything about it.

"She's doing well, mate," Uri says. "She's been working security for Val, but she and the lad have moved back into the compound."

I close my eyes and groan. I had a feeling she would move out of my place. Although I'd been holding onto a little hope.

"Thanks, Uri. I appreciate this."

"Anytime. You know we'll be heading across the pond for a bit, but I don't think she's coming along."

"Okay, I'll keep that in mind."

I hang up and stare down at my phone. Without giving it much thought, I send another text. If only I knew what Missy said to Roni.

"Nephew," Uncle Ronan croons. "What about ye?"

I look up from my phone and stop pacing. The wedding is pretty much over. A glance around tells me that Toby and Kamara have finally taken off.

"Hey, Uncle Ronan."

My tone sound dry to me. Something I've been trying to work on. I've tried. I even got in on ribbing Brax, but my mind is half here. While the rest of the family has been laughing and telling jokes, I've been calling and sending unanswered texts.

"I know ye better than that, lad. What's going on? We don't have enough rope around here for you to truss up one of these birds."

That brings a genuine smile to my lips. "Fuck off," I scoff.

"Aye, there's me nephew." He smiles. "Your brothers have all disappeared. That means you have to spend time with yer ol steamin' uncle."

"You drunk? It looks like you're just getting started," I tease.

He pats my face. "See this is why yer one of my favorites. I have a baldy notion. Come on, take a dooter with me."

I groan. Uncle Ronan and his bright ideas usually mean trouble. I'll take a walk with him, but I'm sure nothing good will come out of it. When he saunters over to the bar and grabs a bottle of whiskey, I know I'm right.

He nods over his shoulder for me to follow him and I do with a sigh as I take one more glance at the unanswered texts on my phone. I tighten my jaw and shove the phone in my back pocket. A number of times I've calculated the flight to New York and back, knowing there's no way I can make it and still be here for my little brother.

However, he's taking a two-day honeymoon before we head to Africa. Maybe… I sigh. Yeah, this is going to take more than the few hours I can squeeze out.

"What's going on with ya? What's on yer noodle?" Uncle Ronan asks as we get a few yards away from the wedding tent.

I blow out a breath. "I got mixed up with this crazy chick. She might actually be stalking me, now that I think of it. Long story short. I found… fuck it. I found *the one*. Her situation is a bit complicated, but we've sort of moved things to the next level—"

"Aye, that's my boy."

"Wind your neck in, Uncle Ronan. That's not what I mean. We've gone from friends to giving things a shot.

"There's just a ton going on in both of our lives. She dropped in on me a few days ago and while I was in the shower, the other girl came by and… I have no fucking clue what happened. When I came out my girl was gone and the nut job I can't seem to shake was there.

"I don't even want to get into the rest. I'm here, my girl is in New York and I have a sick feeling in my stomach that by the time I go to fix this I'm going to be totally fucked," I grumble.

"Next time ya tell me to be quiet, I'm going to cobbler ya."

I snort. "That's all you got out of all of that?"

"Naw, I got the rest. Jesus, Mary, and Joseph. Ye've got yerself into a pickle, ye have. Ye be planning to head to Africa with Toby, aye?"

"Yeah, I want to make sure it all goes smoothly."

He takes a swig from the bottle of whiskey and hands it over to me. I take a drink and wipe the back of hand across my mouth. Staring up at the sky, I can't help wondering what Roni's up to. If Val has taken her under her wing and she's doing security for her, I know she's financially sound.

Not one of the accounts or cards I've given her have been touched in the last five day. She's making her own money the way she wants. At least working for Val, Roni shouldn't accidentally run into her past.

"Well, it seems like yer already in the steamer. I say handle the situation with yer brother. As soon as that's over ye take yer ass after yer girl."

"Yeah, that's the plan."

My stomach churns because nothing is ever that simple for me. I have emails and messages from some detective in regards to Missy's suicide attempt on my phone. I'm going to have to call in a favor on that one. Given Missy's history, I can get this dick to back off and stop calling once I talk to a few people I know in the department, but I'm not naïve enough to think that will be the end of it.

"Anything worth having is worth fighting for. If the lass is willing to put up with ya and all yer kinky shit, she's a keeper."

I stop and take another drink before turning and handing it back. "Okay, how do you even know about any of that?"

"Ya mum can't hold water under a bridge. Me sister tells me everything. I honestly think she's proud of ya." He snorts a laugh and takes a drink. "Besides, remember that one summer I came to visit, and I got your father so luggered he slept half the next day?"

"Yeah, me, Wyatt, and Noah went to that party. Oh shit, that's the night I tied up and gagged Ali Stokes."

"Ya tied a fine knot, lad and I was impressed to see the butt plug. Don't worry, I stumbled into the pool house and right back out." He waves his hand at me dismissing the look of horror on my face.

I burst out laughing. The shit I did to that girl at eighteen is mind blowing. She was two years older and loved it. I had to beat her off with a stick for the rest of the summer.

"You know. I don't think I'll have to give any of it up, but I would if she wanted me to. That's how I know she's the one. I'm willing to wait for her to get a handle on her shit if I have to," I say more to myself.

Not that Roni has allowed everything she's been through to ever get in between us. It's been the opposite. She's allowed space for me. I've gotten to know her in ways I know she hasn't permitted others to. I can't lose that.

Uncle Ronan places a hand on my shoulder and looks me in the eyes. "Ye'll sort this out. Yer a Black. I watched yer dad chase my sister until she was his. Cass didn't make it easy for him at all. Now look at them. One can only hope to find that type of love," he says, his brows creasing for a bit.

"Come on, lad. I feel like a dip in the pond."

I chuckle. "I'm going to call it a night."

"Aye, yer in love."

Everyone knows the pond is a hook up spot for an after party. I'm not drunk enough for that shit. The women down around there are not my type anyway.

CHAPTER FORTY

Framed

John

"Have a seat, Mr. Black. I only want to talk to you," Detective Louis says as if this isn't my damn house to begin with.

I have a headache from grinding my teeth so much. I wanted to be on a plane to New York the moment we returned from Ireland and the short trip to Africa. No such fucking luck.

Apparently, Missy has been telling the police she doesn't remember slitting her own wrists this time. Her timing with this shit is impeccable. Someone's out to fuck with my family, trying to frame Nellie for murder.

It's all bullshit, no body, no real evidence, but it's not the time for me to call in favors for an alleged attempted murder when my sister-in-law has been accused of murder as well. Not to mention, I'm not trying to drag my family into this. They have enough going on.

Mom is going to kick my ass when she finds out about all of this anyway. Seeing how she handled Toby's secrets, I know I should have said something by now. Despite the baby not making it, it's something she would have wanted to know.

"How can I help you detective?" I say as I lean against the wall. "I'm not sure what I can tell you for the third time."

He takes a seat on my couch, making himself at home. I don't like this prick. There's something smug about him.

"Your record as a bounty is outstanding. Never any incidents. Always clear cut and by the book. You don't get that often. You guys like to play cowboys since you don't have to follow the rules," he says as he looks at me and my defiant stance.

I nearly flip him the bird. I don't have time for this shit, but I keep my mouth shut. The sooner this is over with, the sooner I can help clear Nellie's name and then get the fuck out of here to save my relationship with my girl.

"Is there going to be a point here?"

"Tell me, John. If your girlfriend slit her wrists in your kitchen, why would you get on a plane two days later as if you could care less?" he says, leaning forward in his seat as if he's got me by the balls.

"Your first mistake. Missy isn't and hasn't been my girlfriend in over two years. Actually, she was never really my girlfriend to begin with. She was someone I was fucking.

"My brother's wedding was already in the plans. I wasn't going to miss it because Missy decided to show up at my place unannounced to try to fuck up my life," I bite out.

He tilts his head to the side, the beaming smile on his face telling me he thinks he's found something. "You feel like Ms. Hollis is fucking up your life. So, you're angry with her then? She caught you cheating, and you wanted to handle the problem? Knowing her history, a fake suicide would solve all your problems, wouldn't it?"

I go to open my mouth, but my father's voice comes booming through the house. "This bullshit comes to an end here. My son placed the call that saved Ms. Hollis's life. He also accompanied her to the hospital to ensure she received the proper care, both physically and mentally before he left.

"The lass is unstable in the head. You're wasting all of our time with this. As John said, we had plans to attend his brother's wedding. He fulfilled all his obligations and had every right to go on with his own personal life. I've talked to your captain; I think you best be calling in," Dad says as he stops beside me and folds his arms across his chest.

Detective Louis frowns and stands. He takes his phone out and his face turns white as a sheet. I instantly know the calls and questions I've been getting over the last two weeks since I've been back from Africa are going to stop.

"You have a good day," I call out as the pissed off detective storms out of my house.

I don't even bother seeing him out. My father places a hand on my shoulder and gives it a squeeze. Turning to look at him, I sigh.

"How did you find out?"

"One, you've been missing Sunday breakfast. That's not like you. Second, your mother has an emotional GPS on the lot of you. She knew something was going on and asked me to look into it. I stumbled across the investigation after a few calls."

"Do you want to talk about what's going on? I called to check in on your friend. Nate says she's working for the Donatis, but she refuses to even mention your name," Dad says.

"Fuck," I growl. "It's this shit with Missy. Not only is she trying to frame me for her fucking suicide attempt, she said something or did something to Roni while she was here to see me. I haven't been able to go after Roni with everything that's going on and she won't take my calls," I grumble in frustration.

"We'll handle things here. Why don't you take off to see if you can fix things?" He suggests.

"I can't. I promised Wyatt I'd help him get to the bottom of this bullshit with Nellie."

Dad releases a heavy breath. "Sometimes I think we put too much pressure on you to be there for everyone else. Your brothers are big lads. They can take care of themselves. I'm sure Wyatt would understand if you took off."

"He might, but I wouldn't feel right. There's the baby and this bullshit with Nellie. The cops may be backing off, but we still need to know where this came from. I think the last thing I should do at this point is separate from the family.

"Something doesn't feel right. Trust me, I would go if this feeling wasn't so strong. It's like the storm has just begun to brew," I say as my thoughts turn.

"Aye." He sighs, sounding as frustrated as I feel. "You have a point. It's like we get over one obstacle and the next one comes knocking without giving us a breath."

Dad walks over to the couch and takes a seat. He pushes his hands into his hair. It's clear all of this is starting to weigh on him. First Nellie's kidnapping, then Toby's little family of secrets, now all of this.

"Don't worry about me," I say.

He snorts. "When you have a lot of your own, I want you to repeat that to me. I worry about you all. I want to see you happy. That was starting to happen while you were taking those trips."

"Yeah, well, I'm going to have to work extra hard to get through to her once I can get there. It's not like I haven't been trying to call and text," I say as I move to take a seat beside my dad.

"Women are never easy to win over. You have no idea what I had to go through to win over your mother. And when she realized I had plans to move her away from her family, I thought she was going to put my eyes out with a hot blade." He gives a small chuckle.

Tossing my head back against the couch, I turn to the side to look at him. Dad sags back into the cushions too, looking tired. He rubs his eyes before folding his arms over his chest as if he's about to take a nap.

"How about I start the grill? I have some steaks. It's been a while since it's been just me and you. I'd like it if you stay for a bit," I say.

"You had me at steaks. I'm going to sit here and take a nap before your mother calls fussing about you lads. It's becoming an everyday thing." He laughs.

"Take all the rest you need."

CHAPTER FORTY-ONE

Over Him

Roni

"You're feeling like you're losing control again," Val says as she sits beside me by the pool at her estate. She reaches to run her hand over the shaved left side of my hair.

I don't know what I feel. The hair thing was a moment of frustration. I only did the one side before I pulled myself together.

I shrug at Val. "I guess so."

"If you ask me, the hair looks good on you. Makes you look more dangerous," she says.

I turn to her and she has a smile. I don't know when, but I've come to feel safe around this woman. I trust her.

I knit my brows. "What if I wasn't dangerous in my old life? What if I was some timid, shy girl everyone walked over? Will I be able to go back to that when I remember who I am?"

"I'd say fate stepped in. You were never meant to be timid or shy. Who you really are is in your eyes. I think once you find what you're looking for, you're going to be a force to be reckoned with," she says.

I nod as I stare off into space. Everything has changed, but so much remains the same. None of the memories that have surfaced are enough to piece together. We're no closer to finding Natasha, if she's even still alive.

"You carry the weight of the world on your shoulders." I turn to Val as her words pull me out of my head. "I don't know what happened between you and John. I can't say I know him well, but what I do know is things aren't always what they seem. It's important to have all the facts before you make a decision."

I snort. "We were never meant to be more than friends. I was reaching for something I have no right to and I got burned. I have someone counting on me. Chasing after John was only a distraction," I reply.

"Maybe, maybe not. There's something about the way you two are together. Don't be so quick to give up."

Her words sting. I'm no quitter, but I know when to protect me. When it comes to John, I need to guard myself with all I am.

My heart still feels like someone dragged it over a cheese grater. That pretty blonde looked more like his type. Barbie and Ken in the flesh.

Val reaches for the braid resting on my right shoulder. "Maybe John will be into the whole Viking thing you have going on," she teases. She sombers up. I've never seen her look so sad. "My world could be crashing down around me, Roni. I could be losing everything. If he means that much to you. Give him a call. Don't waste precious time."

"Is there anything I can do to help?"

She shakes her head. "Uri will take care of it. My husband has never broken a promise to me. I'm just letting fear get the best of me."

"Yeah, I can understand that."

"Tell me. Is fear what's keeping you from calling John?"

I look at her and think over the question. I'm hurt. A part of me thinks it's because I know that girl has probably satisfied John in ways I wouldn't know how.

Forget all the kinky shit. I don't know if I'd be any good at the basics. I shrug my shoulders.

"Can I tell you something without you judging me?"

She narrows her eyes at me. "Of course, you should already know this."

I chew on my lip for a second. "I believe I'm a virgin. No, I know I am."

Her mouth drops open. I can see the wheels turning in her head. A slow smile turns her lips up.

"I see the problem. This we can fix."

"What?"

She waves a hand. "I was a virgin when I married. Uri was a good teacher, but I learned a few things from the girls. Tonight, we call them over and we'll teach you and my little sister a few things.

"She's been taking my advice to seduce Luca. This will be perfect. All of the ladies could use a distraction. What better way than to teach you two how to give a great blow job," she says.

I choke. "Pardon me?"

"Today me and the girls teach you how to fuck, tomorrow we go to the spa. The two of us," she says as if it's a shopping spree and pamper day.

She continues as if it's nothing. "I don't know how those Irish-Scots do it, but we Italians know how to pamper. We'll have a day on my husband. I'm going in to call the girls."

She laughs and the sparkle returns to her blue eyes. Patting my shoulder, she gets up and returns to the house. I'm left shaking my head, confused by what just happened.

Working for Val doesn't seem like working some days. I'm not complaining. I make damn good money, but I feel like I'm hanging with a friend, not working security. Uri has his own men that guard the family. I know Val only hired me because she knew I wanted to make money of my own.

I get up and stretch, catching one of Uri's men eyeing me in the two-piece bikini I have on. I scowl at him and snatch up a towel to cover myself. Grabbing my gun and holster, I strap it back to my thigh before collecting my phone and following the path Val took to enter the house.

She and Uri are playing with Vita. They make such a gorgeous family. In this moment, you would never know the man and woman sitting before me are trained killers.

Placing a hand over my belly, I grimace. I'd probably make a terrible mother. That is if I ever find someone to want me.

Don't sound so desperate.

I push those thoughts away. Dreams of a life like Val's will get me nowhere. Right as I have that thought, my phone buzzes in my hand. God, why haven't I replaced this thing.

Because you want to know if he'll keep calling, estúpida.

CHAPTER FORTY-TWO

Baby Sis

Roni

"You should always be in control. Allow him to think he is, but you're always topping mentally," Pam says.

"You got that right," Paige says.

"Always. Be. Teasing," Val says, purposely spreading her legs one by one in a seductive way. Leaning forward, she places a forearm on her thigh and licks up one side of the popsicle in her hand as she locks eyes with me. She then takes the ice into her mouth and slurps on it.

"I think you just made my nipples hard," Pam says, fanning herself. She laughs and falls back against the couch next to her twin.

I pull my arms from my sleeves and wrap my middle beneath my shirt. Val gets up and comes to sit beside me. I keep my eyes on the floor as I process everything that's been going on for the last hour.

"Relax," she says in my ear as she strokes my braid. "They have become friends. I wouldn't bring you around anyone I don't trust."

I nod as I lift my gaze to look around Pam's living room at the women Val calls friends. We are sitting here chatting and cutting up while their children are upstairs with the nanny Val called in. This is not my world.

Nate's wife and her twin are no nonsense, but friendly just the same. I guess Pam and Paige are cool. Rita and Marie seem to be besties. They have made me feel welcome, but I haven't decided if I'll fuck with them yet.

Rita used to be in my shit during training, so I'm on the fence as to whether I want to be friends with her or not.

My gaze falls on Val's sister. A lighter version of her. Shannon looks as out of place as I feel, but not because she doesn't belong. She looks nervous and unsure of herself.

Me, I can't recall ever having girlfriends. I've been trying to find a single memory, but I've come up with pieces of lonely moments. Men standing around the room, my father at his desk, but never any friends.

So, this feels way out of sorts to me. These women are sharing so many intimate details as if they trust one another. That's a bit unsettling.

Pam bursts into laughter. "I don't know who's worse. Roni or Shannon."

"I was thinking the same thing," Paige says, holding a cucumber with a condom on it in her hand.

"Give them a break," Marie says, holding back laughter.

I already knew she was Jasper's wife and Jasper is Rita's cousin. However, I've come to learn Marie is also Paige's sister-in-law. Bobby's sister.

He still comes around the training facility. From what I'm told they have two other siblings. I've met Rita's husband Marcus a few times. Not that I care or paid much attention to the people in and out of the Toy Cop Academy.

"I'm going to be honest. Roni truly can't remember a thing about her past and here I am faking. I feel like shit, maybe it's time I tell Luca the truth."

"Good luck with that one," Pam snorts and takes a sip from her glass.

"Why are you lying to him?" I ask, trying my best to be friendly.

"Long story," they all say in unison.

Hey, I tried. *John would be proud of me.* Frowning, I chide myself when the thought pops into my head. I could care less what he thinks. With a pout, I cross my arms over my chest.

"Listen, we are all grown here. We gathered to teach you girls how to keep your men satisfied. Take what you want, leave what you can't bring yourself to do. Just know when you leave here, you're going to have the skills to turn any man out," Pam says with a smile.

Shannon ducks her head, grabbing my attention. She looks up through her lashes to Pam. "This is a little weird for me, but I'm game. If I want to learn from anyone, it's you."

The room falls silent for a second, before they all burst into laughter. Val bumps my shoulder and leans into my ear to whisper, "Pam used to date Luca. My sister is currently engaged to Luca," she says. "He may or may not have been obsessed with Pam at once, but he now knows I will kill him."

"Well, let's go then. I want you two to clean all this peanut butter off these bananas without leaving a single tooth mark," Pam says as she smears peanut butter on one banana and hands it to me.

Paige snorts. "Some men like a little teeth." Val and Rita chuckle. "What? I'm just saying. You have to learn your man."

"Yes, but let's not get anyone punched in the head on the first try, thank you very much."

I actually snort. I'd beat John's ass if he ever—well, not that I plan on going down on him. I start to shift in my seat, feeling like everyone's eyes are on me while also feeling like they can hear and see my thoughts.

"All right, Shannon," Marie hoots.

Looking over at her banana, I find it mostly clean. One thing I know for sure about myself, I'm competitive to a fault. I hate being outdone.

I take the fruit in my hand and stick it into my mouth. A few swirls of my tongue and a tight suction of my lips, the banana comes out clean—no bite marks, no peanut butter. When the room seems to be too silent, I look around at everyone.

They're all staring at me with their mouths open. Then Pam breaks into a wide grin. She leans in and holds her palm up.

"Now that's how you suck a dick. Girl, you don't need me with skills like that," she says and laughs.

"Ah, she can still learn to play with balls," Val teases.

CHAPTER FORTY-THREE

Won't Be Ignored

John

It's been over a month and three weeks since I've last seen or had contact with Roni. When my father announced the family would be coming to New York to stay with the Briggs for a while, I was sure this was my opportunity to finally see my girl and straighten this shit out.

We've been here for four days and I haven't set eyes on Roni once. I've sat through an entire concert that left the whole room charged with sexual energy with no release in sight. Me and Roni need to get our shit together before my balls fall off.

"Thanks for this, Uri. I know how against Val leaving here you were. This means a lot to me," I say as I stand with my arms folded across my chest.

We're standing on the training facility side of the compound, watching as two motorcycles race up the wide driveway heading for us. One carrying the woman I've been looking for.

"It is nothing. Valentina wasn't happy with not having Roni here with everyone else. She was going to drive me bloody crazy until I found a way to drag Roni here," Uri replies. "Good luck."

I grunt. I'm going to need it. Apparently, Roni took off the moment she learned I'd be here. Val made an excuse to head to the Donati residence for a few of the baby's things which meant she needed security. Roni was the one called in to make sure Val made it there and back.

I have a plan. After thinking this all over, I found the solution to all of our problems. It's a simple one I would have thought of sooner if I hadn't had so much going on.

"My sister respects you. It's the only reason she won't put you on your back," Torque storms over to growl at me. "But I don't have that problem. I'll kick your ass."

I pop him upside his head the way I would one of my little brothers and toss a palm into his chest, sending him stumbling back a few steps. He bends at the waist as he gasps for air. Moving in on him I glare down at him.

"You were saying?"

He's grown some more, at least an inch taller than me. I guess that's what made him so bold. I like the kid but I'm not in the mood today.

"Yeah, thought so," I grumble when he's too busy gasping to reply.

It's at that moment that the two bikes stop a few feet away from us. However, only one rider gets off. Val pulls off her helmet and shakes her hair out. Uri pats me on the back before moving to his wife and pulling her into a passionate kiss.

The other rider sits with her arms folded over her chest. Damn, she hasn't taken off her helmet and she still looks sexy as fuck. I clench my jaw when I realize she's not on the Ducati I bought for her.

When she takes off her helmet, I rock back on my heels. It's only been seven weeks, but so much has changed about her. Her hair is the first thing I take in. She has two small braids around her right temple. All the rest of her hair is braided into a larger braid that rests over her right shoulder. The tip of the hair has been bleached to a golden blonde.

However, the thing that makes it sexy is the left side that's shaved. My little warrior looks the part. My jeans grow tight as visions of her on her knees with my cock in her mouth and that braid wrapped around my fist fill my head. I tamp those thoughts down, we're a long way from that.

Oh, but she's testing me. Roni pulls a sucker from her back pocket and unwraps it, popping it in her mouth. The way she sucks and twirls it in her mouth pulls a groan from me.

She pulls it from her lips and points it at Torque. "What did you say to him?"

I turn to look at the kid. His face is red and he's scowling at me. I shrug.

"Nothing," Torque mutters and turns to go into the dorms.

"If he gets out of line come to me," Roni says as she climbs off the bike.

A small part of me registers the laughs coming from Val. Very small because Roni has the majority of my attention as she saunters toward me. I clench my fists as I take in her thick thighs that are revealed by her too short jean shorts.

She has a thigh holster on her right leg and black boots that stop at her lower calf on her feet. Lara Croft has nothing on Roni. The closer she gets, the more drawn I am to her.

When she reaches me, she pulls that lollipop from her lips, the purple coloring stains her mouth. "Hey, boss," she bites out, her lips pinching. "Just so you know this is my two weeks' notice. I'll never work for your ass."

With that, she taps my lips with her sucker and pops the sweet treat back into her mouth. She narrows her eyes at me as she rolls the pop with her tongue. Yeah, my girl is playing with some serious fire.

"Roni—"

She holds her hand up. "I ain't got shit to say to you."

As soon as the words are out of her mouth, she turns to follow Val and Uri into the facility's gym. I just about swallow my tongue when her back is to me. And it's not because of the shorts riding the crack of her big ass.

Her shirt is backless, tying at the neck and waist only. On full display is what looks like fresh ink. Her entire back is covered in the design. I'm seeing red so I can't think clearly enough to focus on making the tat out.

From this angle I can see the sides of her full perky tits that her shirt is doing fuck all to cover. This shit has my blood boiling and I'm ready to spank Roni's ass. Yeah, I'm over this.

I storm toward her and scoop her up over my shoulder without breaking a stride. She kicks and screams, but I ignore her, thinking of the most private place I can take her that's not too far away.

The armory comes to mind. I was in there not too long ago with Uri, checking on the Briggs's supply. Pulling the temporary staff card Thomas Briggs gave me and my brothers from my back pocket, I swipe it to gain entry.

"John, if you don't put me down," Roni growls.

I slap her ass, earning a punch to my ribs. I chuckle as it burns a little, but that doesn't stop me from slapping her ass again. This time I turn my head to lick the sting away.

Her gasp brings a smile to my lips. "If I drop you, it'll be your fault."

"If you put me down you won't drop me," she snaps.

Ignoring her protest, I move to one of the back cages. As soon as I step inside, the lights come up, illuminating all of the weapons and shelves with backlighting. I drop Roni on the island-like tabletop in the center of the cage, stepping between her legs before she can fight me. I grasp her face and crush her sexy mouth with my lips.

Taking my time, I suck and nip at her lips a few times before she starts to respond. Not wanting to disturb her tat as I see it's very fresh, I reach down to pop the button on her shorts and shove my hands into the back of them, palming her lush ass. Dragging her heat closer to the edge of the counter, I start to grind my erection into her. She whimpers into my mouth.

"I've missed you so much," I breathe against her lips.

The words must be like ice water to her. She breaks the kiss and starts to push at my chest. I try to seal our lips together once again, but she grabs me by the throat.

I narrow my eyes at her as she glares back at me. "Back off," she hisses.

I take a step back, folding my arms over my chest. She doesn't release her hold, but I'm okay with that. I lick my lips taking in the flavor from the grape sucker that got lost somewhere in our trip here.

"You have a lot of damn nerve. You come here and cost me my job. Then insist I come work for you. You have to be shitting me," she says with so much heat, her nostrils flare. "And please tell me what the hell makes you think I'll leave Torque behind?"

I step all the way back out of her hold. "This was the plan wasn't it? And I don't expect you to leave him behind. I guess Val didn't tell you everything. Torque will be coming with us."

"Fuck you."

Roni is fast, but I'm faster. I grab her by the arm and pull her from the table, spinning her and pinning her with my hips. She wiggles beneath me, but that only gets her an ass full of my cock pressing into her.

I lean into her ear. "You're forgetting a few things we talked about." I reach into her scrap of a shirt and cover her breasts with my palms. Slowly, I knead the plump flesh, pinching her nipples when she releases a soft moan. Fuck, she's ripe for the plucking. "You belong to me, Roni. There's nothing you can do to change that."

"I belong to no one."

I lick the shell of her ear, causing her to shiver. "You sure about that?"

"Eat shit."

"Very well, baby," I breathe.

I drop to my knees. With one hand I pin her in place and release her holster with the other. It falls to the floor with a thud.

"What are you doing?" she calls over her shoulder.

"Marking what's mine."

Swiftly, I pull down the zipper to her shorts and drag them and her panties down her legs in one quick motion. Biting my lip as her silky-smooth skin comes into view, I marvel at the sight before me. She can protest as much as she wants, I can see her juices soaking her folds.

I spread her cheeks and tease her puckered hole. She gasps and bucks her hips. Craning her neck to look over her shoulder at me, lust fills her gaze.

Leaning in, I graze my teeth across her butt cheek before I give it a hard slap. I move my left hand around her body to play with her clit. My fingers are soaked within seconds.

Roni turns away, her head dropping between her shoulders. She reaches to push my hand away. "Get your hands off me, John," she says in a weak protest.

"What did she say to you?"

"Who?"

She shoves some more at my hand strumming her center. This time she looks over her shoulder again while biting her lip. I apply more pressure.

"Missy. What did she say to make you doubt me?"

She scowls and gets ready to strike me. I slap her right globe before she can, causing her to convulse. A smile spreads across my face.

"Start talking," I command.

"She said she's your girlfriend," she says bitterly.

"Fucking bullshit," I growl, moving lightning fast to spread her cheeks and dive in.

A loud groan comes from my chest as I get my first taste. Roni's eyes darken as I keep my gaze locked on hers. I suck, lick, and devour her pussy.

My angel tries to hold onto her defiant look, but she quickly loses the fight. She collapses against the table in front of her as she starts to cry out. When I start to play with her asshole while eating and fingering her pussy, she begins to rock her hips against my face while she calls out my name.

Her pussy tightens around my fingers and I know she's so close to coming. That's when I back off, pulling my hands and mouth from her body. She lifts and twists to look down at me.

"Why'd you stop? I was so close?" she pants.

"I know, that's why I stopped."

"What the hell?"

I slap her ass and glare at her. "That's your first punishment for doubting me and believing that bullshit lie."

"Are you serious?"

Instead of answering her, I go in for a second round. This time she keeps her eyes on mine as I finger and feast on her. She's so gorgeous as her lips part and she looks at me with so much lust, it's as if I can feel it in my chest.

I palm her cheeks to spread them and lick her inner thigh before sucking the flesh into my mouth. I mean to leave my mark. Continuing to suck, I move my right hand back to her folds and push into her tight core again.

It doesn't take long before I have her on the edge. When she bites her lip and rocks her hips to chase her release, I give a crooked grin. Right as she throws her head back, I back off once more, snatching her climax from her grasp.

"John," she growls.

I swat her ass and watch it jiggle. "That's for ignoring me for almost two months."

Running my palms up her smooth thighs, I watch as goose bumps rise across her skin. When I reach the knot keeping the bottom of her shirt in place, I tug the scrap of fabric free. The ties at her neck are next as I start to stand to my feet.

Tossing the so-called shirt to the side, I drag my body against hers. When I'm at my full height, I spin her and lift her onto the table. Wasting no time, I attack her sexy mouth to devour it and allow her to taste herself.

She moans and it drives me insane. Pressing a hand between her breasts, I push her back. I grab her left leg and toss it over my shoulder. With my eyes on hers, I squat and start to demolish her pussy once more.

"John," she cries out, reaching a hand into my hair.

She has no idea that I'm taking it easy on her even as I pull her soul from her body through her delicious pussy. She once again throws her head back in ecstasy. Freeing her of my mouth, I start to beckon her release with my fingers.

"You better not stop," she warns.

I lick my lips and smile. "My brothers and every other man here had their women put on a show for them. You weren't here, you denied me that pleasure. Do you really think you deserve to come?"

Surprising me, she sits up and leans down to grab me by the back of neck. She seals our lips together, but I take over the kiss like a desperate man. I deepen it as she gives as good as she's getting. Her plump lips are like a dose of heaven.

I'm so lost in the kiss, I almost let her come. Almost. I pull my hand back and grab her backside, bringing her to the edge of the table and into my throbbing cock.

She reaches for my belt, but I block her hands. "Your first time won't be in here," I say tightly.

"Excuse me?"

"I'm not taking you for the first time in a weapons bunker. When I do take you, it won't be like this," I say against her mouth.

She pushes at my chest. "Get this clear. I will choose when and where I want to lose my virginity," she says heatedly.

"Fine, but it won't be here and it's not going to be today," I say just as firmly.

She narrows her eyes, pushing me back as she hops from the table. I go to reach for her clothes, but my girl has other plans. She pushes me back against the wall of weapons behind me, my ass bumping into the short counter space.

She tugs my belt free and drops down before me. I'm thrown for a moment as the vision from earlier pops into my head. Her with her mouth around my cock and her braid fisted around my hand.

It's long enough for her to get me out my pants. She holds me in her palm, looking as if she's in awe. I'm a good eleven inches with more girth than the average dude, so I can't blame her. As if to check if it's real, she drags her tongue over the crown.

"Roni," I say, clenching my jaw.

She locks eyes with me as she slowly takes me into her mouth. I grind my teeth. The sight of her taking me in is perfect.

Roni

As I breathe through my nose, I stare up through my lashes at the man I'm giving pleasure to. John isn't a small man in any way. Watching him tower over me with his massive body and height is as much of a turn on as bringing him to his knees.

Oh, yes, I'm going to bring him to his knees. If he thinks he can *punish me* without consequence, he's sadly mistaken. He set the challenge and I plan to deliver.

"Shit," he growls as I bob along his thick length and reach for his balls.

I can see the flex of his chest and biceps through his fitted T-shirt. He shoves a hand into the front of his hair and tugs, tossing his head back. I continue to take him for all he's worth.

When he lowers his head and looks into my eyes, I grin around him. I bet he didn't see this coming. This is a lesson we'll both remember for a long time. I'm a quick study.

However, the real deal has me drooling a lot more than the banana I practiced on. John is super thick. A soda can comes to mind. Although that might be a bit of an exaggeration, but not by much.

Yet, I bob my head and use my hands as much as I can. He's slick from my saliva, aiding me with each pass. I'm actually enjoying this. Especially when he reaches to wrap my braid around his fist.

It's clear in his face that he's on the verge of losing control. He's trying to take it back, but I'm not having it. Relaxing my throat, I take him all the way in, my nose touching his pelvis.

I make a gagging sound, but I don't back off. I shake my head from side to side while caressing him with my tongue, pulling a roar from him. The sound vibrates through his body and the room.

I back off and repeat. Feeling him swell in my mouth, I think to stop, but Pam and Paige's voices ring in my ear. *You don't let up until you own him.*

I snatch his soul just as I was taught, crumpling him to the floor. His knees give and he drops, popping from my lips as he sprays my throat and my face with his hot seed. I look him in his bewildered eyes with a smile on my lips as I wipe his sticky cum from my face and suck my fingers into my mouth.

His face says it all. His cheeks are flushed and the hair around his temple is soaked. He looks both lost and determined. My pussy weeps for the pleasure it's been denied not once but three times.

I stand and start for my clothes. Using my shirt to clean my face of what I don't catch with my tongue. "Let's be clear. As long as I work for you, I'm not fucking you. That was just to show you what you fucked up," I say over my shoulder.

He roars with laughter from the floor. I don't turn as I get dressed for fear of the look in his eyes. I don't like the sound of that laugh, it's as if it's a challenge.

"Once again, baby. You are mine and I am yours," he says, making my heart twist. "But have it your way. When you're ready, I promise you will be begging me to have mercy. You will pay for what you just did."

I don't reply. I storm out with him laying right where I left him. His laughing trails behind me.

"I won't be ignored, Roni." Is the last thing I hear rumbling behind me through his laughter.

CHAPTER FORTY-FOUR

Your People

John

"I'm thinking about taking advantage of the gym tonight," Noah says. "Any takers?"

We're all sitting around a few tables in the dining hall of the training facility. We've had dinner and haven't moved from our seats yet. Nellie, Bean, Heather, and Kamara are chatting with Mom as Dad, my brothers, and I sit back, sipping a few beers.

Wyatt has Nora in his arms as she sleeps soundly through all our loud banter. Toby's twins took off with Nate after he offered to play them a movie in the theater. That made their night.

"I'll pass. This is my last beer too. I'm going to get Nellie and Nora to bed," Wyatt says, kissing the top of his daughter's head.

"I'm not a baby," Nellie says.

"But the way your lids have been drooping, you might as well be," Brax teases.

Nellie sticks her tongue out and waves him off. I snort and turn my gaze back to where it's been for the last hour. Or should I say on who it's been on. I've followed her every move.

"What are you looking at?" Ry says and tosses a napkin at me.

I haven't taken my eyes off Roni since she walked in with Uri, Luca, Shannon, and Val. Her group all came to join us, but Roni hung back, observing from a distance. She ate alone, not even Torque would enter her space tonight.

He trailed in not long after Roni and the others, but I watched him pile his plate high and leave the same way he came. I have to say, these trainees are spoiled rotten with the meals here. However, it's not the food I'm hungry for.

I'm pissed Roni would rather eat alone than come anywhere next to me. Especially when she looks the way she does. The leather looking skin-tight pants, top that exposes her belly, and stiletto heeled ankle boots have almost broken my restraint.

My mind keeps going back to earlier in the armory. I tighten my fist as I think of the lie Missy told her. Roni is the only woman I've wanted to claim as my girl in years. Not a Sub, my woman.

I narrow my eyes on her as she glares back. She's still pissed at me, despite me telling her the truth. I'll give her space to sort her feelings out. I know she's stubborn as fuck.

I'm waiting for her to come to me. That is until all of my family turns their attention to what I'm hungrily staring at. Roni pushes from the doorway she'd been watching us from and spins on her heels to leave.

"Oh, shit. That's guns," Ry calls out. "Wait, she's here?"

"Who?" Noah says.

Mom laughs as I rise and start after Roni. "Whoever she is, the two haven't been able to stop eye fucking each other."

"Oh my God. That's her. The girl from the wedding," Nellie gasps.

"Our wedding? Wait, that's Roni?" Wyatt replies.

"She's been to Cali to see him too."

"Mind your business, Ry," I call over my shoulder. I can hear the humor in his voice.

He's the one that sees everything. My relationship with Roni hasn't reached a place where prying from my family will help any, if at all. The less they know the better.

A mix of my brother's laughter follows me. "So, it is a woman," Noah says before I'm out of earshot.

Roni

I head downstairs and to the back of the grounds, in need of some fresh air. My mind is reeling. I'm trying to reconcile my assumptions with what I now know about John.

Thinking about Val, she and most of her friends are married to white men. Although I know a few of them are mixed themselves. However, I wasn't expecting to see John with his family and the Black women on the arms of at least three of his brothers.

They have little brown kids with them too. I can't help wondering if I would have felt so out of place at those weddings he invited me to. I step to the stone railing on the massive back deck.

Bending to lean against it on my forearms, I get lost in my thoughts and lift my head to stare up at the stars. I feel him the moment he steps outside. I hate that I always seem to sense his nearness.

John's scent tells me that I'm not mistaken in who has joined me. It's the first thing to envelope me. Stepping up behind me, he places his palms on the railing on either side of my elbows, causing his hips to nestle against my ass. Comfort and warmth settle over me immediately.

With a frown, I straighten and turn to face him. Placing a hand on his chest, I shove him back. He doesn't budge more than a few inches.

As if it's the most natural thing in the world, he cups my face and plants a kiss on my forehead. He remains silent, allowing his lips to linger before taking a step back and crossing his arms over his chest. I glare up at him.

"So that's your people?"

"Yeah, that's my family." He wrinkles his brows. "Why'd you take off? They don't bite."

"They don't know about me. You still haven't told them about me. Why would I come over there?"

I don't know why that bothers me so much. When his brother asked who I was that night in Cali, I was hurt. He's been coming to see me almost as long as I've been here, we'd been talking on the phone practically every day. I thought I meant enough for his family to know he had a girlfriend or whatever I was in New York.

He tilts his head at me. "How do you know I haven't?"

I mirror his stance, tipping my head to the opposite side. "Am I wrong?"

He shakes my head. Those golden eyes become more appraising than ever. Reaching for my hand, he goes to turn for the entrance back inside.

I tug my arm back. "What are you doing?"

"You want to meet my family. I'm taking you to meet them," he says, a grin on his lips.

"For what? I'm nothing to you. There's no need. Not anymore."

He turns on me and grabs the back of my neck, pulling me into him so fast I'm stunned. Our lips are pressed together as he inhales. Then he starts to devour my lips.

The taste of beer and barbeque ribs assaults my mouth. I whimper as he deepens the kiss and my belly tightens. I can't help clinging to his T-shirt. I want to growl when he breaks the kiss. I'm not in the mood for him to play with me the way he did earlier.

"I think it's time I make something clear for *you*. I don't have to be fucking you for you to belong to me. You need this wall, I'm allowing it, but when you learn to trust me again, all bets are off. Forget the bullshit that was said to you, Roni. You could never be nothing to me," he says against my mouth before nipping my bottom lip and tugging it.

I reach to lace my hand in the back of his hair and tug his head back. His eyes light up. I almost lose my train of thought at the sight.

I nip at his chin. "You're not allowing shit, John. If I have to go to California and work for you, fine. Maybe we can be friends. As for your family, they don't need to know me."

He gives me a crooked smile that's both sexy and mischievous. "You're going to need to know my family, baby. I now own a subsidiary of my father's firm, Black and Lock. We'll do what Dad has always kept in the shadows. From time to time, you will have to work with my family."

I purse my lips and tighten my jaw. Releasing my hold on him, I take a step away. The victorious look on his face makes me want to slap him. I'm not going in there to meet his family.

"Maybe some other time," I say.

He snorts. "What? You think all those white folks are going to make you feel out of place," he says with humor in his voice and eyes.

My mind goes back to my earlier thoughts. I look over John in his black T-shirt, khaki cargo shorts, and Jordans. A few of his brothers dressed similar to him.

"So, what? You all think you're woke or something. Y'all date Black girls to prove a point?"

"I thought we weren't dating," he says with that stupid smirk.

I flip him the finger.

"I love women. I've never stopped to think about what color the one I want might be. My brothers have been the same way. We like what we like. You assumed that my family and friends were all a bunch of white folks."

Okay, he's right. I did. I shrug. "Still don't want to meet them."

"Ouch. That hurts."

I look past John to see the brother I met in Cali with his hand over his chest as he mock winces. He must be the one that spoke. The other five brothers are all spread out posted against the house watching us. The four Black women and the small white lady with red hair inch out of the doors next, followed by a man that has to be John's dad. They all look like him.

I suck in a deep breath. I'm cornered. I don't realize I've taken on a defensive stance until the little redhead speaks.

"You can relax, love. We're not into laying boots to our boy's lasses." She pauses and frowns. "Well, the last one he brought around almost did get my boot to her ass."

My lips twitch. I think I like her already. John moves possessively close, but he doesn't touch me. As if having a mind of its own, my body leans toward him. I only catch it because the woman's eyes follow the motion.

"Ma, Dad, guys, I want you to meet Roni. My—"

"New employee. Looks like I'll be coming to LA to work with you guys," I say dryly.

John scoffs. "Yeah, she and her little brother will be working for me."

My heart swells when he refers to Torque as my little brother. He gets it when it comes to the two of us. Others have questioned my and Torque's relationship a time or two. Especially when we moved away from here together. Not Nate or the other bosses. Mostly the trainees that don't know how to mind their fucking business.

"Am I missing some shit here?" One of the two redhaired men says.

"I was going to tell you guys when this is all over, Brax." John sighs. "You know I've been wanting to do a little something of my own for a while. After talking to Dad, I realized this doesn't have to be something completely away from the family. The lease for one of the tenants in the Black and Lock building has expired and they're not renewing. I'm going to take the space and run my team there."

The biggest dude of them all— outside of the dad—gives a low whistle. God they are all fine as fuck. This one has a man bun, which normally isn't my thing, but it works on him. So does the beard.

"That feels like… why wouldn't you talk to us about it?" The brother that now has his arms wrapped around the short nerdy looking chick with the baby says.

"Come on, Wyatt. It's not like I'm going anywhere. I'll be in the office with you guys still. Think of it as Black and Lock expanding," John says.

The Wyatt guy grimaces. He looks a little hurt. Bun guy moves forward with his gaze locked on me.

"Noah," he says holding his hand out to me.

"Yeah, okay," I say, staring down at his hand.

He gives a full belly laugh. "Yeah, I like you already. Welcome to the family."

With that, he turns and wraps an arm around the waist of the tall chick with the strong nose. She's pretty, but that nose does make a statement on her face. She looks over her shoulder at me as Noah tugs her away.

The little woman moves forward. "I'm Cassidy Black. John's mum. Ye can call me, Cass," she says as she locks eyes with me. "We take care of our own. Ye'll learn that in time. We won't pressure ye. We have plenty of time to get to know ye and for ye to get to know us."

She turns to everyone that remains watching us. "Ye think ye fuckers never seen a skirt before. Leave John and his bird be. Let's go. Off with the lot of youse."

His dad is the last one standing as John's mother ushers the others away. He gives a nod. "Joe Black. John's father. It's nice to finally meet you, Roni. I've heard a lot about you from John and Nate. I look forward to have you on the team."

He gives one more nod and turns to places an arm around his wife's shoulders and leads her away. I'm left standing with my mouth hanging open. I'm so focused on the door they all retreated through; I jump when John wraps his arms around my waist from behind.

He leans in my ear. "Still think I told no one about you?"

"Whatever." I push his arms off me and make sure to sway my ass away.

I might forgive him. He doesn't need to know that yet.

CHAPTER FORTY-FIVE

It's Yours

John

Two months later...

"What are you thinking?" I say as I search Roni's face with my gaze.

She has been zoned out for the last few minutes. We've been standing on either side of my kitchen island, drinking wine, and grubbing on the oatmeal and raisin cookies my mother called Roni over to the house to pick up. It's clear Mom likes her. Something I've been secretly stoked about.

Roni blinks and looks into my eyes. "Nothing," she says.

I lean forward placing my hands on the island. She drops her eyes to my biceps and licks her lips. I grin.

It's been like this all night. We've been checking each other out, but I'm playing this cautiously. I know she's still pissed about Missy, but I haven't been able to keep my eyes off her tits in that sundress, or her ass.

The view is grand from any angle. I lick my own lips as I take another glance down at her breasts. Her skin is glowing and looks so damn soft.

"Lose something?" she says with teasing in her voice.

When she folds her arms under her chest, it only enhances the view, causing my shorts to tighten. My smile grows as I take my time lifting my gaze back to hers. Those lips. She has a full smile on them now.

"No, baby, I've found exactly what I need," I reply.

With a snort, she rolls her eyes and reaches for her glass to empty it. The little tease licks the drop of wine that spills onto her lip. I've been on this side of the counter to keep myself from reaching for her and taking her right here on this countertop.

Roni has only been here in Cali for a week, but this is the most content I've been in… ever. Well, for the most part. She has insisted on staying in a hotel since we arrived. I wanted her and Torque to stay here with me.

However, I've been living for these moments when it's just the two of us. I'm building the trust back between us. I want to believe it's happening slowly. I know the time lapse between what happened with Missy and me getting to New York are what allowed her anger to fester.

I get it. For Roni, I've grown a patience I've never known I was capable of. She's my peace, so I'm willing to do anything to keep that.

"Will you let me give you the tour tonight?"

"No."

I chuckle. "Why not? What's that about?"

I pour the last of the wine into her glass, happy to have her in my space anyway I can get her, for now. However, I'm not giving up just yet. She lifts the glass and swirls it before taking a sip.

Interesting.

I've noticed a few of Roni's natural habits. There's something refined about them. Second nature gestures and actions that speak of charm schooling, maybe. I don't think she notices when she does them.

This rough-edged Roni is a contradiction at times. Her tastes and knowledge of clothes, watches, cars, and even fine china have caused me to have Felix narrow the search for missing women that disappeared about the time Roni thinks she was taken.

I'm still looking for her friend, but I also want to find out who this woman once was. It's a gift I desire to give her. A freedom I think she needs.

"If I allow you to show me your home, you will try to draw me in deeper. I've told you, I'm not living with you," she says.

"You can have your own room."

She takes another sip of wine. "I already have my own room."

"In a hotel?"

She shrugs. "I'm looking for a place."

"Why? I have more than enough space here."

Placing her glass down, she stares at me. I wait for her reply as she folds her arms over her chest defensively. That fire is rising within her, but I'm ready.

"We can't always have what we want, you know that?"

"That depends."

"What?" She scoffs.

"If one is determined enough, they get what they want more often than not."

"And you're one determined motherfucker," she mutters. "John, I'm not moving in with you."

"You'd rather waste money on renting a place than live here rent free?"

"Bingo," she exclaims. "You do enough for me. Besides, I'm not your girlfriend. We need to keep that straight. Me living here will only confuse things."

"That bullshit right there shows you're already confused. We're not fucking, but we're together."

She smiles over the top of the glass she just lifted to her lips. "Yeah, whatever you say, Boss."

I bite my lip and groan. With a heated look, I nod. "You might finally be getting the point."

Her eyes widen. "You are a big ass freak. Seriously? Calling you that turns you on?"

We've talked about pet names and titles used in the life. We've also talked a bit about the Dom and Submissive roles. She knows exactly what she's doing when she calls me that.

"More than you know, gorgeous."

She looks at me pensively. Sucking her lip into her mouth. The wheels are spinning, I can tell.

"I'm not moving in and I'm not committing to being in a relationship with you. I work for you."

"But?" I lift a questioning brow, hearing the word coming.

She fidgets a little picking up a cookie to nibble at. "But that place you took me to in New York... I want to go to another place like that. Do they have them here?"

I knot my brows, and in the next breath shoot them into my hairline. "Club Desire. You want to go back there?"

"Yeah, I mean, if that type of thing is here. I want to... I don't know. I'm curious."

"You mean, you like to watch." I grin.

She tears off a piece of the cookie and throws it at me. I laugh at her and round the island. I can't stay away any longer.

Wrapping my arms around her waist, I tug her into my body. She melts right into me. Not mine, my ass.

"If you want to go, I'll take you. There is a Club Desire L.A." I nip her bottom lip, not able to resist. "I like to watch you watching."

She places her hands on my chest and takes a deep breath before releasing it. "Come on, show me your home."

I smile and peck her lips. Patience, that's all it takes. She'll be in my arms every night if it's the last thing I ever make happen.

Roni

This house is amazing. Breathtaking and so inviting. Comfort. That's what I feel when I'm around John. That's exactly why I won't be moving in with him.

I don't deserve to be here in the lap of luxury when Natasha is out there. Or, worse, she could be gone. No, there will be no comfort for me.

"You're lost again," John says as he reaches to rub the back of my neck.

His touch sends firework coursing through my body. I step out of his hold to get away from the feeling. My panties have already been ruined for hours.

Walking to the side door, I grab the knob and place a hand against the cool wood. "The garage?" I ask.

"Yeah, saved it for last."

I turn the knob and push my way in. My mouth falls open. He has at least five cars and three bikes in here.

I grin when I see my Ducati, the one I sold when I was pissed off at his ass. I spin and place my hands on my hips. He's watching me with a smile.

"I have the money for that. I'll write you a check tonight."

He shoves his hands into his pockets. "Keep it."

"How did you find it anyway?" He lifts a brow. I roll my eyes. "Right. Note to self. Burn that bitch next time."

He barks out a laugh. I turn with a smile and walk further into the garage, stopping when a black 1970 Chevrolet Chevelle SS 454 with a white striped hood catches my attention. I know the car clearer than anything I've known since waking on that hard, cold floor. A memory begins to form.

For the first time since I can remember my father is smiling at me. He holds up a set of keys and drops them in my palm. I turn from him to the car and back.

"When I first came to this country, I fell in love with what they call American muscle. I promised one would be the first car I gave to my son. I have no son, but I think this is perfect for you, Princesa," my father said.

I moved to the car tentatively. Climbing inside, I looked around it in awe. Snapping out of shock, I stuck the key in and started it, nearly jumping out of my skin as the engine roared to life.

"Go on. Step on the gas. Rev the engine," my father said as he leaned in the window beaming.

I come back to focus as John revs the engine of the car sitting before me. He chuckles at me as he hangs halfway out of the car.

"You want to take her for a spin?"

"My father gave me one of these for my sixteenth birthday," I say to no one in particular. I wrinkle my brows. "It was black too. Red rims and brake pads."

He cuts the car off and gets out. I catch the keys he tosses at me out of reflex. Looking down at them, I let the memory settle, then look back at John.

"Take it. It's yours."

"Are you crazy?"

"No. Maybe driving it will bring back more memories," he says and closes the distance.

He pinches my chin to lift my face and for the first time since New York, he kisses me with the passion and desire I know him for. My knees go weak and I have no choice but to wrap my arms around his neck.

"Thank you," I say when he breaks the kiss. "But I'm still not moving in with you."

He gives a throaty laugh and kisses my nose. That spark of determination lights his eyes. "Whatever."

CHAPTER FORTY-SIX

L.A. Life

Roni

Three months later...

"How's the L.A. life treating you? If you hate it, you can always come back here with me. Uri has talked about spending some time in Italy," Val says into the phone.

"It's not that bad. I mean, the shopping is great and so is the pay," I reply.

I'll admit, I didn't know how I felt about getting on that plane to move to Cali two months ago. Seeing how dangerous and crazy Val's life can be made me think that maybe working for John was the right change of pace. Not that this job doesn't have its dangers or that I'm not up to handling myself.

No, it's more the odd feeling I got learning who I was surrounded by in New York. My head is still reeling to know that someone I consider to be a really good friend is actually tied up in the mob. I couldn't understand my initial comfort with that.

Seriously, that's movie shit. So, I might as well live out here in Hollywood. Honestly, it's my guilt that pushed me onto that plane. I wasn't there when Val needed me.

I know she keeps telling me it's not my fault. She wanted to rush the baby to the hospital because of her fever. It never crossed her mind to send for me in the gym so I could have her back.

I get it now that I know who she really is. She didn't need me, but still, I should have been there. Nico was hurt because I wasn't there to cover Val's back. That will forever ride my shoulders. It has felt like failing Natasha all over again.

Val's laugh pushes through my thoughts. "Shopping again?" she asks, bringing a grin to my face as I push out of the air-conditioned store.

I put my shades on as the sun beams down on me. "The best way to spend my day off," I sing into the phone.

"Where's the kid?"

"With John and Noah, training."

We've only been on one real mission since we've been here. However, John made Torque hang back. Torque was pissy about it, but Braxton won his attention with some car show or something.

"And how are things going with John?"

I sigh. "Good for us, but weird to everyone else," I say.

"Uri, no. She's had ice cream already," Val says, her voice moving away from the phone.

"Oh, come on, love, do you see the way she's looking at my bowl?" Uri's voices comes from the background sounding pained.

"I hope this one is a boy. You spoil Vita," Val huffs.

I grin. I'm so happy she's having another baby. Val is a good mother.

She then turns her attention back to me. "Anyway, how so? What do you mean by this, *weird for others*? Why are we caring about others?"

"We're not. How can I explain this? We've been to his parents for Sunday breakfast every weekend since I've been here. He does things like handing over his car for me to have, but still picking me up for work and making sure I get home every night—"

"Wait, you're not living with him?"

"No, we fought about it. He wanted me to, but in the end, he gave in and helped me find a place with Torque. He's still not happy about it."

"Okay, so you guys are dating?"

"We're… friends. That's what's weird to everyone else. They don't think we are."

Val snorts. "I've seen you together. You want to tell this lie?"

"What's that supposed to mean?"

"You two are like batteries. When you are in a room together you charge the entire space. I don't believe this friends shit," she says, sounding more and more like her husband.

My cheeks heat. She's right, we are somewhere between friends and… I don't know what. Friends probably don't go to sex clubs together. I told John I wanted to learn more about the life and now we go every Friday night.

And yet, we're still not in an intimate relationship. We're in this awkward, for me, sexually charged place. I say this because John is always comfortable in any situation. I, on the other hand, want to experience all I see at Club Desire, but I don't want to come off the wrong way to John.

"What aren't you telling me?" Val says.

"Nothing I'm going to discuss in the middle of the street."

"Ah. There is more. See, I knew it. I wouldn't blame you one bit for riding that stallion, *bella*. Those Blacks are fine as hell."

"That's it. Your call is done. I will show you fine as bloody hell," Uri growls somewhere nearby.

I laugh when the call cuts off without Val having time to say goodbye. The shoe store I'm heading for comes into view. I get ready to reach for the door when a woman steps in front of me.

I go to curse her rude ass out and that's when I focus on the familiar face. I narrow my eyes behind my shades. It's that bitch from John's house.

"He left me for a gold digger," she snarls looking down at my bags.

I scoff and fold my arms over my chest. I worked for every dime I've spent. John still gives me access to credit card accounts and puts money in savings for me and Torque, but we never touch a dime of it. She doesn't need to know that though.

"Mad I took your place. You look like you could use some coin to get that dye job fixed," I snap back.

"You bitch. You're going to leave him alone and go back to wherever you came from. I can still fix things with him. I didn't know you were what was pulling his attention from me, I do now. You leave and he'll come back to me," she says.

I step into her face and tear my shades off. "You have no idea who you're fucking with. You ever run up on me again and I'm going to put your ass in a body bag," I seethe.

This bitch has the nerve to gasp like she's innocent. "Are you threatening me?" she says in that whiny voice.

"No, bitch. That's a fucking promise."

"We have a problem here?"

I stiffen and turn. In all my rage I missed the damn cop that walks up on us. I clench the bags in my hand. I know exactly what this looks like to him. I'm an Afro-Latina woman threatening this fake blonde princess. Her sudden change in demeanor makes total sense.

I give the cop a smile and shrug. "No, officer. I changed my mind about those shoes. I'm going to head home," I say as sugary sweet as I can.

"Is that right? Ma'am you all right?" he says, looking over my shoulder.

My temper is about to snap when a second officer walks over. "Hey, I remember you," the female officer says. "You Blacks always bring in the big fish."

I'm so pissed, I almost forget John has everyone thinking that my last name is Black too. I'm calm enough to recognize the female cop.

Right, you Blacks as in the family I work for.

"Hey," I say as my lips turn up into real smile. "Yeah, I remember you too. That Reynolds guy, right?"

"Yeah. Real bastard. That was your first official bounty, wasn't it?"

I nod. "Sure was."

John has had me and Torque helping him pick up some of the slack for his dad. With all the drama they've been through, they've been getting the business back in order the last few weeks.

"You know her, Gilmore?"

"Yeah, she works with Johnathan Black. As a matter of fact, I was told to treat her like one of Joe's kids. Especially after that crap with Detective Louis. Man, that almost got him canned. Why, what's the problem?"

The male officer scratches his chin. "Nothing, I guess. You ladies have a nice day."

I can feel Missy's ass seething behind me. I turn to face her and put my shades back on. "Remember what I said. Stay your ass the fuck away from me."

I turn and walk off. In my head, I'm patting myself on the back for not beating the shit out of her crazy ass. She has to be crazy, running up on me like that. John better control his little friend.

John

I pull into my courtyard and the first thing I see is Roni, sitting on the hood of the Chevelle I gave her. I know something is off right away. I'm out of my car faster than I can park it.

I walk over and stand between her legs, cupping the side of her face. She looks pissed. I drop a kiss on her frowning lips.

"What's wrong, baby?" I breathe against her forehead.

"Who is she to you? You said she wasn't your girlfriend when she said she was, but she was at some point wasn't she," she says.

Her voice is so detached, it's as if a human isn't talking to me at all. I squint my eyes as I look into her face. I already know who she's taking about, I'm just not sure why?

In the last two months we've been fine with not talking about Missy. Why start now? Then it hits me.

"Did she show up here?"

"No, I came here after running into her," she says. "Answer my question, John."

"Come inside."

She shakes her head. "No."

"This is a long story. Please, come inside," I say tiredly.

Everything hits me at once. All my family has been through, the shit I've been through with Missy, having my relationship with Roni set back because of Missy. I'm wary to the bone.

Roni nods and starts to lift from the car. I step back and give her room. Relief washes over me when she allows me to place my hand on the small of her back.

I need the contact. I always feel like I'm one step away from losing her before I truly have her. The dance we're doing will hold up for but so long. Roni and I have too much chemistry not to combust sooner or later. That is if something like this Missy shit doesn't come along and ignite the wrong fuse.

I get us into the house, but the foyer is as far as Roni gets before, she spins on me and places her hands on her hips. The fire in her eyes says she wants answers and she wants them right now. I blow out a breath and start talking as I drag my tired body toward the living room.

"I met her at a party. She had a flat tire when I was leaving, and I stopped to help. One thing led to another and we ended up in an arrangement.

"It wasn't anything serious. I had been planning to end it early," I say, blowing out a breath as I sit and run a hand through my hair.

Roni sits in the accent chair farthest away from me. I tighten my lips in frustration. I had thought we were getting somewhere in the last few weeks. Roni had been allowing her guard to come down slowly.

I continue. "That's when she told me she was pregnant. I was shocked to say the least, but I stepped up to help her. We started to really get to know each other—"

"Because as her Dom you weren't interested in knowing her," Roni interjects.

I fix my gaze on her, knowing what she's implying. "Baby, our relationship will be nothing like what I had with her. I want you as more than a Sub. That means, I'm interested in knowing everything you want to share with me.

"But yes, with Missy, we only had an arrangement between us. I didn't want to know much about her. Not that I haven't gotten to know my Subs in the past. Missy was different. I never felt like she enjoyed the life. It was more like she was pretending to please me." I shrug.

"Yeah, okay, whatever. What happened to the baby?"

"A few months went by and things were interesting. One night she started a fight and I was so frustrated and confused. Like, I still can't tell you what the fuck the fight was about. I left, the next morning she called me to say she lost the baby. Since then I've been nothing but guilty.

"Missy latched onto that like a weapon and then the suicide threats and attempts started." I pause and run my hand through my hair again. "So much stopped adding up. No, so much never added up. In hindsight, I don't know what to believe. My gut tells me she's been playing me from the beginning."

"Then she means nothing to you," Roni says coldly.

"No." She nods and stands. "Where are you going?"

"Home."

I stand. "Stay."

"No, we're officially friends, nothing more. We shouldn't be involved anyway; I work for you. Besides, something has gotten in our way every time we've tried.

"Now I have that psycho running up on me, trying to make me catch a case. Handle her. If you don't, I will," she fumes.

"Roni."

"Goodnight, John," she calls over her shoulder.

I drop back down on the couch and cover my face with my arms, too tired to chase after her. I know how stubborn she is, it wouldn't make a difference if I did. Honestly, I'm still trying to process what the hell happened.

"Fuck," I roar as the sound of the muscle car she's driving growls it's way off my property, the tires squealing.

CHAPTER FORTY-SEVEN

We Have a Hit

Roni

Six months later…

"What's up, Kiddo?" I sing as I walk into Torque's room.

I look around and frown. This place is a mess. Torque isn't the neatest kid, but this is insane even for him.

I've been out of town on a mission with John. Braxton and Ryan were supposed to hang with the kid to keep him out of trouble. Yeah, I know he's not a baby, but at nineteen he can be a bit reckless.

He charges into things headfirst. He's too smart for his own good, which leads to him thinking he knows it all. It's a gift and a curse. He makes mistakes because he thinks too much, too fast.

He looks up from his laptop and his blonde locks are in his eyes. With a bright smile, he stands and wraps me in a hug. Damn, this kid has really grown up. He's handsome and so tall now.

He's going to be breaking hearts all over the world and I'll be there to hem those heifers up if they even think of breaking his sweet little heart. However, in this moment, he needs to get his sticky ass in the shower and clean this damn room.

"Dude, what the hell? When was the last time you washed your ass? What's going on? This room smells like a sack of balls," I grumble.

He takes a step back, rubbing the back of his neck as he blushes. He gives me a sheepish smile. "I've had a few days off. I've been working on something. Haven't really cleaned or anything," he says with that voice that has gotten so deep, I sometimes have to do a double take to see who's talking to me.

"Well, it's time to get up from that laptop and clean yourself and this place up," I say, scrunching up my nose.

"Is John here?"

"No, I sent dad home. He was getting on my nerves. I needed a break."

Torque chuckles at that. "You know he's more like my dad and your husband?"

I shrug. "I had enough of him bossing me around."

"Cool, I have about an hour to clean this place up before he shows up and gets in my ass about it," he says and starts to move around to pick things up.

"Wait, are you saying you're more afraid of him than me?"

"Not at all, sis," he says with a mischievous grin.

"Yeah, whatever. Wash your ass," I grumble and head out of his room.

I head for my room and strip down once inside. I'm tired and can't wait to fall asleep in my bed. I snort. Torque was right. John will be here within the hour. The man is in our home more than his own.

I step into my shower and roll my shoulders. These jobs are starting to become more demanding. I'm not complaining. We seem to make more, the more danger involved. I have enough in my bank account to sit pretty for a few years without changing any of my habits.

I frown and turn my face up to the shower spray. I'd give it all away to know where Natasha is. Our team is the best. Torque has become damn good at his job and still we haven't found her. My heart aches with the possible reason for that.

I fight with the tears that want to fall. I should have fought harder to get to her. I should have gone back for her.

"Hey, baby." A weak smile comes to my lips as John's voice fills my bathroom.

I turn and tug the curtain back to peek out. "What happened to you going home to get some rest?"

He frowns as he leans against the bathroom door. He looks exhausted. His hair is a mess and he needs to shave. He looks like a pretty version of Noah at the moment.

"Couldn't force myself to get out of the car. You hungry? Torque and I are ordering something," he says.

"Whatever you guys get, I'm game," I reply as I look him over. "John."

"Yeah," he says tiredly.

"Let the kid order the food. You need some sleep."

He gives me a sleepy grin. "My room is next door to that funk box. I'm sleeping in your bed." He frowns. "What the hell was he doing while we were gone?"

"I have no idea."

He nods. Without another word, he turns and opens the door to leave. I can hear him bellowing for Torque to wash his ass and clean the fuck up. I shake my head.

We really have become a little family. Torque used to be so defiant when it came to John. It took some time, but he respects John now and listens to every word he says as if each one will give him some golden wisdom.

I finish my shower and wrap in a towel. My curls are dripping down my back, but I'm too tired to dry them. Stumbling into the bedroom, I find John face down on my bed snoring.

I smile and shake my head again. I don't bother to wake him and kick him out. I crawl into the bed and pass out next to him.

John

I wake to the scent of something sweet and alluring. Turning my head, I find Roni passed out beside me. Her towel has come loose exposing one of her breasts.

I grow hard instantly at the sight of her brown nipple. I'm so fucking tempted to lean over and suck it into my mouth. Damn, how long has it been since I've had sex?

When the answer to that question punches me in the gut, I groan and roll to sit on the edge of the bed. I push my hands into my hair. It's been months since that incident with Missy.

Missy, she's been too damn quiet. Hopefully she got the point. If only I could be so fucking lucky.

Maybe it's time Roni and I sit down and talk this out. My dick wants her and only her. I release a deep sigh.

The rumble of voices grabs my attention. Roni shoots up in the bed. Why the hell do I turn to look at her?

The towel she was in now sits at her waist. Her entire upper body is exposed. She looks to me confused.

"Sounds like Ry and Felix," I say.

She nods and pushes a hand through her hair. After a moment she seems to realize I'm staring at her. She looks down and covers herself with one arm while trying to get the towel back in place.

I turn my back and pretend to stretch. The bed dips as she moves to climb off the foot of it. When I finally stand and face her, she's in a pair of shorts and a T-shirt.

We both head out of the bedroom together. The living room falls silent as soon as we walk out. I was right, Ryan, Felix, and Brax are all surrounding Torque as he sits with his laptop in his lap.

Ryan straightens from behind the couch. "And you mean to tell me you two aren't fucking," he says.

I give him the finger. "Not that it's any of your damn business in the first place."

"Forget all of that. Come here, Roni. I think the kid is onto something. It's probably a cold lead by now, but it will confirm that Natasha is still alive," Felix says.

Roni moves to Torque's side so fast; I have to do a doubletake. I go over to see what's going on as well. Once I round the couch, I hover next to Ry.

"This is what I was doing while you guys were away. I got this new digital drawing pad. I was able to draw a picture of Natasha and then use digital software to make it 3D. After that, I started to run it through facial recognition software at train stations, bus ports, and airports around the country," Torque explains.

"The kid is smart," Brax says.

"I wasn't getting anything at first. I mean, I had to go region by region, country by country, and I spanned the course of four years. Then I got lucky. I got a hit on a shithole bus station here in the States," Torque says.

"Where?" Roni says as she stands as if ready to jump into action.

"Calm down, killer," Ry says, causing me to pop him in the back of the head. I know how important this is to Roni.

"He's right. No need to get our hopes up just yet. This was two years ago. I doubt we'll find a trace of her there now, but it's hope, right? She's still out there," Torque says, sounding more like the fifteen-year-old that pled with me to help Roni on that truck.

"Good work, kid," Roni says in her detached voice.

When she turns and heads for the bedroom, I can feel the hurt coming off of her. This has been weighing on her shoulders for years. I wish I would have gone back when she asked me to that night.

"Felix, Ry, you guys mind going to Georgia and looking into this. Maybe there are some breadcrumbs still there. It's worth a try. Best lead we've had yet," I say.

"I want to go with them," Torque says.

I nod. "Be safe."

 Warning

Roni

Seven months and two weeks later...

"Hey, you," Val says into the phone.

"Hold on a sec," I reply.

The salty, briny air hits me in the face. The sound of the waves crashing soothes me. I put one earbud in to switch the call to my headphones.

"Hey."

She's silent for a moment. I have to check to make sure I switched over properly. We're connected.

"What's going on? And don't tell me nothing. I can hear it in your voice," she says.

I stop and turn to face the ocean. I drove out to the beach to be alone to think. I'm grumpy and need a vacation.

"John wants us to go to Ireland for his brother's wedding. I don't want to go," I mumble.

"Why the hell not? I'm going to be there. You can see the kids."

"Don't make this about you, big head," I mutter.

"Oh, I'm so going to whip your ass," she scoffs. "Tell me, *La rabbia della morte*. What is the real problem?"

I groan. Death's rage. "That's the thing. I haven't been full of that same rage. It's not gone, it's simmering somewhere in the back of my mind, but not taking over."

"Because of John?"

"*Coger,* woman. Does it always have to be about him?"

"Let's see. Yes."

I sigh. "Okay, yes, it's him. Somehow in the last three months, John has convinced me to start dating him again. It started with dinner one night, then a movie. The next thing, I'm getting flowers at the apartment and kisses goodnight that aren't of the friend variety."

Val laughs at me, causing me to roll my eyes. "I once told you the two of you are inevitable. Why are you fighting it?"

"I don't know," I whisper. "I need to make up my mind. Three and a half years is a long time to be in love with someone and deny it."

Yup, I said that out loud. I've been in love with John since he held my pissy ass on that bus and made me feel like a human again. If it weren't for that crazy ex of his, we'd probably be way more by now.

"Why deny it? Is it this monster that's riding your back? I've been there. You have time? I will tell you about me and Uri. Maybe that will help."

"I have time."

I plop down on my ass in the sand as Val goes into the story of her and her husband. As she speaks things start to become clearer to me. I see a lot of myself in her.

"I've used his ex as an excuse to keep my distance," I say when Val is done. "With all the shit I have going on, it used to make sense. Now, all I know is I want to stop fighting it. But… how do I do that knowing I don't know what happened to my friend? Is it right for me to be happy? She could be living a nightmare."

"One of the things I respect about you most is your loyalty. You're a great friend. The way you look after Torque, this girl you wish to find. I wish you told me about her sooner."

"I didn't know who I could trust."

"I understand." She pauses. "I think she would want you to be happy either way. If it were me… my sister would have wanted the best for me. I know she would. I live every day to the fullest for her and my mother. Watching them die… a piece of me was killed with them, but the rest, the part that's still breathing, they would want that part to be happy. So that's what I'm doing. I think your friend would want the same."

"Maybe."

"So stubborn. Listen, my children and husband are looking at me like I'm neglecting them. I better see you at that wedding. And Roni."

"Yeah?"

"Let him love you. You know you love him. Three and a half years is a long time to love someone. To love them and be patient. See this from his eyes," she says and hangs up.

I'm floored by her words. I feel pretty damn selfish too. I start to wonder when John has time to get some ass. He's either always with me and Torque or with his brothers.

Then it hits me. I don't think he's had sex since we moved here. That's insane. Even I flick the bean at night to fantasies of him.

I sit for another hour before I stand and brush the sand off my backside. I'm still lost in thought as I make my way to my car. My phone buzzes with a text.

John: We're on our way home. Did you eat?

I can't help smiling. We didn't move into his big house, but somewhere along the way he moved into our apartment. I needed an extra bedroom for an office, my ass. He planned on moving in from the time he found us the place.

Me: Nope. Not yet. I want tacos.

"Is that John?"

I look up at the sound of the whiny, irritating as fuck voice. This bitch. Like does she have some type of radar for when John and I are together. She has to.

I fold my arms over my chest and cock my hip to the side as I glare at her. "First, get your ass off my car before I drag you off it."

"So violent. I don't get what he sees in you. You're not even the submissive type," she says in disgust.

"From what I hear you weren't filling the role that well yourself," I toss back.

"Listen. I'm giving you one last chance to back off. Things have changed and I want to fix things with John. We have history. We can make this work."

I look at her, I mean, really look at her. I don't think she's that crazy. It's more stupidity than anything else going on here.

"Yeah, good luck with that. Now get out of my way."

"I'm warning you. Back off or you both are going to feel my wrath. Don't make me play my hand."

I snort. I get up in her face. "Play your hand, your foot, your face for all I care. You keep playing with me, I'm not going to warn you, honey. I'm going to lay you down right where you stand."

With that, I shove her out of my way and get into my car. Enough is enough, let her keep playing with me. John isn't going to have to worry about her, I'll handle it myself.

CHAPTER FORTY-NINE

Last Warning

John

"Baby, just buy a dress. Heck, you can wear pants for all I care. You're getting on that plane no matter what," I growl into the phone.

I walk over to a table of ties, not really giving a fuck about buying one. I'm waiting for Torque to come out of the fitting room in his new Tux. Hopefully, the kid hasn't outgrown it since his last fitting.

"Why is this so important to you?"

"You're family. You and Torque should be there," I reply.

And I love you and want you by my side. The words are on the tip of my tongue. I've been in love with Roni for a long time, something I want to tell her sooner rather than later.

"No one will miss me if I'm not there."

"Bullshit. You may try to keep everyone at arm's length, but that doesn't mean that it works. Not with my family. My mother will have my balls if you're not there and she's coming for your ass next," I say.

It's the truth. Mom will kill us both. Bean and Noah have already asked if she's coming to the wedding. They will be disappointed if she doesn't come as well.

"*Grr,* why didn't you come with me?"

I turn and lean my butt against the display table. "For what? You're like a professional shopper. You never need me any other time." I laugh.

"Don't be a dick, John. I can't decide on anything."

"Why not?"

"Because I don't want to go," she snaps at me.

I laugh harder. "Suck it up, cuteness."

"Fuck you, John. I'm going to show up in chaps and pasties and see how you like it."

I'm really laughing now. I sober up and drop my voice. "We can save that for after the wedding."

"Humph," she murmurs. "Check the picture I just sent you."

I open my text and find the picture she's referring to. She looks stunning. It's a purple, lace dress that molds to her body and plunges down the front. Not too revealing, but it compliments her toned shape and full breasts. It stops right above the knee, showing off her sexy calves.

"You look perfect. Get that one," I say.

"Are you kidding? I was joking. I'm not wearing this."

"Yes, you are. Buy it. If you don't, I promise I'm going to spank your ass."

I know I'm pushing it, but I've been tearing that wall down piece by piece. I want Roni so bad my head hurts. This dance we're doing isn't enough anymore.

"Just so you know, I'm not wearing a collar. An ankle bracelet, maybe," she teases.

I bite my lip. "Have you seen Nick and Sephora's bangles? We could always do something like those."

"Whatever, John." She laughs. "You really want me to get this dress?"

"Yes. I want to watch you in it all day and peel you out of it at night," I reply.

"Fine. I'll get it."

"That's my girl."

I turn to see Torque has stepped out of the fitting room and he's looking for me. I wave to get his attention and head over to him. He looks as nervous as Roni sounds.

Speaking of which, I wrinkle my brows. "Babe, you still there?"

"Yeah, I'm here," she says tightly.

"Everything okay?"

"Peachy. I'll call you back."

She hangs up without allowing me to reply. I stare down at my phone in confusion. Something has been going on with Roni other than not wanting to go to this wedding. She just won't tell me what.

She's been in her head since she said she took that drive to the beach. That was two weeks ago. Something is annoying her, but she won't fess up to what.

"So, how do I look?" Torque asks, grabbing my attention.

I smile at the kid and pat his cheek. "You'll do your sister proud."

His entire face lights up. I once thought he had a crush on Roni. I've come to learn that while her attractiveness isn't lost on him, she truly is the big sister he's never had. He respects and loves Roni and would do anything to make her happy and proud of him.

"Cool," he says and bobs his head, trying to play off how much my words have affected him.

"Come on, we have a few more errands to run. Let's get home before Roni does."

Roni

For two weeks, I've been tolerating this nuisance. Does she really think she's been stealth? I caught her watching me while talking to John.

Little does she know; I'm watching her too. I'm watching and waiting for my opportunity to handle her and get away with it. It's only a matter of time.

"Will that be all, Ms. Black?"

My eyes light up when the salesclerk calls me by my fake last name. I can see Missy in the reflection in the mirrors on the wall behind the register. She's seething.

Hearing my last name is enough to bring her storming over to me. "What did she just call you?"

"Not today, honey. I need to get my nails and hair done. John and I have plans for a date. Don't want to keep him waiting." I lean into her ear. "Although the punishment might be worth it."

When I pull back the crimson color on her face is priceless. I laugh right in her face and turn back to the clerk and hand over my card. I don't have time for the foolishness.

"Yes, thank you. That will be all."

When I have my things in hand, I turn and look Missy over. "You're still here? Last warning, sweetheart. You are barking up the wrong tree. It's going to get you hurt."

CHAPTER FIFTY

My Answer

Roni

"This has been fun," Torque says.

I look over at him as I swing back and forth on the hammock I'm lying in, one leg hanging over the edge. Night has fallen and a light breeze is flowing. Little does he know; I drove us out here in hopes Missy would follow.

However, with leaving for the wedding in three days and all the work I've been doing in the office, this is a nice break. I didn't tell John where we were going because he would have found a way to come along. I need him focused on anything other than me today. My temper has been known to get me in trouble, but I've had it.

"It's peaceful," I say and lift my head to the sky.

Yeah, it's peaceful, but there's the problem. The system I set up two nights ago at this rental property should have gone off the moment someone other than the two of us stepped one foot on the soil. You see, I've been plotting since Missy showed up in that store.

I caught her slipping the other night, watching John and his brothers and not me. While she was watching them, I was watching her. She's up to something. Her patterns are changing and she's becoming erratic. She's doing more than threatening and stalking.

I was sure she would follow me here, but there goes another pattern change. I blow out a breath. I want this handled before I board that plane.

"Hey, can I ask you something?" Torque says.

"Sure."

He pauses for a moment, brushing his long hair out of his face. He's been talking about cutting it. I'll be sad to see it go. I think it's going to take the baby out of his face. I'm not ready to admit he's all grown up.

To be honest, I think he wants to cut it to be more like John. I've noticed that he's been dressing more like John and wearing a similar cologne. I grin at the thought. He's finding himself. There are worse paths he could take to do so.

He exhales. "Once we find Natasha, what do we do next? We both know I'm not as good at the field work as you are. Nellie, Wyatt, and Felix have been covering for both offices. I'm like the backup geek squad. They never let me handle any of the big stuff." He shrugs. "I don't know what I plan to do."

I sit up and rise out of the hammock. Moving to his side by the tree he's leaning against, I gather my thoughts. As I find my words, I sit shoulder to shoulder with him.

I snort. "I still don't know who I am. So, for me, it's one day at a time. It's been so long… I think I've given up on trying to remember who I was, I'm learning to be who I am.

"I'm good with numbers and the field work. Those are the things I'm adapting to. We have money, kid. You don't have to worry about that. If you want to do something else, you say the word. I'll make it happen," I say.

"You mean, you'll get him to make it happen," he murmurs.

I bump his arm with mine. "Torque, are you jealous?"

"Yeah, I am. He's taking more of your attention again. I know it's silly, but… we're a family. What if you and John hook up and… you guys leave to live in his big house, and I'd be alone."

I wrap an arm around his waist and lean my head on him. "There is nothing that can keep me away from you. You're the first person that has given a shit about me and stuck with me. You and Natasha. I'll never forget how you two helped me hold on down there as they tortured me," I say.

"But you're in love with him."

I lift my head and look him in the eyes. He's still a boy in so many ways. I can see the wariness etched in his gaze.

"I'll kick your ass if you tell him."

"I think he knows. Everyone does. You two are the only ones that won't admit it." He frowns at me.

"Stop rushing to grow up, Torque. The team respects you. They think you're smart. You just have to learn to slow down."

He laughs. "Nice."

"What?" I feign innocence.

"Epic subject change. I want to see you happy. If that means you and John ride off into the sunset without me, I'll get over it. I'll get my shit figured out," he says.

"Watch your mouth," I say and pinch his side. He chuckles. "I'm serious, Tor. Whatever the future brings, they'll have to pry my dead body away from you before you live a day without me."

He tosses an arm around my head and tugs me into him, kissing the top. "Don't make promises you can't keep. One of these days we're going to have to live our own lives. I don't think my future wife is going to want you around all the time."

I laugh even as my heart aches. He's right. Two or three years from now he's not going to want me all in his shit. I don't know how much I like that.

"Roni?"

"Yeah."

"I know we're going to find her. I dream about it all the time. She's waiting."

I let his words sink in. "Then John will have a full house," I say, drawing his deep laugh.

My phone rings and I pull away to pull it from my pocket. I don't recognize the number. I answer anyway, in case it's a work emergency.

"Hello."

"You and John think you're so smart. Well, I have something to show you both. Since he chose you, Mrs. Black, I've made a choice too."

"Oh God, you're one rambling ass bitch."

"John thinks I have you. He's going to come for you. If you give a shit about him, you'll come to the address I texted," she seethes then hangs up.

She's full of shit.

I've spoken to John a few times and he's been texting me and Torque all damn day. We've been telling him we're fine and blowing him off. My lips turn up when right at that moment a text from John comes in.

John: Where have you guys been all day? I miss you. We need to have the talk.

I chew on my lip. I don't want to think about the talk he's referring to. Especially not now.

Another text comes in from the number Missy called from. I hand Torque my phone. "Can you get one of your mirrors on her phone? I want to know her every move."

"Got it."

"Good, let's go."

We go to the back of the Chevelle and I unlock the trunk. I hand Torque a Glock and vest. I've been wearing my thigh holster under my mini sundress in anticipation.

Closing the trunk, I nod to Torque to get in. Once I jump inside and turn the key, the car growls to life and I rev the engine. This nut ass woman has played with me for the last time. I shift the gears and gun for the city, heading for the problem I'm about to solve.

My gift to John.

John

"Roni, it's me. You guys okay? Call me back," I say into the phone and drag a hand down my face.

I fell asleep on the couch at the apartment, waiting for her and Torque to come home. I look at my watch. It's pretty late. I have no idea where Roni and Torque have been all day. It's their day off, but I had to head into the office. It's been insane running my own thing and still covering a schedule at the main Black and Lock office.

My crew is solid now with all of my new additions, but I don't know why I thought I was going to be in my own world. My brothers have bled over into my business. All I've done is brought on extra hands.

I'm not complaining. This happens to feel right. Dad and I weren't expecting the unit to open up in the building. It's a full floor of space and only two floors down from the main office. We'd been renting space to those tenants for years. I'd say it was meant to be.

Speaking of meant to be, I look at the text I sent to Roni earlier. She hasn't replied. A part of me says I freaked her out.

At the same time, I want to think it's something else. It's time we talk about our relationship. At thirty-one, I'm watching all of my brothers settle with the women they love.

Wyatt's on his second baby. Toby's twins are growing so fast. I'm sure Noah will have Bean pregnant in no time. Felix is engaged and has an instant family. Hell, I never in a million years thought Brax would be married before me. Ryan is the only one not in a relationship.

I go to call Roni again, but my emergency text alert goes off. It's a text from Wyatt that Noah is in trouble. I jump up without thinking and head out the door.

My adrenaline is pumping. I still don't know what's going on with Roni and Torque. I have an uneasy feeling in my stomach.

"I knew it was too quiet. Roni, where the fuck are you?" I mutter as I jump in my car.

Roni

I pull into the lower level of the garage and come to a screeching stop. Torque already has his laptop open with a visual of the chaos happening on the upper level. I'm seething. The drive back took way longer than I would have liked.

"They've ceased fire," Torque says.

I look over at the screen. My sights are set on one person and one person only. When she comes up on the screen, I'm in motion again. I drive up a few more levels before whipping into a spot.

"That phone is her all right."

"Stay here," I say as I take the comm Torque offers me.

"I can help."

"I said stay here. I've got this."

I shove my way out of the car and look around the level that I'm on. An idea pops into my head and I start for the trunk to get the harness out. I plan to drop in on my little friend Missy.

I take a blade from the stash I have in the trunk and tear it through the fabric of the bottom of my sundress, then rip the entire thing off. Once geared up in the harness, I take off in a jog for the level they are on.

"John's up there. All the guys are," Torque says into the comm.

"Almost there."

I get to the garage level where the action is happening and take a quick look around. It's exactly like the level I parked on. I spot a ladder that leads to the rafters and head for it, my gun aimed for anyone that dares to get into my way.

Once at the ladder, I tuck my gun away and start the climb. I can hear that whiny ass voice from here. Ugh, I don't know what John saw in her.

Moving into the shadows, I inch forward slowly. Everyone's too distracted to notice me up here. I tune out their chatter and keep my focus on the blabbering idiot that has been taunting me for weeks.

I'm almost right above their heads as I vaguely dial into their conversation.

"I don't know. I didn't think that out. If I can't have you no one can," Missy says, causing my blood to boil. "Mr. Coleman promised me one million dollars if I could get you all here. I wasn't sure you would all come for John's little friend, so I brought this guy in once I saw what he was up to."

"Interesting," Wyatt says.

Noah turns to Wyatt and shakes his head. "I told you. Stupid... dumbest plan ever."

"Listen, she promised me half of the money. You've made my life hell. I had nothing to lose. Just leave me the hell alone and we'll all walk away like nothing ever happened," the guy holding Bean says. He looks like he's about to shit his pants.

"I don't think you have that option any longer," Noah says menacingly. "Isn't that right, baby?"

"Absolutely."

"Where is Coleman?" John asks.

They are working this in my favor. The more they talk the closer I get. I want to be up close and personal when I drop this bitch once and for all.

"I don't know. He said he was leaving the country for a while. Once I call him, he is going to wire our money," Missy huffs.

A few of the guys begin to laugh at her reply to John's question and her stupid plan. "Don't laugh at me. You're all always laughing at me. John you just give me the money. Five hundred thousand and I'll walk away."

"Or what?" Wyatt asks.

"Or I'll kill myself," Missy and John recite the words at the same time.

"Oh, my God," Bean gasps. "That's what she's been holding over you all these years?"

John shrugs and frowns. "Sadly, among other things."

"I will, you know I will," Missy whines.

This is it. I'm in position. I quickly hook up my harness, pull my gun, and release the feed to zip down right in front of Missy. She never sees me coming.

I hold my gun out and aim for her head. "No need," I say and pull the trigger.

I told her I was going to drop her ass on sight. My job is done. I don't even care to watch her fall. I'm mildly amused by Bean as she takes out the asshole that had a gun to her head. I already know I'm not the only badass around here.

"I found Roni," Ryan says dryly.

Braxton claps his hands. "I love the women in this family."

"Roni." John sighs.

I look at him and drop down onto my feet, then unhook as if nothing has happened at all. "She's been threatening me for weeks." I shrug.

"And you didn't think to tell me," John says, his tone telling me he's pissed off at me.

I wrinkle my brows in confusion and shrug again. "Why?" I ask.

John throws his arms in the air in exasperation. He then points at me. "You. Let's go. We're having the talk... tonight. I'm not doing this anymore."

The talk. Oh yeah, this has been a long time coming. I definitely can't use Missy as an excuse anymore. It's time we face the music.

"Is that an order, Johnathan," I say, knowing it's going to rev him up some more.

John bares his teeth. "Yes, Roni it is," he growls.

"Whatever you say, Boss." I walk over to him with some extra sway in my hips.

From the energy surrounding us, I know the game has changed. Our relationship is about to take a complete turn. For once, I think I'm ready for it too.

CHAPTER FIFTY-ONE

Boss

Roni

The ride to John's has been silent. I'm still stewing that he forced me to let Torque drive my car home. I hadn't expected John to bring me back to his house. I thought we were all heading to the apartment.

Now we're pulling through his gate and into the courtyard, I have some idea why we're not at my place and why he sent Torque home in my car. This knowledge makes me more nervous than I've ever been, but I refuse to let it show. At least, I think I'm not allowing it to spill through.

Without a word, John gets out of the car. I step out without waiting for him to make it around to my side. When I close the door, he's standing at the hood of the car with his back to me, a hand on his hip and his head bent.

I draw my brows. Is he really that angry with me? Like, come on. That chick was getting on my fucking nerves. I sigh and move to his side.

Once I reach him, John reaches for the back of my neck and starts for the front door, still silent. He gets the door open and we move inside. In three quick moves, he kicks the door closed, spins on me, and backs me into the door.

I gasp and place my palms on his chest. With his face nose to nose with mine, he inhales me. His grip on my neck tightens slightly.

"I've carried nothing but guilt over what happened between me and *her*. It's been riding my back for years. It didn't feel right to have you and know what lingered in the background. That has been the only thing keeping me from pursuing you as hard as I normally would. That guilt has lifted." He moves in so close there's no room between us.

"Guilty for what?"

He shakes his head, a tortured look in his eyes. He lifts a hand to my cheek and swipes it across my skin. Then he shows me his thumb. There's blood on it.

"Not now." His words come out almost pained. He takes a step back. "You can shower in my room."

I reach to grab the front of his shirt. "You're not coming with me?"

Again, he shakes his head. "I won't be able to give you the night you deserve if I step foot into that shower with you."

My lips part, but my heart is pounding too hard to respond. I push off the door and nod. I move in slow motion as my brain tries to catch up.

"Roni." I turn as he booms my name from behind. "Move your ass, baby."

I laugh and turn to rush into his bedroom. I can't strip out of my ruined dress fast enough. Once in the shower, I turn on the spray and start to scrub from head to toe.

Anticipation fills my belly. I try to remember everything the ladies told me to do when this finally happened. I look down at my legs. I shaved this morning, I'm good to go there. Thank God, I went for a wax last week. I'm still in good shape there.

"Shit," I mutter. I don't have any of my own perfume or bodywash.

I smell like John right now. Rolling my eyes, I cut the shower off. I'm not calling this off over a scent.

Wringing out my curls as best I can, I calm my nerves. When I step out of the shower, I look right into the mirror. This isn't the body from when I first met John. Not in the least. It's not even the same body as the first time we were going to have sex or that time in the armory.

All the training has transformed my curves. My thighs are still thick, but way more toned. My tummy is actually flat and tight. When I first started gaining weight back everything moved like jelly. Over the last year, I've pushed myself harder and it shows.

I bite my lip, wondering if John will like what he sees now. Pushing at my wet locks to get them out of my face, I try to shake off the anxiety clawing at me. It's one thing to fantasize about this night, another to know it's about to become a reality.

"Come to me." I turn at the sound of the deep command.

John is standing in the doorway with a towel around his waist. A tented towel. Memories of how thick and long he is come to mind.

Damn, you sure you want to do this?

I push that thought aside and move to him. He lets his gaze eat me up as I do my best to sway my hips. Fear of slipping on the floor and falling face first on his dick taunts me. This would be my moment to become clumsy.

His grip is tight as he settles a hand on my hip and drags me into him. This time he grabs my throat from the front. Like earlier, he hovers just above my lips as I tip my head back.

"I'm going to do this right. As bad as I want you, I'm going to be as gentle as I can be," he says.

"You don't have to be. I'll be fine."

He shakes his head. He's doing a lot of that tonight. I start to get frustrated.

"You already know I'm not a small man. I don't want to hurt you."

I swallow, knowing the lie I'm about to tell. I want all of this man and at full capacity. I've waited too long for him to hold back on me.

"I've used a vibrator for penetration. You don't have to worry about my virginity. I got horny after our trips to the club. I needed to do something about it."

He growls and sucks my bottom lip into his mouth. I whimper as he nibbles and sucks. Tugging my lip between his own, he groans.

"*Tha mo chridhe 'S e deiseil mu dheireadh thall.*"

He crushes my lips before I can ask what he has said. I lock my fingers in the top of his hair. He dips and lifts me onto his waist by my thighs.

Not once do we break the kiss as he turns and heads into his bedroom. I cling to him and savor the way he makes love to my mouth. John kisses with so much passion and hunger.

The cool sheets hit my back and it solidifies that this is happening. He looks down at me with so much want. Palming one of my breasts, he massages it.

He leans into my ear. "We'll talk about your punishment later," he breathes.

"Huh? What? For what?"

"Your virginity belonged to me. You took that from me," he says with a mix of lust and humor.

I don't get to reply as he moves quickly to capture my nipple in his mouth. I bow off the bed, gripping the sheets in my palm. When he moves his hand to start circles around my clit, my eyes cross. I'm already coiled tightly, dripping for him.

"John."

He slips his fingers inside me. "You're still too tight to take me right away. Be patient."

I nod, on the verge of tears. I don't want to wait. I need him, but I trust his words.

John drags his tongue from between my breasts, down my stomach, to my mound. When he joins his fingers and mouth to push me higher, I cry out and plead for him some more. I'm coming so hard and fast.

"Good girl," he croons and sucks his hand into his mouth.

It's the sexiest thing ever to watch him lick his fingers clean as those golden eyes remain on me. He moves up my body with all the fluidity of liquid. With his thumb pressed to my bottom lip, he sticks his tongue into my mouth.

His lips are coated with my essence. We attack each other's mouths with so much passion and heat. This man is so fine. How does he make the taste of my own pussy on his tongue a complete feast?

"John," I cry into his heated cavern as he begins to finger me again.

"Come again, baby. I need you soaked," he says with so much strain in his voice.

I reach to run my fingers down his back, causing him to shiver. His eyes darken. He's starting to perspire with the efforts of his restraint.

I latch onto the look on his face. It's for me. All at once, I admit I'm tired of running. John has always made me feel safe. Just as he has pushed his guilt aside, I do the same.

Pushing the screaming thoughts of betrayal and friendship away, I come again. I nearly weep when he pulls his hand from my body. I turn my head to follow his movement as he reaches for the nightstand.

I look back to John with wide eyes. He has an entire set up. Looking back at the nightstand, I note the bowl of condoms, some sort of plug, cuffs—the wand he picks up is the last thing I get to focus on. He turns it on and places it against my clit.

I claw at his hair as he moves back to feasting on me. My legs are shaking, and my screams are soundless. Holy fuck, what is this man doing to me?

"Come on, baby. The sooner you give it to me, the sooner I can give us both what we need," he says huskily.

He turns the wand up and my eyes roll into the back of my head. I feel the dip of the bed and he lifts above me. The slide of something through my folds has me opening my eyes and sitting up on my elbows. One look down my body and I find the towel gone from his waist and his heavy dick hard and rubbing through my slickness.

I watch with my lips parted. My heart starts pounding harder as my next orgasm takes a hold of me. I tilt my head to the side and let it take me completely.

"Yeah, that's it." He places the wand aside and reaches for a condom. I watch in drained awe as he tears into the packet and rolls it on.

Everything in me tenses up as he lines up with my entrance. Maybe, I should tell him I was lying. That is a lot of dick.

"Relax."

I nod. He takes my right leg and places it on his shoulder. Leaning into me, he keeps his eyes on mine. I truly relax when he captures my lips and kisses my worries away.

A few moments go by before he starts to push into me. I close my eyes tight, trying not to give way to the pain that sears through me. He rocks in and out, slow and shallow, but he's so thick you would think I've had all of him.

John leans into my neck and nuzzles it. Then he flicks his tongue against my skin. "Don't ever lie to me again," he grunts and thrusts forward.

I holler. He freezes, his shaft pulsing inside me. Oh my God. I grab his biceps and dig my nails in. John grasps the sheets by my head and looks into my eyes.

He licks his lips. "You should have taken my offer for gentle."

The thrusting of his hips knocks the smartass remark right from my lips. I press my head back into the bed and marvel at how the pain turns into pleasure. The weight of his body on mine, the feel of his thick length moving in and out of me, feeding me more with each roll of his hips—it's all intoxicating.

"Shit, John," I pant.

"Open for me. Let me in this tight pussy. Fuck, Roni. You feel better than I imagined. Rock your hips for me," he grunts.

I wrap my free leg around his waist and start to grind my hips. He throws his head back and growls as he pounds into me harder, but still not deep. I can feel him holding himself back.

"Damn, that's not what I meant, but don't stop," he grinds out as he palms my ass and changes angles.

I'm crying out louder than before as he lunges into me. He releases the leg over his shoulder and leans into me to kiss me, silencing my moans. Our sweat slick bodies find a rhythm and I rock my hips into him instead of grinding.

He has me so distracted, I yelp when he places the wand between us once again. I tear my lips from his. "John," I holler as my body begins to come over and over again. I lose count as he rolls into my pussy like it's his profession.

With my hands on his tight round ass, I coax him deeper. "You sure you want that," he pants.

No, I'm not sure. As a matter of fact, I'm terrified. I think if he puts anymore dick inside me, I'm going to split in two, but I'm also greedy. I want all of him.

"Please," I plead.

He drops the wand to the side and reaches for both my thighs to pin them to his chest. We lock eyes and he bites his lip. The next thing I know I'm trying to run from him.

He goes deeper and it's like he's hitting shit he has no business hitting. He's biting beneath his lower lip now. This man is just fucking showing off as he practically dances in my pussy.

I mean, for real, for real dancing. He bobs in and out, from side to side. Going deeper with each stroke, not allowing me to move back as he keeps me pinned to him.

"*Fuck*," I scream.

This is insane and it's plain vanilla sex. I look down and watch as he goes in and out. What's truly insane... I'm coating him in my juices, but I'm not taking all he has to give. There's still more dick! How?

John

"John," she says as if she's in awe.

I should not be pounding this pussy out like this, but she lied, and I've waited damn near four fucking years to get inside this pussy. She's lucky I'm not going balls deep. God do I want to, but she's so tight.

Her walls are squeezing the fuck out of me. It's been so long since I've had some pussy, I'm surprised I haven't exploded. I'm going to enjoy teaching her how to fuck. Her eagerness is so sexy.

I drop my gaze to her bouncing tits and can't help but lean in to suck on her nipple. Circling it with my tongue, I relish her moans. When I start to flick my tongue against her peak, her pussy pulses and soaks me some more.

"Fuck yeah, baby," I breathe against her breast.

That tingling sensation starts at the base of my spine. The hairs on the back of my neck stand up. Goosebumps cover my body. I'm going to come soon.

I move to cover Roni's mouth with mine. She cups the back of my head and inhales me. I grin against her mouth. She may not like to kiss in public, but she has no objections when we're alone.

I go to sit up, and she follows, keeping a tight hold on me. Sliding my hands to her ass, I deepen the kiss. With Roni clinging to me, I shift us into a new position.

When I drop her up and down on my shaft, she breaks the kiss and allows her head to fall back. Seeing her exposed sweat slicked neck, I go for it. Licking from the base of her throat to her chin.

"Who's pussy is this, baby?"

"Yours, boss," she moans.

I'm caught off guard. As she comes around me, squeezing me tighter once again, I explode into the barrier between us. So fucking good. I don't even soften all the way. This is going to be one long fucking night.

"You were worth the wait," she says and actually giggles.

I'm thrown by both, but I like it. I made my girl giggle. She has let her guard down and she's trusted me with something she's never given to another.

I know for sure my words in Gaelic were the right ones to say. They are exactly how I feel. The one I've been waiting for is here in my arms. I think the words to myself once again.

My heart is finally complete.

CHAPTER FIFTY-TWO

One and the Same

John

I lift our hands in the air and play with Roni's fingers. I haven't had nearly enough of her, but she needs a break. As I look down at her face, I can't help the swelling of my chest. It was me, I placed that sated look on her face.

"What are you smiling about?" she asks as I lace my fingers with hers.

"I'm smiling?"

"Yeah, goofy."

I laugh. Not answering right way, I glide my hand down her arm, over her shoulder, to her face. Needing to taste her lips, I cup her face and kiss her.

When I pull away, she has a smile on her lips and a dazed look in her eyes. I snort. "I'm not the only one smiling."

"Whatever," she replies and pushes at my shoulder playfully.

I trace my thumb over her chin. My lips turn up more. Roni lifts a brow.

"Why New York?"

She searches my face. I do the same. I was amused by her choice of safe word. Now I'm curious about it.

"It's the first place I remembered, where we became friends, and…" She pauses as her cheeks take color. "It's where we were the first time you took me to a sex club to introduce me to your lifestyle."

"Our lifestyle," I correct.

"Darn it."

"What?" I ask, hearing the teasing in her voice. I know she's about to say something silly.

"I don't remember a red room when you gave me the tour. You have ruined my fantasy of some rich Dom I'm going to run away from," she says, pursing her lips to keep from laughing.

I snort. "I never disappoint, baby. Ever."

I get up from the bed and reach for her to pull her up. Her brows furrowed with curiosity. I kiss her forehead, then turn her and push her forward toward the master bath where the his and hers closets are.

"Okay, what kind of kinky shit can we find in here?" she says once we're in the walk-in closet.

"Hush," I growl and slap her ass.

I lead her to where the hidden panel is and enter the code. The door pops open and I guide her through. She releases a gasp and I laugh.

"It's not red, but if that's the color you prefer, I can paint it."

She turns and wraps her arms around my neck. "You are full of surprises. A whole ass playroom hidden in your closet. I have to say I'm impressed."

"There's a weapons room in the other closet."

"The perfect his and hers closets."

"It's like I always knew I'd get you in this house," I say with a smile.

"Oh, no. I said nothing about moving in with you."

Quickly, I toss her over my shoulder and swat her ass again. "Torque is already packing. You're mine now in every sense of the word. We're not living in that apartment when we have a home," I say firmly.

"I multiply after midnight when wet. Trust me, you don't want me to move in."

"I'll take my chances. It's time we try to make it through a meal," I say.

We tried breakfast and lunch. Both times we ended up feasting on each other. When we enter the kitchen the mess we left is still there.

I place Roni on one of the stools at the island and go to look through my refrigerator for something to make for dinner. Once I've done inventory, I turn and look at her. She's watching me with her elbows on the island, her face in her palms, and her lips turned up.

"I can make us spaghetti. Or chicken cutlets with fettucine," I offer.

"Wait." She frowns. "What's the point of dating an Irish-Scot if he's going to offer me Italian food?"

I pick up the dish towel and toss it at her. "Shut up."

"You know I'm right. Do I have to call Cass?"

I roll my eyes. "Fine, I have to go to the store."

"Can I just say that it's so sexy that you're going to cook for me."

I round the counter and move between her legs. Cupping her face, I look her in the eyes. She leans in and I kiss her soft lips.

"I love it when you're like this."

"Like what?"

I kiss her nose. "Open, your guard is down."

She wraps her arms around my waist. "You're my safe place. I can *be* around you. No watching, no calculating. I like that."

I capture her lips in a deep kiss. Soon I have to force myself to break it before we never eat. "Come on. I'll put you in the tub while I make a store run."

Roni

Dinner was nice, but this is so much better. I think something is wrong with me. Two baths and three naps and I still want more.

Who wouldn't want more of this? I grin as he places a kiss to my stomach. My body is already coiled tightly from this sensory torture that's proving John isn't the only freak.

He has placed a blindfold over my eyes and headphones on my ears. However, it's what plays in my ears that's makes me question so much about myself. John teases my body as the sound of porn plays through the headphone.

Some chick is going crazy as the guy grunts and coaches her and it's all so fucking hot. Not knowing where John will touch me next, if he'll slip inside me and feed this ache—I'm almost overwhelmed with anticipation. I can't help squirming as I wait for him to make me scream like the woman in my ears. I part my lips and moan when he takes a nipple into his mouth.

"John," I hiss when he moves away yet again.

I don't even know how long this teasing has been going on. All I know is I want it to stop so I can feel him once more. Almost twenty-four hours ago, I put a bullet in a woman's skull over this man and I have not a single regret.

"Babe," I whimper as he starts to suck on my inner thigh.

I can't believe he's calmly feasting on my body while I'm losing it from the simplest touch. This isn't fair, but I don't want it to stop. I'm panting and wiggling as he has his way.

Suddenly, I'm turned onto all fours. Face down, ass in the air, my body his for the taking, and take he does. With his finger on my clit and the symphony of sex in my ears, it doesn't take long for him to bring me to my climax.

He tears the headphones from my ears and places his mouth to the shell of one. "We are one and the same. You were made for me."

"Maybe," I say sleepily, my lids already drooping.

He groans as he finds his own release. The swell and hot sensation, causing me to come again. Nap number four is welcomed with a smile.

CHAPTER FIFTY-THREE

Small Assignment

Roni

I wake and stretch. Looking to the side John had been sleeping on, I find the bed empty. I smile. John likes to run in the mornings. He skipped his run yesterday.

My body is sore, but I smile at the reminder of the previous day I had. I'm not complaining at all. Damn, I need to get to the apartment to pack. We leave the day after tomorrow.

"I still don't want to go," I mutter to myself.

I frown and climb out of the bed. I avoid John's family when I can. Cass doesn't make that easy.

It's not that I don't like them. I don't know them. The Blacks have this dynamic that makes me uneasy with longing. I can understand why Missy was so hard pressed to be a part of their clan.

You're afraid to get close because you're afraid of losing them.

"Oh, shut up," I say to my thoughts.

I climb into the shower to avoid the truth running through my head. I want what the other girls have—the connection to Cass, Joe, and all the brothers. I just don't know how.

I press my forehead to the tile wall. Honestly, I think I was damaged before I ever ended up in that place. They only stepped on the broken pieces that were left over.

Can this work with John?

It's like all my evil thoughts begin to attack. Guilt consumes me as I see Natasha's face in my head. Here I am in this house, this gorgeous bathroom and I have no idea what happened to her. I don't know if I can truly say I tried my best to find her.

I punch the side of my hand against the shower wall. I gasp for air as my thoughts threaten to take me under. It's like a weight that's being pressed down on me.

Cutting off the water, I end the shower and go to step out. I grab a towel and wrap in it. That's when something feels off.

I move for the bedroom and grab my guns. Voices rumble from the front of the house. Instincts tell me not to assume that it's John.

I grab the shorts I washed and tug them on. Not releasing my guns, I find one of John's tank tops and pull it over my head. Dressed, I slowly inch out of the room with both guns aimed.

The voices get louder as I move forward. They seem to be arguing. I don't hear John and I don't know the two accented voices I pick up on. When I get to the living area, I have a clearer view of the open floor plan.

Standing in the kitchen stuffing his face with a sandwich is Noah. Two other guys sit at the island going at each other with thick Irish accents, although, they sort of have a hint of New York to them.

Noah freezes, a smile comes to his face. "Good morning, Roni," he says after he swallows.

I have a gun aimed at the heads of the two I don't know. They turn and I'm startled. I'm looking at two version of Wyatt with green eyes. One as big as Noah. He's the one with the pissed as hell expression.

"What the hell is in you guys' genes? Like, how?"

Noah laughs and the smaller one smiles. The mountain doesn't look amused as I haven't lowered my guns yet. He glares and I glare back.

"This is Cole and Logan," Noah says. "You can put the guns down."

I mutter to myself and lower the guns, placing them back on safety.

"Nice to meet, ya. No one calls me Cole. You can call me Brooklyn."

The other one with his mean looking ass, narrows his eyes on me. It's like he isn't looking at me but through me. He tilts his head and narrows his eyes.

"Ya have a familiar face," he finally says.

I shrug. "You don't know me."

"Aye, didn't say I did."

I dismiss him and look to Noah. "Where's John?"

"Right behind you, watching you try to blow my cousin's heads off." I turn to find John with a smirk on his lips.

"It's a family trait. We love 'em violent."

"Speak for yourself," Logan's gruff voice makes me turn to glare at him.

What's he so pissy about? His eyes are on me again. My hand is twitching at my side. I'll shoot his ass if he keeps looking at me like that.

"I don't know. I agree with Brooklyn. We do tend to fall for shooters," Noah says.

"You need to put some vitamin E on your face, and shouldn't you be getting ready for your wedding?" I say.

Noah chuckles. "I'll look into that. We had some business with you guys first."

I lift a brow. John moves to walk by me, tapping my ass as he passes. I whip my head in his direction, but he acts as if nothing happened.

I glare at his back. We'll be having a talk later. It looks like we need outside the bedroom rules as well.

"I'm going back in the room. You fellas enjoy your talk."

"I could have talked to my cousin over the phone. I didn't fly all the way from New York to talk to him. I came to talk to ya," mean ass says.

"Me." I hold the gun in my right hand against my chest.

"Yes, *you*. Ya've already proved what I heard about ya is right. I have a job. I'll pay extra because of the timing and the inconvenience."

"Yeah, I think you have the wrong person. Thanks though." I turn to leave.

"Val said ya have an attitude. She also said she trusts ya with her life. Better yet, the lives of her wee ones. That's why I'm here."

I turn back slowly. I'm not quite sure I like this Logan guy; he has a chip on his shoulder or something. He oozes anger.

"What's up? What's the job?" John asks as he takes a seat in the middle of Brooklyn and Logan.

Logan seems to take a calming breath. He turns that mean glare on Brooklyn. "As you and Noah might already know. My brother here has been keeping little secrets from me while I was away." He looks at me.

"I have a daughter. She's two and a half years old. There are reasons I shouldn't return to Ireland at the moment, but nothing will keep me away for my cousin's wedding. I've been away for long enough," Logan says.

"What does that have to do with me?"

"Shauna is the most important thing in the world to me. There are people who are finding this out and that could pose a problem. I'm asking you to help look out for my wee one during the time I'm in Ireland. I won't be staying long. The few days before and the day of. We'll be out of your hair before you know it," he replies.

"You don't have to do this. She has her nanny and we'll all be fine to look after her," Brooklyn grumbles.

"Cole, you're lucky I haven't cobblered ya yet. Leave me be," Logan says.

"Fine, suit yourself."

"Let me get this right. You want to hire me to look after your little girl?"

"Aye, Uri and Val say you're a natural. I asked them for one of their best hitters, one they trust, and they told me to come see you. That you work for John."

"You know there will be tons of family there. No one will allow anything to happen to her," Noah says.

"It's yer wedding. I don't want to take attention away from that." Logan turns his gaze on me again. "My daughter is with my aunt Cass and uncle Joe. Aunt Cass mentioned your name. I knew you were the one I needed to talk to, love. Do this for me and there will be one million in your bank account before the plane lands in Ireland," Logan says.

I sigh. It's the plea in his eyes. I think I understand the anger coming from him. He's concerned about his little girl. My heart twists. If someone were that concerned about me—I cut the thought off.

A glance at John and I can see that he wants me to do this. Not for the money, but for his family. His family that trusts me. Cass mentioned me. She talks to people about me like I'm already one of her daughters-in-law. I've heard her do it.

"Fine. Give me the details of what you need. I'll do it."

John

"You're a da," I say to Logan.

"Aye, I'm as shocked as you sound," he says gruffly.

"I bet. You know they only did what they thought was right."

He grunts and nods into the living room. "What do you know about her?" he asks, changing the subject as he watches Roni talk to Noah and Brooklyn in the living room.

"Only what I've learned over the last few years. She doesn't remember anything before that," I reply.

"You believe this?"

"Aye, I do." I nod. "Roni may be a lot of things, but she's not a liar. At least, she's not able to lie to me. I see right through her. Val was right, you can trust her."

"It's not trust that I'm having a problem with," he says and squints in Roni's direction. "There's something about her. Something about her face."

I sit up a little straighter. "You think you know her?"

He shakes his head. "Naw, I don't think I've ever seen her in my life, but her face reminds me of someone. I've yet to figure out who."

He says that as if he's frustrated about the fact. He purses his lips and turns back to me. "Anyway. Thanks for this."

"I'm not doing anything. Do you really think they would come at you during the wedding?"

"I'm not willing to chance it."

"You know Brooklyn and the others would never let anything happen to her."

"I'm too angry to say what my siblings will or won't do. You know me well enough to know I'm covering all the angles. The one time in my life that I didn't it cost me more than I could afford to lose," he grumbles.

I nod. "Yeah, I understand. Although you know you didn't have to offer money. I would have asked her to do it for free," I reply.

"If I'm right, she's family. She should be enjoying the wedding with you guys. She deserves the pay."

I snort. "I'm practically dragging her kicking and screaming. You might have helped me out more than you know."

Logan turns his gaze on me. "Ya look happy. I don't know if I've ever been able to truly say that about ya over the years. It looks good on ya. Do what ya need to keep her. I will regret my mistakes for as long as I live. Never let her down, ya hear," he says slipping deep into his accent.

"Yeah, I hear you."

He stands and pats me on the shoulder. "Good. We'll be getting out of your hair. See you soon."

I watch Roni as the guys say their goodbyes and leave. I don't plan on letting her down or letting her go. She turns to me and for the first time today that smile is out.

My Roni.

"Come here. It's been too long since you've been in my arms," I say.

She gives me this sexy look. "You got it, boss."

Oh yeah, I'm definitely never letting her go.

CHAPTER FIFTY-FOUR

Cared For

Roni

"Nice," I murmur to myself. "Almost done."

I'm lying in the middle of the bed working John's books for the business. He is not about the books, scheduling jobs and getting the job done is his thing. I'm getting things in order and setting it up for his dad to have access to the account John created to send Black and Lock their cut of the business.

Black Confidential has been doing great. We're able to do jobs here and there while also helping out Black and Lock. John seems to be happy with the workflow, but my head almost exploded when I looked over his shoulder as he looked at all this last night.

With our flight leaving in the morning, I want this done. I hit send on the email for Joe and Rob. I've finished the task of linking their access. I save and start to look over my work.

That's when a gift box is tossed on the bed. I look up to find John standing before the bed staring back at me. He reaches for his shirt and begins to strip out of his clothes. Sitting up and crossing my legs in front of me, I take in the show he's putting on.

Once he's butt naked, he stands with his legs set wide and arms across his chest. "Put that on," he commands.

"Put what on, Mr. Black?" I say with a grin.

"Open the box, smartass."

I reach for the box and take the lid off. Peeling the tissue paper back, I find a sheer scrap of fabric. I hold it up and look over it at John.

"You needed all that box for this little bullshit?"

He drops his head back and blows out a breath. "Only you," he snorts. He looks at me and barks the command again. "Put it on."

I toss it back into the box and stare at him. He shakes his head at me, but I don't move. Yup, I'm defiant for the sake of it.

He bends at the waist and places his palms flat on the bed. "You want this as bad as I do. We've been talking about it for the last two days. What's the problem, princess?"

I get on all fours and claw to him. Wrapping my arms around his neck, I place my forehead to his. "This handing over control thing. It may be a problem."

He lifts to his full height bringing me with him. I wrap my legs around him, and he captures my lips. The taste of something citrus bursts into my mouth, pulling a moan from my lips.

"You said that wasn't a problem for you. What's changed your mind?"

"I like watching you try not to be annoyed when I don't listen." I pout.

He releases a laugh. "Is that right?"

"Yeah."

He kisses my nose. "How about this? For today, this will be all about your pleasure and yours alone. We go inside and do whatever you want. One day of you having full control before you hand it all over to me."

"You...give up control? Yeah, right."

He nips my lip. "The only way to find out is to put that on and follow me."

He gets the biggest side eye ever from me as I slide down his body. However, I take off his T-shirt I've been wearing and peel off my panties. Making a show of it, I turn my back to him and reach for the teddy in the gift box.

With a grunt, he walks off toward the master bath. I get the scrap of fabric on and follow after him. When I get into the closet, the door to the playroom is already sitting open.

I try not to drool over this man as he sits back on his elbows, on the bench in front of the bed.

"Well, where do you want to start?"

Where do I want to start? I want to do it all. Everything I've watched and been curious about when we've gone to Club Desire. The whole nine yards.

I chew my lip trying to decide on an actual answer. This place is larger than his master bedroom and fully equipped for a sex play dream.

I don't know why I was so surprised the first time he brought me in here. This place is better than any red room. I like that it's dark and sensual. Mixes of black and gray make up the wall colors and furnishings.

The four-poster bed sits on a platform in the center of the room, anchoring the space. It has a black leather tufted headboard—the masculine feature gives the room a bold statement. Actually, it's the bed and the mirrored half wall that rises up behind it.

A large boxed like mirror that spans most of the bed is suspended above from black chains similar to a light fixture or something. All the other bondage furniture fits in the room as if a designer strategically placed them into the design. Pleasing to the eye and functional.

This place puts Club Desire to shame. There's a bondage board, swing, a bench, bondage cross, a sex wheel, this box like table that has grabbed my attention a number of times. The thing looks like a piece of normal furniture—a simple coffee table—but with its padded base and the hole in the center, I know it's anything but.

That's just the start of what's in here. This room was built for pleasure and tranquility. Water features run in front of the display shelves that hold toys and accessories.

Does he think he can purify himself before and after the kinky shit he does?

I snort at my thoughts.

"What?"

"Nothing," I say.

He gives me a curious look but doesn't push. I look around the room, still deciding. When I turn fully, the water and platform behind me come into view.

You should always be in control. Allow him to think he is, but you're always topping mentally... Always. Be. Teasing.

"I want you in ties," I say without turning.

"Is that right?" The lust in his voice causes me to face him. He's now leaning forward as if he's ready to pounce. The desire in his voice is reflected in his eyes. "What do you plan to do with me?"

"You said this is about my pleasure, right? My one free day to control before I hand it all to you."

He nods and licks his lips.

"I want to break you," I say with a slick smile.

He releases a laugh that lights his entire face. Laugh lines around his eyes, head back slightly, Adam's apple bobbing, sparkle in his eyes and all, so sexy. That golden gaze takes me in from head to toe.

Seeming pleased with what he sees, he nods his assent. He reaches for the controller he tossed on the bed and presses something. Suddenly, one of the water features slows to a stop, fully revealing the wall behind it.

"The silk ties are in the top drawer, rope and zip ties in the second and third," he says, not taking his eyes off of me. I start to move for the drawers and shelves. "Oh, and Roni."

I look over my shoulder. "Yeah."

"Good luck, princess," he says with a wink as he leans back against his elbows once again.

I scoff and rock my jaw. Challenge accepted. I'm determined to make him lose it. John is able to hold back orgasms for hours. He prides himself on it. I want to own his ass.

With a smile on my lips, I open the top draw and pull out two ties. I laugh to myself, those stupid app videos I watched out of boredom pop into my head and I put one back. Silk in hand, I prance back over to John.

I climb onto his lap and he grasps my waist. His dick pulses against my butt cheeks. We lock eyes and I know I have this in the bag.

"Do you have music in here?"

"Yes." He grabs the controller and hands it over, then taps at the buttons. "Music panel comes up when you press this. It syncs with our phones. I added yours earlier."

"You knew I'd want to play music?" I lift a brow.

He gives a short laugh. "No, smartass. The system feeds the house. It will pull your device from the connection to the main house sound system."

I shrug. "Wouldn't have been the first time you've read my mind."

"Maybe," he says teasingly.

I tap at the screen and pull up my phone. It allows me to unlock my device from the controller and get into my phone's playlists. I find the song I want and press play, placing it on repeat. "River" by Bishop Briggs pours through the speakers.

I toss the device down on the bed behind John and hand him the tie. He gives me a smug look. I look at him pointedly. He talked shit about beginning able to tie the same knot as the guys on the videos and better than they did.

He takes the silk and effortlessly creates the two loops and knot. He sticks his hands in the loops and bites the end to tug the loops tight around his wrists, winking at me when it's done. I grin and kiss his lips. It is sexier when he does it. I stand up on the bench to reach for one of the hooks fastened to the intricate canopy part of the bed frame.

John kisses my thigh. "The keypad will release them for you. That one is FM3 on the screen," he breathes against my skin.

"Oh," I say and feel my cheeks heat.

I should have known he had this bed rigged up to that thing too. Squatting back down, I allow my breasts to hover in his face, teasing him. When I press the keypad, the hook I want releases with a gasp. The chains rattling as it drops. I have to press the arrow on the screen to lower it to the level I want.

"You're like the fucking inspector gadget of kinky shit."

He releases a deep laugh. "I've always known I'd find someone perfect for this room."

I turn to find his face close to mine. His eyes searching. Oh, he's trying to place me under that spell. I'm not gonna do it.

Instead of getting lost in his gaze, I lift his arms and place them on the hook. He has an amused look on his face as if I'm an amateur. Well, I am but I plan to show him.

I move to his feet and reach for the restraint I noticed tucked away beneath the bench he's sitting on. The chain releases, revealing its length. This will do. I fasten the first one around his left ankle.

"Very observant," he murmurs.

"I learned from the best." I wink at him to mock him.

I move to the right ankle and reach for that restraint. Once I have it fastened as well, I rise and take a step back to eye him. His muscles bulge as his arms are trapped above his head. Slowly, I allow my eyes to move down his gorgeous body. His collarbone is already glistening with sweat, putting his Brothers Black tattoo on display.

Traveling lower with my gaze, his abs come into view. I lick my lips and slide my hand down my stomach to where the sheer fabric of the teddy dips. Slipping my hand inside, I bite my lip, then touch myself.

The chains clink and I smile. I lift my eyes to his and the heat I see almost buckles my knees. He's looking at me through his lashes and hooded lids. To have this beautiful man look at me with so much passion places a fire in my belly.

He leans back slightly, bringing my attention back down. His legs are spread wide due to the restraints. My lips part. He's so hard and it looks like all the blood has rushed to the fat mushroomed tip.

"Like what you see?" he asks, his voice a deep rumble that divulges the depth of his want. "Come get it, Roni."

My pussy is already weeping, but I'm not ready to free us of this torment. He promised me control. Clearly, he doesn't know how to submit. He still thinks he's in control.

"Do you remember being mad at me for not being around for the ladies' performance at the compound?" I say.

His forehead creases for a second, then recognition comes forth. He narrows his eyes. "Yeah, I remember."

I spin on the balls of my feet and make a running start for the waterfall. Leaping in the air, I reach out for the two rings that hang above the platform the water runs over. John calls out my name to stop me. I'm sure because the rings are wet and slippery, but I grab them and hold tight.

Once settled, I release one ring to turn and face John, before securing both hands once again. Water cascades down on me as I lift and balance on the rings. I look at John and he's still staring with the same intensity. I have his full undivided attention.

Good.

John

My chest heaves as I watch my girl. She almost gave me a heart attack jumping for those rings. I would have cut the water off if I knew she wanted to play on them.

She's a work of art as she holds herself up. When she drops out from the position she's been holding, she throws herself into a spin, water sprays out from her body as she spirals. Her braid circling her with the action.

I tug at my restraints. I never should have agreed to this. I'm so hard it hurts. I want to toss her on this bed behind me and fuck the shit out of her.

"Shit," I mutter.

She spins back the other way, then she drops down to the balls of her feet like cat. When she lands, she lifts her head slightly and looks up through her wet lashes. Water drips down her face and from the tip of her nose.

Standing, she keeps her eyes on me and stretches her arms out to her sides. Roni begins to roll her hips to the beat, teasing me with every gyration.

Precum beads at the tip of my cock. She might actually succeed at breaking me, she keeps this up. As if reading my thoughts, she places a hand on her belly and tips it in time to the song.

If she means to make up for that show in New York, she's forgiven. I almost forgot about that. It was almost two years ago, clearly my words stuck with her because she's putting her all into this show.

"Damn," I growl, when she turns and bends at the waist to show off that plump ass. The string of the teddy lost in all that sweetness.

I bare my teeth. If she was closer, I'd bury my face between her cheeks and pull the thong out before sucking on her sweet pussy. I drag my tongue across my lips as if tasting her on them already.

I say a prayer of thanks as she starts to dance her way to me. I hate to ruin her show, but she didn't make the anchor on my restraints taut enough. If I wanted, I could get my hands free.

I still consider it as she gets nearer. She turns her back to me and moves like she's going to sit in my lap. Instead, she plants her hands on the sides of me and leans back, taunting me some more.

I stick my tongue out and lick her cheek when she turns her face to the side. That brings a smile to her lips. In a quick motion, she's facing me, straddling my lap as she looks down at me. Bringing her lips inches from mine, she breathes me in.

It takes everything in me to remember that I've given her control. Otherwise, I'd take her mouth and devour her. Those lush lips are tempting me.

"Not bad," I say to goad her.

She tilts her head to the side a bit. "Oh, you thought that was it?"

She reaches between us and grabs my cock. A curse is on the tip of my tongue as she moves to her knees and take me in her mouth. I drop my head back and ball my fists.

"*Gah*, baby," I groan.

Is she sucking my dick to the song? I look up at the mirror above and she has her eyes on me as I watch our reflection. I drop my gaze to Roni in the flesh. Fuck yeah, she's damn near swallowing my cock to the rhythm of the song and that shit is so fucking hot, I start to lift my hips to match her efforts.

This seems to egg her on. I roll my hips and she bobs her head, working her hands at the same time. Pure natural talent.

Shit, she can have control anytime she wants with head like this. My eyes roll in the back of my head. My thighs start to burn from the position we're in, but you'd have to shoot my ass to stop this.

Roni reaches to run her hands up my abs and I jerk. "Fuck," I hiss out.

She lets me pop free from her mouth. "Too much for you, boss?"

"Not at all, princess. I'm still with you, baby."

"Mm, let's fix that."

She wipes her forearm across her mouth, then lifts to straddle me once again. This time she captures my lips. It becomes a battle of wills as we use our tongues to fight for control of the kiss.

I'm so consumed by our power struggle, I don't realize she's seating herself until her tight, hot pussy has sheathed me, pulling a groan from my lips. She cups my face and holds me to her, preventing me from telling her that she forgot to put a condom on me.

As she starts to ride me, rocking and rolling her hips, all is forgotten. The feel of being inside her bare draws out something animalistic inside me. I tug at my wrists to unhook them. Once, twice, the third time is a charm.

"John," she gasps when I cage her in between my bond arms and thrust into her.

I stare into her eyes and she looks down at me. Yeah, I tried. Moment of truth, I never really thought I had it in me to be the bottom.

Sweat pours down my face as I guide her body on top of mine. However, my girl isn't ready to lose complete control. She tugs my head back and rides me harder.

"That's my princess take it. You're soaking my cock, baby. You like riding me, don't you?"

She sucks my lip into her mouth. "I'm not the only one enjoying this. You're so hard. I feel you heating up inside me. Come, John. Give me what I want?"

I give her a devilish smile. I come inside her, that's it. She's sealing her fate. My heart pounds at the thought of her swollen with my child.

"You sure you want that?"

Her reply is to suck my tongue into her mouth, and she does this slow roll of her hips, again, moving in sync with the song. As she wishes. I finally free my hands. It's time I give my baby what she's asking for.

Roni

I'm taken by surprise when John grabs the thong of the teddy and tears it. I had pushed it aside in my eagerness. I don't get much time to react as he wraps my braid with one hand and palms my back with the other.

He instantly takes over. Thrusting into me and tugging my head back. I'm bowed backward as he rocks into me.

"Do you realize I'm going to come inside you?" he growls before he captures one of my nipples in his mouth.

I tighten and gush all over him. My screams fill the air as he drills my body from beneath. The bite to my scalp from him tugging me backward only increases the pleasure.

"Yes, yes."

"Fuck me, princess. Don't stop now," he hisses through his teeth.

He lets me up a bit, but he doesn't stop thrusting up into me and he still has a tight hold on my braid. I can tip my chin down enough to look into his face. His face is soaked in sweat. He releases a groan and his nostrils flare. The sweat from his nose flies onto my breasts as he releases a harsh breath. The sight is so fucking hot.

I've never seen John so unhinged. I flex my walls around his shaft. He growls and slaps my ass so hard I come. My eyes widen as he smiles with all his teeth and pistons into me harder.

Then it happens. It's as if I leave my body and I'm hovering above our sweaty connected ones. The look in John's eyes reveals more than desire and the determination to make me come again.

I see… love? Is that what it looks like? He places a kiss to the center of my chest that's such a contradiction to his fucking. It's tender and reflects the look in his eyes.

"You sure you want me to come inside you?" he whispers.

His words caress my soul like a plea. It is in this moment that I want to be his, I need to be marked by him, to know he'll always be this for me. If that means he needs me to be submissive for him, I think I can do that.

I'm determined to try all I can. Yet, I know that's not what he's asking for. This goes beyond submission. He's asking for a different trust. The kind that you plan for. A decision that builds a future.

"Give yourself to me," he pleas, placing a hand over my heart.

I nod, relishing the feel of him swelling even more. "Yes."

I throw my head back as his hot seed fills me. He kisses between my breasts and finally releases the hold he has on my hair. My mind reels as I come down from the best high of my life.

"You know... I could end up... that might have been stupid," I mutter.

"I have no regrets. Blacks play for keeps. Whatever happens from this moment, I'm conscious that I want it all. All of you and all of what we are to each other. It's my job to care for you. Let me."

I say nothing to those words. Not because I have nothing to say, but because I want to wrap myself in them. I want to be cared for.

CHAPTER FIFTY-FIVE

I Love You

John

Ireland for Noah's wedding…

I stumble into the house. It's time for me to call it quits if I'm getting up for this wedding tomorrow. My brothers and cousins are still at it, but my mind is elsewhere.

"Hey, John," my cousin Connie says as she walks toward me.

I lean in and kiss her cheek when she stops in front of me. "Hey Con."

She giggles and purses her lips. "I see ya boys have been hitting the black stuff."

"Aye, a wee bit. The Guinness is always better here. You seen Roni?"

"This is true." She laughs and tosses a thumb over her shoulder. "She's in the theater with Shauna and yer mum and da."

I nod and tug her into a hug, kissing the top of her head. "I love you, Con. We have to see each other more."

She pats my cheek. "Go find your bird. Let her put you to sleep," she says.

"How do you know she's my girl?"

Connie's face lights up. "It's in the way ya guard her with yer body, as if ya can shield her from the world. And the way the two of ya look at each other. She's in love with ya, ya know this right?"

I grin like an idiot. "You never know with Roni. She shows her emotions when she wants to."

"Don't be a stook. Anyone can see it. She's a tough one, but she's soft for you."

I hug her again. "I'll see you tomorrow."

"Mmm," she says with a smile. "See ya bright and early, I will."

I stumble around Connie a bit and her laugh reaches me as she walks away. The theater room is down the stairs, but it might as well be in New York for all the effort I have to put in to get there. I make my way inside as my mother and father are on their way out with a Shauna on my father's shoulder.

I bend and kiss my mom on the cheek. "Yer fluthered," my mother says.

"Nah, I'm not that drunk," I say and try to straighten up.

Mom laughs. "The boy is totally langered. Where are the rest of the eejits? Ye'll all be useless in the morning."

"I plead the fifth."

Dad laughs low. "Come on, Cass, leave the lad be. Let's get this one into bed and call it a night so we're not useless in the morning."

"Fine."

I watch my parents go before I turn to head down the rows in search of Roni. I find her three rows from the top, slouched down in one of the large loungers. A quick glance around and I see we're here alone.

Tugging my lip into my mouth, I can't help thinking about popping the button on her jeans and bending her over the seats in front of us. However, lacking the coordination for that, I more so flop down beside her and fall onto my back in her lap. She doesn't even pull her eyes from the screen as she reaches to start combing a hand through my hair.

The gesture is so soothing, I close my eyes and bask in the feeling. It takes a moment for the sound from the movie to break through my drunken fog. When the music registers, I snort.

"Really? Grease?" I slur.

"Don't make me dump your drunk ass on the floor. This is a classic and you will respect it."

I smile and look at her pretty face. "Does my mother know you feel this way?"

"Maybe. I find I have a lot in common with the little lady," she says with a teasing grin.

"I think that's why she likes you."

I close my eyes again and take in the moment. I'm fucking shitfaced. It wasn't my intention to get this drunk.

And damn, I'm horny as fuck. I shift my head to nuzzle her belly. "You smell *so* good, baby."

She laughs. "Your ass is *so* drunk, *baby*."

"Mm, maybe," I say and reach under her shirt to palm one of her breasts.

The cup is in my way, so I tug it down. I smirk and begin to roll her hardened peak between my fingers when it tightens from my caress. I'm growing stiffer by the second which means I'm not as drunk as I think I am. I groan when the sound of her panting fills the air.

"I wanna fuck."

"Are you serious?" she says incredulously.

"Yeah, come here. Sit on my cock."

"That would be a no," she says. I pinch her nipple, causing her to take in a sharp breath. "John."

"See, you want it too. Come here," I breathe against her stomach, flicking my tongue out.

She tugs my hand from under her shirt and places it on my chest. I reposition my head so I can look up at her. She's glaring at me.

"I'm going to finish this movie. If you're still coherent after, then I'll think about it."

I laugh and lock my fingers together over my stomach, settling in again. My lids have a mind of their own and won't stay open. Oh well, I let them have their way and tap my feet to the music as my legs hang over the arm of the seat. I grin to myself.

"You know, you're already showing signs of being a terrible Sub. So defiant. I'm going to enjoy spanking you until we get that fixed."

"You can kiss my ass, you know *that*, right."

More laughter spills from me. "This is why I love you."

Roni stiffens. I open my eyes and look up at her. It takes a
moment for me to focus on her face. When I do, she looks like
she's seen a ghost or something.

"What? What happened?"

"Nothing," she says and turns back for the screen.

I'm drunk, but I still know my woman. Not willing to let
this go, I sit up and drag her into my lap. I cup her face and
search her eyes as I try to think over what I said before the
change in her demeanor.

She drops her gaze to my chest, and it clicks. The realization
sobers me up a bit and I capture her lips. Deepening the kiss, I
pour my soul into our connection.

"I love you," I say into her mouth and tug at her lip. "I love
you." I kiss her again. "I love—"

"I love you," she says before I can finish saying it again. She
looks me in the eyes. "And that scares the shit out of me."

I nuzzle her nose. "Why? What are you afraid of? Do you
have any idea how much I love you? If you would let me, I'd
make sure the world knows how much I love you every day."

She smooths a finger over one of my brows and gives me a
weak smile. "John, I don't care about anyone else knowing how
you feel about me. That's not what I need."

"What do you need?"

She looks as if she's searching her feelings. "To know you're
here to stay. I… this can't be a mistake."

I scoff. "Mistake? The only mistake between us was waiting
too long to become us. I'm not going anywhere."

"If you hurt me, I'm going to kill you slow. I like Cass. I
don't want to have to take one of her sons."

"Tell me what's actually on your mind. You already know I
would never hurt you, so what's really going on?"

She places her forehead to mine. "We fucked up."

"We're both adults."

"I can't stop thinking about the other night. I could be pregnant. What's wrong with us?

"We've talked about safe words, collars, we even talked about me starting birth control, which to me says you don't want children. And yet, we've never once talked about if you want a family with me."

"Come here." I bring her to straddle my lap instead of sitting in it. "I want you and if you're not pregnant already, I plan to fix that as soon as the room stops spinning."

"I'm fucked up. Can you seriously say you want to have a family with me?"

I turn completely serious. "All my life I've been the pretty brother. Women don't stop to think about what they are getting into with me because they can't stop ogling me.

"For the first time in my life, I've found someone that's nothing but honest with me. You call me on my shit, and you treat me like I need you, not like you need me.

"I haven't been too pretty for you to speak up and tell me what you do like and don't like. You like the same shit." I pause and shake my head.

When I look deeper into her eyes, I see everything I ever wanted, and I continue. "I've always known you were out there. Somewhere, waiting for me to find you, to love you. I'm not going anywhere, Roni."

"You're drunk. You don't know what you're saying."

"I'm drunk so everything I say is true."

"Everything I've been through has brought me here. I don't deserve—"

"You don't deserve to be happy?" I shake my head. "No matter how many times you say that it's not going to be true. You're not to blame for what happened that night. The other team was supposed to get the others out safely. There was no way to know Natasha wasn't going to get out with the others.

"God, baby, that has haunted me since you told me she never made it to New York, but we can't live our entire lives unhappy because of it. You deserve to live and be happy," I say.

"I'd probably make a terrible mother; you know this right?"

I place my hand over her belly. "Our son will be the luckiest kid in the world. His name will be John by the way."

"Whatever," she says and rolls her eyes.

"You can trust me. I will show you how good your future can be. Let me in." I smile as the song in the background registers with my brain. "Do you hear that?"

"What?"

"The song."

She listens as Sandy and Danny sing about being the one that they each want. A smile beams across her face. She's so damn beautiful.

Roni kisses my lips. "This is my favorite song in the movie. And yeah, you're the one that I want too."

CHAPTER FIFTY-SIX

Wedding Duty

Roni

Noah and Bean look so happy. She makes a gorgeous bride. This wedding was more than I expected, but as I look around, I think it's perfect for them.

The wedding is in full swing. Music is blaring, laughter rings out around the room. Everyone looks so happy and normal.

Normal. It's an odd word when you think of it. Here I sit with Shauna in my lap while she plays with Torque's phone. Torque is on the dance floor, soaking up all the feminine attention.

The kid looks good. He cleaned up well in his tux. And yet, I can't help thinking about why I've made sure to have Shauna as close as possible when she's not in her father's arms.

"What's the deal with those two?" I nod over at Logan and Brooklyn as they lock their heads together in a heated discussion.

Cass turns to look over at the two, then back at me. She tilts her head to the side as her eyes twinkle and she reaches to run a hand over Shauna's hair. It's not lost on me that Cass is both a gentle woman as much as she's a hard ass.

"Me nephews and their sisters are as close as me boys are. This wee one means the world to the both of them, but her father has only just learned she exists. His brother did what he thought was the best thing for them both. I believe he was right. However, it's going to take time for Logan to feel that way. For the moment, he's like a bear that wants to rip all his siblings apart," she says.

"Why do I get the feeling Connie and Kate could have done this… looked after her?" I say and look down at Shauna.

"Because the O'Briens would turn this place upside down if anyone breathed so much as a foul breath in this tiny lass's direction."

I nod and look back to the brothers. Brooklyn is now smiling at Logan, but Logan still has a slight frown on his face. I follow the line of his gaze and find Camille on the other end. From what I know, she's Bobby's assistant or something.

She and Paige seemed to be close, the few times I saw them together back in New York. Proving my point, the woman I've been seeing clinging to Sam and Paige walk over to Camille and her eyes light up. Again, I remind myself that these people aren't normal.

"I can always tell which women will be right for me boys." Cass says, bringing my attention back to her. "The ones that can handle *everything* about us. The first time I met you, I knew you would be the one that understands it best."

"Understands what?" I lift a brow.

"Don't make me bop ye upside your head. Yer just like me little fuckers." She narrows her eyes on me, then smiles. "Be patient with John, love. Everything we know is changing and the more change that comes, the more they're all going to become more protective. I'm warning ye now because I see it coming."

"It's not my patience I'm worried about. It's his."

"Johnathan Dillion Black has been waiting for you all his life. Someone to call his own. Being not quite the middle child of seven, but almost has taken its toll on him. Nothing is ever truly his. He has shared and nurtured when it comes to his brothers. Always the peace maker," she replies.

"Always the one doing the fixing," I murmur.

"Aye, see. Ye get me boy so well."

I look out at the dance floor and my gaze lands on John. He's hovering over a little boy that's having a tantrum on the floor.

"Ah, shite," Shauna says as she apparently loses the game.

I look back at Cass, widening my eyes. Her shoulders shake with laughter as mirth shows in her eyes. She shrugs it off.

"She wouldn't be the first," Cass says.

"Oh God. Not my babies. I need to start cleaning my mouth up now," I groan.

"Are ye pregnant?"

I freeze. I can't say yes. It's too soon. However, I'd feel like a liar if I said no.

Thankfully, John comes to save the day. He has the little boy in his arms from the dance floor. He's the cutest little guy. Gray eyes and dark hair. The moment they reach us he almost leaps into my lap and wraps his arms around my neck.

Shauna moves over, but I see the little frown on her face. John must pick up on it too. He reaches for Shauna and she goes to him.

"Now this looks like a future," Cass says and stands. "I'll leave you be. Maybe ye'll catch the fever from giving all these wee ones attention."

With that, she floats off humming. John takes the seat she left, holding Shauna in his lap. He gives me a brilliant smile.

"I'm not going to lie, I've been watching you with her all day and thinking what it will be like to have our own," John says.

"This isn't insane... you want this? Like now," I say.

"Nope, and I'm pretty sober today." He winks. "You have no reason to doubt me."

Suddenly, the little boy in my arms starts to hum. At first, I think he's humming something random. I used to hum to myself when I was younger. It drove my father crazy.

I freeze. That memory came so easily. Me humming, my father's face as I hummed to myself.

However, I'm brought back to the moment as the little guy cups my face. He stares at my chin as he hums some more. The song clicks and I draw my brows.

"Say yes. No scared. Yes, okay?" he says reaching for my hand and John's and linking them together. "*Bella*, say yes to everything."

I look to John. I'm sure all the blood has drained from my face. John has a surprised look on his as well.

"He's humming "You're the One that I Want". Who is this kid?"

"Hey, Sammy, where'd you hear that song?" John says.

The kid doesn't answer. He jumps off my lap and races across the room to wrap around the leg of the woman with Paige and Camille. I look back at John.

"Could he have been there last night? Oh my God, John, after the movie we—"

"He and his family arrived this morning. No, he wasn't there," John says. He shrugs. "Coincidence. After all, you said it yourself. It's a classic."

When Logan calls it a night and collects his daughter, I need a drink.

John

"You look tired," I say as I walk up behind Roni and wrap my arms around her.

She shrugs. "A little."

"What are you thinking about?"

"I remembered something about my father today. It was something small. The little kid humming triggered it.

"I had pretty much given up on remembering more of my past. Sometimes... there are days when I think I should leave it all where it is. You know, like it's all going to come back and bite me if I finally figure out how to pull the fog back," she murmurs.

I turn her to face me. "Hey, if you remember nothing, I will be here to help you make new memories. If you remember everything, including the day you were born, I'll be here to help you deal with how you feel about that.

"It will always be my sole mission to see you happy and safe. Don't get lost in your head. I'll be your anchor. Use me."

She smiles at me. "Yes, boss." I growl and palm her ass. "See, I can be a good submissive."

"We have the rest of our lives to prove that's a lie."

She reaches to cup my junk. "I was wondering how I can get one of those spankings. Is this enough?"

I throw my head back and laugh. God, I love this woman. I'll do anything to protect her and make her happy.

CHAPTER FIFTY-SEVEN

Present Fire

Roni

Back to the present…

"It will end the way I want it to end, Cherone."

The words ring like a bell as the bullet from my gun pierces through this son of a bitch's skull. After all I've been through, it finally all falls into place. It's clear as day as if I've lived it all over again. I remember every single detail, including the day this fucker groped me and demanded I marry Darius or be sold off.

Even over the last nine months, I've suffered because of this man. Or better yet, because of the people who sent him for me. Rage courses through me as his body drops to the ground.

I run over and empty my clip into his chest. Tears blur my vision. The more I remember, the more I become unhinged.

"Is this how you wanted it to end, you fuck?" I scream. "I'm going to kill you all. I'm coming for every single one of you."

"Roni, Roni," John calls out as he wraps me in his arms.

"What the fuck?" Ryan says somewhere close by.

I bury my face in John's chest. "I remember. I remember everything. I know who I am."

"Holy shit," Ryan says.

"I'm going to kill them, John. I'm going to fucking kill them."

John

When I say I'm coiled tight enough to spin, I'm ready to explode and I've yet to hear the truth. She remembers. That means that I can finally close this chapter for her.

With her.

I work my jaw. I understand Roni, she's not going to allow me to do this for her, but I'll be there with her. That's a promise I can make.

"You guys all right?" Wyatt asks as he comes through the doorway panting.

"We're good. Are we all clear? Roni and John need a moment, she remembers," Ryan says.

Wyatt pushes a hand through his hair as he takes in a sobbing Roni. "We're all clear here. Felix, you have an update for me on the rest of the family?"

"Toby's getting mom stitched up. She was hit in the shoulder," Felix says into the comms.

"*No,*" Roni screams, causing my heart to feel like it's going to give out as my brain glitches from my brother's words.

"She's okay," Felix adds, calming the storm in my head only slightly. "Toby said these fuckers got it worse."

"Noah?" Wyatt asks.

"His place is shot up, but they're fine. He says we're going to want to hear what he and Bean learned."

Wyatt nods. His lips tight. He looks to Roni still sobbing in my arms.

I already know what he's thinking. He needs me to clean this mess up, but I have my girl in my arms, falling apart. I catch his eyes and nod.

"This is going to take a hell of a lot of favors," he says.

"Yeah, but I'll handle it. My team will cover. Get everyone out of here and be careful."

This is definitely one of those times I'm grateful that I've expanded the team and have my own clean up crew. Our lives are leaving bigger messes in their wake. This needs a personal touch with finesse.

"The baby," Carmen says.

"Safe," Felix replies. "Tell her that Omid has her. She's safe."

Ryan tightens his hold around Carmen and murmurs something in her ear. I still have my woman locked closely to my chest. I think I'm the only thing holding her up at this point.

"Felix, I can use a little assistance with this if you can," I say. "I'm going to need eyes in the sky for the guys."

"You got it."

"John," Roni whimpers.

"Shh, first, let me get you in the bird. Then, I'll make some calls. After that, I'll get you home and you can tell me everything. Okay?"

Roni nods and sniffles. She's in that detached mode. I can feel it. This is a huge blow.

In the back of my mind, I know this all comes from the Alliance. We've been waiting for it. However, as I move Roni toward the chopper, I have one question.

How does this all connect to my woman?

CHAPTER FIFTY-EIGHT

Let Me Heal You

John

We're sitting in the back of the Chevelle where I found Roni after I finally got our little girl to sleep. Roni has been like a hollow shell since we took off from that rooftop. It's going to take time to get through to her and I haven't had a second to breathe yet.

This has been a shit show. Half of my family will be splitting between my place and Wyatt's since Mom, Noah, and Toby all had their places shot up. I guess I understand why Roni has been hiding out here.

"More damage control," Roni murmurs for the first time in hours.

"LaSalle is a true friend. He sent Bobby in to help. Felix has been working with him to get shit done," I reply.

I'm still fielding text messages from my contacts that are making this go away. I can't put the phone down before it's buzzing again. I'm grateful to Torque for the blackout text system he built just for our network. All of our communications are ghost.

"Do we need to go help?"

I kiss her head as she sits between my legs with her back to me. Tightening my embrace, I lend her my strength. "We're right where we need to be. You ready to talk? No rush, I'm only asking."

She fiddles with her phone a bit and then moves from my hold to turn the key in the ignition. The sound system I placed in the car as an enhancement comes to life. "I Wanna Dance with Somebody" by Whitney Houston fills the car.

Roni settles back between my legs and blows out a breath. "There's one time I remember my mother and father together. My first and last memory of them as a couple. I can't believe I can remember it now, it was so long ago and I had to be so small."

She snorts, then continues. "My dad swayed my mother to this song. They laugh and danced together like something out of one of those movies.

"I think that was the last time they saw each other. They fought like cats and dogs that same night. My mother was never happy again after that. I can't remember my father being happy after that either."

"Do you remember where they are now?"

"Dead. My mother died when I was ten and my father..." She stifles a sob. "His death was the beginning of all of this. He had a sudden heart attack."

I wrap my arms around her again and start to sway her to the music. "We don't have to do this now," I murmur against her shoulder.

"Yeah, we do. I need you to know what happened on that roof and why I'm about to become the epitome of death's rage. Val was right, there were people who hurt me. People before those Russians. I wasn't someone random like the others."

"What are you saying?"

"My father was a powerful man. I believe all of this was because of his power. His death might have put a target on my back. I need to go see Misha. I think he has the missing pieces that I need."

"Misha?" I say in surprise.

"Yeah, he once told me that we have common enemies. I don't want to be right, but my gut is telling me I know where all this started. I need to be sure before I start knocking at doors.

"I think that's why Misha's so pissed about Torque. Misha knows something he's not telling me, he wanted Torque to stop pushing."

"But you knew Torque was up to something."

"No, I knew he was taking a trip, that's all. You were so angry with me this morning; you wouldn't let me explain. I didn't know what the trip was for or where. I told him to back off. I warned him."

"But he ran face first into Misha instead."

"Yeah, thank God it was Misha. I don't know what I would have done if he went after someone else. He thinks he's protecting me. I could have told him Misha isn't my enemy, but his hardheaded ass ran off like he's some freaking superman."

"He's lucky Misha called LaSalle instead of killing him."

Roni stiffens for a moment. I move a hand to her shoulder to massage it and help her relax. "What? What is it?"

"Nothing. I... I... nothing."

"Don't worry about Torque, he'll be fine. LaSalle reassured me he's fine."

She's silent for a moment before she sighs. "I swear, John, I didn't know. I warned Torque off. I told him not to follow anymore of the leads he thought he had and to stay out of it. I guess he thought Misha was threatening me. I didn't want to get his hopes up, so I didn't tell him about Misha's promise to get me to Natasha."

"Okay. You need to see Misha and he's hell bent on seeing you. We need to collect Torque anyway. We'll head out first thing in the morning. We'll get you the answers you need. I promise."

"John, if I'm right, you, Torque, and munchkin are the only family I have left."

"You know that's a lie, baby. Mom would kick your ass for it too."

Roni snickers a little. "You know what's crazy?"

"What's that?"

She links our fingers together. "I know why I am the way I am now."

"What do you mean?"

"My father was always distant and cold. I thought I had to be that way for him to want me around. I was always so afraid he'd leave me again.

"That he never wanted me in the first place. So, I had to be perfect for him to want me. To this day I don't know why he left me behind and didn't come back for me until my mother died.

"I don't want to be this way with our baby—detached, cold, cautious. I never want her to feel the way I did with my father. Oh God, John, there were times I thought my mother hated me too. I think some part of her blamed me for losing my father."

I free one hand and reach for her face to turn it up toward mine. "We are not your parents. I know how much you love that little girl in there. This is the first time you've been in the same house with her and you haven't hovered over her or watched everyone around her like a hawk. That alone tells me how much you're hurting right now."

"I... I... when the doctor told me about the damage to my womb from my injuries and all the torture, John, I didn't think she would make it." Tears start to fall and her lips tremble. "She's everything to me. Why wasn't I everything to them?"

I kiss her lips. "I don't know, baby. But you are everything to me. I love the two of you so much. I love you with everything I am."

"Which is why you can't do this with me. You need to be here for—"

"Did you bump your fucking head?" I seethe before I catch myself.

"No, but you must have talking to me like that."

"Roni, you're not doing this alone. *We* are going to handle this *together*. You've been around long enough to understand the type of man we're dealing with when it comes to Misha.

"There's no way I'm sending you into that fire without me. You need to go see Misha; *we* go to see Misha. You need to right this wrong; *we* right this wrong."

Roni

I purse my lips. I should have known he wouldn't see this my way. The look in his eyes tells me this is the one time my defiance isn't going to fly. While some part of me wants to protest, I want him with me.

If I'm right… Oh my God, if I'm right this is so much bigger than me. Logan and LaSalle's names have never rung in my head so loudly. Now John's causal mention of them bangs like drums inside my skull.

The meeting I never set up before leaving for DR. The two associates from New York. I'm not ready to tell John what I think I know. I don't know how he will feel about any of it. Hell, I don't know how I feel about it.

"What if this is too much? What if what I need to do crosses that line?"

"If you haven't noticed, I'm the line crosser. Which means, I was made to be here for you."

I pause to think and nod my head. He leans in and crushes my lips. His soft but firm mouth grounds me and all the emotions floating around inside me.

"Let me see that," John says as he breaks the kiss, reaching for the phone in my lap.

Plucking the device up, he splays our linked hands on my belly. He opens my phone and taps at it until the song changes. "For the Love of You" by The Isley Brothers starts.

I turn my lips up into a small smile and lift a brow. He gives me a crooked grin and kisses the tip of my nose. "This is what I remember my parents for," he says in reply to my questioning look.

"Really?"

"Yeah, my father wasn't home a lot when we were little, always away on a mission or away on a case. But when he was home, on any given Saturday you could walk in on Cass and Joe Black swaying to songs like this or something from back home. We got it all in our house," he says.

"I've always wondered where you and your brothers get so much rhythm and skills from." I laugh.

He does too. "Interestingly enough, it's because of Dad."

"Joe? You have to tell me this one."

He shrugs. "It was Uncle Ronan that told us the story. Apparently, Mom has two left feet, but she loves to dance anyway. She, Uncle Ronan, and some friends were on holiday and went dancing."

He stops to laugh and shake his head. "She was on the dance floor flailing around and Dad walked up and started to guide her around to the beat. From how Uncle Ronan tells it, Dad danced his way into her heart. She was gone from that first dance even though she gave Dad a hard time and made him chase her," he explains.

"That's sweet. So, your dad taught you all how to dance?"

"No, mom put us in classes and had teachers come to the house. She was adamant we learn to be as smooth on our feet as Dad. And I repeat: *when you little fuckers are old enough, nothing will get your dicks wet faster than being able to show a lass you can dance.*"

I bark out a laugh and it feels so good. Some of the burdens on my shoulders seem to lift for a moment. John's laugh grows.

"That sounds so like Cass. I love her."

"She loves you too."

"Are you guys sure we shouldn't have taken her to the hospital?"

"Mom is tough as nails. She'll be fine. She's been fussing over everyone else."

"I would have lost my shit if something happened to her."

John smiles and drops a kiss on my lips. I search his eyes when he pulls away. The love I see there makes my heart squeeze.

He turns the music up, then pushes the front seat up to open the passenger's door. He tilts his head to gesture for me to get out. I look at him curiously but climb over him and out of the car. He follows and closes the door.

The next thing I know, I'm in his arms and he's swaying us to the music. I can't help smiling. I place my head on his shoulder and allow him to distract me from reality.

This is exactly what I need. To be made to feel normal before the concept floats right out the window. His scent wraps around me like a comforting blanket.

"I love you, John."

"I love you too, princess and I plan to spend the rest of my life making sure you know that."

I smile. Does he know how sexy this is? He has this two-step down. When he slips his leg between mine and moves my hips with his, my panties are ruined. He lifts my hand he has in his to his lips and kisses my fingertips.

I lift my head to look up at him. My heart aches. I don't want to lose this. I know what he has said, but I wonder if he'll stick to his word when the full truth comes out. I have no idea what the impact of being Eliam Pérez's daughter will be.

"Promise me something," I say as I stare into his eyes.

"Depends."

I cup his jaw. "Val once told me that Uri had to bring her back from the darkness. Promise me, you'll never allow me to lose myself in all of this."

He draws his brows in. "You know I will always take care of you. Whatever level you need me to take you to, I'm here to do it. I'll set you free whenever you need."

I can't say the words that are caught in my throat.

"I see you, baby. You don't have to ask, just let me heal you," he murmurs against my forehead.

I close my eyes and nod, basking in all that is this man. It's in this very moment that I know I have the perfect man for me. I may push the boundaries of our relationship, but without his dominance, John would never be able to handle me. Especially now that the real Cherone Pérez will be resurrected.

CHAPTER FIFTY-NINE

Tell Me Now

John

As Roni and I are led into Misha's office and I swear I'm counting to ten to keep my head from exploding. I glare at Torque as he sits on the leather sofa with his head down. When he looks up his eyes grow wide and pleading.

"Roni and John, I'm sorry. I didn't know he was going to help us find Natasha. I thought Roni was in danger," Torque jumps up and says.

"Sit. Down," I snarl.

He clamps his mouth shut and sits. When I turn my focus to Misha, he's staring at Roni with his eyes narrowed. Something about the look raises my hackles.

He definitely knows something more about Roni. However, it's not lost on me that Torque's the initial reason we are all here in Russia. I still have no clue why Torque's actions have garnered so much of Misha's attention.

This kid has really stepped in it this time. My head is still reeling with how I fix this, whatever it is. Roni nor Torque can come out of this with a single hair harmed.

"Welcome, John. It's good to see you, my friend, da."

"Yeah, wish it were under different circumstances," I say, shooting Torque another glare.

Misha nods his head at Torque. "He is problem yes, but I have things I want to see clearer."

"What does that mean?" Roni says.

"You remember nothing, not even who you are, da?"

Roni tenses up beside me, balling her fists at her sides. I place a hand on the small of her back to remind her that I'm with her. She shrugs her reply.

"Sit," Misha says. "Your guard is up. We are not enemies."

I guide Roni into one of the chairs in front of Misha's desk before I take the other seat. He is still watching her closely. Curiosity lights his eyes.

It hasn't slipped my notice that Roni hasn't told him what she has remembered. I hold my tongue to see what she's up to. However, Misha gets my attention with his next words.

"Does the name Eliam Pérez ring a bell for you?"

Roni narrows her eyes. "Maybe."

Something about the name tickles my brain. Misha sits back in his seat and steeples his fingers in front of his mouth. He pulls a face and shrugs his shoulders.

"You can leave. I have no time for this. You haven't kept your part of deal. I owe you nothing."

It's clear that we're being dismissed. However, Roni isn't quite done. I cover my face with my hand.

"Are you shitting me? I had no idea what he was up to. You can't hold that against me. I told him to stop. I have a two and a half month old; I can't run after him every time he runs off. You said you would help me. Where's Natasha? What did you find out about me?"

"I know everything," Misha barks. "Be grateful for gift I give and go back to life you know. You don't want the one you can't remember."

"What does that mean, Misha? What aren't you saying?" I speak up.

"This is her past and her debt. Not yours," he says to me.

"Her debts are mine as are the kid's. Whatever they owe you is now mine. You call me from now on."

"John," Roni snaps.

Instead of turning my attention to her, I don't take my eyes off of Misha. He gives a grin that looks sinister. Roni is burning a hole in the side of my face as she stares at me, but I need Misha to understand how serious I am.

"Are you sure you want to take that on?"

"Tell her what she wants to know. We'll discuss the rest later, between you and me."

He sits silently for a few beats. I can tell the wheels are turning. There are a million ways this could go bad. I know that, but I'm not allowing Roni to get in any deeper with Misha.

"I will tell you where to start looking for your truth. If you still wish to know everything else, I will help. Not for favor, not for friendship, I do for knowledge of pain." He turns to gaze to Roni.

"What pain?"

"Pain you have yet to know. You have choice to make." He turns to narrow his eyes at Torque. "Although, I don't think truth will stay hidden for much longer."

"That's not good enough," Roni snarls.

"For now, it is. Trust me, you thank me later."

"Misha," I say firmly.

His lips thin. "I do you favor this way. I do us all favor. If I tell you now, all our problems get worse. Take what I give."

"John. Take Torque. Let me talk to Misha, *please*," she says the last part pleadingly.

Working my jaw, I finally turn to her and glare. Her eyes are what give me pause. There's a desperation I've never seen from Roni. "Please," she repeats.

Against everything in me, I stand and nod. Moving to the couch, I grab Torque and shove him toward the door. I hesitate briefly at the exit. Looking back, I see my girl sitting before a killer king like a queen ready to overturn him and his empire if she has to.

Baby, don't make me start a war.

Roni

I watch Misha as he tilts his head to the side examining me. I appraise him right back. I'm not leaving here without what I came for.

"Speak," he says dryly.

"Yesterday, I was able to remember some things. I know that I'm Cherone Pérez, the daughter of Eliam Pérez," I reply.

A smile spreads across his face. "Your father was interesting man. A wise man among thieves."

"You knew him?"

"*Da,* I know many things. I know story of man and of you. You are ghost that has become ghost. He hid you for years and then you appeared and disappeared within months."

"Why did I disappear, Misha? Or should I be asking how?"

He sits with his eyes narrowed on me. I don't realize I've been holding my breath until he speaks. "You are asking the wrong questions. Tell me, was father's death suspicious to you?"

I gasp and clench my fist. "Yes, it was. Why do you ask?"

He tilts his head to the side. "Are you sure you want to know what I know?"

"Yes," I say in frustration.

He sighs and leans forward to put his elbows on the table. "Woman you grow up thinking was mother, was not. When you were baby men were sent to kill you and your family.

"They underestimated your papa, but the attempt was not total fail. Your papa took you to his mistress in New York—"

"Wait, what?"

"*Da,* Eliam loved your birth mother, but having power like his makes for foolish decisions. Anyway, you were safe with mistress. She loved Eliam and wanted nothing more than to please him.

"However, Eliam wasn't the same. Your father didn't want to compromise your safety and he was heartbroken man. Soon mistress grew tired.

"Nothing was same. Eliam stopped coming to visit, she could not live good life out in open. He made sure you both had money, but she could never spend on lavish things as she used to," Misha says.

My mind is reeling. I feel like I just walked onto an episode of the *What the Fuck* game show. I can't even follow him fully as question after question forms.

"Where is this going?"

"Mistress threatened to expose you and sell you to highest bidder, thinking this would get papa's attention. It did. As he should, your papa took her life. But here's problem.

"Betrayal warps mind. Secrets have bigger secrets. Your father put trust in wrong people. He could never prove who was responsible for your mother's death. He had suspicions, but no proof.

"He left snakes to wonder in garden. Now you have infestation. Not good for safety of daughter he spent life protecting."

I squint at him, trying to see through his cryptic words. "Like who?"

He reaches for his cigar box and cutter. Clipping a cigar, he stares at me and lights it. I fold my arms over my chest while he blows smoke out.

"You have many heads to cut off, but the first part of problem... two brothers, last name García. Your father trusted their uncle, but never should have trusted them. I get his plan; what he was thinking. I just don't agree. Especially when you add those fuckers," he says.

I clench my jaw; I already know that I'm going to kill Darius and Richie. My question: is how deep does this go? This all had to start somewhere.

"Misha, what happened in DR?"

He pauses and his eyes turn into slits. "You go knocking at doors, they will open."

"Knock, knock," I huff.

"Everyone was told you were dead. A plane accident on your way to DR." He's eyeing me for my reaction, but I reveal no emotion just like my father taught me.

"Who else am I looking for?"

He sits back again and allows more smoke to billow. "You will tie yourself to bigger problems. This what you want to hide from John, da?"

"I still don't know what I'm hiding from him. I never figured out the depth of what my father left in my lap."

"Maybe you should start there. Not on this mission you seek," he says.

"It's been what? Four years or more. Where do I begin? Won't I be rattling the same cage?"

His face lights up. "See you are smart. Know this, little warrior. You will have to fill seat you vacate. This is something to think about. Be sure you are ready for storm you want to cause. If I finish story you will have to finish road it paves."

"You know, I'm geting tired of your ass talking in riddles," I grumble.

He bursts into laughter, transforming his handsome face into a more gorgeous version—almost welcoming. "*Da,* I see why Val likes you. Listen to me, go get friend. She is priority for now."

"Finish the story, Misha," I say tightly.

"I just did," he says with a smug grin. "I will give green light when time. As I told you, we have connected problems. You can't solve yours without exposing mine."

I purse my lips, trying to hold in my anger. I want to make those fuckers pay. Darius and his brother are going to meet with hot slugs from my gun. I promise that.

However, knowing I can finally get to Natasha does simmer down some of my anger. Although something about Misha's unfinished story leaves me unsettled. I weigh his words chewing on what I do know.

"Fine, where is she?"

CHAPTER SIXTY

Best Distraction

John

I sit in our suite with a tumbler of Brandy in my hand, watching my woman. So many thoughts run through my jet lagged brain. We flew out from Russia to come back to the States as soon as we collected the baby and our things from the hotel. Mom insisted on coming along with us to help with the baby, even with her healing shoulder.

I only agreed because Mom threatened my life a number of times and I could see she needed to get away. I could see how stressed all this has made her. With Dad detouring to New York to get some answers, I figured we'd head here once we had Torque. It's going to take a while for everyone to get back to normal after this one.

I take a sip of my drink and grimace at the burn. "You going to tell me what you and Misha talked about?" I say after I swallow.

Roni looks up from watching our daughter sleeping. She's been sitting staring at our little princess since she fed her and put her to sleep. Roni is a great mother. I still don't get how she can doubt that.

"Not much to tell," she lies.

I nod. "That's one."

"One what?"

"Who's Eliam Pérez?"

Her eyes widen for a split second before she puts that mask in place. I take another sip of my drink and lick my lips as I wait for her next lie to spill from her mouth. Instead of answering me, she goes to the door and cracks it.

"Torque, come get the baby and take her to Cass. Help her if she needs it," Roni says.

She hands over the baby and closes the door. When she faces me, she leans her back against the door and folds her arms over her chest. I wait. I've cultivated my patience at this point.

"We don't need to talk about this."

"That's two."

"What the heck are you counting?"

I finish my drink and put it down. "I'll ask again, baby. Think before you answer."

"Who is Eliam Pérez?"

"No one you need to be concerned with. I've got this, John."

"That's three."

"Three what? What the heck are you talking about?"

I crook a finger at her. "Come here."

She side glances me, but I keep my face expressionless. The moment she realizes my intention, her eyes light up, she releases a heavy breath, and starts back across the room to where I'm sitting. The little sweat shorts she has on are perfect for what I have planned.

When she gets within arm's reach, I tug her across my lap. It's been a while since I've given her a good spanking. I'm going to enjoy this.

I grow hard as I caress her full globes, building the anticipation. "Now, you have avoided my questions and lied to me. I think you are forgetting who I am."

I lift my hand and bring it down on her plush left cheek. The way it bounces is nothing short of perfection. Roni moans and squirms.

"John," she gasps as I rub the sting away, brush my fingers close to her inner thigh, but not close enough.

"One," I breathe. "You still not ready to talk to me?"

"Babe, let it go," she grunts.

"Two," I call out as my hand comes down on the other cheek. "I can do this all night, baby. You ready to test me?"

Roni

I bite my lip. I don't want to tell him about my dad or the craziness that's going on in my head, but I know where this leads. If John doesn't get answers, I'm not going to get the release he's building me toward.

His hand comes down again and the loudest moan ever comes from my lips. I wiggle in his lap, but he plants a hand in the center of my back to hold me still. Once I stop squirming, he guides his hand to the waistband of my shorts and peels them away.

"Damn," he groans. "You're soaked."

With my shorts discarded, he slips his fingers between my cheeks and gently caresses my folds. The teasing is always the worst part. I'm panting for him to give me what I need.

"Eliam Pérez is my father," I relent.

"Now was that so hard, Cherone?"

I suck in a breath and turn to look up at him. His eyes are filled with a mixture of knowing and lust. "How do you know my name?"

"You have forgotten who I am. While I waited in the hall for you to finish with Misha, I started to search for anything I could find on Eliam Pérez. The death of his daughter, Cherone Pérez, four years ago was only one of the things I came across," he replies.

"John, there's so much I still need to figure out. I didn't want to drag you into my mess."

He lifts his hand and brings it down again. "When will you understand that I'm here to take care of all your needs. Stop trying to push me out. Stop being so damn stubborn."

A keening sound comes from the back of my throat. I roll my eyes at my own weakness when it comes to this man. "If your dick wasn't so good."

"Like you don't like being spanked. Look how wet your pussy is." He chuckles. "What did you and Misha talk about?"

"He told me where I can find Natasha. I'm going after her, John. I'm not asking, I'm telling you that I'm going to get her."

"I already know this. I have one request. Now that we know where she is, you let me do what I do best. I want to know

everything there is to know about her. Why the fuck was it so
hard for us to find her?"

I take a moment to think that over. He's right. We need to
do some recon before storming in and bringing Natasha to
safety.

"I've been wondering the same thing. I'm not going to argue
with that."

He caresses my stinging ass. "This conservation isn't over.
For now, strip for me and get on your knees. Let me get your
mind off of all of this."

I smile and hop up from his lap. Maybe I can do something
to get me another spanking tonight. When I lock eyes with
John, he grins as if he's reading my mind.

"Don't worry, I'm sure I'll be spanking your ass before the
night is over," he says.

I woot and tear my shirt over my head. John can only shake
his head at me with a smile. I shrug as I release my bra and drop
to my knees.

"Hands behind your back," he commands.

"Yes, boss," I purr.

It's as easy as that with John. He's the best distraction I
know. For the next few hours, I turn it all off and get lost in the
man I love.

CHAPTER SIXTY-ONE

Answers Found

Roni

A week later…

I try not to look at Torque, the pain in his face only increases the rage inside me. We were betrayed. A part of me doesn't know why I'm here.

I guess it's because I want to hear it from the horse's mouth. Misha's riddles are starting to unravel right before me. As the apartment door opens, I hold my breath. In this moment, I know so much is about to change.

"Holy shit," Natasha exclaims as she drops the plastic cup in her hand.

Ice coffee spills across the floor as the cup hits it. The brown liquid splashes up against Natasha's expensive looking jeans and starts to surround her red heels. I snort, I guess she has to look the part.

"Hello, Indigo," I say. "Good to see you looking so healthy."

With a hand over her heaving chest, she turns to look behind her and rushes to close the door. When she looks back at me, a new panic has set in. I home in on this new reaction.

"Did anyone see you guys come in here?"

"Not likely," I reply.

She pushes a hand into her hair. "They'll kill me if they find out—"

"Cut the act. I already know you were a plant. You've been helping them from the beginning."

Her mouth drops open. "What? Wait." She shakes her head. Her brows furrow.

I lift a brow. "Are you really going to act like you weren't working with them?"

She lifts her hands. "Oh, you've got this all wrong. One, let me be clear. They will kill me if they find out I've had someone here without permission, so let's make this quick. Second, all that evil wench told me was that she needed me to do this for her. I'd be in and out."

I frown. "What evil wench?"

"The bitch that birthed me."

"Nice way to talk about your mother."

"Mother?" she seethes and makes a face like she's smelling shit. "Let me fill you in on the lovely woman that birthed me. She doesn't give a shit about anything or anyone but herself.

"All my life I had to hear about how her brother got everything while she was passed over. How she was going to right that wrong.

"Dude, do you know why I know so many languages? That bitch has been dragging me around the world while she plotted her master plan," Natasha says as tears come to her eyes.

She continues, her voice full of emotions. "My own mother sent me into trafficking as a *favor to a friend.*" She makes air quotes. "I was supposed to get my assignment once I was there. My *mother* is the one that was supposed to get me out of there after whatever it was had been done."

She wraps her arms around her middle and starts to sway. I bite back the words on the tip of my tongue and let her continue.

"Instead, she left me to rot and be sold off just like all the rest of you. That power-hungry bitch is off somewhere living her life and left me to fend for myself."

"Good story, but you don't look like you're hurting. Rumor has it you have these guys wrapped around your finger."

"Don't fault me for being smart. I've done everything I've known how to survive. Everything except kill." She scoffs. "I never want to be like my mother and her friends when it comes to that."

"But you helped them. Didn't you? I feel so stupid. I can see it all now. The access you had. How you always came to us with information. You knew things you shouldn't have," I snap.

"I agreed to go into trafficking out of fear she and her friends would kill me. Yes, they knew who I was. I helped them because I thought she would want me to.

"Then the longer I sat there, the more it started to become clear she wasn't coming back for me. Besides, I'm no fool. I played nice for as long as I had to," she replies.

I'm ready to kick her ass, but the next words out of her mouth strike a chord. They hit my heart like a well-aimed arrow. I know the pain I hear for its truth.

"It wasn't hard for her to move on with her life like I didn't exist. She hid me from everyone for my entire life. I was nothing but a burden for her. That cold bitch could care less about me," she says and frowns.

"It seems we could have been spawned from the same family," I say bitterly.

"I never knew my dad. I used to pray he was out there somewhere. Then I gave up," she says and shrugs.

I watch her and calculate. If this is true, some things still need to add up from what John found. Natasha is as much of a ghost as I am.

"And if I were to believe all this? How are you living so lavishly now?"

"You don't have to believe a damn thing. You see lavish, I see a freaking gilded cage." Tears start to roll down her cheeks. "You guys were freed, but I didn't have that same luck."

"What happened?" Torque asks in a calm that doesn't match the tears of rage in his eyes.

"The Russians, it was their job to get me back to my mother. When they called her to tell her about the raid, she told them I was their problem. She wasn't willing to settle up on whatever the deal was.

"I had to think fast. I made myself useful for a while. Then, I was so close to getting away, another raid. I was so sure that was my chance, but it was snatched away and now I'm here," she says sadly.

"Helping them sell drugs to college students and recruit girls for their sex ring?"

She looks away as shame covers her face. "These girls all want the money and the lifestyle. They see my clothes and car, I'm the black girl with connections and big money.

"All of that draws them in to find out how I'm doing it. None of the professors question a thing because I'm a straight A student and the college damn sure hasn't asked any questions since my tuition is paid for the year, including nice donations. We just switch colleges every six months to a year, no matter if the tuition is paid or not.

"New college, new name. I keep them in money and girls, they keep me fed and clothed. That's how I've served," Natasha almost whispers.

"So, you didn't betray us?" Torque says, hope lacing his words.

"You two were the first and only friends I've ever had. I never thought I'd see you again. You guys have to go. I can't have anything happen to you. Gidden will lose his mind if he finds you here. He's possessive and crazy about me. You need to go."

"Gidden. That's the blonde?" I ask.

Her eyes nearly pop out of her head. "Did he see you?"

"My boss took care of him, turns out he likes to filet shit. I needed to get answers, now I have them." I shrug. I might have a few questions about John's sanity after this. "You can either get your shit and come with us or you can stay here, and figure shit out," I say and start for the door.

"Wait, what? I can't leave. He'll find me," she says, once again she's in a panic.

"Dead men can't find shit," I call over my shoulder. "Make a decision, chick. My breasts hurt. My little girl is hungry. I'm done here."

When I step out of the front door, John is standing there waiting for me. I wrap my arms around his waist and bury my face in his chest. It's like a weight has been lifted from my shoulders.

"Misha knew. He knew it was my aunt that set me up," I breathe.

"Did you tell her?"

"I don't know how," I breathe.

"Your aunt is the head of your family business," John says what I'm thinking. "You're going to have to address it."

"Yeah, because she won't be for much longer. It's time for this to end."

CHAPTER SIXTY-TWO

Get Ready

Roni

Two months later…

"Vita, I'm going to pluck you right in your mouth if you stick your spoon in Nori's ice cream one more time," Val calls over to her daughter as she and her twin brothers sit in the kiddie pool.

"Mama," Vita says and pouts, giving her version of an angry face.

"I will take you out of the water and place your little butt in timeout," Val says, sending a motherly glare at her little one.

Vita pokes her lip out more and bats her lashes. Oh God, she's so adorable. She sneaks a peek at her two brothers still finishing their ice cream, then looks back at Val to bat her lashes again.

"My name is not Daddy. Those eyes don't work on me. You had your own ice cream, it's gone," Val chides.

"You are so mean," I say as I try to stifle my laughter.

Val waves me off and settles back in the lounger next to mine. A group of us have been hanging out by the pool with the kids at John's house. Yes, I've been living here with him, but I've yet to call it my home.

That seems weird. Especially without Torque here. He moved back into the apartment so Natasha would feel safe there. She still spends most her time looking over her shoulder.

"Now back to you," Val says. "You really want to do this, huh?"

"Yeah, she started this. I'm going to finish it."

"Mm, things have been too quiet."

I shrug. "She's not a very bright woman. I'm sure she'll try again."

"You know what they say about letting sleeping giants lay. She fucked up," Val says thoughtfully.

My aunt sure did. She never should have sent her men and the Russians to come for John's family and me. I hadn't known a thing about her before then.

Heck, it took a while for me to connect that asshole I killed on the roof to her. I've only ever seen him a few times before he kidnapped me in DR. However, one day it clicked, he was the guy that would lurk in the shadows around my aunt.

When you are taught to hide, you notice those hiding with you. I've heard his voice from his whispered conversations with my aunt and wouldn't have remembered a thing about him otherwise. Yeah, my aunt is a dumbass.

Lifting my sunglasses, I watch Carmen as she stares at Kaye and Dae-Dae. She's been eyeing them and chew on her lip as she holds her daughter in her lap. I frown, I hope she's not turning into a weirdo on me.

I shake my head. "You know what's crazy to me. We're all connected. Way before this all started, we were all connected in some way. Now it's like it's all coming full circle," I say.

"I've heard Logan call it the degrees of separation. The Alliance was built on it."

The Alliance. The name alone feels so heavy. "I can't believe she had my father killed to keep him from sitting at the table," I muse aloud.

"I can't believe she's been plotting with Misha's aunts for all these years. I've been begging him to let me at those old bitter hags," Val snarls, causing me to turn my head to look at her.

She's glowing from the sun. Her lips are pinched as her eyes are hidden behind her sunglasses. Even in her anger, my friend is a gorgeous woman.

"I'm growing impatient waiting for him to give me the okay. I'm ready to get this all over with," I say tightly.

"Call him. Tell him what you told me. I'm sure you will get what you're looking for."

"I don't know. LaSalle and Logan still don't know who I am. Why? What is Misha trying to hide and why?"

"Beats me, but if my husband asks, I'm not going to lie. I think he'll be asking soon. He knows something is up."

I roll my eyes. "Don't get me started on that. John is growing suspicious. He's bound to figure out I'm leaving a gaping hole somewhere in all this."

"I figured. Are the girls ready?"

"They will be." I look around the pool at the other women. They all look so innocent. However, innocent they are not.

My gaze falls on Carmen again. I can't take it anymore. I get up and murmur that I'll be back. A peek inside the house tells me that John and my little monster are still fast asleep on the couch.

My lady parts tingle at the sight of my man shirtless with our little girl curled up on his chest—her sole protector and warrior, ready to get up and go into battle for her at any moment. She loves her father already. She's sure to be a spoiled little brat.

Turning back to Carmen, I move to her side and sit at the edge of the pool next to her. With a bump of her shoulder, I grab her attention. She looks at me as if she's startled to see me here.

"Hey," she says and smiles.

"Hey, weirdo. What's going on with you?"

She bites her lip. "I don't know how to apologize to Kaye," she says.

Confusions covers my face. "For what?"

She sags her shoulders. "I ruined her wedding. She and Felix were supposed to get married during the time Ry had to hide me away. They postponed the wedding because of me."

I twist my lips at her. "If you don't go somewhere with that. I think that baby is what made them postpone. I've seen the dress she was planning to wear. It was not going to hide that bump, no matter how hard she tried and she refused to get anything else."

"I still feel bad."

"Don't," I say and then whisper. "He's giving her a surprise wedding."

She turns to me, this time with her own confusion. I smile and put her out of her misery. "I only know because I walked in on the guys talking about it. Stop stressing."

"All right." She murmurs and gives me a tiny smile. "Hey, I think I have some time to go to the range this week. You down?"

"I knew I'd convert you from those blades." I laugh as she sticks her tongue out at me.

As I look around again at the women, I now call family and friends, I know I'm making the right decision. Perhaps it is time I call Misha. We're ready.

CHAPTER SIXTY-THREE

This Could Be Us

John

Four months later...

"Proud of you little brother," I say with a smile as I pat Felix on his back.

My little brother is married, and it looks good on him. I reach to fix his tie, then slap a hand against his cheek. We're all standing around the bar for a toast as brothers. Kaye and the girls are on the dance floor taking more pictures.

"Damn, I thought this day was never going to happen," Felix says and laughs.

Brax reaches to mess Felix's hair. "Delay is not denial, big brother. Welcome to the club. Now, we have to get John here engaged and Ry down the aisle and we'll all be married men."

Wyatt laughs and turns his mischievous gaze on me. "I don't know if Roni is the marrying type."

"You took the words right out of my mouth," Ry says.

"I don't know. They have their weird shit, but I got five hundred on him proposing before the year is out," Noah says, shooting Wyatt a warning glance. These two are up to no good.

"What's so weird about us?" I challenge.

"Come on," Ry snorts. "We know you're into that Dom shit hard, and yet, Roni's ass has to be the worst Sub in the world. She doesn't listen to a damn thing anyone says to her."

"Not to mention, you guys don't do couple shit. What's that about? I don't know if I've ever seen you kiss in public or hold hands," Felix says.

"I figured it's his stinky breath. As pretty as he is, that breath has to be his downfall. Never did believe he's as perfect as he tries to play off," Ryan says.

I glare at him. "Fuck you. When's the last time you washed your ass like an adult. I bet Carmen keeps changing the baby thinking it's her taking a shit."

"But she still lets me put my tongue down her throat whenever I want," he tosses back.

I lift my shoulders. "Not everyone has to display their affection in public."

"Yup, weirdos," Ry says.

"First, you've been hanging with Roni too much with that weirdo shit. Second, to each his own. We work for us."

Noah pats me on the back. "You're right. We all have what we need. I wouldn't change Bean for anything, but I know what we have wouldn't work for everyone."

"Nothing but truth," Wyatt says.

"I'll drink to that," Brax says and starts to pass around beers.

We continue our banter and laughter. The party is turning up on the dance floor. My face hurts from smiling so much. I truly am happy for Felix. For all of my brothers actually.

"Dad," Dae-Dae runs over to Felix.

I can see from the look in my brother's eyes that hearing Kaye's nephew call him Dad means the world to him. Dae-Dae has only ever known Kaye and Felix as parents, so I'm not surprised that he's started to call Felix Dad. This all looks good on him.

"Unbelievable. They didn't even invite us to the toast." I look over my shoulder to see the O'Brien brothers headed our way. Things are about to get lively now that my cousins are joining us.

"Whatever, Brooklyn. I didn't think we'd be able to pull you from DJ's side," Felix says.

"Anything to back pedal your way out of this one," Brooklyn retorts.

Logan moves to Felix's side to place a hand on his shoulder and give it a squeeze as he hands him an envelope and whispers something in his ear. Felix laughs and throws a punch at Logan's shoulder. Something in the back of my mind reminds me that this is a rare moment.

Things have been tense. We're always on high alert. It's only been two weeks since the fire at DJ's bar. It's good to see smiles on everyone's faces despite the drama lurking in the background. This wedding is a much-needed distraction.

"I think they're all hiding from changing diapers and crying babies," Dylan teases.

I scoff. "I know I am. I love her, but my little girl is teething. She spent last night trying to gnaw on my nose and fingers," I say. "She's as cranky as her mother."

Jamie winces. "Ya sure are talking a lot of shit. Roni will have yer ball in her palm you keep it up."

"Speaking of Roni. When are ya going to let her make an honest man out of ya?" Brooklyn says.

"What is with everyone trying to marry me off today?"

"Tell me you haven't thought about it," Wyatt says with an amused look in his eyes. "Don't you want to be a husband?"

I freeze for a moment. I'm not going to lie, as I watched Kaye walk down the aisle to Felix, I couldn't help imagining that she was Roni making her way to me. At the same time, I couldn't help wondering of all of this would be Roni's thing.

Felix followed Kaye's original wedding plan to a T. This was everything she dreamed of. Roni can be full of surprises. I don't know if this is something that she wants. Although I wouldn't mind if we did have a huge wedding with all my family there to have our backs.

"Honestly, if I thought she would say yes, I would've proposed already. I'm just not ready to push her into anything yet."

Toby gives me a shit-eating grin. "You think she would say no?"

"We've never talked about it. So much has happened. I don't know what she wants."

"You suck ass as a Dom," Ry taunts.

"Fuck you. You know good and damn well her needs come first. I'm not going to force her into marrying me. Stop reading Mom's romance books. Life doesn't work that way."

It's right as the words finish coming out of my mouth that I know I've been played. I look around at the mirth in my brothers' and cousins' eyes. I purse my lips and make a face at them all.

"She's standing right behind me, isn't she," I huff.

"Have been since you talked trash about our poor baby teething, asshole," she says.

Everyone around me bursts into laughter. I toss them all the finger and turn to face Roni. She has our sleeping daughter in her arms with a scowl on her lips, but what I love is the twinkle in her eyes. She's not really pissed at me, but I know she's going to give me shit.

I close the distance between us. "Come dance with me," I command.

Defiance lights her eyes, but the moment Noah plucks our little princess from her arms, I have my hands on her waist, backing her toward the dance floor. The yellow dress she has on compliments her skin. However, the best part of the night will be getting to watch it slide down her curves.

Roni

I play with the hairs at the nape of John's neck as I look up into his eyes. He sways me to the music while holding my gaze. I should give him shit, but I'm too stunned by his words to rib him about them.

He was right, we've never talked about getting married. It's always been inferred that we'll be together. Do I want to marry John?

As I look into his golden eyes, the question rolls around in my head. He places his forehead against the bridge of my nose, his breath tickling my skin. I breathe him in and instantly know the answer.

Yes.

"What are you thinking?"

"You don't think I want to marry you," I say.

He pulls back and looks me in the face. "You never do or say what I think you will. I'm not going to make any assumptions."

"I've never thought of you as the marrying type," she says.

"Why not?"

I roll my eyes. "Maybe because you've been unconventional in your relationships."

He rumbles a laugh. "Okay, but how many married couples have I introduced you to that are unconventional? I've never been against marriage. I've only been waiting for the right person. Now, I think I'm only waiting for the right time."

"What does that mean?" I side eye him.

"Your last name is already mine. We only need to make it official at this point."

"My last name is Pérez," I say with a smile.

He growls at me. "You haven't changed your ID."

"For safety reasons," I try to say with a straight face.

"Hm. I think you're telling me a lie. My palm is getting twitchy."

This time I laugh, placing the side of my face against his chest. "Whatever, John."

We fall silent as the music fills in the gaps. I get lost in my thoughts, imagining my own wedding. I never knew I wanted one like this until I watched the look in John's eyes as I walked down the aisle as a bride's maid. It was in that moment, I realized I want to pick out colors for dresses and dress up to meet John at the altar.

"John?"

"Yeah, baby."

I sigh. "Just so you know. I am into all of this. I would want it all and I would say yes."

As if by divine design, "For the Love of You" comes on. I've never been the shy type, but I can't help shying away from the beaming smile that crosses John's face. He pinches my chin and lifts my face to his, I know what's coming before it happens.

With tears in my eyes, I nod my consent. John crushes my lips with his in a soul-searing kiss that has me feeling like I'm floating in my heels. That feeling of longing that I've had all my life lifts from my chest.

I finally have someone that loves me and is willing to show it. That's when it dawns on me. I'm not against PDA, I'm afraid of it.

I've never known public affection to be genuine—not until now. My father only patted my shoulder for the few people he allowed me around. It was always for show. This... this is John showing me love.

When he pulls away, I feel dizzy. He brushes a finger over my lip and smiles back at me. "I'm going to hold you to that, Princess. You've sealed your fate tonight, Mrs. Black."

I wrap my arms around his neck and return his smile. When I look around us, Cass and Joe are on the dance floor as are a few other couples. My heart swells as I realize we're surrounded by people we love that are sharing the same energy I want to have fifty years from now.

This is what's been missing. This is love.

CHAPTER SIXTY-FOUR

Strange Meetings

Roni

My feet are killing me. The Blacks know how to party. I've enjoyed the cultural mix of Felix and Kaye's families. It has made for one of the best weddings I can remember going to.

I shake my hands over the sink and dry them. Looking in the mirror, I brush a hand over my hair. It crosses my mind to grow my hair back out for my own wedding. With a frown, I roll my eyes at myself. John hasn't even proposed. I won't be that girl.

As I chide myself and exit the bathroom, I debate going barefoot. It's time to collect my child and head to bed. Maybe she will sleep long enough for me to take a long soak in the tub.

Doubt it.

I stumble to a stop as I walk out into the hallway. LaSalle, Logan, Uri, and Val are all standing around casually as if this hallway is a part of the reception area. I cock my hip to the side and fold my arms across my chest.

"What's all this about?"

"Is that way to greet friends?"

I whip my head in the direction of Misha's voice. I didn't know he was here. I haven't seen him all night or at the ceremony.

"Let me ask you something," LaSalle says, pulling my attention.

I look at him and nod. "Do you remember any of the meetings you had planned after your father's passing?"

My expression turns thoughtful as soon as the question hits me. My lips part as I remember the two names I kept forgetting even back then. Logan and LaSalle.

"Yeah, I do."

"I had planned to look into what happened to ya before I ended up in a cell. Never believed that bullshit story that came to us. I wish ya never postponed the meeting in the first place. It would've kept me from making that trip to Ireland," Logan says gruffly.

"Papa was a fan of Alliance. Auntie, not so much," Misha says. "I might have gotten something wrong in story. Now, I know whole truth."

"Okay, but what's this all about?"

"We have problem. It's time we fix," Misha replies.

LaSalle pushes off the wall. "I have a gift for you," he says. "In turn, I would like you to fill this box. If you can do this, we will talk more about your future. You didn't find your way to us by accident. For whatever reason, I believe you are destined to be around. This will only tell me in what capacity."

He hands me an ornate gilded box. I look down at the little rectangle box in my hand in confusion. I turn it over and examine it, finding the latch. When I flip it open, it's lined with velvet.

"What am I supposed to fill it with?" I ask, looking around at all of them.

Misha hands me a knife, but it's Logan who speaks. "You will know when the time is right."

"I will give the call when my gift is ready," LaSalle says. "I'm sorry, Roni. Know that no matter what you choose to do, we are all here for you. You are family."

"Bloody right. Val and I will be there when LaSalle calls. You will not be doing this alone."

"Wait, doing what?"

"You have green light for the brothers. I deliver them with LaSalle's gift. Goodbye, Roni. We are even. Hope to see you on other side," Misha says and turns to leave the same way he came.

Logan pushes off the wall. "I don't mind the way this is going at all," he mutters and pats LaSalle on the shoulder. "It's getting a wee bit interesting. If you need anything, love, John knows how to find me."

With that, Logan starts down the hall toward the winding down reception. I turn to Val and give her a puzzled look. She grins at me.

"I told you to be careful what you ask for," she says. "As Uri said, we will be by your side. I'm always one phone call away. Always."

She comes over to kiss my cheek. Uri moves behind her, placing a hand on her back and leads her away in the same direction Logan went. I'm left staring at LaSalle.

He narrows his gaze on me. "I'll be here in Ireland for a bit after this, but if you need anything, you can reach out to me as well."

Without another word, he leaves to join the others and I'm left wondering what the hell just happened. I look down at the box in my hand. What the heck am I supposed to be placing inside of this?

"What was that about?"

I nearly come out of my skin. "Torque," I hiss. "What the hell?"

He blushes. "Sorry. What happened? Did we get the green light?"

"Yeah, *I* got the green light."

He smiles and it lights his entire face. "Doing this with you will be my last job. I already talked to John. I'm taking a break."

His words tug at my chest. It's been feeling like he's changing, as if we're pulling away from each other and going in two different directions. I don't know how I feel about that.

"Listen, Roni. I'm not a kid anymore. I'll be fine." He pulls me into a tight hug.

"I know. I'm proud of you. Never forget that."

He pulls away and beams at me. "She shows emotion and John is nowhere in sight. Yup, you're human after all," he jokes.

"Shut up and stop acting like a weirdo," I sniffle.

"You're the one having secret meetings in hallways. What's that in your hand?"

I move the box out of his sight. "Nothing. Come on, let's get the family and get out of here."

CHAPTER SIXTY-FIVE

Silenzio

John

A month later...

"You okay?" I say and kiss Roni's forehead while I massage the back of her neck. She's filled with tension as we sit in the back of this SUV. I know the waiting has been driving her crazy. First, the wait for the green light from Misha to get to this very point.

Now we're waiting for the call from LaSalle. A call I have to say I've been curious about. All I know is that Roni sat me down and told me that it was time to put this all to rest.

I'll be more than happy to put this behind us. The climax of things with the Alliance hasn't even come to a head—I know that as well as anyone. Therefore, placing all of Roni's drama in the rearview is at the top of my list.

"Yeah, I'm fine," she says.

I know right away she's somewhere else. She's doing that detached thing. I don't push.

I'm agitated as well. It's hot as fuck out and this bullet proof vest under my suit and dress shirt isn't helping. The air conditioning might as well not be on, that's how much it's good for—and the sun has fallen, but you're still cooking. The faster we can get this done, the better.

My phone rings and relief washes through me. This is the moment we've been waiting for. Time to plug in those holes and be done with all of this. I answer and bring the phone to my ear.

"Listening," I say into the line.

LaSalle speaks a simple word. "Go."

I hang up and rap my knuckles at the hood of the car, signaling for my father to take off. He starts the engine and pulls out of the alley we've been sitting in, setting the convoy behind us in motion. When I turn to look into Roni's eyes her face is completely expressionless. I cup the back of her throat to get her attention.

"Whatever happens in here, we get home to our little girl in one piece. When this is over it's over," I say.

She shakes her head. "That's just it, babe. It's not, this is only the beginning. I don't know how to explain it, but I get that now. Whatever Misha was waiting for had more to do with me than he let on. This doesn't end tonight. It's only a choice of how it will begin," she says, her voice haunted.

I want to groan because as her words ring out through the vehicle, they ring true deep down in my soul. "Well, whatever's waiting for us, I'm here to make sure it brings you no harm. I'll make it better," I reply and lean in to kiss her neck and nuzzle it.

"While I feel like I'm about to walk into a den of lies, those words are what I believe most," she murmurs.

"I haven't told you a lie yet, and don't plan on starting."

"Showtime," she says as we pull up to the party, we'll become famous tonight.

I don't feel bad about this at all. There's not a single innocent person left inside. Felix looked through the entire list to see if we'd need to extract any innocent bystanders. My stomach railed at most of the crimes of these men and women—heartless, careless, and greedy are only a few of the flaws on the list.

Those that were here simply to party were sent home before the real action came into play here. These are the low lives that think what was done to Roni, Torque, and Natasha was okay.

Music is blaring through the restaurant as the party has been in full swing for some time now. "Silencers on. We want to make this messy, but not loud. Your gift in the back building should be surprised once you enter their little private party," Felix says into our comms.

"We're on it," Roni says.

We climb from the SUV as the rest of our team does as well. Wyatt and Noah emerge from two cars back and head in our direction. Their eyes are hard, letting me know they are as focused as I am.

Felix, Brax, Ry, and Torque are already in place, waiting for the signal. Dad, Rob, and Chase are holding down the vehicles for us to make a smooth get away back to the airport where our plane is waiting.

Uri and Val step from the SUV directly behind us. I shake my head. Val and Roni both have on red heels that are made for anything but what we're about to do.

The black wraps they're wearing are covering more than their tight black dresses underneath—don't ask. We're all dressed to the nines, however, I wasn't expecting Roni's knee length black dress with the shear overlay or to find Val in something similar. Anyone watching us walk into this fancy restaurant shouldn't question why we're arriving to the party so late—with men dressed in long dress coats in this hot ass heat nonetheless—but I'm sure the sight of all of us heading in their direction has caused pause for a very different reason.

Male and female, jaws drop as we head to the door. We clean up nice. They probably think we're a group of models or entertainers come for the after party.

"Nice restaurant," Val says as we move for the all glass front. She's right, the place is huge.

"Yeah, too bad we're about to fuck this shit up," Roni says, tossing off her wrap as we walk through the entrance.

Roni pulls her guns and starts to fire. The guards at the front are taken by surprise as we all open fire with her. This isn't my style, but LaSalle and Misha want to send a message.

"Dialing up the DJ's frequency from here. Got to love these new DJs and their electronic rigs. Team two is coming in," Felix says into the com.

The sound of the music has increased, and right as Felix's words cut off, glass shatters above our heads as Ry and Braxton's team of four comes to crash the party. The tall ceilings are not as majestic as my brother's, Torque, and one of my guys comes through like avenging angels. I'm sure the García brothers are sorry they made a house of glass for themselves as we bring it tumbling down.

Knowing this is their restaurant spares me one. There is a huge chance they will be here tonight. Because of that I've called in a few favors for this, in the form of a couple of snipers and shooters, courtesy of the Briggs and Slaughter House. We won't be leaving anything at risk on the table.

Val signals to Roni to head for the back of the restaurant. Stunned men begin to pull guns and fire back. I frown, hoping the music is enough to muffle the action in here, but not banking on it, I follow Roni and Val to cover them once they make it out back.

Uri is right beside me, probably thinking the same thing. I don't have time to marvel at Roni and Val in their stilts as they drop bodies left and right. We wanted to make a scene; we're making it.

Roni

The closer I get to the back of the restaurant the more my rage builds. The answers to everything are back there. My revenge, my freedom... yeah, my freedom. I hadn't realized that I've been looking over my shoulder until I watched Natasha—or should I say Indigo, don't ask long story—do it for months.

That stops. I won't be free until I set a blaze to my past. I fire, wanting each bullet to release the tightening in my chest, but it never comes. Every bullet carries more fury with it. I reload and keep moving.

"You should have just let me torch this motherfucker, none of these fucks deserve to live," Brax says through the earpiece.

I bare my teeth. That's when something in my gut calls my attention to the right side of the room. Once again, like the day on that roof, time slows. Water from the sprinklers has been triggered leaving us all to get soaked beneath them.

When I turn toward the feeling pulling me, my ponytail whips with the action, sending water across my vision. On instinct, I move both arms in the direction I'm now facing—one across my front, bent as if I'm pulling a bowstring. A second later, my target comes into view.

"Bingo, motherfuckers," I murmur as both Richie and Darius stand staring at me. "I bet you didn't get what you wanted this time."

Shocked expressions mixed with recognition cover each of their faces. However, it's Richie that acts fast to pull a gun. He never gets the chance to fire. I send a bullet through both of their skulls. The satisfaction from their bodies dropping at the same time sends a roar from my chest as my knees almost buckle.

It's like I'm giving a praise dance, with my hands clenching my pistols in front of me in triumph as I release another scream. Val spins to wrap around me and fires at someone behind me. I'm shaking as I look up at her through my lashes.

"We're not done. Pull it together," she growls. "They're not who you're here for."

Her words sink in and confusion keeps me frozen for a second. It's clear she knows a lot more than she's told me. I quickly snap out of it as John shields us both with his body and fires as three guys came out of nowhere.

"Channel it, use it, *La rabbia della morte*," Val says.

I brush one hand under my nose and nod. John turns his gaze on me. I reassure him with my eyes I'm fine. Not wanting to see the worry in his eyes, I'm in motion for the back door again.

"I have a party of ten at our final destination. They're in the back building. It's the brick structure. When you step outside, make a right and you're going to find two guards as soon as the building comes into view," Felix says. "That leaves you eight inside."

I nod to Val as we head for the back exit. With a swiftness that speaks of my hours of training and preparation for this, I drop both empty clips and reload again. Once we're all clear, we step out of the exit, Uri and John are right on us. I follow the path Felix has laid out.

First thing I notice is that the doors to the building sit partially open. If we fire now, those inside may see the two guards fall. We all take cover, Uri signals for Val to follow him and for me and John to wait.

We nod and watch as they circle the building. "John get the one closest to you to start in your direction," Uri's voice comes through the com.

"Got it," John replies.

John pulls something from his pocket and tosses. The sound vibrating through the night. I tuck my guns away and pull a blade from my thigh. We wait for the guard to get to us.

When he's right up on us and out of the view of the entrance, I saunter from the shadows, bringing a grin to his face. At the same time, I can see Val doing the same thing with the other guard.

However, she moves faster, and her guard's gurgles catch the attention of the one I have in my sights. He goes to turn, but I grab him around the throat and hold him to my chest as I pull the blade clean across his neck. I drop his body and step right over him as John places a hand on my back and kisses my forehead.

I clean the blade on the side of my dress and put it back away before I draw my pistols again. We move flush to the building and meet at the entrance. I have the better view from my side. I can partially see a table as I cautiously peek my head in.

The first thing I note are the two guards that come into view. The next thing that stands out to me are the pale well-manicured hands folded on the table. Lastly, the sight that makes me stifle a growl and the bitter taste in my mouth, my dear aunt Grissel.

However, it's the voice and words that are barked inside the room that send me into a blinding rage.

Eliam Pérez

"I should kill you with my bare hands," I snarl as my sister sits across the table with a smug grin on her face. She thinks the Krupin family will keep her safe from me.

"I did exactly what you asked me to," she says with no remorse or inflection. "If you ask me, I tried to do her favor. If she would have married Darius, I could have done this nicer way. *You* wanted her to fall into enemy hands and make her way back."

"I wanted you to use her brain to get her out of a tough situation. Not be tortured for years and forgotten," I fume.

"All the same to me."

I don't know what made me trust my sister with this task. She is as cold as my father made her, exactly what I tried to instill in Cherone. The ice queen sitting before me was an ice queen way before her betrayal, I only took too long to learn this.

"*Estúpido*, I was so focused on trying to prepare Roni for things like this, it backfired. You meant to allow me to rot in that prison and you wanted to ruin her. I never should have trusted you and your little boyfriends. I was betrayed by my own sister. How could you do this?"

"You wanted a seat with that Alliance. I told you it would make you look weak." She makes a disgusted face. "You want to hand over everything *my* father built. Over my dead body."

"You know I can arrange that," I seethe.

"With what army? You have no power," Grissel says through her thick accent. "I have been running this family since I got rid of all of you. If I would've known you were not incinerated like I ordered, I would have come to that hell hole to kill you myself."

"You betray everyone around you, your own daughter? The walls have ears. I know about Indigo, Grissel," I say.

"What about her? She was a causality of war as was your brat," she replies.

I shake my head. "I have been cold to Roni for her own good, to make her strong in this world. Love makes weakness, I couldn't afford to show her affection. Unlike you, you are simply callous, *sin corazón.*"

"You think you're better than me? Mamá told me how you treated her. Made her cry for your affection that you never gave," she tosses back at me.

"I did what was right for her."

"You have no balls. You should have left her to die. I would have."

I grin like *el diablo.* "And now she comes for your head." I tilt my head when she looks surprised. However, she quickly tries to hide it. "You don't know do you? The person that set me free said I could tell you goodbye before Cherone is set free to end your sorry *pequeña vida sucia.*"

Grissel lifts a hand and shoulder as if she has no fear, but I see it in her eyes. "I may allow her to live. I hear that your plan for her worked out after all. She is ruthless bitch you wanted. The Russians broke her and made her savage that you set out for."

Anger threatens to scorch the hair on my head. I sat in the bowels of that rat-infested prison for years not knowing if Roni was alive running the family or if she had a similar fate to mine. I was only to disappear to give her some responsibility and allow her to learn the real world and empire I had built. To make her hard in a world that would see her as soft. A year or two tops.

What my sister planned for me instead almost made me lose my mind. If she were anyone else, I would have slit her throat from the moment I walked in. She deserves nothing less.

"Almost five years," I roar. "I meant for this to toughen her skin, not break her completely. This all belongs to *me* and *my daughter* and here you sit as if it's your throne. You were to help prepare her for the Alliance not try to take what's ours."

"You have always been weak," she screams. "This is why I killed her mother."

The room goes silent. It's as if I'm in a tunnel and a bomb has just exploded. I've been suspicious about this for years.

"Enough," Irina Krupin shouts. "I've not come for this. You have family problem you solve on your time. My job is to find out who Pérez family will be loyal to. Me or nephew. He's becoming too strong. You forget Alliance, I give you back family business."

"What?" Grissel gasps, causing me to grin.

"You have made mess at every turn. It is time we end partnership. You and boy toys are not worth trouble," Irina waves her off.

"What makes you think I need you or her?" I say tightly.

"My sisters and I are ready to put pressure on coup that has started. Only matter of time before all implodes and we crush them like bugs they are. Choose right side."

"What about all I've done?" Grissel hollers.

"What have you done? Send your men and mine to California to be slaughtered. What did you accomplish? My nephew has been like dog with bone since. Your friends, Serbians were useless. Again, too worried about young men you are fucking to get job done," Irina says dryly. "You and García's are pointless and are now problem for me."

"If I side with you, my daughter must never know about this," I say.

"Why should I grant this silly request?" Irina replies, turning up her nose in disgust. "I should kill you where you stand. Your family has no loyalty in you."

I laugh. "I am loyal to the options in my favor. That used to be the Alliance.

"From what I hear now, you are at a pivotal point. You are the one with a nephew that wants your entire family dead. I have an ear to the ground that Cherone has a foot in the Alliance. This will be how we take them down," I say.

"But there's one problem." I spin to face the voice at my back. Standing before me is my little girl all grown up. Her eyes are hard, she looks more like me than ever. "I now know everything."

Roni

He has the nerve to look at me with a smile as I round the table moving closer to Grissel and Irina Krupin. My own father. That's where this all came from. He wanted to make me tough? That's his reason.

I would never do something like this to my baby girl. Not even if it was only to toughen her up. The cruel bastard never showed me love. Not like a real parent should. Is this how they would have taught me to raise my child? So much deception and deceit.

"What is this?" Irina says going to lift from her seat.

"Sit the fuck down," I bellow.

For good measure Val places her gun to the back of Irina's head. John moves behind two of the guards, placing his gun to the head of one and pulling the trigger.

Just as swiftly, he shoots the other in the leg, before pulling a knife and slicing his throat. Uri makes quick work of taking care of the last of Irina's men.

"Give me reason," Val hisses close to Irina's ear as she watches in horror as her men lie lifeless.

"Do you know who I am?" Irina seethes.

"I don't give a fuck," I say, without taking my eyes off my father.

The two guards I assume to be my aunt's, go to draw their guns as my aunt signals them. I pump two in each of their chests. Moving behind her lightning fast, I holster my guns and pull my knife. I don't even blink as I open this woman's neck as if she's nothing more than a stranger to me.

She is.

"Roni," my father says, with a mixture of hurt and disbelief.

"Your mission was accomplished," I say as I begin to move around the table in his direction. I stop before my father and look at him impassively. "They tortured me until I felt nothing. I was broken mentally and physically."

"Roni, I wanted you prepared for anything that would come your way—"

I cut my hand across my throat. "Silence. You have no idea," I bark, my chest heaving. I tilt my head as I glare at him. My voice fills with so much emotion as I think of the biggest cost of the ordeal I went through. "My daughter…my daughter almost didn't make it. My insides were so broken from the torture, I wasn't able to hold her full term. Do you understand what I just said? Years later I'm still suffering from what happened to me. You did this to me."

"I'm sorry, *princesa*."

"Don't call me that. You never treated me like a princess. You don't know what that word means. I've only ever been a possession that you've held this warped sense of protection over. For what? Money? Power?"

"It was the right thing to do. Look at you now. You are stronger than me."

"You're motherfucking right. I don't trade lives for power or comfort. I don't sell my own for a means to an end," I challenge.

"Roni—"

I move swiftly to slam him down on the table. In the next breath, I cut his ring finger right off. His screams fill the room. "I hope I've finally met your expectation, Papi. See you in hell." I pull my gun and blow his brains out.

Irina jumps in her seat, reminding me she's in the room. I lift my gun to put a bullet in her forehead. "*Net*, this one is mine. My blade will be the one that starts the war."

I turn to find Misha standing there with a sinter grin on his lips. He's looking at Irina like she's the prey he's been waiting to catch all his life. He continues to speak as he unbuttons his suit jacket to reveal a vest of blades.

"We good?"

"*Da*, but you should be one to take gift box to LaSalle in Ireland face to face. I told him you would make the right choice. He thought you would bring him finger of your aunt and allow father to breathe. I warned him you are one of us."

"Then, I pity us all."

I say nothing else as I exit the building and head home. This chapter is closed.

CHAPTER SIXTY-SIX

Happy Birthday

John

One months later...

When Roni wraps around my arm and holds on tight as we walk down the New York street, I know she's somewhere far away. I don't think she's aware of the action at all. It makes my heart swell and causes me concern all at the same time.

"This trip was meant for you to have fun," I say, hopefully pulling her from her thoughts.

She releases my arm and wraps her limbs around her middle. I take a chance and tug her into my side by the waist. She comes willingly and sinks into my side.

"I'm having fun," she says and looks up at me.

I narrow my eyes. "Mm, hadn't planned on spanking you tonight."

She gives me a nudge and a small smile. "I am having fun. The food was good."

I can't help the smile that comment brings. I took her to our spot. Mom told me to go all out, but I did what felt like Roni. The jerk chicken placed a smile on her face.

"But your mind is everywhere but here. Mom kept the baby for the weekend so we could come here and kick back," I remind her.

"I'm sorry. I still can't believe she's my family. From the first time I met her, I was drawn to her. I had my doubts when you found out we were relatives, first cousins at that. I'm still trying to process so much," she says.

"Which is why we're here. It's okay to let it all go for a bit. It will all be there when we get back and you can work your way through it then."

"Do you think she will ever forgive me?" she asks in a small voice so unlike her.

I release a heavy breath. "I think Indigo has nowhere to place her anger and because of that she's turning it on you. She's young and confused. Give her time, it will all work out."

She wrinkles her little nose. She looks gorgeous tonight in black wide bottom slacks, black blouse, and heels. About a week ago, she cut the hair at the nape of her neck, giving her style more shape and a bit of a different look. I love it on her. It calls attention to her face.

When we reach the entrance to our old building, Roni gives me a curious look. "What are we doing here? I thought you let the place go?"

"I had, but it came back on my radar and I decided to purchase it. We have a few memories here I wouldn't mind keeping," I reply.

She groans. "Don't turn into a weirdo on me, John."

"What are you talking about?"

"A sentimental apartment? Really?"

I press for the elevator before turning to her and cupping the sides of her head to kiss her forehead. "Yes, and I plan to make more memories here."

She makes a face at me, but I can see the smile behind it. The elevator dings, and I lace our fingers together as we step on. Roni looks down at our linked fingers and her smile grows.

"I've been wondering if I would change things about my past," she says. "I don't think I would. Not if it meant losing you."

I lean for a sample of her full lips. "Does that mean you are going to get soft and mushy on me?"

"No, and I'm probably going to do my best to top from the bottom tonight," she says and wiggles her brows.

I burst into laughter. "I'll allow it. You've been so well behaved the last few weeks."

She pouts. "It's no fun when you allow it."

I shake my head and lead her off the elevator. My nerves kick in as we near the apartment. Roni is either going to really hate this, or she's going to absolutely love it.

Here goes nothing.

Roni

My mind starts to wonder off again as we walk to the apartment door. As I thought, knowing the truth has only brought on more decisions and uncertainties. Things I'm still wrapping my head around.

However, all of that skids to a stop as we enter the apartment. My mouth drops open and tears start to build. It's right here, right now, I know with all my heart that this man knows me better than anyone.

There are roses and balloons everywhere with a banner hanging up. *Happy Birthday*, it reads. It's my birthday, but I hadn't made a big deal about it. I didn't know John knew in the first place. We don't talk much about my life before I met him and the things I now remember.

"Do you like it?" he says by my ear.

Speechless, I take a few steps forward and the champagne colored balloons dance around my ankles, only to reveal a thick blanket of white rose petals covering the floor beneath. There's no way he has lined this entire apartment with roses. I move further into the living area and spin in a circle to confirm that petals are indeed covering every inch of the floor. This place looks like a fairy tale.

Music comes softly through the sound system. I grin as Bootsy Collins version of "I'd Rather Be with You" plays. This is so some smooth John shit.

Looking up at the banner, I ask, "You did this for me?"

He moves behind me and wraps his arms around my waist. "One of my jobs is to know you better than you know yourself. It's not that you don't want affection, you're confused by it. I'm going to spoil you, Roni. When I know you need to be loved on, I'm not going to let your stubborn ass keep me from giving you what you need," he murmurs against my neck.

"Yes, I love it. That's the answer to your question. This is…" I cover his arms with mine. "This is everything to me."

"But I'm not done. Happy twenty-seventh Birthday, baby."

I turn in his arms to look at him. The weight of the love in his eyes is like a punch to the gut. I caress his jaw with the back of my hand.

Suddenly, he drops to one knee and my brows lift into my hairline as my mouth drops open. I take a step back, always that push and pull with me and John. However, when he reaches for my waist and pulls me close, I don't fight it.

"I figured your birthday would be the perfect day to let you know how grateful I am that you graced this world with your presence. You couldn't have been made more perfectly for me. I knew you were mine the first time I saw you... That's not right." He shakes his head as tears gather in his eyes.

My knees are ready to give. I've never seen John this emotional. He held his shit together during the birth of our daughter because of all the complications. He was my rock then.

He swallows hard and continues. "I had so much crazy shit going on, but I knew your spirit. Your heart talked to mine from day one. I've needed to be there for you like I've never needed to be there for anyone else. There wasn't a single word to be said or an action that I could perform.

"With you, I needed to be as present as I could be, in hopes that the rest would work out. I've never been patient until I met you." He reaches into his pocket and pulls out a ring box.

"John," I gasp when he opens the box. "Are you fucking serious? Where am I wearing that thing to?"

He laughs. "Let me finish this. I knew your ass was going to complain about the ring," he murmurs to himself. "You've become my best friend. I've done shit with you before we were in a full-blown relationship, stuff I never thought I'd get a female friend, let alone a girlfriend to be willing to do."

I shrug. "When it comes to kinky shit, you're the man. I'm just saying."

"Shut up, woman. That's an order."

I clamp my lips shut and throw the key out.

"Where was I? Yeah, okay. It's never been awkward to be us, not for us. We've grown into who we are. I'm willing to grow into who we need to be, as long as I get to do it with you," he says.

He has broken out into a sweat. It's too adorable. I can't help the tears that fall.

Linking our fingers together, he looks up at me through his damp lashes. Those golden eyes arrest all brain function. Every word that follows is a struggle for me to keep up with. "I like that we're us. Raw and unfiltered. I hadn't been sure at first if you wanted to be a wife with all the conventional shit that comes with it. Then one morning, I got my answer.

"You were in the kitchen with the baby, making me bacon and eggs. The entire time you cooed to her about our family and how much you loved us both. I stood in the shadows watching you two. You were happy, we had a mission to go on later that day, but you were happy with our life. Our unconventional life. At the wedding you only confirmed what I had already seen.

"What you overheard me say to my brothers and cousins wasn't entirely true. I had every intention of proposing. I just couldn't allow them to ruin the plan. Wyatt and Noah already knew, which is why they were giving me shit." He pauses and clears his throat.

"Roni, I'd rather be with you than without. You know you're the one that I want. Will you marry me?"

I smirk. We're unconventional so this deserves an unconventional answer. Reaching for the belt on my pants, I keep my gaze on him.

I release the belt first, then the button and zipper on my slacks. When the pants hit the floor, I kick them out of the way, causing balloons to fly and float around us. With my fingers hooked into my panties, I shimmy out of them.

John smiles and folds his arms over his chest. I sway to the music as I release the buttons on my blouse. His eyes grow dark as I allow the top to fall. Releasing my bra, I bite my lip and drop it to the floor.

However, my answer is in my next action. John and I have never had a true Dom and Sub relationship. I…I've never been able to bow my head to him or give over my complete submission. It's been embedded into my subconscious for my safety to defy him and hold on to that piece of control.

Today, I drop to my knees and bow my head before John. I exhale before I say, "Understand the power in this action. I've just taken back all of my power in it. I've given you all of me, but I also allow my crown to rest with the one person I trust to cover me, my heart, and my throne. If I can't rest with my king, I've chosen a joker and I deserve to have my head cutoff.

"I'll be your best friend, your wife, and on any day, anytime, anywhere, I'll be the escape you need, mind body and soul," I say.

I can feel more than see him stand to his full height over me. He caresses my hair as my head remains bent. "I've never heard anyone explain our relationship better. I'm so in awe of you. That totally outdid my proposal just now, but yeah. That says it all."

Only a man that understands me can be the man who earns all of me. I remain silent, awaiting his next command. He lifts my left hand and places the ring on it before planting a gentle kiss over the ring. I can't help marveling at the intricate design and all the diamonds surrounding it as I drop my hand back to my lap.

He steps from his shoes and the sound of his belt is next. My mouth begins to water when he moves around. The whooshing of my own breath becomes so loud as I wait for him to completely strip down.

He moves behind me and leans into my ear. "I'm going to give you a choice. We do this sweet because we're engaged and I'm trying to be gentle, or we fuck hard and dirty. You already know what that means. I'm going to abuse this body and knock your ass out for the night," he whispers.

I grin. "Why are you asking, boss? I haven't complained about our sex life once. Do you?"

John palms under my chin and tips my head all the way back until my back is arched and I'm face to face with his pulsing shaft. I open my mouth as he goes to feed me his long fat length. He pulls out after one pass but guides himself right back in.

"Hold on to my thighs and relax your throat," he breathes.

I do exactly as he instructs as he thrusts his hips forward. I'm making that sound he loves, causing him to groan and grunt. I'm just getting started when he backs off. Saliva makes a trail from his tip to my lip.

He brushes it with his thumb and sticks his finger in my mouth. His face is so tight with lust. I'm praying he'll pick me up and let me lock my legs around his neck while he eats my pussy upside down and I suck him off. It's one of my favorite positions.

I know the moment something else comes to mind. We have to be pretty limited on what we can do here without our playroom and toys. He winks.

"Stay here, I'll be right back," he says.

I'll never tell him how sexy he is when he puts all that bass in his voice and exudes dominance. I'm wet from the vibration of his voice alone. I wait, hoping like hell he'll hurry up.

While he's gone, I take another moment to look down at my ring. I'm getting married. After all the time I've spent in a box all to myself—not even when I was with Darius did I feel like I was with someone—now, I have my person.

"I knew you would like it. The size will grow on you," John says when he returns.

"Where am I wearing this thing to?"

"Wherever you want. As long as you never take these off. I had planned to wait, but things changed," he says, holding a pair of diamond cuffs in front of my face.

I reach for them but he snatches them back. "Oh no, baby. You're going to earn these."

"Here you go taking shit too far," I say and look over my shoulder at him with a smile on my face. He laughs and shakes his head at me. "What do you need me to do for them?"

"Good girl," he purrs. "Stand up for me."

I stand and turn to face him. He has a few things on the coffee table that weren't there before. My gaze bounces between him the dildo, butt plug, and wand.

"Wait, you've already filled this place up?"

"What do you think?"

"Oh, okay, we're getting nasty, nasty, all right, John. I'm up for your naughty ass challenge," I say.

He closes the gap between us. "Are you sure?"

"Try me."

He stands the dildo up on the marble coffee table until the suction on the bottom adheres to the surface. With his gaze on me, he changes the song to "Bed" by J. Holiday. I laugh and he winks.

"Nice playlist," I say.

"Thanks. Now get your ass on that table. I want you to bounce on that dildo for me."

I tilt my head to the side and point. "On that one?"

He rolls his eyes. "You stayed in role for all of two seconds."

"Oh, be quiet. I'm with you."

I test the table with one leg, then climb on with the other. The trust I have for this man. Facing him, I lower onto the dildo and slide down. It's not as snug a fit as when he's inside, but it's enough to pull a moan from my lips.

I start a tentative bounce at first. John hovers over me, cupping the sides of my face as he captures my lips. The more he consumes my mouth the wetter I get.

I shove my hands into his hair and tug as he moves his hands to my hips and begins to guide them. I'm good and slick when John slaps my ass hard.

"Babe," I groan as he frees my mouth.

I think I actually get scared as he turns on the wand. John can be relentless. From the look on his face, this is relentless John. He's not going to let up until I've soaked this damn table and every toy he has.

With the wand to my clit, he slaps my ass again and moves his lips to my ears. "That's it. Come all you want."

"John, please."

I don't think I'm going to stop coming as my first climax hits. My legs are shaking, and my chest feels like it might explode.

"I think you want the cuffs more than the ring, baby. You're so wet. I want you to come again."

"John, please don't. I don't think I can take anymore. Move the wand, give me a break," I whimper.

He kisses my temple. "Come, Roni. Don't give up on me now. You only get the cuffs if you come on me. I'm not inside you yet."

"Then you better lift my ass and dive in," I say in a cross between a plea and a sob.

"You can do it. One more," he pants, turning up the wand.

"Holy—" I open my mouth to say more but my words are caught in a silent scream.

"That's my baby."

This night turns into one I will always remember. I'm near lifeless when John wraps my body around his as he thrusts into me. I didn't think I could take anymore, but that's a lie. I found my second wind and rode him for all he's worth.

Not that he allows me to get the best of him. All I know is that John's entire mission for this night had to be to rip my brain out through my vagina because I'm mindless by the time I pass out.

Although I earned both cuffs. John locks them each in place around my wrist and to my surprise, he ended up with his own around one of his own. I locked it with my very own key that will forever dangle around my neck. The initials RB in the center.

Perfect.

CHAPTER SIXTY-SEVEN

Full Circle

John

Roni is knocked out and has been for a few hours. We've been out of the apartment once. Long enough to get some food, eat and fall right back into bed.

I can't keep the smile off my face when I look at her wrist across her face as she sleeps. Her ring is smiling back at me. I've never seen a more beautiful sight.

"Stop staring at me, dork," she murmurs, half asleep.

I lean in and kiss her lips. "I thought you were sleeping."

"I was. Then I felt you staring at me."

"Whatever, we should start dinner soon," I say and pull her into me to hold her to my chest. "What do you want to have tonight?"

"I was thinking that pepper steak and rice you do. I could tear that up right about now," she hums.

"Hold that thought," I say as my phone rings.

I look at the phone and want to throat punch Wyatt. I told all of my brothers that if they call it better be life or death. I freeze as that thought goes across my mind.

"Hey, everything all right," I answer right away.

"I'm not entirely sure yet," Wyatt say, bringing on my curiosity.

"What's going on?"

"We got a call from LaSalle's son. Sammy wants us all in New York to help out with an attack that's on the way," he says.

"Did you call LaSalle?"

"No, the kid said not to. This has to play out a certain way. LaSalle needs to finish the night exactly as planned, but we need to be there. Shit has us all freaked out, but I've heard what Sammy's capable of so we're getting on the plane."

"Okay, I'll see if I can get us a chopper. It will be faster once you land," I say, thinking aloud. "I'll be there when you guys arrive at the airport."

"See you in a bit," Wyatt says and hangs up.

"What's going on?" Roni says.

I drag a hand down my face. "It seems Sammy's called in the cavalry for his dad," I say and knot my brows.

"I'll call Val."

"No, don't. We're not supposed to interfere with this," I say and shake my head. I can't believe I'm going to fly blindly into this according to a kid's word, but I am.

"I'll get dressed," Roni says.

"Baby, you should stay here."

"Yeah, okay, right, babe."

I glare at her the entire time as she climbs from the bed to get ready to head out once my family arrives. "So much for submitting," I mutter.

She saunters back over to me. "You can't have all the things all the time," she says with a smile and kisses my lips. "That's a five-hour flight, come shower with me."

"I should cuff you to the bed," I say as I get up.

"You want to try for another baby. I don't advise that. Besides, I want to see that kid in action."

"You and me both."

Roni

"Will you look at this. They look like roaches," I mutter as our enemies come into sight.

We come in hot as we land on LaSalle's property. They're lighting the house up from inside and out. I frown and jump out of the chopper with my gun blazing. I'm working with muscle this time. Noah has brought in the big boys.

"Let's make this fast. We all have shit to do," Wyatt barks into the com.

"Judging from that rock, John has some celebrating to do. Let's get Roni tied back up to his bed," Ry replies.

I shake my head, but I don't stop firing. "Head in the game and out of my fucking business asshat," John's voice is the next one I hear.

I ignore them all. My girls are at that house. Tasha texted to give me a heads up that they were about to be under attack. She probably thought she was sending me a warning for the girls in L.A.

"I still can't believe the kid was able to warn us," Brax says as if reading my thoughts.

"Thank God, he did," I say as I air out a handful of motherfuckers.

"Looks like things are slowing down inside. I'm still trying to hack their comms to let them know friendly fire is coming in," Felix says.

"Man, fuck this," Toby grumbles as he goes in.

He starts to clear a path as me and John keep close to each other and do the same. Brax and Ry are the first to get close to the back door and block it as we all form around our targets and box them in. We finish them off right as the lights come back up.

Felix must get through to the other's comm as his next words aren't meant for our team. "Y'all can relax. This is Felix. We're here for back up. That kid is amazing, by the way."

My mind takes me back to the wedding. Sammy had been what, two? However, even then he was trying to tell me something. I've heard about his mother's gift.

I sigh, knowing that I can no longer war with the conversation I had with LaSalle only a few weeks ago in Ireland. Placing my gun over my shoulder with one hand, I brush at my black slacks and blue dress shirt with the other. Straightening my shoulders and lifting my head, I walk into the house behind the others.

"You know this has only begun," Uri says. "It is time to make them Hush. I will handle it from here. It is time the hitters step in."

"Yeah, but not before everyone around here comes clean," LaSalle says as looks in Misha's direction.

Misha looks at his nails and ignores LaSalle as he picks his fingernails with one of his blades. LaSalle shakes his head. "Don't worry about me. Worry about answer you need from her." Misha points his blade at me.

As he does, his words seal my fate and I accept what they mean. This is who I've always been. This is what Val really saw, what that little boy Sammy meant by yes to all.

At once, Tasha, Val, and I move to the center of the room, revealing the powerhouse we are. The links that have been moving together all this time. I look them in the eyes one by one and nod. We then turn to LaSalle.

"It looks like you have your general. I'm claiming my seat at the table."

Come to Collect

Weston

Fourteen years later…

Jordan Black is the prettiest girl in school. She's also the smartest and the nicest. She's never makes me feel dirty or poor like the other kids.

"Get out of the way, spaz," one of the older kids snarls as he pushes me into the lockers.

One of these days I'm going to be strong and I'm going to kick all of their asses. I hate them all, all except for Jordan. I smile as I watch her in the courtyard of our school, surrounded by her friends.

Friends that would never welcome me into their conversation, let alone their space. That's why I'm waiting. My hands are growing sweaty as I watch them and pray she comes this way soon.

My heart begins to race when she turns my way and smiles. I slowly smile back, not sure if she's smiling at me at first. When she waves, my heart feels like it might explode.

Looking around to see if she's waving at someone else, I smile wider when I turn and wave back. She turns to her friends and says something before she grabs her backpack and starts over toward me. I lick my dry lips and start to fidget with my shirt sleeves.

It's pretty hot for the long sleeves, but I have my reasons for wearing them. I tug at the front of my shirt and wiggle a little as the fabric and sweat stick to my body. Being nervous isn't helping my situation.

Then she stops a foot away with that bright smile on her pretty face. Her golden eyes light up with it. She's so pretty. Her springy dark curls are thick and frame her heart shaped face. Her brown skin glows like polished bronze and she always smells so nice.

I'm already six feet tall so I tower over her at what's probably five feet. I love the way she looks up at me. I've imagined so many times holding her hand as we walk the hallways.

"Hey Weston," she says and all I can do is stand here like an idiot.

I wipe my hands on my jeans and her gaze drops to the action. Her lashes are so long they fans across her cheeks. Cheeks that have been losing the chubby plumpness they had when we were in elementary.

She reaches into the pocket of her backpack and pulls out a pack of tissues and holds them out to me. "My palms get sweaty sometimes too. Mom always gives me a couple of packs of these. Here, you can have these," she says when she holds them out and looks back up to meet my eyes.

I reach out nervously and take them. "Thanks."

"No problem."

"Um… I was waiting for you. Our science project. Um… We're supposed to work on it together."

"Oh right," she says, her eyes growing wide. "I totally forgot about that. The flood in the library made it slip my mind. I'm headed to my family's office. We can work down in the gym if you like."

"Um… I can't. I'm supposed to head straight home after school." I don't mention that I'm already late and hope to God I get there before I get into trouble.

"Oh, no problem. I'll call my mom. She should be cool with me coming to your place to work. After all, this thing is due at the end of the week," she says and rolls her eyes.

I go to tell her that's a bad idea, but the thought of spending time with her causes me to keep my mouth shut. I look around for her cousins. None of them are in sight. They're never dicks to me like some of the other kids, but they aren't what I would call my friends either.

The Blacks have a clique of their own. They're the cool kids on campus and the guys will kick your ass for fucking with one of their girl cousins or sisters. I'm not in the mood to get my ass kicked today.

Jordan follows my gaze and giggles. "Don't worry. The guys already took off for the gym at Black and Lock. It's training day for the boys with Uncle Noah. Come on. I'll text my mom. She said it's fine. I just have to text her your address," she says.

I nod and take her phone to enter the address. I know I'm skating on thin ice. I'll have to get us to my house soon and we'll have to work fast before my dad gets home.

I start for the bus stop, but Jordan places an arm on mine to stop me. She gives me that bright smile again, nodding her head toward the parking lot. My dick twitches in my pants from her simple touch and I can feel the heat in my cheeks.

"I have a ride. My driver, Shep, is waiting for me. Come on."

Oh yeah, I forgot that all the Blacks have cars at their beck and call. Some of the older ones drive their own cars to school. The others arrive in SUVs and shiny expensive cars.

Every time I see them come to school it reminds me that I've only been in their world because of a scholarship. A scholarship that gets my ass kicked almost daily and not only by the kids at school who hate having me here.

I'm a lot smarter than I look. Or at least that's what my father says. My mother took a chance when my kindergarten teacher told her to have me tested. I've been getting a free ride to places like this ever since she did.

When we walk to the shiny Mercedes and the driver opens the door for us, it's one more reminder of how far out of my league Jordan is. She's gorgeous, super smart, and rich. At fifteen, Jordan is a grade ahead. Yeah, I'm smart, but I've never been skipped a grade.

I slide into the back of the car beside her thinking that in all my sixteen years, I've never been inside a car that cost anywhere near this much. Turning, I watch Jordan put lip gloss on her full lips. When she turns those amazing eyes on me, I don't feel like the bummy kid at school.

It's like Jordan sees more. She sees me. That's one of the things I love about her.

"Stop looking so nervous, Weston," she says with a small giggle. "I promise not to ruin the project. I plan to do my share. I'm not like those slackers in our class."

"I know. I don't think you're going to slack."

"Honestly, I was so glad you were assigned as my partner. Swear to God, if I would have gotten one more assignment with a partner that did nothing but pick their nose the entire time while I did all the work, ugh," she says with a grimace.

The way her little nose wrinkles is adorable. I wish I could lean in and kiss her. I've daydreamed about it so many times over the years. Each year Jordan becomes prettier and prettier.

"Shit," I say when my phone rings in my pocket.

The smile drops from her face and her lips flatten. I don't have time to analyze what just happened. I rush to take the phone from my pocket.

Boy do I sigh in relief when I see it's my mom informing me that my dad will be coming home late. The tightness in my chest releases. Great, not only will I avoid getting in trouble, we'll have time to really work on the project.

I turn to Jordan and she's now looking out of the window. Something caused her mood to shift. I sneak a sniffle at my armpits.

Not so bad.

Feeling awkward, I start to fidget with the sleeves of my shirt. I breathe the biggest sigh of relief when we pull up in front of my home. That is until Jordan steps out of the car.

She looks around the trailer park and I want to vomit. I'm sure her home looks nothing like this. The cute sneakers on her feet probably cost more than everything I have on.

I've had the same five uniform shirts since last year. I've been literally threatened not to grow anymore. Too bad my body hasn't planned on listening to that.

"We don't have to do this today," I murmur.

She turns to me with her brows drawn. "What?"

"We can do this another day. You know at your place or
something. I'll try to get permission—"

She grabs my hand and tugs me forward. "Come on. We're
wasting time. I have so many ideas. We'll need all the time we
can get to plan and execute by Friday," she says her smile back
in place.

I try not to show the relief on my face. I may never have a
shot with this girl, but I want to absorb the light that comes off
of her for a few hours. If only an hour, I'll live with that.

Here goes nothing.

Jordan

"You kids want some more Kool Aid?" Weston's mom asks for
the millionth time.

You would think he never had a friend over the way she's
been acting. Although it wouldn't surprise me. Weston has
always been quiet in school and stays to himself.

"No, thank you, ma'am."

Her face lights up. "You're so well mannered. Weston, you
went and got a pretty little thing with manners as a girlfriend,"
she says happily.

I look at Weston and his entire face is beet red. I suck my
bottom lip into my mouth. I've always had a crush on Weston.
Some of the other girls at school used to as well, but then they
found out he doesn't come from money. I hate that they call
him *Scholarship Kid*.

Weston is such a nice person. With his blue eyes, dark hair,
and those dimples. He even has one in his chin.

He almost reminds me of my uncles Uri, Nico, and Michael in New York. They're not my real uncles, they're all handsome. Sure, he's not as built as my cousins or my little brother for that matter, but Weston makes up for all of that with his gorgeous smile.

"She's not my girlfriend, Mom. She's my science project partner."

"Oh, I don't know. She's been giving you the eye."

Weston turns to me, blushing harder than before. I can feel my own cheeks warm. I duck my head and turn back to my notebook.

"I'll let you two have some alone time."

Once she's gone, I peek over at Weston and he's watching me. I give him a small smile. If I had been eyeing him, I didn't mean to make it so oblivious. Sticking my pencil into my mouth is all I can do not to say something stupid.

He drops his eyes to my mouth and clears his throat. "Are you going to that dance?"

I nod and start to get excited. "Yeah, my mom and aunts are taking me shopping for my dress. I haven't decided what color to get yet. I've been looking at hairstyles to try." I clamp my mouth shut when I realize I'm rambling.

"Yellow or blue. You're always so pretty in those colors, on dress down days," he says, red creeping up his neck and face again.

I smile. "I'll keep that in mind."

"Has anyone asked you to the dance yet?"

I frown. "Yeah, a bunch of guys I'd never say yes to," I reply, rolling my eyes.

He starts to play with the edges of his notebook while searching my face with his gaze. I've never noticed the grey in his eyes. Up this close, I can see all the colors and hues as they blend together.

"Why not? I mean, you don't have to answer that."

I cover his hand with mine. "No, it's okay. I sort of like someone. I was hoping he would ask me."

His shoulders sag and his expression turns defeated. I don't think he gets that I'm talking about him. Auntie Bean says I should be more outgoing.

What the heck?

I lean in and kiss him on the cheek. Weston's head snaps up and he looks at me with wide eyes. I smile at him and squeeze his hand.

"Why'd you do that?" he asks.

"Duh, I'm trying to tell you that I want you to ask me to the dance. I smile at you all the time. When are you going to get the—"

My words are cut off as he cups my face and really kisses me. I gasp and he slips his tongue into my mouth. It's my first kiss.

My heart races. It's not as bad as all the girls at school made it seem it would be. Weston knows what he's doing. At least more than I do.

He pulls away and looks at me with a big smile on his face. "I… I don't have anything fancy to wear, but I want to take you. I've been saving for the tickets. I'll get them tomorrow. I mean, if…if you want to go with me," he stammers out.

"Of course, silly." I lean in and press my lips to his once more.

We don't get carried away. I turn back to my books, wanting to do a little dance. Weston Ash is going to be my date to the dance. I want to squeal.

He reaches for me hand and locks our fingers together. Oh my God. Should I ask if we're a thing now. No, I need to play it cool.

Weston seems to relax, and we get back to our project. Time has been slipping away. When I text my mom, she informs me that the entire family is at Black and Lock and they've started a barbecue. I'll head there when we wrap up here.

Suddenly, light flashes through the window and all the blood drains from Weston's face. His mom comes out with a nervous look across hers. An uneasy feeling settles in my stomach.

"Is your ride still outside?" Weston asks nervously.

"No, I have to text Shep and he'll come back for me. He had to run an errand."

"Fuck," Weston mutters.

I frown at the foul language. It's not the first time I've heard him curse. Doesn't mean I like it.

However, that's forgotten when a man in a dirty jumper comes into the house. He's covered in grease and oil. I think I remember once hearing that Weston's dad is a mechanic.

The man turns cold blue eyes on me and snarls. Weston moves as if to shield me. A glance at Mrs. Ash and she's wringing her hands.

"Who the fuck is this?" the man says.

"She's a friend from school, Dad. We had a project to finish. She's just waiting for her ride to come get her," Weston rushes to say.

His dad looks me over, causing Weston to move to shield me more. I don't like this guy. He's rude and the way he looks at me says a thousand words.

"They better be quick. I have enough mouths to feed," he grumbles.

Weston turns to me. "Come on. Text your ride," he says sadly.

"Okay."

I text Shep and start to place my things in my backpack, but not without watching Weston and his mom. They're afraid. I mean, really scared.

"Honey, why don't I feed you. Weston can eat after his friend is gone," Mrs. Ash says.

"Bitch, why the fuck is she here? I told you that boy thinks he's better than us because he goes to that fancy school. Now he's bringing those uppity fucks into my home," his dad snarls.

Yup, I don't like this guy. Someone needs to teach him some manners. I ball my fists at my sides.

Weston has started to sweat. He wipes his hands on his pants. Suddenly, I take notice of details like Grandpa Joe teaches us to do. It's hot. Yet Weston has on a long sleeve shirt and his mom tugged on a sweater as soon as I came inside.

I swear she had a bruise on her arm. This dude hits them. I know he does.

"Jimmy, the girl is only here so they can finish a project for school. Leave the boy be. Don't embarrass him in front of company," Weston's mom says soothingly.

It seems to work. He grunts, tossing me a dismissive look before turning to head in the dining area. Weston turns to pull me into his arms immediately.

"I'm so sorry. I should have gotten you out of here sooner. I lost track of time," he whispers.

"It's okay," I whisper back.

"Come on, we can wait outside."

I nod and we go to stand up. That's when chaos breaks loose. Mrs. Ash screams as Mr. Ash slams her head down on the table.

"You don't have any respect for me and that's why that boy has no respect. Bringing that little tramp into my home," he hisses as he hovers over her face.

"Mom," Weston cries out as he rushes over to his parents.

Before he can do anything to help his mother, his dad has him by the throat, slamming him down on the table. Mash potatoes and gravy fly everywhere. Weston grabs for his father's arm, but he has Weston pinned down good.

"You see this. He thinks he's the man of the house or some shit. You keep coming at me, boy. I'm going to show you what it's like to be a real man."

"Get off my mom," Weston yells.

He does release Mrs. Ash, but only to punch Weston in the face. I've had enough. I'm Jordan Black, I might be many things, but a coward isn't one of them.

Weston

I turn my head to tell Jordan to run, but she already is. Only it's not from my dad but straight for him. She's so small, I can't believe my eyes as I watch what she does next. She leaps into the air, wraps her legs around Dad's neck and with the momentum of her run and jump, she flings him against the wall.

Dad falls to the floor, but she's not done. She grabs him by the hair and slams his face into the old credenza.

"You like beating on the defenseless. Try me," she growls.

She slams his face into the credenza again. I sit up gasping and rubbing at my neck, completely in awe. However, Jordan isn't done.

"You little bitch," Dad says as blood flies from his mouth.

"You're going to watch that filthy mouth. Is that where your son gets it from?" Her voice is so small yet menacing.

She releases his hair and throws a combo punch that knocks Dad on his ass. I don't know if I want to dance or hug the shit out Jordan. Instead, I race to grab her arm and rush for her backpack.

"Go, get away from here," Mom cries out. "Hurry, Weston."

"Mom, you have to come with us," I say.

"No, you get out of here. I'll be fine. Don't you argue with me. This was the plan."

I nod, knowing this is what we talked about happening someday. I'll come back for her when I can. I promise I will.

Grabbing my backpack with the money I've been saving, I hold Jordan's hand as she grabs her bag. We rush out the door just as her ride pulls up. I jump in after Jordan, hoping I can bum a ride to the bus station or something.

"Shep, get me to my dad and uncles," she says angrily.

"What's going on?"

"Get me to Black and Lock," Jordan demands.

Shep groans and starts to mutter to himself, but he pulls off. I tug Jordan's trembling body against mine and hug her tight. Inhaling her strawberry scent, I allow it to calm me.

She turns her face up. "Hey, I'm sorry. I just couldn't stand there and not do anything," she whispers.

I brush my lips against hers, still not able to believe that I got to kiss her. When I look into her eyes, I try to memorize every single feature of her face. I want to remember the girl that kicked that bastard's ass.

When we pull into the underground garage of the building, it's like all of Jordan's cousins are there as well as a bunch of adults. They have the backs of their cars open and two grills are being manned. It's like a tailgate party.

"Don't worry. My uncle is the fixer around here. He'll make sure you're safe. Your dad won't ever hurt you or your mom again," she says and rushes out of the car.

I follow after her and she grabs my hand, tugging me with her. We move for the group of guys talking and laughing together. They're all huge. I swallow and squeeze Jordan's hand.

"Uncle John, I need your help," Jordan says.

All heads turn in our direction. They don't look at all surprised to see us. Jordan releases my hand to run forward to wrap her arms around the tallest guy in the group.

"Daddy, I'm sorry. He made me so mad. He was hurting Weston and his mom."

"Aw man, baby, come get your little Samurai before someone tries to sue my ass again," her dad groans.

"He won't be suing anyone. Not after I handed him his whole life," Jordan replies.

"I swear to God, you're just like your mother. Please tell me you didn't cut anyone up? Carmen, Carmen, are you letting her take blades to school?" Jordan's dad bellows.

"No, Dad," Jordan pulls away and places her hands on her hips as she frowns.

"Ry, give me a break. I lock all of their swords away. They know not to take them out of the house," I turn to see the pretty lady that must be Jordan's mom.

"I didn't need any blades. Uncle Noah tell him. I don't need my swords." Jordan turns to the big scary looking guy.

"Did you do me proud?" Her uncle Noah asks.

She gives him a nod. He winks, holding his hand up for a high five. Watching Jordan's small hand slap his reminds me of how small she is and all she did to my dad.

Suddenly, a tall guy dressed in all black with black hair and gray eyes steps from the center of the other seven guys. He looks younger than them all. Closer to my age.

"Hey kid, catch," he says to me and tosses an ice pack.

"Sammy," Jordan sings and runs to hug him around the waist. "What are you doing here?"

"I came for him," he nods at me. "Get your stuff, kid. I'm taking you home."

"He can't go back home," Jordan says in a panic.

This Sammy guys looks down at her. It's not lost on me that only moments ago she was beaming up at him like he's her favorite older brother or something. He then leans to whisper something in her ear before saying out loud to me, "Say your goodbyes, Weston. We have a flight to catch."

"What the fuck?" I gasp.

"You'll understand. We all had to get used to it," Jordan says knowingly. "You'll be safe."

"Most of all, I won't have to kill you. *Yet*," Jordan's dad says. "Say so long, baby girl. Sammy needs to get his little ass out of here before I change my mind."

"Dad," Jordan pouts.

Jordan drags her feet as she comes to stand before me. When she looks up at me something tightens in my chest. I cup her face as my heart breaks. I've had a crush on this girl for forever and now, when I know I'm not in this alone, I have to leave. I hate my dad so much.

"I promise, one day, I'll see you again," I say.

She lifts onto her toes and kisses my cheek. "Yeah, I know."

Blue Collection Character Tree

Legally Bound 1

Bobby Mairettie and Paige Kemble-Mairettie *father and mother of:*
* *Peyton and James Mairettie (*twin boys*)
* *Sydney Mairettie and Maria Lynn Mairettie (*twin girls*)

Legally Bound 2

Marcus Mairettie and Rita Briggs-Mairettie *father and mother of:*
* *Daniel Mairettie
* *Hannah Mairettie

Legally Bound 3

Nathaniel (Nate) Briggs and Pamela (Pam) Kemble-Briggs *father and mother of:*
* *Tiffany and Tracey Briggs (*twin girls*)
* *Nathaniel Briggs Jr.

Legally Bound 4

Jasper Briggs and Marie Mairettie-Briggs *father and mother of:*
* *Clay Briggs

The Mairettie Family

Grandpa Marcello Mairettie and Grandma Marie Ann *father and mother of:*
* *Marcello Mairettie Jr.
* *Andrew Mairettie

*James Mairettie
*Jessie Mairettie
*Lynn Mairettie
*Gianna Mairettie
*James Mairettie and Minnie Mairettie *father and mother of:*
    *Bobby Mairettie
    *Sam Mairettie – (Ellen Kensington-Mairettie, *wife*)
    *Marcus Mairettie
    *Marie Mairettie

The Briggs Family
Thomas Briggs and Raquel Marinos-Briggs (**Deceased**) *father and mother of:*
    *Nathaniel Briggs
    *Rita Briggs

Earl Briggs (Thomas' younger brother) and Caitronia Marinos-Briggs (twin sister of Raquel) *father and mother of:*
    *Kelly Briggs-Fecteau (Alexie Fecteau, *husband*)
    *Jasper Briggs

The Kemble Family
Peyton Kemble and Davina Kemble *father and mother of:*
    *Pamela Kemble
    *Paige Kemble

Other Important *Legally Bound* **Characters**
Camille (Cam) Mc Wien-Carter (Seth Carter, *soon-to-be ex-husband*) *father and mother of:*
    *Seth Carter Jr.
    *Eddie Carter

*Aiden Carter

Austin Mc Wien (*Camille's father*)

Baroness Olivia Kontos (Baron Kontos' widow; Jasper's ex-lover; Thomas Briggs' new love interest)

Vanessa (Julissa) Smith-Mims (Patrick Mims, *husband, Deceased*)

Hush 1
Uri Donati and Valentina Caprisi-Donati *father and mother of:*
   *Vita Khayla Donati
   *Nori Donati
   *Inzo Donati
   *Eva Donati

Hush 2
Luca Donati and Shannon Caprisi-Donati *father and mother of:*
   *Carlo Donati (Introduced in **Ballers 2**)

The Donati Family
Angelo Uri Donati (**Deceased**) and Donatella Manzo-Donati-~~Zuko~~ *father and mother of:*
   *Uri Donati
   *Nico Donati ~~Zuko~~
   *Annabella Donati ~~Zuko~~ (*Nico's twin sister*)
   *Michael Donati – ~~Zuko~~

Nicholas Donati (Angelo Donati's brother) and Ava Donati *father and mother of:*

    *Luca Donati

The Caprisi Family
Vincent Caprisi and Khayla Grant-Caprisi (***Deceased***) *father and mother of:*
    *Valentina Caprisi
    *Lissette Caprisi (***Deceased***)
    **Shannon Caprisi (*Vincent's daughter*)

Other Important *Hush* Characters
Uncle Valentine Caprisi (*Vincent's brother, head hitter*)

Iman Grant (*Khayla's sister;* ***Shannon's mother;*** **Deceased**)

Roberto Donati-Zuko (*Donatella's husband;* ***Deceased***)
***Posed as Dale the accountant from Legally Bound 3*

Cole 'Brooklyn' O'Brien

DJ

Ballers 1
Bradley Monroe and Tamara Hathaway-Monroe *father and mother of:*
    *Brielle Monroe
    *Ashley Monroe and Ashton Monroe (*twins*)
    *Corey Monroe (*Baby Tam is pregnant with at end of **Ballers 1***)

The Monroe Family
Vernon Monroe and Gloria Monroe *father and mother of:*
  *Trevor Monroe (Donna, *soon to be ex-wife*)
  *Bradley Monroe
  *Ann Monroe (*Bradley's twin sister; Tom,
  husband*)

Trevor Monroe and Donna Monroe *father and mother of:*
  *Jessica Monroe
  *Toby Monroe and Paige Monroe (*twins*)
  *Jonathan Monroe
Tom Rivers and Ann Monroe-Rivers *father and mother of:*
  *George Rivers and Melissa Rivers (*twins*)
  *Amy Rivers

The Hathaway Family
Byron Hathaway and Fiona Hathaway *father and mother of:*
  *Ellerie Hathaway
  *Tamara Hathaway

Other Important *Ballers* **Characters**
Stacey (Tam's best friend)

Reese (Tam's best friend; Nico's girlfriend in **Ballers 1**)

Alee (Tam's best friend)

Cyrus Pierson (Tam's boss) *father of:*
  *Tommy Pierson
  *Carey Pierson

*Stephanie Pierson

Ballers 2

Nico Donati and Reese Bridges-Donati *father and mother of:*
  *Nico Donati Jr.
  *Lanya Donati
  *Orso Donati
  *Santo Donati
  *Stefano Donati

Other Important *Ballers 2* Characters

Tiberius Roman (Reese's ex-husband)

Symphony (Michael's right-hand)

Brothers Black 1

Wyatt Black and Lanelle (Nellie) Bryant-Black *father and mother of:*
  *Nora Black
  *Evan Black

The Black Family

Joseph Black and Cassidy Black *father and mother of:*
  *Wyatt Black
  *Noah Black
  *Johnathan Black
  *Felix Black
  *Toby Black
  *Braxton Black
  *Ryan Black

The Lockhart Family
Rob Lockhart and Faith Lockhart *father and step-mother of:*
  *Heather Lockhart

Steve Lockhart and Nora Bryant-Lockhart (*Deceased*) *step-father and mother of:*
  *Lanelle (Nellie) Bryant-Black

Chase Lockhart and Jennifer Lockhart *father and mother of:*
  *Rebecca (Bean) Lockhart (Noah's best friend and love interest)

Other Important *Brothers Black 1* **Characters**
Missy (Johnathan's ex-girlfriend, *Deceased*)

Lucy (*Heather's girlfriend*)

Barry Coleman (*Deceased*)

Brothers Black 2
Noah Black and Rebecca (Bean) Lockhart-Black *father and mother of:*
  *Brodie Black
  *Connor Black
  **Baby on the way*

Other Important *Brothers Black 2* Characters
Joshua (*Deceased*)

Carmen (Nene) Nash (*reporter; niece of Mariah Briggs from Yours Series; Ryan's new crush*)

Logan O'Brien

Brothers Black 3
King Toby Black and Queen Ogeima Feechi (Kamara) Abioye-Black *father and mother of:*
    *Lulu Black
    *TJ Black
    *Baby on the way

Other Important *Brothers Black 3* **Characters**
Missy (Johnathan's ex-girlfriend, ***Deceased***)

Lucy (*Heather's girlfriend*)

Barry Coleman (***Deceased***)

King Elijah Abioye aka Mr. Naidoo

Queen Ada Catherine Naidoo-Abioye

King Kwäzē Naidoo-Abioye

Celeste (Kwäzē's ex-girlfriend)

King Afafa (***Deceased***)

Missy (Johnathan's ex-girlfriend, ***Deceased***)

Lucy (*Heather's girlfriend*)

Barry Coleman (**Deceased**)

Joshua (**Deceased**)

Carmen Nash aka Nene (*Reporter, Mariah Briggs, from Yours Series, Niece, Ryan's new crush*)
Logan O'Brien

Dylan O'Brien

Jamie O'Brien

Cole 'Brooklyn' O'Brien

Uncle Jonah McGowan

Uncle Jack McGowan

Uncle Raymond McGowan

Uncle Ronan McGowan

Carrick McGowan

Malcolm McGowan

Graham McGowan

Jeremiah McGowan

Reilly McGowan

Brothers Black 4
Braxton Black and Heather Lockhart-Black _father and mother of:_
  *Riley Black
  *Rowen Black

Other Important _Brothers Black 4_ **Characters**
  Debbie ~~Lockhart~~-Kline (Rob's ex-wife, Heather's Mother)

  Lucy (_Heather's pretend girlfriend_)

  Amanda Kline (Heather's half-sister)

  Ernest Kline (Heather's Stepfather, **_Deceased_**)

  Eugene aka Crooked Nose

  Logan O'Brien

  Dylan O'Brien

  Jamie O'Brien

  Cole 'Brooklyn' O'Brien

  Uncle Jonah McGowan

  Uncle Jack McGowan

Uncle Raymond McGowan

Uncle Ronan McGowan

Carrick McGowan

Malcolm McGowan

Graham McGowan

Jeremiah McGowan

Reilly McGowan

Nicholas Lincoln

Sephora Lincoln

Thomas Briggs

Brothers Black 5
Felix Black and Kaye Porter-Black aka Kaye Blaze *father and mother of:*
   *Dashawn Black
   *Second child unannounced

Other Important *Brothers Black 5* **Characters**
   Lakia Redding (*Kaye's writer friend*)

   Dean (*Kaye's writer friend*)

Hayidah (*Doll for Club Desire*)

Pastor Wayne Porter (*Kaye's father*)

Danesha Porter (*Kaye's mother*)

Danny Porter (***Deceased*** *Kaye's brother and Felix's best friend*)

Grandma Reid (*Kaye's grandmother*)

Grandpa Reid (*Kaye's grandfather*)

Alberto Perez (*Felix's best friend*)

Jacob McTavish (*Lead actor in Kaye's movie*)

Mona Richards (***Deceased***, *a fan)*

Logan O'Brien

Dylan O'Brien

Jamie O'Brien

Cole 'Brooklyn' O'Brien

Connie O'Brien

Kate O'Brien

Uncle Ronan McGowan

Carrick McGowan

Brothers Black 6
Ryan Black and Carmen Nash *father and mother of:*
    *Jordan Black
    *Second child unannounced

Other Important *Brothers Black 6* **Characters**
    Kiyoshi Matsumara-Nash (*Carmen's father*)

    Paloma Matsumara-Nash (*Carmen's mother*)

    Nelson "Ne" Matsumara-Nash (*Carmen's Brother*)

    Yui (*Nelson assistant*)

    Bekia

    Calu

    Mariah Briggs (*Carmen's Aunt*)

    Gigi (*Carmen's roommate*)

    Torque

    Alexander (*Oldest Triplet*)

    Maximilian aka Mil (*Middle Triplet*)

Tobias (*Youngest Triplet*)

Austin Mc Wien (***Now Deceased***)

Logan O'Brien

Misha Krupin

Dr. Omid V-Shah

Connie O'Brien

Kate O'Brien

Don LaSalle Locatelli

Tasha Locatelli

Valentine Donati

Uri Donati

Brothers Black 7
Johnathan Black and Cherone "Roni" Pérez -Black *father and mother of:*
   *Mena Black

Other Important *Brothers Black 7* **Characters**
   Natasha "Indigo"

Grissel Pérez (**Now Deceased**)

Eliam Pérez (**Now Deceased**)

Irina Krupin (**Now Deceased**)

Yours Series
Nicholas Lincoln and Sephora (Sophi/Soph/Lilla du) Emilsson *father and mother of:*
   *Nicole Lincoln
   *Nadia Lincoln
   *Nicholas Lincoln Jr.

The Lincoln Family
Dean Lincoln and Shelly Lincoln (***Both Deceased***) *father and mother of:*
   *Nicholas Lincoln
   *Rick ~~Carbon~~ Lincoln
   *Gavin ~~Carbon~~ Lincoln

The Emilsson Family
Liam Emilsson (thought to be deceased) and Faraz Emilsson father and mother of:
   *Lucian Emilsson
   *Ettie Emilsson
   *Sephora Emilsson

Lucian Emilsson and Kimberly Ann Clove *father and mother of:*
   *Lilla Emilsson

Other Important *Yours* Characters

Mark Fienberg (Sephora's best friend)

Ivana Graves (Nick's ex-girlfriend; *Deceased*)

Bianca (Liam's mistress; *Missing*)

Winton (Nick's driver and security)

Jillian Carver (Nick's ex-temporary PA; *Deceased*)

Harvey Carver (Jillian's father; Nick's family friend; *Deceased*)

Bailey Wilder (waitress; Mark's girlfriend)

Dylan O'Brien

Nick's Crew
Wyatt Black
Kevin Briggs (Mariah Briggs' husband; Nick's PA)
Craig Hilton
George Ligal
Lucian Emilsson
Andrew Connor (Ettie's husband)

Be Yours Series
Prince Omid Arman Vahid (Dr. O.V-Shah) and Divine Favors
father and mother of:
   *Prince Firuz Arman Vahid
   *Princess Fairuza Araz Vahid

The Vahid Family

Javed Vahid and Hana Vahid (**third wife**) *father and mother of:*
  *Prince Omid Arman Vahid
  *Prince Bazar Vahid
    Padma Vahid *first wife and mother of:*
      *Prince Paiman Vahid
      *Princess Yasmin Vahid

Other Important *Be Yours* **Characters**
Prince Jahan Vahid

Prince Remi Vahid

Prince Ramses Vahid

Sassa Vahid (*First wife of Javed Vahid*)

Marica Thompson (Divine's cousin)

Dr. Nobi

Gretta (Medical Assistant)

Navid (Omid's advisor)

Dada (Divine's best friend)

Blue's Queens', Divas', and Readers' 2021

BLUE'S 40TH BIRTHDAY BASH
JULY 15TH TO JULY 18TH 2021

WILD DUNES RESORTS
SOUTH CAROLINA

Want to Meet the Authors of Perceptive Illusions in Person?
Come join us in South Carolina for
Blue's Queens' Divas' and Readers' Retreat 2021.
July 15th -July 18th
Join Blue and the ladies for Blue Saffire's 40th birthday bash
weekend at the luxury Wild Dunes Resort.

Blue's Queens', Divas', and Readers 2021 Retreat Itinerary

Here's a look at the tentative itinerary.

Thursday, July 15, 2021

4:00-5:30pm Check-in and Registration

6:00 pm-11:00 pm: *Buffet Dinner and 20's party*
  ❖ Special Welcome Event

Friday, July 16, 2021

10:00-11:00 am: *Breakfast Buffet All Invited*

11:00am-2:30 pm Trip to the outlet for shopping (Tentative in planning)

3:00 pm -4:00 pm: *Lunch Buffet All Invited*

4:00 pm -6:00 pm: Book Signing and games time with Blue and Ivy Harper

7:00 pm-12:00 am: *Blue's 40th Birthday Party*
    ❖ *Dancing, games, and more*

Saturday, July 17, 2021

10:00-11:00 am: *Breakfast Buffet All Invited*

1:00 pm -2:00 pm: *VIP Private Author Lunch Big Hats*

4:00 pm -5:30 pm: Belly Dancing lessons with Blue and KT Adler

6:00 pm- 7:30 pm: *Dinner on Your Own*

7:30 pm- 11:00 pm: Book Signing with KT Adler, Ivy Harper, and Tiya Rayne and games

Sunday, July 18, 2021

10:00-11:00 am: *Breakfast Buffet All Invited*

2:00 pm – 4:00 pm: Paint and Sip with Blue and Tiya Rayne
    ❖ *Paint and Sip*

4:30 pm – 6:00 pm: Beach Hang out with Blue

10:00-11:00 am: *Dinner on Your Own*

8: 40 pm-Until
  ❖ ***Diva's Ball*** Final Party with live DJ

  ***All Itinerary subject to change.

Registration closes for tickets on June 1, 2021.

http://bluesaffire.com/blues-queens-divas-and-readers-retreat-2021

Get your copy today!
Calling on Quinn and In Deep
are now Available.

ACKNOWLEDGMENTS

I'm laid out y'all. This book and this year has been out to get me. However, I refused to put this book out until it was everything I wanted. I mean, I hollered and clapped my hands when I got to the end of the edits.

This book, John, and Roni became everything *I* wanted, saw, and more. They had a story to tell and it was important to me to tell it right. There are always so many ways to tell a story and this was theirs. I love them both. I'm so sad to see the Blacks' series end, but I do have plans to see them again. Hint, hint.

Thank you, guys so much for coming on this journey with me. I had so much fun waiting to tell you who Jordan is. I can't wait for the next generation. However, I am exhausted from all the details and timeline matching it takes for the connecting series so we will see what's up next. This is not easy to do. This year has through me curveballs and I'd rather be happy writing than miserable and fighting against myself. So bear with me.

Big love to my team. They have been going through it with me. There were days I was ready to be like forget this and they all come together to talk me off the ledge. Muah, to my husband. It's never easy dealing with me and my crazy.

God has pushed me to my limits and told me to fly. I'm spreading my wings. It may not be smooth, but I'm finding the right height to soar to. Thank you, Lord for your guidance.

Next! Man, I'm not even going to tell all I'm up to. For real, it might attack me. LOL .

ABOUT THE AUTHOR

Blue Saffire, award-winning, bestselling author of over thirty contemporary romance novels and novellas, writes with the intention to touch the heart and the mind. Blue hooks, weaves, and loops multiple series, keeping you engaged in her worlds. Blue is a hybrid author, writing for Sourcebooks and for her own publishing company Perceptive Illusions as Blue Saffire as well as Royal Blue.

Blue and her husband live in a house filled with laughter and creativity, in Long Island, NY. Both working hard to build the Blue brand and cultivate their love for the artists. Creative is their family affair.

Blue holds an MBA in Marketing and Project Management, as well as a MED in Instructional Technology and Curriculum Design. She is also an NLP Master Practitioner.

Wait, there is more to come! You can stay updated with my latest releases, learn more about me, the author, and be a part of contests by subscribing to my newsletter at
www.BlueSaffire.com
If you enjoyed Brothers Black 7: Johnathan the Fixer, I'd love to hear
your thoughts and please feel free to leave a review. And when you do, please let me
know by emailing me TheBlueSaffire@gmail.com
or leave a comment on Facebook
https://www.facebook.com/BlueSaffireDiaries or Twitter
@TheBlueSaffire

Other books by Blue Saffire
Placed in Best Reading Order
Also available….
Legally Bound

Legally Bound 2: Against the Law

Legally Bound 3: His Law

Perfect for Me

Hush 1: Family Secrets

Ballers: His Game

Brothers Black1: Wyatt the Heartbreaker

Legally Bound 4: Allegations of Love

Hush 2: Slow Burn

Legally Bound 5.0: Sam

Yours: Losing My Innocence 1

Yours 2: Experience Gained

Yours 3: Life Mastered

Ballers 2: His Final Play

Legally Bound 5.1: Tasha Illegal Dealings

Brothers Black 2: Noah

Legally Bound 5.2: Camille

Legally Bound 5.3 & 5.4 Special Edition

Where the Pieces Fall

Legally Bound 5.5: Legally Unbound

Brothers Black 4: Braxton the Charmer

My Funny Valentine**

Broken Soldier

Remember Me**

Brothers Black 5: Felix the Watcher

A Home for Christmas

Be My Valentine**

Doctor Feel Good

Wicked Prince Charmings**

Brothers Black 6: Ryan the Joker

Brothers Black 7: Johnathan the Fixer

Title from Blue Saffire and Sourcebooks
The Blackhart Brothers Series***
Calling on Quinn
In Deep

Coming Soon…
Wild Hearts
A**holes Club Series (Book 1 Pit)
A**holes Club Series (Book 5 Kelex)
A Black Christmas: (A Black Special) Book 8

**Blue Saffire Exclusive on the
BlueSaffire.com Site****
The Lost Souls MC Series
Forever

Never
Always

The A Million to Blow Series
A Million to Blow
A Million to Stay
A Million Blown Coming 2021

Coming this August 2020
His Miracle Baby**

Other books from Evei Lattimore Collection Books by Blue Saffire

Black Bella 1**

Destiny 1: Life Decisions**
Destiny 2: Decisions of the Next Generation**
Destiny 3 coming Winter 2020/Spring 2021**

Star**

**Book not connected to the Legally Bound Spinoffs.
***Books published by Sourcebooks

www.ingramcontent.com/pod-product-compliance
Lightning Source LLC
Chambersburg PA
CBHW051055030726
47504CB00006B/1636